❦ ❦ ❦

R*ARELY has a storybook family swept
into life with such breathtaking reality as
the famed Whiteoaks, who from the moment of their creation enchanted millions
of readers all over the world.*

*"The Jalna saga," says one famous critic,
"has an almost phenomenal sustaining interest. It is doubtful if any recent tale of
comparable length . . . can match the con-
sistent pace and surging vitality of this
long, rich story."*

*The novels, which span four generations
of this fascinating and unique family, rank
among the most enduring works of modern
fiction. Their appearance in a paperback
series is an event hailed by American
readers.*

Fawcett Crest Books in the Jalna series
by Mazo de la Roche:

CENTENARY AT JALNA

Mazo de la Roche

FAWCETT CREST • NEW YORK

CENTENARY AT JALNA

THIS BOOK CONTAINS THE COMPLETE TEXT OF
THE ORIGINAL HARDCOVER EDITION.

Published by Fawcett Crest Books, a unit of CBS Publications,
the Consumer Publishing Division of CBS Inc., by arrangement with Little, Brown and Company in association with The
Atlantic Monthly Press.

Copyright © 1958 by Mazo de la Roche

ALL RIGHTS RESERVED

ISBN: 0-449-23691-9

Printed in the United States of America

10   9   8   7   6   5   4   3   2   1

Contents

The Whiteoak Family

CAPTAIN PHILIP WHITEOAK (of the British Army)
b. 1815 (deceased)
m. 1848

ADELINE COURT (of Ireland)
1825 — 1927

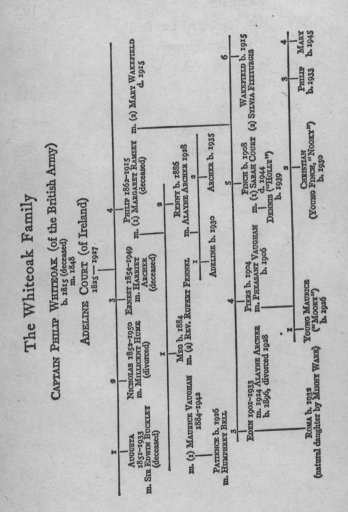

CENTENARY
AT JALNA

One

Mary Whiteoak's World

This little Mary was eight years old, rather small and tender for her age, more puzzled than pleased by what she discovered around her, yet, at times, swept on the wings of a wild joy. But this always happened when she was alone, when there was silence, except for perhaps the sound of leaves being tumbled by a breeze or a sudden burst of song from an unseen bird. Then she would raise her arms and flap them like wings. She would utter a little cry, as though her feelings were too much for her.

There was nothing to give her special joy on this cold morning in early May. There was a north wind that made the growing things in the garden tremble. Some of them were about six inches tall but the leaf buds of the maples had barely appeared.

"My God," exclaimed Renny Whiteoak, coming into the studio where Mary was, "it's as cold as charity in here! Why are you hiding yourself away?"

He took her small icy hands in his to warm them but she gave an enigmatic smile.

She said, "I'm not cold."

Her hands were hidden in his sinewy horseman's hands. "The trouble with women," he said, "is that you never wear enough clothes. Look at that skimpy little dress you have on."

She did not quite know whether or not her feelings were hurt. She liked this uncle better than any other male, even her father, who doted on her. She had him in the studio, all to herself, yet—lumping her in with all women, as he had, appeared to thrust a responsibility on her that she could not, without tears, accept. . . . The tears were ready, somewhere in the back of her throat, but she swallowed them.

"I didn't choose the dress," she murmured. "It was put on me."

"By your mother?"

"Yes." She did not say how pleased she had been when the

sunshine of this May morning had seemed to warrant a cotton dress. And it was her favorite color, light blue, the color of her eyes.

"But your mother did not tell you to come into this cold studio, did she?"

"I came to see the cocoon." She led him to a window sill where the cocoon had lain all the winter. One end of it was open and out of it had crawled (no more prepossessing than a worm) a moist brown moth.

Renny lifted Mary to the window sill as they might watch it together. The sill was dusty and rather rough, for the studio had once been a stable, but the tender flesh of the little girl's thighs accepted it without a shudder.

"It's going to be a beauty," said Renny, as the moth stretched its wings. They opened and closed like fans, and new colors (pink, blue and glossy brown) were discovered as the wings dried.

The moth gained strength. It crept to Renny's finger and slowly made the ascent to his knuckle. He opened the window and a shaft of sunshine entered.

"It's wonderful," said Renny, "how growing things prosper in the sun!"

"Prosper?" she questioned, somehow connecting the word with making money.

"Flourish," he replied, "grow plump and strong. You could do with some sunshine yourself."

"Should I grow wings?"

"Heaven forbid!"

"Why 'Heaven forbid'?"

"Because you're angel enough as you are."

This pleased her. Indeed, conversation with him was always a pleasure to her. She bent her head closer to the moth to watch its progress along his hand. Her fine hair separated and fell forward, explosing her tender nape. His eyes moved to it, away from the moth which, with a quiver of new life, prepared to fly.

"Why does it take so long?" she asked.

"Well, it took you more than a year to learn to walk."

"Had I been in a cocoon?"

"Sort of." She turned her head sidewise and gave him a slanting look.

"Tell me," she said, "all about—everything."

"You ask your mother." His tone became brusque. "I wouldn't know."

"I think you know everything," she said.

Together they watched the moth's progress from a lumbering movement to a confident preparation for flight. It had become more brightly colored, its body smaller, its wings larger, capable of flight.

Renny Whiteoak lifted it from his hand and set it outside on the sunny sill. "Come along," he said, "you'll freeze if you stay here."

"I like this studio. I come here to think."

"About Christian?"

Christian was her brother, the owner of the studio, who was studying in Paris.

"No. About all of us. Do you know how many houses there are, with us in them?"

He pretended not to know. "How many?"

"Five," she cried in triumph. "First there's ours—"

"You should put Jalna first," he interrupted. For a moment she looked downcast, then strung off the names quickly.

"First there's Jalna, where you live. Then there's my house—"

Again he interrupted—"You should say *my father's house.*"

Instantly she brought out, for she was a regular church-goer, *"In my father's house are many mansions.* What's a mansion, Uncle Renny?"

"A large residence."

"How could there be a lot of large residences in one house, Uncle Renny?"

"That particular house is heaven."

She pondered over this as she hopped beside him through the door into the sunshine.

"Is Jalna a mansion?" she asked.

"Good Lord, no. It's just a fair-sized house."

She hid her disappointment and went on with her list.

"First there's Jalna. Then there's my father's house. That sounds silly to me. Does it sound silly to you?"

"Rather. Better say *my house,* as you did the first time. That's two, isn't it?"

"Yes. Jalna and my house and Uncle Finch's house and Aunt Meg's and Patience's. That's five houses, all belonging to us. Shall we call on them, just you and me together?"

"All right," he said. "It's rather a good idea. We'll go to Jalna first. I've already told your mother that I'm taking you to see the new foal."

She was so happy to do this that she wanted to reward him. She said, "There's a starling's nest under the eave," and she pointed it out to him. The starling had just gone in, with a bit of string dangling from his beak. He was quite hidden, now that he was under the eave, but a pigeon had seen him and had flown to the roof to peer in at the happy householder. As though that were not enough he hopped down from the roof and went in to observe the progress of the nest-building. His feet showed clean and coral-colored. His pouting breast was the banner of desirous conjugality. Deeply he cooed as he stood half-hidden with the starling.

"Poor old boy," said Renny. "He's dying for a nest of his own and is too lazy to build one."

Mary's eager sympathy, where birds and beasts were concerned, overflowed in a tear or two. She wiped them on the back of her uncle's hand that she closely held.

"Let's go," she whispered, as though unable to bear the sight of the pigeon's frustration.

Together they strolled along the road and entered a field across which a path, newly thawed, led to Jalna. Mary's shoelace was dangling and Renny bent to tie it. Consciously feminine, she savored his attitude of service to her. She sniffed the good smell of tweed and pipe tobacco that rose from him. As he had looked down in tenderness at her white nape, now she gazed in wonder at his weather-beaten one. All the long winter it had been shielded by a collar; still it looked weather-beaten. With curiosity she examined his high-colored, pointed ears, his dense red hair.

She asked, "Why is your hair a different color in spots?"

He sat on his heels and stared at her in surprise. He was astonished. "A different color? Where?"

"There," she touched the hair at his temple with her forefinger. "It's sort of gray there."

"Gray," he repeated. "Gray. I hadn't noticed. You mean really gray?"

She was proud to have discovered something about him that he himself hadn't noticed. She danced up and down and chanted—"Gray! Gray! Gray!"

"Well, I'll be dashed," he said, rather to himself than to her. "I hadn't noticed more than a few scattered gray hairs, but *really* gray, you say, at the temples? Hm—well—I'm past sixty. I suppose it's to be expected." He tried to sound resigned, then burst out: "Why, my grandmother lived to be a hundred, and she *never* went gray. But, of course, her hair was hidden by a lace cap. I couldn't very well wear a lace cap, could I, Mary? Would you like to see me in a lace cap?"

"You look nice," said Mary, in a comforting tone, for she felt that he was troubled.

Hand in hand they crossed the brown field, he leaving the path to her and walking alongside in his thick-soled brown boots that left their imprint on the rough grass. They came to another field, into which gave a five-barred gate. The field beyond was somehow greener and more springlike. A benign cow stood there, wating for the grass to grow. Renny Whiteoak laid his hand on the gate.

"See this gate, Mary?" he asked.

She nodded, her fine fair hair blown by the north wind.

"Well," he went on, "I've been in the habit of vaulting this gate, just for the fun of it, when I cross this field. I haven't done it since last fall. Now I'm going to make a test. If I can vault over this gate—well and good. If I can't I shall realize that gray hairs are a sign of decrepitude."

"What shall you do then?" she asked, only half-understanding.

"I'll burst into tears," he said emphatically. "How would you like to see me burst into tears?"

The thought of seeing him in tears brought the all too ready tears into her own eyes.

He saw them and declared, "We'll cry together."

He took a clean neatly folded handkerchief from his pocket and put it into her hand. "We can share this," he said. "It's large but we'll need it." Near the gate he halted. "Now—be ready, Mary—go!"

He took a few quick steps to the gate, laid a hand on it and vaulted it smartly, turning on the other side to face his niece with a grin.

"How was that?" he demanded.

She clapped her hands, with the handkerchief between them. She gave a little laugh of delight. "Oh, that was good," she cried. "Do it again!"

The grin faded from his face. "How like a woman," he said, opening the gate for her to pass through. "A man does his damnedest and all she can find to say is—'Do it again.'"

Mary wiped her eyes, then her nose, with the handkerchief and returned it to him. The cow moved a little closer to watch them pass. They were observed also by Renny Whiteoak's son, Archer, a University student, home for the week end.

"Well, Archer, and what did you think of that for a jump?" Renny's eager brown eyes sought his son's cold blue ones.

"Very spry," returned the youth judicially.

"I'll bet you couldn't do it."

"I never have pretended," said Archer, "to be athletic. It's all I can do to find the path and, when I have found it, to stay on it. But I admire high spirits—never say die—all that sort of thing." Archer liked a Latin quotation and now added—*"Nec mora nec requies."*

He joined the other two, taking care that they should be between him and the cow.

Renny had not liked the word "spry." To get even with his son he remarked, "That's a nasty-looking pimple you have on your chin."

"It may not add to my appearance," said Archer, "but it has added considerably to my comfort, as, because of it, I am excused from a tea party Auntie Meg is giving at the Rectory. I was to have helped pass the tarts but she thinks that pimples and pastry are too apropos."

"That's the Women's Institute," Mary piped up proudly. "I'm going to the party to help."

They passed from the field into the apple orchard, where the trees, after valorous effort throughout the month of April, had produced only the tiniest leaf buds, where the path was half-hidden by last year's dead grass, where a few dying snowflakes huddled in the deepest shade.

"Will spring ever come to us!" Archer exclaimed disconsolately.

"In a few weeks this orchard will be white with bloom." The word "white" touched the master of Jalna in a tender spot. He bent his head in front of Archer. "Do you see anything wrong with my hair?" he demanded.

Archer examined it without interest. "Nothing," he said, "except that it's red."

"Well, I like that!" exclaimed Renny, affronted.

"I admit that it suits you," said Archer. "You were born and bred to what it indicates, but I have always been thankful I did not inherit it."

Renny straightened himself and gave a disparaging glance at his son's dry pale thatch.

"I know it's not handsome hair," said Archer, "but it will see me through courtship and marriage. By that time I shall probably be as bald as a doorknob."

"I had not thought of you in connection with marriage." Renny spoke with respect rather than unkindness.

"Why not?"

"Well, possibly because you're so highbrow."

"I may be highbrow," Archer said stiffly, "but I believe I shall be capable of propagating my kind."

"That's just it. Your kind isn't suited to the life we lead here. I can't picture your kind as breeding horses and farming. You've said that yourself."

Archer spoke with an edge to his voice. "I suppose you have my sister in mind for the job. . . ."

"I had thought of the possibility."

"Have you a mate for her in mind?"

"I have my ideas."

"For what they are worth," said Archer. "Where she is concerned you can't be certain of anything. To wit, she's a female."

When conversing with Archer, Renny sometimes found himself using pedantic expressions quite unlike his naturally terse manner. Now he said, "What I was endeavoring to elucidate is whether you notice any change in my hair."

"Elucidate," repeated Archer, drawing back.

"Yes. Find out."

"I've noticed it's a bit gray at the temples."

"You have—and you didn't tell me!"

"It seems natural, and—" here Archer gave his singularly sweet smile—"looks rather nice."

Renny returned the look glumly. "I don't understand," he said. "My grandmother's hair was still red at my age."

Mary was dancing from one foot to another, hugging herself to keep from freezing.

"Come along," Renny said, taking her hand. He swept her over a puddle at the edge of the orchard and they made their way across the sodden lawn, round the house to the front door.

Inside the hall the three dogs, having too much sense to go out on such a morning, rose to greet them with overdemonstrative affection for Renny, tolerance for Mary, and cool curiosity for Archer. He remarked:

"Funny to meet you without the dogs."

Renny took the cairn terrier into his arms. "This little one," he said, "is not as hardy as he used to be. He's promised me to take care of himself. One of the others has a sore paw, and one a touch of rheumatism."

"Poor things," said Archer, without sympathy.

Alayne Whiteoak, Renny's wife, came out of the library, a book of essays in her hand. That room had been no more than a sitting-room, with few books, when she had come, as a bride, to Jalna, but now its walls were lined with well-arranged volumes. It also had a television set which Alayne deplored. Little Mary at once went into the library and turned it on. A seductive baritone voice came into the hall. Alayne could imagine the face from which it issued. She called out:

"Mary, you did not ask permission to do that." Mary did not hear her.

"She loves it," said Renny.

"It gives her a sense of power," said Archer, "and that's why she turns it on."

"Well," Alayne spoke sharply, "go and turn it off, Archer."

He went into the library and closed the door after him.

Alone with Renny, Alayne avoided looking at his muddy boots by looking at his attractive face, with its well-marked aquiline features, adroit mouth and amber eyes. However, she so well concealed her admiration that he thought she was annoyed at him—as indeed she all but was.

"Little wife," he said, and made as though to kiss her, but she moved away. If there was one form of his endearments she liked less than "little wife," it was "wee wifie," which he occasionally produced when he happened to remember that he had had a Scottish grandfather. But "little wife" was bad enough to make her reject amorous overtures from him.

"Why did Mary come?" she asked.

"That's very interesting. She suggested that we should call at all five of the houses belonging to our family. I think that's rather clever of her. What I mean is, she's the youngest of the tribe. She's just beginning to understand what it is to belong to a family, to . . ." He hesitated.

"To be a Whiteoak," she finished for him, with a touch of irony.

He did not notice that. He accepted what she had said, as wisdom.

"So," he went on, "Mary and I are making the rounds, and I'm going to tell her a little about each of the houses as we visit them. And about the families who live there, of course."

"I must go into town this afternoon," Alayne said, feeling little interest in Mary's education. "Will you drive me or shall I ask Hans?" Hans was the husband of the cook. A Dutch couple had served the household well while Wragge, the

Cockney houseman, was, with his wife, taking a prolonged holiday in England.

Renny amiably agreed to drive Alayne into the city, though he hated and feared the traffic. "I have no business there myself," he said. "I can start at whatever time you like."

A little later he and Mary were standing, hand in hand, on the gravel sweep in front of the house. She was sorry to leave the television, but she was so pleased to be going about with Renny that nothing else really mattered. Even the wetness and cold of her feet did not matter, and the hand that lay in Renny's was warm as toast.

"This house," he was saying, "is where your roots are."

"My roots?" she repeated, looking down at her small wet feet.

"Yes. Your beginnings. Your father and mother came here when they were first married." His mind flew back to that homecoming and the hot reception the young pair had suffered. He saw, as clear as though it were yesterday, the passionately excited group, the grandmother in their midst. She'd given Piers a sound rap on the hand with her stick. The poor little bride had cried, and no wonder.

"It's the most important house of the five, I know," Mary said, looking up into his face.

"You're right, and it's soon going to have a birthday—its hundredth birthday. That's what they call a centenary. And it's going to have a celebration!"

"A party?"

"Yes. A really splendid party."

"Shall I be there?"

"We'll all be there. And let me tell you, Mary, there's nothing in the world so strong as a close-knit family group. It gives you confidence. It gives you good cheer. It may give you a bad hour occasionally but it's always there to go to in time of trouble and it's there to share your joys."

Mary nodded agreement, even though she did not understand half of what he said.

Looking down into her child's face, he said, "You'll remember this later and it will mean a lot to you."

To show that she understood, she said, "The house will soon be a hundred years old."

He exclaimed eagerly—"And for the occasion, all the woodwork, shutters, porch and doors will be freshly painted. The woodwork's paint always has been green, but I'm seriously thinking of ivory paint this year. It would set off the rosy color of the brick and the green of the Virginia creeper."

The Virginia creeper, at the time, showed not a single green leaf. Its leaves were tightly rolled and looked like little red tongues, stuck out in derision.

"Will you paint the front door ivory?" Mary asked.

"No. The door will keep its natural oak color. The brass knocker looks well on it, don't you agree?"

"It's a very nice house," said Mary. "Our family has five homes and it's the best."

The house appeared to absorb all this attention and praise with great self-satisfaction. If a house could be said to look smug, certainly it did. It seemed to say: "I will remain here, to justify your lives, as long as this country survives."

Seven pigeons slid down the sloping roof and stood poised for flight, their jewel-like eyes, their burnished throats, bright with the promise of the season. The steps that now came running along the drive were those of Renny's daughter, Adeline. She was five years older than Archer and though slim was exuberantly formed, as compared to the stark austerity of his youthful frame. These two were in every way a contrast: his fair hair, dry and inclined to stand upright, while hers, of a rich auburn that in sunlight glowed red, curled, as though caressingly, above her vivid face; his eyes a constant blue, hers a changeful brown; his lips composed in a thoughtful and almost satiric (or so he hoped) line, hers ready to smile or be sad.

"I heard your voice, Daddy," she excalimed. "Where are you going? To the stables? Hello, Mary." She kissed the little girl with warmth and a certain possessiveness.

Renny said, "Mary and I are making the rounds of the family, just to see that everyone is in their place and behaving themselves and to let them know we are on the spot if they want our advice or our help."

Mary looked important.

"Good," said Adeline. "I'll go with you as far as the stables." She wore riding clothes and already had been exercising her favorite horse. That was what had brought the brilliant color to her cheeks.

In the stable they inspected the foal—weak, rough-coated, timid of eye, but standing on his legs. A whicker of warning and pride made him move closer to his mother, who showed no sign of the ordeal of giving him birth. At this time she was the heroine of the stables. Nothing was too good for her.

Mary sniffed the scent of clean straw and hay. She remarked, "It's warmer here than outdoors. Why is it warmer here than outdoors?"

"It's animal warmth," said Adeline. "It's the healthiest kind of warmth."

"I wish," said Mary, "that I might go to see East Wind. . . . He's my favorite of all the horses."

Renny and Adeline exchanged a look over the child's head. The look said: What an amazingly clever child she is. The things she thinks up!

"He certainly should be my favorite!" Renny spoke with warmth, for all his present prosperity, so long delayed, was due to the prowess of East Wind on the race track.

The thoroughbred stood now in his loose box, eying them nonchalantly. He was big, brawny, without elegance, but full of confidence. No sudden contingency alarmed him. He enjoyed racing. He had an impeccable digestion and iron nerves. Renny Whiteoak had spent a large part of the legacy from a loved uncle in acquiring East Wind. He had bought him in the face of bitter though almost silent opposition from his wife. And how well had that purchase turned out! The rangy colt had won race after race. Wealthy racing men had offered large sums for him, but a kind of stubborn loyalty caused Renny to refuse even the most tempting offers. East Wind's place was at Jalna as long as he lived.

It was this same loyalty that led Renny now to the side of his loved old mare, Cora. She was approaching forty years of age but was in fine fettle—her teeth tolerably good; her intelligence, so Renny thought, amazing. She loved him with the ardor of a strong, one-track nature. He now submitted to her moist nuzzling, her pushing and her nipping, giving her in return a playful cuff, as well as a kiss.

After the visit to the stables, uncle and niece went down a path, through a ravine and across a rushing brown stream that not long ago had been frozen. Now it flowed only a few inches below the small rustic bridge spanning it. "I won't walk across," cried Mary. "I won't! I won't! I'm afraid!"

"I'm surprised at you," said Renny. "Every spring you see this little stream in flood. Why should it frighten you now?"

"It never came so close before." Mary looked at it askance. "It's turned into something different. I don't like it. I'll get my feet wet," she said, as though they could be any wetter. He picked her up, strode across the bridge with her, set her down on the other side. Happily she clambered up the path on the far side of the ravine. Passing through a bit of woodland in whose shelter the first hepaticas, the snow-white bloodroot bloomed, and the crows were cawing, they came to the small house known as the Fox Farm. Here lived Renny's niece, Patience, married to a writer named Humphrey Bell. She opened the door to them and it could be seen at once that they had called at an unpropitious time. After kissing them she whispered:

"Humphrey is desperately working on a radio play. He must finish it by evening. I'm so sorry he can't come down. He'll be sorry too."

"O.K.," said Renny, "if he's not able to come down, I'll go up and see him."

"Oh, no!" She tried to intercept him, but he was already on his way up the uncarpeted stairs that creaked at every step.

When the two cousins were left below, Mary remarked, "I like television better than radio."

"I like radio best," said Patience, "because Humphrey makes more out of radio. I do wish Uncle Renny hadn't gone up."

"Shall I go up and tell him?"

"Goodness, no. It's very bad for a writer to be interrupted in his work."

"We're making a tour of the family houses." Mary looked important. "You are second on our list."

The two men now descended the stair together, their boots clumping in unison. Patience, who looked on her husband as an artist to be protected and cherished, searched his face in anguish to discover what damage this interruption might have done him. But his was an inscrutable face, principally because of his extreme fairness. He had narrowly escaped being an albino.

"We're going to have a drink," he said to Patience and went to the pantry and brought out a bottle of rye.

Patience and Mary looked on in a kind of speechless disapproval while the two men, having produced a completely masculine atmosphere, sipped their drinks and talked about the weather.

"Have another?" Humphrey invited, suddenly looking carefree, as though he had not a living to earn and his wife were not pregnant. On her part she placed her bulk between him and her uncle, as though to protect him.

"No second drink in the morning," said Renny. "But this was just what I needed to warm me up."

"You never look chilly."

"It's my coloring. Now *you* never look warm."

"I suppose it's my coloring—or lack of it," said Humphrey Bell ruefully.

"Have you," asked Renny, as he finished his drink, "noticed anything about my hair?"

"Only," answered Bell, "how thick it is and—how red."

"Uncle Renny can't help that," put in Patience. "I'm used to it and I like it."

Renny gave her a hug. "Thank you, Patty. However, this child tells me I am going gray at the temples. I don't want to be self-centred like my poor old grandmother, but it came as rather a shock."

Was he being funny? Patience wondered. She said—"I had noticed."

"Had you noticed, Humphrey?" Renny demanded.

"I had noticed," said Bell, with the air of a man who says—I can face life as well as you.

"But it was Mary who broke the news to me." Renny's dark eyes were fixed on the little girl with an accusing look that brought tears to her own eyes.

"Give the little one a Coke, Patience," said Bell kindly. He knew nothing of children but supposed it was the thing to do.

Renny intervened. "No—never a Coke. My brother Piers said, when Mary arrived, she was never to see a comic or taste a Coke, and he's stuck to it."

"Well, I'm awfully glad you dropped in," said Bell, wistfully thinking of his work upstairs.

"We are on a tour, Mary and I, of the family houses." Renny put an arm about Mary and went on to inform her, "This house, as you know, was once lived in by people who bred foxes." He looked thoughtful for a moment, thinking of those people.

"Funny," said Patience, "how the name stuck to it."

"No family has lived very long in this house," continued Renny, instructing Mary as though in a matter of importance, "but all have been connected more or less closely with Jalna."

"Humphrey and I hope to live here a long while," said Patience.

"Of course you will," said Renny cheerfully. He glanced at his wrist watch. "Well, Mary and I must be moving on if we are to complete the tour before lunch."

When the Bells were left alone together Patience took his hand and led him back upstairs to his study.

"Poor dear," she said tenderly. "Poor, poor dear! What an interruption! Your day's work will be ruined, I'm afraid. I try so hard to protect you," she mourned.

He could not tell her that she tried too hard, that all he wanted was to be let alone.

He was a source of wonder to her. She would raise herself on her elbow in bed and brood over his face, as he slept, in mingled curiosity and delight. She had been brought up surrounded by males but they were uncles and cousins. Humphrey was different. He was an enigma. When she heard, on the radio, something he had written, she was almost overcome by pride and her desire to protect him from intrusions on his work. But Humphrey, hearing it broadcast, was ashamed to acknowledge that it was his. Still more ashamed was he of his lack of appreciation for her care of him, his longing to be not fussed over.

Now he heard her go slowly down the stairs and he had a sudden fear lest she should fall. He ran to the top of the stairs and called, "Be careful, dear!"

She looked over her shoulder. "Careful of what?"

"Of falling."

"You dear old silly," she said and plodded on down the stairs.

He returned to his writing.

Hand in hand Renny and Mary passed through a gathering of noble oaks, embosomed by evergreens, crossed a stile and were on a new path across a field.

"That is a nice little house," said Mary, "where Patience and Humphrey live."

"Yes, it's not a bad little house."

"Who owns it?"

"I do. Why do you ask?"

"Daddy says they should pay more rent."

"Well, I like that."

"Then why don't you ask for more, Mummie says."

"Mary, you tell your parents that when I want their advice I'll ask for it."

"Yes, Uncle Renny." She felt rebuffed. She had tried grown-up conversation on him and it had failed. For a short space she plodded beside him in silence. She rather wished she had not come, and she was beginning to get hungry.

"Where are we going now?" she asked.

He stopped stock-still to say, "Do you mean to tell me you don't know?"

She hastened to say, "It's Vaughanlands, where Uncle Finch lives."

As they drew near the house that was built in a hollow, Mary timidly asked, "Do you own this too?"

Gazing at it without admiration he replied, "God forbid."

"God forbids lots of things, doesn't He?" said Mary.

"What I mean is that I don't like the style of this house—its architecture. It's a new house, built to take the place of a fine old house that once stood here. It was burnt to the ground—do you remember?"

"Oh, yes, and Uncle Finch built this new one. It's pretty." She saw the large picture window in the livingroom and, looking out of it, a woman wearing a white pullover.

"That's Sylvia," said Mary. "Must we go in?"

She was shy, but Sylvia Whiteoak came out to meet them. Mary had a strange feeling, an uncomfortable feeling about this new wife of Finch's, possibly because she herself was so patently shy. Also she had heard it said that Sylvia had once suffered a "bad nervous breakdown." Mary did not at all like the thought of that. It was mysterious, and Mary half-expected to see Sylvia come to pieces before her very eyes. Also Mary was becoming colder and hungrier. Much as she liked to be with Renny, she almost wished the tour were over.

He was telling Sylvia about it. "You are the third on our list," he was saying. "I picked Mary up at her own home. First we visited Jalna. Next the Fox Farm."

"How are Humphrey and Patience?" said Sylvia. "I like them both so much."

Even that simple remark made Sylvia seem strange to Mary. You did not say you liked or disliked anybody in the family. They were a part of it, so you neither liked nor disliked them. They were just there.

"You are the third on our list," repeated Renny, not noticing her remark. "After you we shall call at the Rectory—then to Piers's in time for Mary's lunch." Mary wondered if that time would ever come. Her little cold hand lay acquiescent in Renny's. She curled and uncurled her toes against the damp sodden soles of her shoes.

"How interesting," said Sylvia in her pleasant Irish voice. "But what is the object of the tour?"

"It's to make Mary conscious of the connection—the family bond that—well, you know what I mean. She goes to each of our houses in turn. She sees some of the family in every one of them. It gives her a feeling of what we are to each other."

For the first time Mary spoke up. "It's a tour," she said.

"Now I understand," said Sylvia, "and I'm proud to be included, even though Finch is not here. Won't you come in and have a drink? I can make a quite good cocktail."

Renny looked at his wrist watch. "It's half-past eleven. Too early for a cocktail. But I shouldn't mind a small glass of sherry, if you have it."

Inside the music-room that was dominated by the concert grand piano, Sylvia brought sherry in a plum-colored glass decanter. The window was so large that the newly awakened trees crowded almost into the room. Mary saw how one maple tree had young green leaves and a kind of diminutive bloom, while the tender leaves of another were of a strange brownish shade, but in time they would be green.

Sylvia was holding a box of chocolates in front of Mary. She took one but, when she bit into it, discovered that the filling was marzipan. This she disliked above all flavors. It made her feel positively ill, yet she had to swallow the morsel she had bitten off.

"I had a letter from Finch this morning," Sylvia was saying. "His tour is nearly over and I'm sure he will be thankful. These tours are so tiring!"

They are indeed, thought Mary. She too would be thankful when her tour was over. She kept the sweet hidden in her hand. She could feel her palm getting sticky from the melted chocolate. She wondered what she could do to be rid of it.

"Do have another," Sylvia was urging her.

"No, thank you."

"But surely you can eat two chocolates!"

"Of course, she can," said Renny. He took one from the box and put it into Mary's hand. She bit into it and it was marzipan.

"Thanks," she murmured and might have added "for nothing."

She sat, holding the two chocolates in her two hands, while Sylvia and Renny sipped sherry and ate biscuits. At last, in desperation, she asked, "May I go to the bathroom, please?"

"I'll show you where it is," said Sylvia.

"I know." Mary thought of how she had watched this house being built, before even Sylvia had married Uncle Finch and come there to live. In the bathroom she put the two chocloates into the lavatory and turned the handle. A great rush of water swept them away. Not a decent little rush such as came at home, when you turned the handle, but a cataract like Niagara that swept the chocolates out of sight for ever. But Mary's palms were still sticky from them. She wiped her hands on a white damask towel and was troubled to see the brown stains left on it. These she folded out of sight and trotted back to the music-room.

When Sylvia and Renny were left alone she said, "What a shy little thing Mary is! It's a wonder, with three older brothers. One would expect her to be forward."

"She's very like her paternal grandmother. She's named for her. She came as governess to my sister Meg and me. Then she married my father."

"I want so much to be friends with the children of the family," said Sylvia.

"There are only two. This one and Finch's boy, but before long Patience will make her addition to the tribe."

"Finch's boy. . . . Tell me about Dennis. I did not see much of him in the Easter Holidays. Finch and I were busy settling in, and Dennis seemed always to be off about his own affairs. He's not a very friendly child. Is he shy too?"

"Quite the reverse. A self-possessed little fellow—small for his age. He'll be fourteen next December and looks eleven."

"He has no resemblance to Finch." Sylvia spoke wistfully. If the boy had been like Finch she was sure she would have understood him—sure that he would have been easy to make friends with. Finch was such a friendly soul. Finch reached out toward people.

"Unfortunately Dennis takes after his mother," Renny said cheerfully. "She was a bit of a devil. You'll make Finch happy. She only made him miserable."

Mary had returned to the room. She overheard these last words, from the strange talk of grownups, from which she shrank. Sylvia now took her hand and said:

"You do like me, don't you?"

Mary despairingly searched her mind for an answer.

"I like *you* so much," went on Sylvia.

She was at it again, talking about things that Mary preferred to keep private. She looked into Sylvia's lovely pale face and murmured, "I think I must be going. Thanks for the nice chocolates."

"Have another."

Mary drew back from the proffered box.

"Better not," said Renny. "It's her lunchtime. But first we must go to my sister's. We're making the rounds, Mary and I."

"Is she walking all the way?"

"A walk like this is nothing to her, is it, Mary?"

"Oh, no," said Mary. "Are we going now?"

Sylvia kissed her and soon they were outdoors again.

Striding along the path Renny remarked, "That's one of these newfangled houses. All very well, if you've never lived in anything better."

"I'd not like to live there," Mary said stoutly. "I'd rather live at home."

"Or at Jalna," he suggested.

She agreed with an emphatic nod. She was suddenly happy. The wind had ceased, the sun come out warm and almost springlike. Suddenly on a mound a cluster of trilliums rose out of the wet earth, their white blooms held up like chalices, as though they had that instant sprung up from pure joy.

Renny and Mary stood looking down at them.

"You know better than to pick, don't you?" he said.

"I've known that all my life." She was proud of her knowledge of growing things. "It kills the bulb. . . . Is Sylvia Dennis's stepmother?"

"Yes."

"I thought stepmothers were cruel."

"Nonsense. I myself had a stepmother, and a very sweet woman she was."

"Does Dennis like her?"

"He will when he gets used to her."

Mary was thankful when one of the farm wagons from Jalna overtook them and they rumbled in it, behind the two stout percherons, and were deposited at the gate of the Rectory—which, behind its tall greening hedge, looked the proper cozy setting for Auntie Meg. She met them and enfolded them in a warm embrace. She was having a cup of tea from a tray in the living-room and at once brought two extra cups and poured some for each of them.

"And I have some thin slices of fruit loaf—really nice and

fresh, with good raisins in it that you might like. You know how it is with me. I eat scarcely anything at table but must have a little snack now and again to keep me going. This is really the first food I've had to-day."

"I know what you are about meals," Renny said sympathetically. "It's a wonder you don't starve. Mary and I are due for lunch in a short while, so we don't need anything to eat now but we'll gladly drink a cup of tea with you."

Mary was hungrily eying the slices of fruit loaf but she politely began to sip her tea. Renny was explaining to his sister the reason for the tour, while she, without seeming to do so, was sweeping clean the tray. Every now and then she would smile at Mary, a smile of such peculiar sweetness that the little girl forgot how hungry she was and how wet were her feet.

Renny, drinking a second cup of tea, was saying, "With the centenary of Jalna coming next year, I thought it a good thing to give the youngest of the family an idea of what it means to us."

"You couldn't do a better thing," said Meg. "Modern times are so strange. One can't be sure what children are thinking. One must guide them as best one can."

Renny spoke firmly to the child. "Tell Auntie Meg what you know about the centenary at Jalna."

With a slight quaver in her voice Mary answered, "Everybody's got to come."

Meg gave a pleased smile. "And who is everybody?" she asked, helping herself to another slice of fruit loaf.

"Everybody in the family."

Meg now said, in the dictatorial tone of someone hearing the Catechism, "Name them."

"All the ones that live—that live—"

"Convenient." Renny supplied the word.

"Convenient," Mary said with a pleased smile at her aunt, who, taking another large bite of fruit loaf, mumbled through it:

"And who comes from a distance?"

"My brother and Uncle Wakefield and Roma."

"Isn't she clever?" exclaimed Renny. "She knows everything."

"It would be nice," said Meg, "if we could celebrate the centenary by a wedding. Adeline's, for example."

"It would indeed, but whom is she to marry?"

"There's that dear boy, Maurice, who loves her to distraction and always has. How would you like to see your favorite brother married to Adeline, Mary?"

"I have no favorites," said Mary. "My brothers are all just men."

"I know, dear," Meg spoke patiently, "but you must have a man for a wedding. Whom would you choose for a bridegroom—a fairy prince—for Adeline?"

Mr. Fitzturgis," said Mary promptly.

Renny and Meg groaned in unison. They had unhappy memories of Adeline's engagement to the Irishman. Renny took some credit to himself that it had been broken off.

At that moment the Rector entered the room. He had a genial greeting for the two visitors and a look that was half-admiring, half-reproachful for his wife. They had been elderly widow and widower when they married. He still had not grown accustomed to encountering her and her relatives always about the house, and he deplored her habit of frequent little lunches from trays.

"She never eats a proper meal," he said to Renny.

"She never has. Yet she thrives. She how plump she is, while I, who eat like a horse at table, am thin as a rail."

"What is a rail?" asked Mary.

"A rail," observed the Rector, "is a kind of water bird—rather rangy and thin." He went and opened a window, exclaiming. "How stuffy it is in here!" During the years after the death of his first wife he had lived in a pleasurable draft from open windows; now in his second marriage he was always complaining of the stuffiness of the rooms.

This open window affected Meg and Renny not at all, but it was right at Mary's back. She grew colder and colder. Shivering, she watched her aunt empty the teapot, demolish the last currant from the fruit loaf; heard her uncle and the Rector discussing the lateness of the season; she thought of the different houses she had visited that morning and longed for home.

At last they were on their way there. Holding tightly to Renny's hand, getting out of the path of motor cars, every yard of the way familiar to her, her blood moved more quickly, her spirits rose. She enquired:

"Uncle Renny, why do some ladies get fat?"

"It's the life they lead."

"Does the life they lead make them get fat in different parts of them?"

"It certainly does."

"Auntie Meg is fat all over."

"She certainly is."

"But Patience is fat only in her tummy. Why?"

"Ask your mother."

"Don't you know?"

"It's none of my business."

"Do you always mind your own business?"

"I try." After a little he said, "I hope you're not tired or cold or hungry."

"Oh, no. I'm all right." But he could feel that she was lagging.

"Good girl," he said, and to encourage her began to sing, in a not particularly tuneful voice, an old song he had learned from his maternal grandfather, a Socttish doctor:

> Oh, hame came oor guid man at eve,
>   And hame came he,
> And there he spied a saddle-horse
>   Whaur nae horse should be.
>
> "And hoo came this horse here?
>   And whase can he be?
> And hoo came this horse here
>   Wi'oot the leave o' me?"
>
> "Horse?" quoth she.
>   "Aye, horse," quoth he. . . .
> "Tis but a bonny milch coo
>   My mither sent to me."
>
> "Milch coo!" quoth he.
>   "Aye, milch coo," quoth she. . . .
> "But saddles upon milch coos
>   Never did I see."

By the time he had finished the song they had arrived at his brother's house. The wicket gate stood invitingly open, the fox terrier Biddy came in rapture to meet them, and Piers Whiteoak opened the door.

"We're holding back lunch for you," he said to Renny. "I suppose you'll stay. Have you any idea what time it is?"

"To tell the truth I haven't. Mary and I have been on a tour. Tell Daddy about it, Mary."

Seated on Piers's knee, the warmth from his robust body reaching out to comfort her little thin one, the beam from his fresh-colored face encouraging her, she could think of nothing to say but—"We saw all the family."

"Well," said Piers, "there's nothing very new about that, is there?"

"Oh, but we saw them in a different way," said Renny. "In the past we took it for granted that our kindred was the most important thing in the world for us. Now the youngsters must be taught."

"What about Archer?" asked Piers.

"That boy's an oddity—but, beneath his oddities, he's a Whiteoak all right."

Piers grunted. He took off his daughter's shoes and socks and held her little cold feet in his warm hands. "So you visited all the family houses," he said to her.

"Yes, every one."

"And which do you like best? I mean including our own home."

Certainly Piers expected her to choose her own, but at once she answered—"Jalna."

Renny gave a delighted grin. "There," he exclaimed, "she chooses Jalna! I've explained to her about its centenary. Now, Mary"—he looked at her intently out of his dark eyes—"tell us why you like Jalna best."

Without hesitation, she answered, "Because it has television."

Crestfallen, the brothers stared at her in silence a moment, then broke into a shout of laughter.

Piers's wife, Pheasant, setting a platter of lamb chops on the table, heard this last. "There's a modern child for you," she said, and added wistfully—"When I was a child, how romantic Jalna seemed to me! All the family who lived there were glamorous."

"Even me?" Piers asked flirtatiously.

"Even you."

After twenty-seven years of marriage, they still were lover-like.

While they were enjoying the lamb chops a persistent ringing came from the telephone. Piers answered it and, returning to the table, said, "It was from Jalna. Alayne, wanting to know if you were here and why you had not sent word. She sounded a bit annoyed."

"By George, I forgot."

For a moment Renny was subdued, but soon his naturally good spirits were restored. He liked being with Pheasant and

Piers. The brothers had many interests in common: the live-stock, the farm with its orchards and small fruits. Since Renny's unprecedented success with the race horse, East Wind, Piers had troubled his head less and less about being in debt to him for the rent of the farmlands. Renny was a generous elder brother. If he had money on hand for his needs, he gave little thought to what was owing him. On the other hand he had not been scrupulous, when he was hard up, in days past, about acquiring the wherewithal from his wife's private means or from his brother Finch who had inherited a fortune from his grandmother.

Seated beside her brown-eyed, brown-haired mother, Mary dallied with the hot food on her plate. So long had she gone hungry, she had lost appetite. Now that she was warm and no longer straining to keep up with Renny's strides on the wet paths, the windy road, she could look back on the tour with pride and even pleasure.

"You should have heard us singing as we came down the road," Renny was saying. "Do you remember that old song, Piers?" and he sang:

> Oh, hame came oor guid man at eve,
>   And hame came he,
> And there he spied a saddle-horse
>   Whaur nae horse should be.

"I had it from my maternal grandfather. He was a self-opinionated old Scotch doctor. Do you remember him, Piers?"

"I can't very well remember him, for he died before I was born."

"Well, you've heard of him often enough—Dr. Ramsey—your own grandfather."

"You forget," said Piers, "that we are half-brothers?"

An unpleasant reminder that, to the master of Jalna. He wanted the relationship to be intervolved, with no break. He frowned and asked, "Then who was your maternal grandfather?" He would not do him the courtesy of remembering him.

"He was a London journalist—drank rather heavily, I believe."

"Oh, yes. I remember now. Well, never mind—we had the same paternal grandfather, and what a man he was! Philip Whiteoak!" He mused on the name a moment, then added:

"I'm glad you named one of your sons for him and that the boy is the very spit of him."

"He's a rascal," said Piers. "He'll be coming home from college soon and I have a thing or two to say to him about his extravagance. Christian will be coming from Paris, too."

"And Maurice from Ireland," cried Pheasant. "All three brothers at home! Won't that be lovely, Mary?"

Mary was not at all sure it would. In truth, home seemed pleasanter to her, more her very own, when those three, unruly, loud-talking young men were away. After lunch, with clean dry socks and shoes on, and a warm sweater, she wandered again into the garden. Somehow there was a difference in all the growing things. It was as though they heard spring singing in the distance, and were poised to listen. She discovered the moth, that morning freed from the prison of its cocoon. It was clinging to a newly opened leaf, in a ray of pale sunlight. It attracted the attention of a bird which hovered above it. But the moth, in self-protection, raised its wings, vibrating them. From its hind wings two spots like eyes glared in threat. The bird, alarmed by this insect ferocity, flew away. Yet it did not fly far. Somewhere by its hidden nest it burst into a cheeping song that was the only one it knew.

Mary thought of all the houses she had that morning visited, of the people in them. They all were parts of the family. They were the family—her world. They were separate, yet they were one. Their faces were distinct, yet merged into the weather-beaten countenance of her Uncle Renny.

Two

Finch's Return

Home-comings, thought Finch, were the very best things in life. Home-leavings, a kind of death. Though he had faced the publicity attendant on the life of a concert pianist, he had shrunk from it. In the exhilaration of a public performance he would, for the time, forget his audience. Would, in fact, feel himself one with them. But, at the end, they were his enemies. Then he did not face them in courage but, exhausted, with a smile that women reporters would describe as a "naïve, friendly grin" or a "shy, boyish grin." One thing was certain, audiences liked him. They liked his gangling boyish figure as he crossed the platform. They liked the shape of his head, the expressive movements of his long bony hands.

Now, at the end of a tour (and at this moment he hoped he would never have another) he had come home to his own house, his own wife. He had possessed neither for very long. The paint on his ranch house was still fresh. The house had been built on the site of one which had been burned. This new marriage was built on the ruin of his first marriage. His house, he was willing to admit, did not harmonize with the other houses of the neighborhood—or Jalna, with its faded red brick, almost covered by vines, its stone porch, its five chimneys, rising from the sloping roof where pigeons eternally cooed and slid, where their droppings defaced the leaves of the Virginia creeper and the window sills, where smoke was always coming out of one or more of the chimneys and where the old wooden shingles so often managed to spring a leak.

This house of Finch's was something new, something different. The family must get used to it. As for himself—he was proud of it. He loved it, he told himself—returning to it. He loved his wife and was hoping, with all the fervor of a nature too often swept by hopes and despairs, that his family would love her and she them.

Now he and she were together in the music-room. To-

gether as they always would be in the future, he thought—
and she tried to believe, for she took no happiness for
granted. Now, in wonder, she held one of his hands, with its
beautifully articulated fingers, in hers.

"I'm thinking of the power in it," she said.

"I should like to dig in the earth with it." He clenched it,
as though on a spade. "I'm tired of taking care of myself. A
kind of beastly preciousness—that's what one feels of one's
body on a tour. God, when I think of the rough-and-tumble
of my boyhood! When I think of the life my two older brothers lead—it's natural—"

"But you're doing what you've always wanted, aren't you?"
she said gently.

"Yes," he granted. "I guess it's just that I'm tired. You've
never seen me at the end of a tour. I shall be different in a
day or two. . . . Oh, Sylvia, if only you could know what it
is to me to come home and find you waiting for me! . . .
You do like the house, don't you?"

"It's perfect. There's nothing I would change in it. And
nothing could be more different from my home in Ireland—I
was so ill and unhappy there."

"Do you see much of my family?" he asked, as though he
felt that seeing a good deal of them would complete her cure.

Certainly she knew them quite well, for she had visited at
Jalna. Now she said, "I have had dinner there twice a week
and have had them here. All the family have been sweet. I've
told you in letters."

What a charming voice she had, he thought, and he
remembered how sweet had been the voice of his first wife,
Sarah. Both of them Irish. But how different! Sarah—with
her odd gliding walk, her jet-black hair and green eyes, al-
mond-shaped. Something rigid about her body—while Sylvia
was loosely put together, pale-colored as a wandering wood
spirit. So he thought of her, as he sat holding her hand—
thought of her as elusive, where Sarah had been so relentlessly, almost desperately yet coldly clinging. . . .
Looking into Sylvia's blue eyes, he sought to put Sarah out of
his mind for ever.

But now Sylvia was speaking of Sarah's child. She was saying, "Dennis will soon be coming home for the holidays. It's
so exciting to picture a child in the house."

"He's thirteen. Will be fourteen next Christmas. We used
to call him Holly. An odd little fellow. Small for his age.
Looks about eleven."

When in a few weeks Dennis returned from school, that was Sylvia's first thought: how small he was—how compact, firm, and yet how guileless—with his pale hair and green eyes, he was veiled in her mind—the child of another woman by Finch, yet now to be hers to care for, to love. Why, he looked small enough to tuck into bed at night—to snuggle up to one and tell his boyish troubles. She felt, at the moment, quite ridiculously sentimental about him.

As he sat on the arm of Finch's chair, with an arm about Finch's neck, she looked into their two faces with affectionately critical eyes.

"There's no resemblance," she said. "You two are as different as you can be." She rather wished the boy had looked like Finch. His unlikeness seemed to set him apart. Suddenly she wondered how she would talk to him. She'd had no experience. But she would find out. Bit by bit they would draw close to each other. She and Finch were setting out with a ready-made family. Three of them! A family to be reckoned with.

Finch removed his son's arm from his shoulder.

"Shouldn't you like to run off for a while?" he said.

Dennis from his perch looked down into Finch's face. "Where?" he asked.

"Oh, anywhere. To Jalna. To the stables."

"I've been there already. I'd rather be here with you."

Sylvia asked, "Are there any boys of your age in the neighborhood?"

"I've had enough of boys," returned Dennis. "I've been with over a hundred of them all the term."

Finch got up and gave his shoulders a restive twitch. He went and looked out of the window. The cool unseasonable weather had given way to glowing summer heat. The flowers, as though weary of waiting, had burst into bloom—had, with undue haste, matured.

"The border looks well," said Finch, "considering it's been made so short a while." His eyes were caught by a mass of pansies. He said: "You might go and pick some pansies for Sylvia. You'd like them for the table, wouldn't you, Sylvia?"

Dennis went off obediently. They watched him, as he squatted by the pansy bed. "How sweet he is!" she exclaimed. "Most boys would think it a great bore." She added suddenly, "He's very reserved, isn't he?"

Finch stared. "Reserved! The opposite, I should say. Too clinging. Don't let him pester you."

"What I want is to be friends with him," she said.

In a surprisingly short while Dennis returned with a neat bunch of pansies. He marched straight to Finch and offered them to him. "Take them to Sylvia," said Finch sharply. "Don't be stupid."

Dennis laid them on the small occasional table near Sylvia. She gathered them up tenderly. Dennis's eyes were on the table. "That table," he said, "belongs to Auntie Meg."

To Finch it seemed that Dennis had purposely spoken of the occasional table because its ownership had been the subject of heated discussion at the time when this house was being furnished.

Now Finch said, "It does not and never did belong to her. Can't you go off somewhere and amuse yourself?"

"Nothing amuses me so much as being with you."

Finch gave him a swift glance. Was it possible the boy was ragging him? But no—the small, cool face was gently reflective—the green eyes fixed on Finch's face with longing. Sylvia took the pansies to the pantry to find a vase for them. Finch steadied his nerves and sought to produce a fatherly tone.

"Look here, old fellow," he said, "if you will leave Sylvia and me for a bit—we have things to talk over, you know—then you and I will go to Jalna to see Uncle Renny, who has been away ever since I came home. Will that be all right?" To Finch the fatherliness in his voice sounded hollow and forced, but Dennis smiled in pleasure.

"How good you are!" he exclaimed.

Now surely that was an odd remark for a modern boy of thirteen to make. It sounded positively Victorian. And the way he said it, with his small hands clasped against his chest and his eyes shining! It was almost funny.

Anyhow he went, and Finch followed Sylvia to the pantry and admired her arrangement of the pansies. They were in two amethyst glass bowls. "One is for the music-room," she said, "and the other for Dennis's room—if you think he'd like it."

"Good Lord," exclaimed Finch. "If anyone had put flowers in my room when I was a boy I'd have dropped dead from astonishment."

"Then perhaps I'd better not."

Sylvia set the second bowl of pansies in the dining-room. She felt oddly, purposefully happy as though a new invigorating element had come into her life with the coming of the boy. When she saw him set off in the car with Finch to go to Jalna she called out, "Don't be late for lunch, you two."

"We two," repeated Dennis to Finch. "That's the way it used to be, when we had the house to ourselves."

Finch stopped the car with a jolt. "Just what do you mean by that?" he demanded sternly.

"I mean I'm not used to women." Dennis had flushed but he answered with composure.

"Of course you're used to women. You've always had a woman in the house with you."

"Not in our new house."

"Now, look here, Dennis, you are to be specially nice and friendly toward Sylvia or—I'll know the reason why." Finch made no effort to keep the irritation out of his voice. He longed to enjoy his home without the pushing presence of this odd child. He had been an odd sort of child himself, but God knew he had never been pushing.

"Oh, I shall be friendly all right," said Dennis. "I only thought—"

"I don't want you to be—well—pushing."

"Oh, I won't be pushing," said Dennis. "I know how to be quiet. Is Sylvia delicate?"

"She was—once."

"How delicate? Did she have to stay in bed?"

Without answering Finch drove on. Dennis glanced up shyly at him but Finch's expression was enough to prohibit further questioning. Even a child would be conscious of that. With his hands, palms together, pressed between his bare knees, Dennis sat quietly thinking. It was as though he tried to make himself as inconspicuous as possible. But his very smallness, his compact paleness, made his presence more noticeable to Finch. If he had been a different type of boy, thought Finch, he would have been easier to ignore, or perhaps easier to get on with.

But the boy's peculiar presence seemed no barrier to Renny Whiteoak. They found him at Jalna, watching on television a horse race in Florida.

"One of the best things I've seen on TV," he said, turning it off. "They do horse races well."

"Don't let me interrupt you," said Finch.

"It's over." He got to his feet, took Finch's hand and kissed him. He had in him abundant power of enjoyment, though combined with it he was capable of deep depression. Now he was all pleasure in his brother's return.

"You look well," he said, "for you. Was your tour a success?"

"I had good audiences."

"How much did you make?"

From this practical question Finch resolutely shied. He knew that Renny had done well with his colt, East Wind, but it was an expensive thing to maintain a race horse. Perhaps Renny was short of money and was considering the possibility of a loan from him. However, that apprehension was dispelled.

"I've had a good year," Renny said tranquilly. "But show horses are my line, not race horses." He sat down and drew Dennis on to his knee. The boy looked confidently into Renny's brown eyes.

"How do you like having a stepmother?" Renny asked with his genial grin. "Has she beaten you yet? Does she make you eat in the kitchen? And sleep on the floor?"

"I've just come. She hasn't yet." The boy laughed, his face close to Renny's.

"But she will," said Renny. "Just give her time." His expression was now ferocious. "I had a stepmother and she did all those things to me, didn't she, Finch? Made me eat from the dog's dish off the kitchen floor, while Finch ate from a gold plate in the parlor. Isn't that so, Finch?"

Finch nodded, without amusement. This teasing of Dennis, as though he were a six-year-old, bored him, but it was easy to see that Dennis liked it. He snuggled up to Renny, sniffing him with animal pleasure.

"Who's he like?" Renny asked, studying the child's face.

"Certainly not me," said Finch.

"Nor *her*," said Renny, referring to Sarah, Finch's dead wife.

"Eyes and hands," Finch spoke almost in a whisper.

Dennis blinked his eyes and spread out his hands.

"I've been taking violin lessons at school," he said proudly.

Renny groaned. "Another artistic one. Oh, Lord, what's the family coming to! Talent on all sides. Thank goodness, Adeline has none."

"I have none, Uncle Renny," laughed Dennis.

"Splendid! Fiddle away for all you're worth—so long as you've no talent."

"My father is a genius," said Dennis.

"It's time you went." Finch could bear no more. "Clear out."

"See you later," Renny said to Dennis, as man to man. "Go over to the stables and then tell me what you think of the new foal. Here's Adeline. She'll go with you."

Adeline had that moment come into the room. Greeting her, Finch was struck afresh by her beauty. This he remarked to Renny when they were left alone. "She's really stunning," he said.

Renny agreed. Then, moving close to Finch, he said, "I have a wonderful scheme." He fell silent, as though overcome by the splendor of his scheme.

What was it—Finch wondered—to enlarge the stables? He hoped not. He would not put any of his hard-earned cash into that all-engulfing maw. He looked with curiosity into his elder's eyes which, through all vicissitudes, had retained their brightness.

Renny took his arm and led him into the dining-room where hung the portraits of their paternal grandparents. He said:

"Take a good look at them. What do you see?"

But Finch looked at him rather than at the portraits. He thought, What is it in him that fascinates me? Is it his vitality? His zest for living? Yes—but even more it is because he is mysterious. That's the quality in him that fascinates me. Yet he looks on himself as a simple, uncomplicated fellow!

"Tell me what you see," repeated Renny.

With something between a sigh and a groan Finch said, "I see a handsome blond officer in the uniform of the Hussars, the uniform they wore over a hundred years ago."

"Yes—and the other?"

"Well, of course, it's Gran, when she was about twenty-five."

"Who is like her—the very spit of her?"

"Young Adeline—without a doubt."

"And who resembles him? Who's a chip off the old block?"

"Piers, I suppose."

"Yes—but much more than Piers."

"Who then? Whatever are you driving at, Renny?" Renny gave a shout of laughter, that was not all pure enjoyment, for it had an undercurrent of defiance, as though he were expecting criticism. He said: "Just this. If we were to place my young Adeline and Piers's young Philip under these two portraits, what should we find?"

"A remarkable resemblance."

"Right. A truly remarkable resemblance. And what is the

moral? The point of it? The point is that they should marry. Another Philip and Adeline!"

Finch gave a brief ironic laugh. "It would be fine, if you could persuade them, but I make a guess that they've never thought of each other in that light."

"But they soon will. I'll see to it that they do."

"You can't make people fall in love, especially strong-willed, rather spoilt, young people like those two."

"I've every hope." Renny spoke with confidence. "Already they admire each other."

"If it turned out badly you'd never forgive yourself."

"It couldn't turn out badly, any more than the marriage of those two turned out badly." And he cast a confident look at the pair in the portraits who, impersonal, elegant, of a different world, gazed blandly out of their gilded frames.

"The boy," Finch said, "is only twenty. Give him time to grow up."

"He'll be twenty-one next year—the centenary of Jalna—the centenary of Uncle Ernest's birth. . . . What a celebration! But mind, not a word of this to the youngsters."

"Have you spoken of it to Piers?"

"Yes. He's all for it."

"And Alayne?"

"I haven't mentioned it to her yet."

"She'll never agree."

"And why not, I should like to know? Why, it's destined—ordained—there never was such a suitable match. All I wonder is that I never thought of it before."

"You, Renny—a matchmaker?" laughed Finch.

"I've been making matches all my life. Successful ones!"

"My dear fellow, this isn't the stables."

"It's thoroughbred stock."

"I can't decide," said Finch, "whether you're a romantic or a hardheaded materialist."

"Neither. Just a man who loves his family."

"And is willing to subject them to risks?" But what use was there in talking? Finch turned away, and Renny turned to a high-pitched, somewhat acrimonious telephone conversation concerning the behavior of a horse he had recently sold.

Finch wandered through the house, so dear to him, and came upon Alayne in the drawing-room. She was putting out of sight a china figure that she had always disliked but which the family cherished. Finch kissed her and said:

"Ah, there's the dear old shepherdess I've always loved. I haven't seen her in a long while."

"Take her," said Alayne, "I'm sure Renny would be delighted to give her to you." She tried to put the figurine into his hands but he drew back.

"No, no," he said. "I couldn't bear to take her away from Jalna. She's always been here."

Alayne replaced the ornament on the mantelshelf, with a sigh of frustration. They talked of the concerto which Finch was composing. Alayne was the one above all others of the family with whom he could speak with freedom of his work, knowing that from her he would have sympathetic understanding.

When he left he found Dennis waiting for him in the car.

The boy gave his small sweet smile. "Isn't it fun," he said, "to be together again."

Three

The Promising Boy

Piers Whiteoak and the youngest of his three sons stood in the green freshness of morning in the cherry orchard facing each other. Piers wore an expression of embarrassment, just lightened by amusement. Young Philip looked completely dumfounded. He really could not take in what had just been said to him.

"Don't be stupid," Piers said, but kindly.

"But—Dad—why—she'd never do it."

"That's for you to find out."

Philip's bright blue eyes opened wide. His mouth opened and his jaw dropped. His legs, which were as strong as two young pines, suddenly felt weak under him. He stared at Piers, who said, "You're fond of Adeline, aren't you?"

Philip just nodded.

Now very much in earnest, Piers went on: "Renny and I have talked this over. Mind you, it was his idea in the first place, not mine, but I agree that it would be a first-rate match for both of you. You'd be compatible. It would be establishing the family all over again—in a fine sort of way. Another good-looking healthy pair—in love with each other and with life at Jalna. As things are going now, you'd have plenty of money to get on with. Not to be rich, certainly, but enough to get on with quite comfortably."

Philip found his voice. "But hell, Dad. I'm only twenty."

"You'll grow up fast enough. This marriage would make a man of you." A smile, with a touch of malice in it, lit Piers's ruddy face. "Your brother Maurice would envy you. Adeline has refused him, time and again. He has told your mother so."

"She'd reject me too," Philip broke out, almost as though he'd be glad if she did. "She looks on me as a kid."

"She'll soon look on you in quite a different light if you approach her in the right way. You have no objection to the thought of marrying, have you?"

44

Philip, looking like a beautiful, bewildered rustic, scratched his head and said, "I've always thought—well, I haven't thought much about it—but always that I'd like to be head over ears in love when I married. As you were."

"Naturally," said Piers. "But let me tell you this—your mother and I had a very tough time of it after we married."

"Did you?" Philip was surprised.

"Yes. We had a tough time. Everyone was against our marriage."

"Why, Dad?"

Piers flushed. "Oh, I can't explain. It was just what any young couple might suffer, when their family thought they were too young and with no means for marrying. But it would be quite a different affair for you and Adeline. Everyone would be delighted. . . . As for love—marriages are very comfortably arranged in Europe and wear better than many of the love matches made in this country. You and Adeline would be bound to get on together. But—remember, I don't want to urge you. Just think it over. And think how you'd enjoy being master of Jalna."

"What about Archer?"

Piers gave a derisive chuckle. "Archer will never be what I call a man. Not that I mind a chap being studious or talented. Christian is artistic, certainly—but he has blood in his veins. Archer will never really enjoy life. You and Adeline could have a happy life at Jalna."

"Has she been told anything of this? Because, if she has—I can't face her. I'd be too embarrassed."

"Don't worry," said Piers. "Adeline has been told nothing. But I can see that you're not against the idea." Piers lighted a cigarette, took a puff, then added, "Don't let anything your mother may say prejudice you. She's hopelessly romantic. But a man has to be practical in these days. Remember. Here is Jalna—right in your hand—if only you steer your course properly."

"Adeline doesn't care a damn about me."

"You can make her care. Come, Philip," Piers patted the boy on the shoulder, and gave his jolly laugh, "don't take it so seriously."

"I can't alter my nature," said Philip.

Philip found his mother in the pantry washing up the tea-things. He took a clean towel from the rack and began to dry them for her.

She slid a glance toward him and receiving it he burst

out—"I suppose you know what Dad and I were talking about."

"Yes," she said, "and it seems to me that a lot of trouble is being laid up for you young people."

"Dad told me you'd probably take it like this."

"Who do they think they are?" she cried. "Arranging other people's lives! Pushing them about like pawns! Why—you'd think Jalna was a dukedom instead of just an Ontario farm!" Her eyes were bright with anger.

Philip dried a cup and set it carefully on a shelf. He said, "I've heard that you and Dad had a chilly reception at Jalna after you married."

"Chilly!" exclaimed Pheasant. "Chilly! It was just the reception that any young couple might have who'd eloped and married without the consent of their people. But we were in love. We were desperately in love. Adeline's a girl who might make a man miserable if she didn't love him. Oh, Philip, I know you both so well, and I don't want you to be rushed into a union you'll regret—just to please the fancy of your Uncle Renny. Surely Jalna can celebrate its centenary without a wedding."

Philip dried the last of the teaspoons and put them neatly in a drawer. He turned to find little Mary peeping in the door.

"Why are you always spying on people?" he said crossly. "This is a private conversation."

"You think you're private," said Mary, "but you're not."

"Not with you around—spying."

"Children!" admonished Pheasant, and Mary fled to her room. "Now you've hurt her feelings, Philip."

"Please don't call me a child in front of her. She's conceited enough already."

"Mary conceited! Well, I never."

"She manages to hide it, but it's there."

"I suppose all females are conceited, Philip. But I think it's because they know they have a better understanding of the problems of the world."

"They're the cause of most of them," said Philip.

"Oh, darling, you sound about forty." Laughing, Pheasant clasped him to her.

That same evening at sundown Philip and Adeline met on the path through the pine wood. These trees were a small remnant left from the primeval forest, their trunks red in the blaze of the fast disappearing sun, each needle glittering as though varnished, the cones sending out a captivating resinous scent.

The two young people were in white, the beauty of their flawless complexions enhanced by it. She knew nothing of their elders' scheme for them, but his heart was in a tumult.

"Oh, hello," she said, and he answered—"Hello."

"Isn't it nice here?" she said, sniffing the scent of the pine. "Do you smell the pines?"

He too sniffed. "It's a healthy smell," he said.

"How did you do in your exams?" she asked.

"Not too badly."

"You don't look worn out from study."

"Look at yourself. You're fairly bursting with health."

She was insulted and showed it.

"What I mean is," he said, "you look wonderful."

This was something from Philip. She gave a little amused laugh. Now he felt insulted and showed it.

They walked together in silence, the last sunny shafts of the day pointing their path. They saw coming toward them the figure of Renny Whiteoak, his dogs at his heels. As they were in white, so was he in black, for he had just returned from a funeral.

After greeting them he exclaimed, "What a miserable thing to die in this lovely summer weather!"

"Was it a friend, Uncle Renny?"

"No, no. I thoroughly disliked the man. But I should never wish my worst enemy dead . . . and he was only eighty-eight."

"That is considerably younger than Uncle Ernest and Uncle Nicholas were," said Adeline with understanding.

"I can't imagine being that old," said Philip, beginning to romp with the dogs.

"I expect it gets easier to imagine, as time goes on," said Adeline, putting her hand into her father's.

"I'll tell you what I was imagining, as I saw you two coming along the path," said Renny. "I was making a picture in my mind of this pine wood as it was a century ago, when the foundations of Jalna were laid. I pictured my grandparents walking here in the evening—just as you two—and then I saw you coming—another Adeline and Philip! I can tell you I was fairly staggered by the likeness."

Philip stopped playing with the dogs and came close to Renny, looking into his eyes with the expression of a child learning its lesson. In truth, Renny's influence meant much more to him than that of either parent. Adeline was still ingenuously watching the dogs, her mind on them rather than on what Renny was saying. Now he went on:

"A hundred years have passed and here, you might say, was a reincarnation of the originals. You know, it gives me tremendous pleasure to see you two, walking here together. There's no denying I'm sentimental. I'm not ashamed of it. I'm full of sentiment about Jalna and the coming of my grandparents to this new country. I hope you have a feeling about it too, because—oh, you know what I mean." His manner, usually incisive, became gentle, almost wistful. He blinked, as though feeling tears behind his eyes, but they did not come. Indeed, his eyes looked bright and even calculating as he took in the points of the young couple before him.

"Yes, I know," said Philip, trying to talk wisely—"changes come, but feeling remains the same."

"My feelings don't," said Adeline. "They change all the time." After a moment's thought she added, "But about certain things I never could change. For one thing, I mean my feeling for Jalna."

The two young people turned to look after Renny when they separated. Then Philip reached out to take Adeline's hand. Her fingers closed amiably on his and she said, "Poor little boy—he wants his hand held by his big cousin."

This reference to his youth was too much for Philip. Angrily he snatched his hand from hers.

"I'm going home," he said. "You can finish your walk alone."

"That's what would please me," she said.

The last of the sunlight was now gone. The wood was suddenly enveloped in twilight. The three who had stood there together were now separated by growing darkness, by intervening branches. The separation was made the more complete by the call of the whippoorwill repeated many times from the depth of the wood.

Four

In the Basement Kitchen — and After

He was affectionately known to the Whiteoaks as "Rags" and his wife as "Mrs. Rags," though their name was Wragge. Alayne felt little affection for them, or so she thought, for her Dutch couple had been admirable. Yet, when the Wragges were once more established in the basement, she experienced a kind of inner glow, as though their presence had brought back to her something that she had thought lost—an excitement in living, an earthy appreciation of the rough-and-tumble side of days at Jalna. For one thing, both Rags and his wife had a lively sense of humor, where the admirable Dutch couple had none. The Cockney pair were zestful observers of all that went on about them, while the Dutch couple were absorbed in their own affairs. Renny, on his part, was delighted to have Rags again with him at Jalna. Together they had passed through two wars. They had racy memories in common.

On this summer afternoon the basement kitchen was the scene of a reunion. From a glaring recipe that occupied a full page in the evening paper the cook had made a cake which now sat in the middle of the table and was sprinkled thickly with coconut, its layers held together by jam, and there were chopped nuts through it. Also on the table were ham sandwiches, radishes, sliced cucumbers and a large pot of tea. At one end of the table, which was covered by a red-and-white-checked tea cloth, sat the cook, even more florid and stout than before her stay in England. At the other end Rags, even grayer of face and thinner. Both were in high spirits. At one side sat Wright, who for many years had been the head of the stables at Jalna, a fine man of stocky frame and intrepid nature who spoke in a deep resonant voice and was always seen in leather leggings. Opposite him Noah Binns. All his long cantankerous life he had lived in this neighborhood and found little to please him. From the time he was old enough to hold a hoe he had been a laborer, adept in wasting time,

49

self-opinionated as any town counsellor. Now, through the
sale of his cottage on the highway and his old age pension, he
had retired. He had never married, had a poor regard for
women but kept on the right side of the cook.

She said, "Have another radish, Mr. Binns. It's grand to see
you able to champ them hard things, for you used to be a bit
short on teeth."

"No thank *you*," said Noah. "It's true that my dentures
can tackle anything but my stomach ain't that plausible. It
prefers soft food."

"Another sandwich?"

"I've ate several of them. I think I'll start on the cake."

The cook helped him to a generous slice which he attacked
with avidity, shreds of coconut clinging to his straggling gray
moustache and the bristles on his chin.

"Delidgious," he said. "I've never tasted cake like that
since you went away. I didn't think much of that Dutch
couple. They were terrible penurious with the refreshments.
You'd a thought they'd have paid for the food themselves the
way they doled it out. The last time I came to the door they
never answered my knock, though I could hear them jabber-
ing away in their own lingo at the same time. Well, I says to
myself, I can be standoffish as well as you. So I never called
on them again. I'm a proud man. Pride hasn't been my downfall. If it wasn't fer pride I'd like to know where I'd be."

"Hans and Frieda," said Wright, "were always nice to me.
I guess they sort of looked on me as one of the family."
Noah Binns grinned. "Danged if I'd want to be took fer one
of this family."

"And why not, I'd like to know?" demanded Rags.

"Because of mortality," said Noah. "I was raised in a
mortal home and I never forget it."

"I don't want to hear anything said against this family."
Wright looked squarely at Noah.

Unperturbed, Noah replied, "I like the family or I
wouldn't visit here, but danged if I want to be took fer one
of them."

"Not much danger of that," grinned Wright. "Not with
your face."

"Danged if I'd call the boss handsome," said Noah.

"Put him on a horse and there's no one in the country can
equal him for looks," said Wright.

"Then the credit goes to the house, don't it?" said Mrs.
Wragge.

"What would Noah look like on a prancing thorough-bred?" asked Wright.

At the thought of that spectacle Rags and his wife could not restrain their mirth. To ease the moment, she said, lolling a little in her chair, "Ah, it's good to be back."

"This here country can't be beat," said Noah. "It's the best in the world."

"And the way it's growing! Whatever way you look there's hundreds of new little houses and wherever you go you hear foreigners talking," she continued.

"Them's new Canadians," said Noah. "They was born and bred to be new Canadians. You couldn't stop them if you tried."

"Who's trying to stop them?" she demanded.

"London ain't what it used to be," said Rags. "So my missus and me moved to one of them new villages, developed on an old estate, but life there wasn't as 'appy as we'd hex-pected."

"I bet it wasn't," said Noah.

"What was the trouble?" asked Wright.

Rags answered solemnly, "It was the nightingales."

"They'd drive you crazy," said the cook. "There was no peace for them. Babies—invalids—working folk that needed their rest. They couldn't get it, for the nightingales singing."

"That was bad," Noah mumbled, through lips fringed by coconut shreds. "Very, very bad. Worse than motor traffic. Danged if I'd not sooner have motor traffic than birds piping away in the dead of night. It's unnatural. Motor traffic is natural."

"I've always fancied a bird in the house," said Mrs. Wragge. "Then you can cover the cage with a cloth if necessary. But them nightingales you couldn't control."

Down the stairs from above Dennis appeared and was greeted affably by the cook.

"You haven't grown as fast as you might," she said. "Do they give you plenty to eat at school?"

"I'll shoot up later," he returned. "We get plenty to eat but not cake like that."

At once she placed a slice on a plate for him and he drew a chair to the table beside Wright. All four adults regarded him with concentrated interest as he ate.

"I haven't seen your new ma yet," said Mrs. Wragge. "I suppose you love her dearly." She gave a knowing look at the men.

"She's a lovely young lady," said Wright.

"I haven't seen the woman yet I'd want to share my home with," said Noah.

"If one of these modern girls got after you, you wouldn't have a chance," observed Wright with a wink at Rags.

"Is that the way it is?" asked Dennis.

"Oh, they've been after me these many years," said Noah, "but I know how to circumference them."

"I was caught young," said Wright, "and I don't regret it."

"I'll not get caught," said Dennis. "I shall live in a ranch house with my children—and no wife."

He was pleased by the laugh this brought. He continued, "Just as my father and I settle down to enjoy ourselves, my stepmother says for me to make myself scarce because she wants to be alone with my father."

"Well, of all the cruel things I ever heard!" cried the cook.

"You wouldn't think it to look at her," said Wright.

"Would you think I was a desirous man to look at me?" asked Noah.

Wright answered, "If you mean desirable, I have my doubts."

Mrs. Wragge leaned across the table to say firmly to the little boy, "Don't let yourself be put upon, dearie. Stand up for yourself. Reely, it's shameful the things some women will do."

"Don't go putting notions in the child's head," said Rags. "It'll unsettle 'im."

Noah Binns tapped the table with his teaspoon. He said: "Organize—that's the way to get things done. All my life I've organized. Whether it's ringin' the church bells or diggin' a grave, I organize." He stared hard at Dennis.

"Now, young man," he went on, "you've got to organize against the schemes of that woman or she'll get the best of you."

"What's organize?" asked Dennis.

"Organized labor," said Noah, "is what has kept this country from being ruled by danged aristocrats and Tories."

"The Tories are in power in the province now," said Wright. "Don't forget that."

"The way you men get off the track is terrible," said Mrs. Wragge—"while here's this little boy waiting for advice."

"Thanks," said Dennis, rising, "but I think I'll go."

"My advice," said Noah Binns, "is: Organize, plan, lay a deep scheme, and don't let nothing stop you."

Wright left with Dennis. Outside he said, "Don't you pay any attention to what Noah Binns says. He's not worth it. You mark my words. Your stepmother means well by you, I'm sure of that. But she's delicate. She's nervous, and she had a great shock in the war."

"What was that?" asked Dennis.

"Perhaps I oughtn't to tell you," said Wright, "but I think I will. It may sort of help you to understand her better."

Dennis's eyes were on Wright's face. "What was it?" he asked.

"Well," Wright said, almost whispering, "she was in London, with her first husband, at the time of the Blitz. You know what the Blitz was?"

"Yes. I know."

"I don't suppose I ought to tell you this. If your father wanted you to know, I guess he'd have told you."

"I think he'd rather you told me."

Wright was longing to tell him. Now he got it out. "Well, what she saw was—her husband blown to pieces before her very eyes. It was a terrible shock for a sensitive lady and I guess she's never been the same since."

Dennis ran home through the shadows cast by the tall trees. This summer the leaves seemed larger than usual and of a more intense green. This color was strangely reflected in the little boy's eyes.

He found Sylvia in the music-room writing a letter. She smiled at him and said, "I've just been writing a letter to my mother, telling her about our lovely house, and now I find I have no stamp for it."

"I have stamps," said Dennis. "I have a stamp collection. When my father is on a tour he sends me valuable stamps from everywhere he goes."

"I'd love to see them," said Sylvia.

"I keep them under lock and key. They're too valuable to be left lying about."

There was something unfriendly in his tone, Sylvia thought. She drew into herself. "I only want an ordinary five-cent stamp," she said. "Surely that's a simple thing to need."

Dennis regarded her intently. He appeared to want to ask her something important. She smiled at him and said, in her voice that was like music, "Yes, Dennis, what is it?" She raised her hand as though to touch him.

"Have you ever," he asked abruptly, "seen anybody killed?"

The color retreated from her face. "Yes," she breathed. "Once—I did."

"So did I," he said. "It was my mother. In a motor accident. I was only four but I remember. Her blood was on the road. It was on me too." He raised his voice. "Do you see blood, when you think about the one you saw killed?"

"Don't! Don't!" She covered her eyes with her hands. "I can't bear it." She gave a cry as of one in pain and her slender body was shaken by sobs.

Finch's steps were heard running along the drive.

Dennis moved lightly out of the room.

"Sylvia!" cried Finch. "For God's sake, what's the matter?"

She made a desperate effort to control herself.

He took her in his arms. "My darling one," he kept repeating and soon she was quiet.

"I was writing to my mother," she said, "and something I wrote was upsetting to me . . . Oh, nothing that has happened here . . . Something out of the past . . . It's all over. See how steady I am." She achieved a smile, then hid her face on his shoulder.

"Was Dennis here?" asked Finch. "I thought I saw him through the window."

"He was here—a moment before—I think."

"Did he say anything that upset you?"

"No, no. He was telling me of the wonderful collection of stamps you've sent him."

"Stamps!" Finch exclaimed. "I've never sent him a stamp in his life." He wheeled and turned toward the child's room. "What the devil does he mean?"

Sylvia caught his arm. But now again she was overcome and could not speak. "There, there," he kept on saying and patted her on the back, as one would comfort a child. Not till she was calm did he detach himself from her clinging hands and go to Dennis. He was hot with anger at the child. Either he had deliberately been the cause of Sylvia's distress or he had not. But he was entangled with it, whatever his intentions.

Finch strode to Dennis's room. He went in and closed the door after him. The child had remained unmoved by Sylvia's outburst but he flinched when he saw Finch's frown. He stood up straight in front of the window.

Finch said, keeping his voice low with an effort, "Why did you tell those lies to Sylvia?"

"I thought there was only one lie," said Dennis.

Dennis had a surprising power of angering Finch. He found himself with a hot desire to take hold of his son roughly. That would not do and he said, in a controlled voice, "You said you had a stamp collection *and* you said I'd sent you stamps for it. What does it matter how many lies? You lied."

Dennis hung his head. "I thought you had."

"You knew I hadn't. Why did you lie?"

"I don't know."

A silence fell that seemed almost fearful to Finch, for his nerves were shaken by Sylvia's distress.

Through the window Dennis was watching a red squirrel. Finch asked suddenly, "Was Sylvia upset before you spoke to her? I mean did you say anything to upset her?"

"I couldn't know how, could I?"

"Well, I just wondered. You were with her."

They looked into each other's eyes—each trying to fathom what lay hidden.

Finch drew a sigh. "Sylvia is very delicate," he said.

"Is it a misfortune to have a delicate wife?"

"She must be taken care of."

"By you and me?" Dennis asked eagerly, moving a little toward Finch.

"You must not make yourself troublesome."

Dennis said at once: "I won't be troublesome."

"As for your lying," said Finch, "for that you'll stay in your room for the rest of the day."

He left Dennis and returned to Sylvia. He was very anxious about her, and puzzled because she had seemed particularly well and gay all that day.

"There's one thing I have made up my mind about," she said, "and it is that I'm never going to be the cause of trouble between you and Dennis. He is your only child and nothing must spoil your relationship." She spoke with vehemence, as though she had thought anxiously on the subject.

"You must not look for trouble," he said, sitting down beside her. "As for the bond between Dennis and me, I'm afraid I'm not much of a father—but he does irritate me with his clinging ways and now—this lying."

"If only he will cling to me!" she exclaimed. "That's what I should love. It will be tragic for me, if he holds something against me. He always speaks of you with such a possessive air."

"Possessive—yes," said Finch. "That's his mother all over again."

"Finch," she said, "Dennis remembers that tragedy. He remembers it clearly. It made a terrible impression on him."

"Did he tell you that?"

"Yes."

"That's what upset you, then?"

"I was very much moved. How could I help being moved? It brought back . . ."

"It's a lie," Finch said loudly.

"Hush. He'll hear you."

Finch spoke more quietly. "It's a lie. Dennis remembers nothing of that accident. He doesn't remember his mother. I'm sure of that. I've a mind to go back and face him with it. He ought to be punished."

"No, no, no." Sylvia laid a restraining hand on his. "You would turn him effectually against me. If I'm to be a good mother to him—Oh, I do want to be a good mother, and you can help me, darling."

"I had no mother," said Finch, "and I can tell you I was roughly treated sometimes."

"Then you must be all the more understanding with Dennis." She spoke with confidence, almost with authority. "Remember the little boy you were."

After a little she arranged a tray for Dennis and carried it to Finch for his inspection. On it were sandwiches, strawberries and cream and sweet biscuits.

"May I take it to him?" she asked.

"Good Lord," Finch said, "it looks like a treat rather than a punishment."

"It's not a punishment. Dennis is just having a tray in his room." And she repeated, "May I take it?"

"If you wish," Finch said indifferently.

Dennis was lying flat on his back on the neat white bed. There was a strange austerity in the outline of his narrow shape beneath the sheet. His eyes were closed and he did not open them when Sylvia entered. She set the tray on a low table beside the bed.

"It's turning much warmer," she said, as though casually. "I think it's going to be a hot night."

How pale he was! Surely he never could look really warm. He did not open his eyes. He scarcely seemed to breathe. It was as though he were listening with his whole body—with every bit of him.

She laid her hand with a caressing movement on his forehead. She had, ever since they were together, longed to touch his hair. Now she found it fine and silky, rather long for a boy's hair but becoming. Her heart went out to him.

"Dennis dear," she said, "aren't you hungry?"

Still without opening his eyes he said: "Go away. And take the tray away."

Five

Seen Through a
Picture Window

The night did indeed turn hot. It felt breathlessly hot in Dennis's small room. There was no slightest breeze to stir the curtains. The sheet that covered him no longer felt pleasant to the touch. He threw it off and raised his legs straight into the air. He was naked.

He could hear the daily woman and Sylvia talking in the kitchen. Now the table was being laid in the dining-room. The woman was a good cook and an appetizing smell pervaded this part of the house. But Dennis was not hungry. He listened, tense, as he heard Finch go into the bedroom he shared with Sylvia. With all his might he wished that those two did not share a room. He wished that Finch would come in to see him, but he trembled with fear at the thought of Finch's frown.

He had no visitor all that long evening but a mosquito. It had got in, despite the wire screening, and hovered about him incessantly buzzing. It seemed not able to make up its mind to bite him but never stopped singing of its intention. He hated it and longed to kill it.

He held up his bare knee in the twilight and said:

"Come on—come on—bite me if you dare!"

But the mosquito refused to be tempted.

Sometimes it sang close to his ear. Sometimes it became tangled in his hair. Then its buzzing was maddening. He struck at it in a fury of resentment.

"You devil—you devil—you she devil," he said between his clenched teeth. For he had learned at school that it was the female mosquito which stung. "You she devil," he growled. "Why doesn't your husband kill you?" He had a picture in his mind, then, of the female mosquito being killed by the male and he forgot everything else in the pleasure of witnessing that death—the wings torn off, the sting ripped out.

But it was only for a moment. Soon the mosquito was buzzing about his lips and nostrils. He became intolerably hot,

58

even though he was naked. With the increasing heat, darkness descended. But he knew it was light where Finch and Sylvia were eating their dinner. He could hear the clink of dishes and the rather heavy footfall of the daily woman. Then at last she left for her home. He heard her footsteps on the path.

Now the mosquito was buzzing about his body. Twice it alighted on his leg but though he struck at it he failed to kill it. He lay still scarcely breathing, till he felt the tickle of it on his knee. Then out shot his hand and he struck it and crushed it.

There came the peace of silence. No more buzzing. He sprang out of bed and turned on the light so that he might discover the corpse of his tormentor. . . . Very small it looked, crushed there on his knee. A trickle of blood, his own fresh blood, stained the paleness of his skin. He turned out the light and flung himself again on the bed, savoring his victory.

He was wakened by the itching of the bite on his knee. He could hear the piano being softly played in the music-room and pictured Finch with his hands on the keys and Sylvia sitting close by. He began to scratch the mosquito bite—rhythmically, as though in time to the music. The more he scratched the bite, the more it burned and itched. He could feel the blood trickling down his leg.

So curious was he to see the bite and the blood, he again turned on the light that he might examine it. "Whew," he exclaimed in surprise, and again, "Whew." Certainly he must have scratched hard to draw so much blood.

It was on his hand too. . . . He could not stop himself from putting his hand to his forehead to leave a bloody imprint there. He stood in front of the looking-glass, gloating over his reflection with the bloodstained forehead. He ran his fingers through his hair, so that it stood upright. He was almost afraid of his reflection, it looked so strange. He wished the pair in the music-room could see him, could see what they'd done to him.

As he had been unable to stop himself from smearing his forehead, so now he could not stop himself from putting first one palm and then the other on his bleeding leg. After that he carefully made a mark on his side, just beneath his heart. Now he knew what one who had been crucified looked like. He examined himself in the mirror and found himself growing a little sick.

It was so hot in the room he made up his mind to go out-doors through the window. The sill was low and it was noth-ing to him to climb over it onto the smooth grass. The grass was deliciously cool to his feet, the night air to his feverishly hot body. The light from a young moon was just touching the petals of a white peony. Sylvia was proud of this, its first bloom. It was a single variety, looking and smelling like a large water lily. Dennis ruthlessly pulled off the flower, scat-tering its petals as he went toward the picture window. The fresh air made his body light and daring, but his mind was sunk in resentment. Incoherent thoughts of vengeance, for he did not know what, possessed it.

The picture window framed the one who played the piano and the one who sat listening. Sylvia's eyes were on Finch's hands that moved quietly, as though conscious of their power. Finch's back was toward the window but Sylvia sat facing it. Dennis threw the last of the peony petals toward her face against the pane. He threw them as though he wished they were stones.

They fell only softly against the pane but the movement of his arm caught Sylvia's eyes. She moved them startled to the window. Now she and Dennis were face to face. She saw him raise his arms and extend them, as though on a cross. She saw his bloodstained forehead and the hair in sharp golden points, like thorns. She saw the red prints on the palms of his hands, and the blood on his side. When he was conscious of her look of horror he allowed his chin to drop and rolled his eyes upward to the night sky.

"Dennis!" With a strangled cry she repeated his name, then covered her eyes with her hands.

Finch sprang up from the piano, and he too looked out and saw the ghostly figure of the child. He ran out to him and Sylvia followed.

When Dennis saw them he said loudly:

"I'm crucified! Don't you see? I'm crucified!"

Finch picked him up and carried him into the house and laid him on his bed. Dennis relaxed there, gazing up into Finch's face with a possessive look.

"What do you mean," demanded Finch, "by saying such a thing? Where are you hurt?"

"Shall I telephone for the doctor?" Sylvia asked from the doorway.

"Wait till I find out where he is hurt." He stared at the bloodstained figure of his son in perplexity and dismay. He went to the bathroom and returned with a sponge and basin of warm water. Sylvia, her face drained of color, leaned against the side of the door for support.

Finch wiped the blood from Dennis and discovered the mosquito bite. "This is all play-acting," he said. "He's not hurt—but, by God, he deserves to be."

Dennis lay looking up at them with an expression almost blissful. To be the focus of Finch's attention, even though in anger, was enough to bring that look to his face.

"You got yourself into that disgusting mess," said Finch, "to frighten us. You scratched that mosquito bite again and again, didn't you? You smeared the blood over yourself purposely, didn't you? You were out to give us a great fright, weren't you?"

"Yes." Dennis still wore that blissful half-smile.

"I'll take that smirk off your face," said Finch and roughly turned him over. He administered a dozen stinging slaps to the boy's small round buttocks. At the impact of the first, Sylvia fled.

She stood, with wildly beating heart, looking out into the darkness of the trees. This house, she thought, which should have been so happy, so peacefully welcoming to Finch, was disturbed, unhappy, because of her presence. She turned a wan face to him when he came to her.

"Is Dennis—" she began, but could not go on.

"He's all right," Finch said tersely. "He'll not bother us again tonight. What a young viper he is! It's a damned shame that you should have been so upset." He put his arm about her. She could feel that he was trembling.

"It was terrifying to both of us," she said, for she wanted to feel that they both were in the same boat. "And—*crucified!* How ever did he come to think of that?"

"I tell you he's vicious," said Finch.

"I won't hear you say that about your child. But—I do think he is rather morbid—poor little boy."

"Let's go out into the air and forget about him," said Finch. "It's a lovely night. See where the moon has climbed. Above the treetops."

They went out into the garden. Finch saw the blood-stained petals of the white peony. He picked them up, trying to conceal them from Sylvia, but she had seen them. "I don't mind," she said. They did not look in the direction of the window of Dennis's room.

It was early daylight when the sound of crying woke them.

It was a loud, wailing, unrestrained crying such as Finch had never before heard from Dennis. He sprang out of bed and—"You are not to come," he said sternly to Sylvia. He laid his hand on her chest and pressed her back onto the bed. "You've borne enough from him. Stay where you are." Miserably, and with the feeling that this was but the prolonging of her troubled dreams, she obeyed. She put her head under the bedclothes to dull the sound of the crying, but it went through her like a knife in spite of that.

Shortly afterward the telephone extension in Renny Whiteoak's bedroom rang persistently. He might well have refused to wake, because he was at that moment in the midst of an enthralling dream in which he was judge at a show where all the entrants were unicorns. He was hesitating between a beautiful blond unicorn, with a horn of pure gold, and one which was striped like a tiger, with a lovely body and challenging eyes. He did not want to be waked but the little old cairn terrier lying against his back climbed over him at the sound of the bell and firmly pawed his face.

With a groan he reached for the receiver. "Hello," he said.

"Sorry to disturb you so early," came Finch's voice, "but I'm wondering if you can tell me what to do for a mosquito bite young Dennis has. I guess it's infected. It looks pretty bad. The leg's swollen."

"I have the very best remedy for that," said Renny. "I'll bring it right over."

It was a marvel, thought Finch, how Renny could have got into his clothes and so soon appeared at the door. He went straight to the little boy's room. Dennis at once sat up in bed. "Look," he said, "how fat my knee is! It was paining like anything but my father heard me and he came to see, and now it doesn't hurt so much."

Finch sat down on the side of the bed. He said, "Feel how hard and hot the leg is."

"Yes, feel, Uncle Renny."

Renny examined the leg. "It's infected," he said. "We must have the doctor to it. I'll bet you've been scratching it, young man."

"Scratching," Finch echoed bitterly. "He got himself into a horrible mess last night. Bleeding."

Dennis, his possessive eyes raised to Finch's face, put out his hand to press it into Finch's, who quickly drew his away. As though to make up for this retreat, he said, "I'll bring you a cold drink."

The result of the doctor's visit was that Dennis was kept in bed and treated for a serious infection. It was a painful time, but he was uncomplaining, gentle. Yet when Sylvia carried a tray to him or offered to read aloud he would turn his face to the wall and ask to be left alone. It was different when Finch appeared. Dennis would gaze at him with what seemed to Finch a calculated devotion, as though he strove, with all his small strength, to build a wall about the two of them. If Finch were present when Sylvia came to the sickroom, Dennis would meekly accept what she offered, meekly reply when she spoke to him, but always he kept those jewel-like green eyes of his, in which the whites were not noticeable, averted.

To be with him was enough to make Sylvia tremble. Small and suffering as he was, she felt in him a force dominant over her. She realized that he was aware of this, that he saw and savored her trembling. In the days of his illness she gave up hope of winning him over. The long weeks of his holidays loomed as a threat. She might have borne his presence with ease, if she had not seen its effect on Finch. They could not speak of the boy without constraint. Try as they would they could not be natural about him, could not treat him as the child he was. Yet, when he lay sleeping, Sylvia would sometimes long to take him into her arms. At other times she was startled by her anger against him. Almost, she felt, she hated him. Once, she found to her horror that she was imagining him dead and the relief it would be.

All the family came at different times to see him, to relate their experience of insect bites and to give advice. Meg's advice was the most pleasing to Finch. She said, "As soon as Dennis is completely recovered you must send him to camp. I know the very place for him and, as the owner of the camp is an old friend of Rupert's and a good churchman, nothing could be more suitable. The child will be made completely happy and your minds will be at rest about him."

So it was arranged, and the day came when Meg and the Rector, themselves going in the direction of the camp, took the little boy with them. Dressed in gray flannel shorts and blue pullover he set out to say good-bye to the family. At Jalna the only one he found at home was Archer, who shook hands with him formally.

"Good-bye," he said. "Have a good time, if you can."

"Why do they send children to camp?" Dennis asked.

"So they may have peace."

"Is it better to have peace than children?"

"Children are always listening. Grownups like a little privacy."

"I'll have no privacy at camp."

"You will have everything you need," said Archer. "At your age you are not supposed to need privacy."

"What I like," Dennis said, looking up at two pigeons on the roof, "is to be with my father. And he wants me to be with him. It's Sylvia who sends me to camp."

"That is because she feels insecure when you are about."

"My father belonged to me before he belonged to her."

Archer regarded him judicially. "I foresee quite a struggle," he said, "but I think you'll come out on top."

"Noah Binns says to organize."

"You couldn't have better advice. . . . Well—run along now and say your good-byes. When you come back from camp I shan't be here."

"Where will you be?"

"In England. I've been chosen as a Rhodes Scholar and I'm setting out in time to travel round a bit."

"Will it make you different—being a Rhodes Scholar?"

"I've always been different."

"Will it be fun?"

"I hope not. Your camp will be fun."

Adeline and Philip now appeared, carrying tennis racquets. Dennis said good-bye to them and set out to visit the rest of the family. At the Fox Farm he found that Patience had the day before given birth to a daughter. Humphrey Bell was so pleased and excited by this that he tucked a five-dollar bill into the little boy's pocket. "For you," he said, "to spend at camp, to celebrate the coming of Victoria."

"Thanks very much," said Dennis, and he added, for politeness' sake, "Is that what you're going to call her?"

"Yes. Victoria, for my mother. She'll be Vicky Bell. Don't you think it's a pretty name?"

Dennis thought it was, but thought a baby girl was a quite unnecessary addition to any family. Still he was pleased by her arrival, as it had produced such munificence from Humphrey. He found little Mary in the studio and showed her the crisp new bank note.

"I have more money than I know what to do with," he told her. "My father said how much money did I want and I said just what he could afford and he said I can afford as much as you want and he took out his wallet and said to help myself and I did. My father makes a terrific lot of money. Do you know how? He makes it playing the piano, that's how."

"I knew that," said Mary, "long ago."

"Does your father make a terrific lot of money?"

"No," said Mary. "He's very poor. But he doesn't mind. He likes it. Will you be long in camp?"

Dennis gave her a look that somehow was not comfortable. "I don't think so," he said. "My father will miss me. I'll not stay long."

"My daddy would miss me, if I went to camp, and so would my mummie, but she'd miss me even more," said Mary, who thought Dennis was too boastful and even a little tiresome.

"I have no mummie," he said. "Just a stepmother. And do you know what she is? I'll tell you." He put an arm about her neck and whispered into her ear: "She's a she devil—that's what she is." He drew back a little, laughing, his eyes close to hers.

His words—a combination new to her—sent a thrill of excitement through her nerves, but she only said, "Why are your eyes that funny color?"

Laughing at they knew not what, they sauntered along the country road together, for Mary was accompanying Dennis as far as the Rectory to see him off. At last she said, "I know what devil is but not she devil."

"You'll find out soon enough," he said. "When you have a stepmother."

"I couldn't have one, because my own mother is living." No longer was she laughing. A flutter of apprehension brought the color to her cheeks. "I couldn't have a stepmother," she added decisively.

An enigmatic smile curved his lips. "That's what I used to think."

"Till when?" she asked.

"Till one day my mother—died. Yours might die any day, you know. Then you'd get a stepmother."

"I'm going home." Mary spoke with vehemence. "You can go on alone."

"All right," he said tranquilly, "but don't tell."

"Tell what?"

"What I said about—anything. Good-bye."

The Rectory was in sight, the car standing at the gate. Meg saw the small figure coming alone down the road and called out, "Hurry up, Dennis! Uncle Rupert and I are waiting.

Your father has brought your suitcase and your rubber sheet, and"—by this time the little boy had come close—"the strange thing is that I'm almost positive this suitcase belongs to me. I've been missing it for some time and I can't imagine how he came to get hold of it. I don't mind your taking it to camp, Dennis dear, but I do hope you'll take good care of it, for I really think I must ask your father to let me have it back when you return."

"Has he gone?" asked Dennis.

"Yes. He just left your things and then drove off."

"He didn't say good-bye to me." Dennis stood looking wistfully down the road. "I hurried because I expected to find him here."

The Rector was behind the wheel and growing impatient. "How long am I to sit here waiting?" he demanded. "We're already late in starting. I don't know why it is, but I used always to be on time."

"Rupert, dear," said Meg, "don't fuss. It's so bad for you."

They were in. The car started with a jolt, for it was an old one and the Rector was not a very good driver.

Six

Father and Daughter

Renny Whiteoak was not a man to let the grass grow under his feet. Even though his mind was firmly fixed on circumspection in the planning of a marriage between young Philip and Adeline, try as he would to keep himself from urging it on her, he did not succeed. Sooner or later, she was bound to discover how ardently he hoped for it. Better speak now and exert his influence in the open. He was sure that Philip was agreeable to the union. Never a day passed but he came to Jalna on one pretext or another. Alayne had remarked this, but supposed he was drawn by the tennis court, the stables, and his affection for Renny as much as by the charms of Adeline. Though Renny had dropped hints to her of his desire, she had thought of it as fantastic and even dangerous. Both of Piers's olders sons (one in Paris, one in Ireland) were more congenial to Alayne than Philip. She would have preferred either, if she had been consulted, as a son-in-law.

No one knew what were Adeline's feelings toward Philip—least of all Philip himself. He held himself aloof from sentiment, with adolescent aloofness. Yet in solitude he never ceased to toy with the idea of marrying Adeline, of sometime being master of Jalna. He never took Archer into account as a rival in its possession, dismissing him as one whose sole ambition in life was to pass examinations with the highest marks possible. He was immensely flattered by Renny's choice of him as a husband for Adeline and by Piers's optimistic agreement.

On this particular July morning Renny, discovering his daughter leaning on the fence of the paddock where a pair of two-year-olds were being schooled, took her by the hand and said, "Come into the office for a bit. I'd like a word with you."

Indolently she turned with him. "How muggy it is," she exclaimed. "The colts are lazy. I'm lazy. The rain last night

didn't clear the air. All it did was to beat down the hollyhocks and delphiniums. Mummie is mourning over them."

"Is she?" he returned absently and, still with fingers inter-
laced, they entered the little room, next the tack room in
the stables, that was his office—the scene of many a deal
in horseflesh, of much perplexity in the squaring of accounts,
of interviews where privacy was important. Adeline loved
this room. She could look back to the days of early childhood, when to sit opposite Renny in his shiny swivel chair,
with the littered writing table between them, filled her with
pride. She never tired of admiring and comparing the points
of their most distinguished horses, the framed photographs
of which covered the walls.

Renny offered her a cigarette which she refused.

"Thanks," she said, "but I've given up smoking—for the
time being."

"Self-discipline?" he asked.

"No. Self-indulgence. I'm tired of it."

"I find it very comforting," he said.

"I don't need comforting."

She studied his face. His expressive eyebrows told her that
something was in the wind. To help him out she asked,
"What is it, Daddy?"

"I've been thinking."

"How extraordinary."

"Don't laugh. I was thinking seriously about you."

Her eyes were earnestly on his, as without again speaking,
she waited. "I've been thinking," he repeated, "how hard it
was on you—that disappointment in your Irishman, Fitzturgis, I mean."

She tried to speak lightly. "For goodness' sake, what put
that into your head? It's all in the past. I never give him a
thought now." But the quivering of her lips, the darkening of
her eyes, rejected this quick denial.

"That's well," he said. "I admit I have been pretty anxious
on that score."

"That sounds as though I've been acting the part of the
jilted maiden."

"That's ridiculous," he said testily. "You've been so
natural, it's seemed too good to be true." He paused, picked
up a small bronze horse that was a paperweight, and
considered it. This had been a birthday present to him from
Adeline and Fitzturgis. "As for him," Renny went on, "he
never could understand or appreciate a thoroughbred—horse

or woman. It simply wasn't in him. He was too damned self-centred."

"Why do we have to talk about him?" Adeline broke out.

"We don't. What I've been wondering is whether the thought of marriage—in the future—ever comes to you. You're young, healthy, good-looking. It would be natural."

"I never give it a thought."

"Never?"

"I have enough in my life, as it is. I have you, Daddy. I have Jalna *and* the family. Why should I want another man hanging about?"

"Not if he were the right man?"

She turned to him squarely. "Don't imagine," she said, "that I can't guess what's in your mind. I know you too well."

So flabbergasted was he by this remark that he was speechless for a space. Then he got out, "But why—how?"

"I should have been pretty dull," she said, "if I hadn't guessed." She laughed, almost derisively, it seemed to him, and he felt his well-laid plan had fallen through.

"Poor darling," she said, and came and sat on his knee. "Poor darling." She toyed with his dense unyielding hair. "What a disappointment for you."

He caught her hand and held it. "This is no joke," he said angrily. "It's a very serious affair. It's your future—if you will consent—*and* it's my dearest wish."

"Do you expect me to consent? How can I consent to anything so vague?"

"It isn't vague in my mind," he said eagerly. "It's solid. It's as real as flesh and blood. It's the very heart of all I hold most dear."

"What about Philip and me?" she said, bringing their two names out into the open. "We don't hold each other dear. We're just two cousins. I've had experience. I've loved and been disappointed. Philip is just a boy."

"I'm sorry," said Renny, "that you should have guessed what I have in mind, because I wanted to tell you of it in my own way."

"You think you could persuade me, Daddy?"

"I'd never try to persuade you to acquiesce in any plan of mine unless I were confident it would make you happy." He tried not to sound high-flown.

"I suppose," she said, seriously now, "Philip and I have a right to be happy."

"And that's what I want," he exclaimed, "above all things! The pair of you are cut out for each other. It would be a perfect match."

She had got off his knee and was walking nervously up and down the little room. Even in that restricted space it could be seen how graceful was her walk. In truth the grace of her walk, the musical quality of her voice, were her greatest charms. Now she demanded:

"Have you spoken of this to Philip?"

"Yes."

"You shouldn't!" she cried. "Not before you spoke to me."

"I thought it should be first in the mind of the man."

"The *man!* The *boy*—and only twenty! How did he take it?"

"Calmly. Seriously. Like the nice chap he is."

"I suppose he's thinking of Jalna—with me thrown in. What of my brother?"

"Archer will never settle down to country life."

"Would Philip?"

"I'm sure he would. I'm sure he'd like nothing better. What better life could a young pair have than the life you and he would enjoy here? Another Philip and Adeline—after a hundred years! And you two the very incarnation of the other pair."

"Life is different now, Daddy. There isn't the same *belief*."

"Belief doesn't need to be conscious, Adeline. There's too much said and written about our feelings nowadays. If we just go ahead and *live* we can be as happy as ever people were. There's the great thing about this marriage I propose. You and Philip have it in you to live and be happy."

"*You* propose," she repeated. "That's funny—when one comes to think of it. *You propose* and Philip and I do the marrying." She faced him almost accusingly and he noticed how pale she had grown and how large and darkly tragic appeared her eyes.

"No need to look at me like that," he said. "Put the whole affair out of your mind. Forget what I have said. Only remember this, my pet, that your happiness is what I crave, above all things. And I'll be honest with you. The thought of losing you is almost more than I can bear. If you and Philip married I'd have you safe at Jalna."

"I don't want to marry anyone." Without warning she burst into tears.

He took her in his arms and kissed her trembling lips.

"Not now, perhaps, but—the day will come. Then some brute will appear on the scene who will captivate you and off you'll gallop with him and never a look behind."

Now her tears were mixed with laughter. They clung together. Noises from the stables reached them, then a sudden shower sounded on the roof and a distant roll of thunder. These sounds enclosed them. They smelled the rain, heard the thunder, and wished for nothing but to be together.

Seven

Adeline and Philip

The summer was lush, the leaves broad and darkly green.
Paths were overgrown, grass sprouted up in the gravel of the
drive. There was a hushed, humid resignation in the midsummer air. The stream moved darkly, slowly beneath its
little rustic bridge. And there on the bridge sat Adeline, lost
in thought. Even on the bridge the unusual growth was noticeable, for a wild grapevine had secured a hold on one of
the handrails and, with leaf and tenacious tendril, was pursu-
ing its way to the other side of the stream.

Adeline wound a tendril round her finger like a ring. The
green of the crowding foliage cast that hue on the golden
brown of her dreamy eyes, so that it would have been difficult, even for those who knew her best, to pronounce what
was their color. She was living these days in a strange confusion of thought—at times reliving the experience of her
engagement to the Irishman, Fitzturgis; more often, dwelling
on the proposal made to her by Renny.

She had thought herself to be free of those recollections, so
poignant, so capable of shattering her peace, but now they
had come back to her. The meeting with Fitzturgis in Ireland.
The budding, the blossoming of her first love. The days they
had spent together in London, she under the guardianship of
Finch. The return to Canada. The two years of waiting for
Fitzturgis to come out to her. His coming to Jalna. That exciting, disturbing, disappointing time. The scene by the lake
when she had discovered him and her cousin Roma bathing
together. Her fierce anger at seeing their embrace. If she lived
to be a hundred, as her great-grandmother had done, never
could she forget the fierce violence of that moment—the
moment that had changed everything. She could not recall it
even now without a smile of triumph at the discomfiture of
the pair in the lake and her hurling stones at them.

Bit by bit she had put that time out of her mind. It lay dis-
carded like a torn-up illustration out of a book. But, now and

again, she would take out the scraps, piece them together and form again that haunting picture. Renny, understanding her all too well, had given her a new picture to dwell on—the picture of Philip and herself at Jalna. Always it glowed, at the back of her mind, as though illumined by a secret light. Then again she would see the two of them, framed as were the portraits of their great-grandparents in the dining-room, in ornate gold frames.

Love? What matter if they were not "in love"? Once she had known what it was to have her life transfigured by love—broadened into a new spaciousness, yet strangely narrowed to the passionate employment of her powers upon one individual. She felt that she had discovered all there was to know of such an entanglement. She wanted no further experience of that sort. Once was enough. Often she had pictured her future—free as the wind that blew among the trees, across the fields of Jalna. She would belong to no one but herself—and the family. But Philip was part of the family. If they two . . . but she could not bring herself to give words to the picture that was now so insistently in her mind, the picture which Renny had made for her—herself and Philip, gilt-framed, beautiful and silent, gazing out upon a placid world . . .

This world, she knew, was in a troubled, uneasy state. Often she heard her mother and Archer discussing it, sometimes heatedly, and felt uncomfortable, and wished they wouldn't. Philip and she could live in a world they would make for themselves. There would be no love in it. Just comradeship and love for the countryside. She amused herself by playing with these thoughts, never bringing them too close, always keeping Philip safe within his gilt frame.

But now, as she sat on the bridge, the live Philip came down the path, whistling as he came, like the boy he was. He did not see her till he was close upon her, then he stopped short and the whistle died on his pouting lips. He stood looking down at her, mildly surprised.

"Oh, hullo," he said.

She also said, "Hullo." Then they regarded each other irresolutely, as though they had sooner not have met and now would make the encounter as brief as possible.

The stream dominated the scene. It came out of the shadow of the trees and flowed, bronze and golden, into the sunlight that surrounded the rustic bridge. In the pool beneath, minnows darted above the yellow sand or hid themselves in the watercress, their noses safe in the dimness, only their flirting tails visible. A dragonfly in glittering armor hovered above the pool. All was in miniature. Indeed, if the pair on the bridge had suddenly descended into the pool, they would have disturbed it as two giants. Yet the time had been when, as infants, they had gazed from the safety of grown-up arms in wonder at its depth. Now, after the interchange of a swift glance, their attention was focused on the stream.

"Pretty, isn't it?" said Philip.

"Yes, isn't it?" she agreed, and on that subject they had nothing more to say.

But the stream made fluent conversation for them, with gurgling vowel sounds and hissing consonants against the reeds. The dragonfly had recklessly touched the water. His wings were wet and he might, like many another aircraft, have met his end, had not Philip scrambled down to the brink and rescued him.

"Thanks," Adeline said tersely but with a warm look.

"Why thanks?" said Philip. "He wasn't yours."

"I feel as though all wild things were," she said. "Especially those that fly."

"Stinging insects?" he asked with a teasing look.

"Every one of them," she said, "unless in the act of stinging."

"There's no use," he said, "in being too softhearted."

"Why did you save the dragonfly?" she demanded.

"I'd as lief drown it," he said.

"Naughty boy." She gave him a suddenly coy look and he scrambled back on to the bridge and sat down beside her. She glanced down at his strong brown hand lying on the rough boards of the bridge and withdrew her own hand a little distance from it.

That seemed to him a dismissal and he said:

"Well, I guess I'll be going." He gathered up the last notes of the song he had been whistling, repeated them, then continued in a remarkably sweet series of variations. Like a male singing bird he appeared to be showing off his accomplishments to the female.

"Pretty," she remarked. "I wish I could whistle."

"Try."

She gave out one long clear note.

"Good," he said encouragingly. "Go on."

She made an attempt but her lips refused to be pursed.

They parted in a smile and she said, "I can't. There's no use in trying." He did not again urge her.

They sat in a dreamy silence, the dark green of the summer leaves casting a shadow on them. But there was nothing of youthful romance in the heart of either; there was instead an image planted by Renny Whiteoak which pleased their fancy, gave them an almost ennobling sense of security. There was no need for speech. No need excepting to say the few words that would take them out of the gilt frames now enshrining them, transform them into flesh and blood.

In spite of herself Adeline could not keep from speaking these. She wanted things to drift on as they were, but her lips that had been unable to constrain themselves to whistle now had no power to restrain those words.

"There's one thing we could do—both of us," she said, "if we wanted. . . ." Those words, the assertion of their right to choose, repeated themselves in her stubborn heart. Did she *want* him? Did he *want* her? Surely not. There would be nothing new to discover, each in the other. They who had romped together as children, she the older and stronger of the two . . . Yet—no matter how her heart rebelled—her lips could not keep from saying the words, so eloquently desired by Renny.

He kept his eyes averted but asked, "What could we do?"

"We could get married."

"Yes," he said, under his breath. "We could."

"If we wanted."

"Certainly. If we wanted."

Now her eyes looked straight into his. "What about you?" she asked. "Do you want to?"

His face was suffused by color, while she looked remarkably cool.

"Yes," he mumbled, gazing down into the stream.

"Really?" she asked, with a scornful look for his mumbling.

He could not speak but nodded violently.

"Very well," she heard herself say, "let's."

"When?" he got out.

"Next year—for the centenary, of course."

There followed a silence, empty rather than pregnant. Yet Adeline was not disappointed by this emptiness. It was as though a burden had been lifted from her and in its place this empty buoyancy.

"Shall we go and tell . . ." *Daddy* she had been about to say, but, instead, she said, "everybody?"

As though electrified by the prospect of activity, Philip in one agile movement was on his feet. He took her hand and for a moment they stood linked, then darted from the bridge and up the steep to the lawn above. Facing the lawn rose the house, richly clothed in its mantle of Virginia creeper. So dense was the growth of the vine that the principal upstairs windows were half-overhung by it, giving the effect of eyes half-hidden by a wink. The house seemed to be saying: "Well, in my time I have seen a number of affianced couples, of brides and grooms to be, but—this engagement beats all!"

Eight

How They Took the News

The announcement of the engagement of Adeline and Philip ranked with the family as a major event, one of the same interest accorded to the events of the outer world, such as an alliance of two great powers or the collision of two great ships at sea. To some it was an announcement of pure happiness and promise. To others the reverse.

There was little harmony between Renny and Alayne in this affair, he viewing it as a personal achievement accomplished by his own finesse. He considered that he had been delicately artful in his handling of the young people, while Alayne felt that he had been ruthlessly impulsive. Both boy and girl, she thought, were far too much under his influence. There was no clear judgment on the part of Philip and Adeline. Neither was there passion. Passion, in spite of her cool exterior, she could have understood, for once it had played havoc in her own life. Adeline's former fiancé, Maitland Fitzturgis, had possessed qualities which had appealed to Alayne. She had been eager to welcome him into the family. But this unformed youth, this Philip, she could only regard in puzzlement and dismay.

So Renny took his triumph to his sister for understanding. She received him in a flood of happy tears.

"Isn't it wonderful?" she cried. "Really I don't know when anything has made me so happy. And how delighted dear Gran and the uncles would have been to see another Philip and Adeline at Jalna! It might have meant little if the young pair had resembled the families of their mothers, but there is Philip, the image of our grandfather; and there is Adeline, the very picture of Gran—though I do hope she will have a nicer disposition as she matures. I can never quite forget how Gran put me off in her will with an old-fashioned watch and chain, and an Indian shawl that her parrot used to make his nest in."

"I know, I know. It was a shame," Renny said soothingly,

though certainly he had had more to complain of than Meg in that will. But it was far in the past, and the betrothal of the young pair was in the glowing present.

"We must have a celebration," he went on. "A dinner party for the tribe—with plenty of good food and drink. I will provide champagne, and Alayne will buy a new dress for Adeline. I am glad Finch is home after his tour and that Patience has had her baby. Wakefield may possibly come from New York, and Piers's two older boys from abroad. Then there is Roma in New York. She'll naturally want to be here."

"Dear me," said Meg, "such a gathering is almost enough for the wedding itself. It will be thrilling to have such a reunion." She dried her tears and gave her incomparably sweet smile. Together they went into the garden to tell the good news to the Rector; but he was more concerned by the plight of his hollyhocks, which had on the previous night been blown over by wind and rain.

"Flat on their lovely faces," he mourned, "and I have only myself to blame, for I could have staked them up. Many people," he went on, "think of hollyhocks as rather common flowers. That is because they will flourish with little or no attention in the workingman's garden. But to me there is something regal in their height and their simplicity. They do not realize that they can so easily be toppled—"

Meg interrupted—"Rupert dear, surely you are thrilled by the news Renny brings us? Just think. Adeline and Philip are going to be married next year and right now we are to have a dinner party at Jalna in celebration."

"Very nice. Very nice indeed," said the Rector. "I am glad Adeline got rid of Fitzturgis. He was too experienced . . . A divorcé and all that. Too experienced altogether for Adeline. Not really nice. But—if I have an objection to Philip it is that he's not experienced enough. Why—it seems only yesterday when I held him in my arms at the font, and he looked such surprise out of his big blue eyes. Let's see, what names did I give him? Philip . . . yes, Philip Vaughan. . . . Do you think you could hammer these stakes into the ground for me, Renny, to support the hollyhocks? Dear me, their stalks appear to be cracked. I do hope the sap will be able to find its way through to the blossoms."

He put a hammer into Renny's hand. With stakes and raffia they rescued the hollyhocks, which, standing again upright, looked serenely unconscious of past downfall.

"Well," said Renny, "I'm glad you are pleased by the engagement. On my part I think nothing so heartening has come my way for many a year."

"Not East Wind?" asked the Rector.

"There's a wide difference between a race horse and one's only daughter," Renny said in an admonishing tone, a tone almost clerical, as though he were the clergyman and Mr. Fennel the layman.

The Rector's mind, however, was on his garden. "See those hydrangeas," he said, lifting one great white bloom. "How well they bore the storm! They bend but they do not break."

"They look good enough to eat," said his wife. "They always remind me of a delicious dish of curds."

Though Meg had (or pretended she had) little interest in food where she herself was concerned, she took great pleasure in the arrangements for the dinner party at Jalna. In the immediate family there were thirteen to sit down at table, but word came that very week that Piers's second son, Christian, who had been abroad studying art, would be returning in time for the party.

"Let's hope," Piers said to Pheasant, "that he will be able to sell some of his pictures. It's been an expensive business sending him abroad to study, and I must say he doesn't appear to appreciate what I've done for him. He takes it all for granted."

"Oh, he appreciates it all right," said Pheasant. "He's often said what a generous father you are."

"Has he? Well, you have never told me that before. It's a good thing for a father to hear occasionally that he is something more than a mere provider."

As a matter of fact, Piers was proud of his artist son and never grudged what was spent on him. Neither did he consider that Renny was really the loser, though Piers was badly behind in his payments for rent of the farmland of Jalna. Occasionally the brothers had what they called a "business talk," in which Piers was able to convince Renny that to run a farm was much harder work and much less profitable than to run stables. Now the engagement of Adeline and Philip had drawn the two men closer.

Little Mary was not sure that Christian's return was pleasing to her. In his absence, his studio had been hers to do what she liked in. With his coming all was different. New canvases he had brought with him lined the walls. He was here, there and everywhere, his light pleasant voice bringing its atmosphere of the outer world. He had been home for less than a week when he wrote a letter to his elder brother in Ireland.

He carried it to his mother and said, "I've written to Maurice. Have you a message for him?"

"Tell him I shall be writing before long. Tell him we're looking forward to his coming this fall. Be sure to say that."

"Should you like to read what I've written?"

Pheasant was staking a larkspur. She pulled off her gardening gloves and took the letter from him. As she read, he studied her sensitive face with an artist's interest.

"Well," he said, "is it all right?"

"I suppose so. But why do you pretend that you think Maurice has ceased to care about Adeline? I'm sure he hasn't."

"It was easier to write that way."

Pheasant returned the letter to him. "I suppose so," she said, then added: "It was very hard on Maurice—leaving home when he was only a child—even though it turned out so well for him, in a material way. And—it nearly broke my heart." Christian kissed Pheasant tenderly.

He had often before heard her say this sort of thing, but he himself felt that Maurice had been lucky.

What Christian had written was:

My Dear Maurice:

Here I am—home again and, after the first excitement, feeling as though I had never been away. Everything is so exactly the same. You of course have had the experience of returning after a long absence, time and again. But this is my first. One of the things I most enjoyed abroad was my visit with you. I feel as though I had not thanked you enough for it but I really am tremendously grateful. I have said everything is the same but it is not—quite. In fact I have one startling bit of news. Mother agreed that I should be the bearer of it. For some reason she seemed to shrink from writing it. I think the reason probably is that she is against the project. But myself I think it is rather a good idea. It certainly is picturesque and traditional and all that.

I know, Maurice, that you were more than a little in love with Adeline. What man wouldn't be! I was myself—that is I was in love with her graceful walk and her lovely hair and those eyes of hers. And I still am—as an artist. But in spirit she and I are miles apart and always shall be. When I was in Ireland with you I felt that you too had quite got

over your early infatuation or whatever you like to call it.
You spoke of her so seldom and, when you did speak of
her, you seemed so natural, so uninterested, that I don't
think this news will trouble you . . .

Maurice Whiteoak was lounging on the sun-warmed steps
in front of Glengorman, his home in Ireland, and he was
reading the letter aloud to his close friend and confidant, Sir
Patrick Crawshay, a young man in his thirties and a neigh-
bor.

Maurice interrupted himself to exclaim: "What the devil is
the fellow driving at? Why doesn't he get to the point?"

"Certainly he is mysterious," said Pat Crawshay. "But read
on. Let's discover who is the happy man."

"Happy man?" repeated Maurice, as though dazed.

"Obviously he is trying to tell you of Adeline's engagement
to someone."

Maurice's eyes returned to the letter, but for a moment he
seemed to have trouble in making out the words. Then he
read on:

> If I had been asked who was the most unlikely suitor I
> could think of, I should have said this boy. But perhaps he
> has already written to you himself and made the affair clear.
> I believe and I'm sure Mother believes that it was engineered
> by Uncle Renny—you may imagine why—I can't.

Maurice broke off to say: "For the love of God, get on
with the news! What *is* the fellow's name?"

Yet a sinking of the heart made that name less of a surprise than he would have thought. He read on:

> Philip and I were pals, as you know, but the three years
> between us seems much more since I have been away. Now I
> feel closer to you. Philip's just a big boy.

Now it was Patrick Crawshay who interrupted. "Philip
. . . He's your youngest brother, isn't he?"

Maurice raised sombre eyes to his friend's face. "Yes. A
big lump of a boy and, though he's as pretty as a picture, it's
unbelievable that Adeline should fall in love with him."

"But why," demanded Patrick Crawshay, "should your
uncle favor the match?"

"Family pride. Worship of family traditions. The boy
hasn't a bean. He's not very intelligent, but—Oh, I can't talk

about it." Maurice threw himself on his back and stretched out a hand to pull off the infant buds of flowers which bordered the steps. He held the buds to his face from which all color had fled, and sniffed them, as though he hoped by their scent to revive his spirits.

"This is a blow, Pat," he said. "There's no use in denying it. You know—I've never tried to hide my love for Adeline. I still love her, without hope. And now—to get this news! My young brother. It's a hell of a situation. I don't know how to bear it. I can't imagine what she sees in him. Why—it's not so long ago that I laid him across a bench (it was my last visit home but one) and warmed his behind for him. God, I wish I might lay hands on him now!"

"Surely he's not to be blamed," said Pat Crawshay. "Adeline is a lovable girl."

Maurice interrupted—"She's far from lovable. She's never been loving toward me. Yet I can't put her out of my head and I'd forgive her everything if—"

"Forgive?" questioned Pat Crawshay, gently stressing the word.

"Forgive her what she's put me through. I can tell you I *suffered* when she got herself engaged to that fellow Fitzturgis."

"I never liked him. He always behaved as if he had something to hide."

"I'll bet he had a lot to hide."

"Haven't we all?" laughed Crawshay, who had lived a particularly transparent life.

Maurice answered gloomily, "To hide ourselves from ourselves is the problem. We want to feel brave and unselfish, don't we?"

"I'm afraid I've done just what I've wanted to—without thinking."

"If it had been you who was to marry her," said Maurice, "I could have borne it, but that whippersnapper—that puppy!"

"I wish it might be me," said Pat Crawshay. "I fell in love with her, truly I did, when she visited you here—at first sight. I had been fishing and when I climbed the bank to the path, there was she with the two Labradors—looking so proud and so innocent—good Lord, I've imagined happy endings for that meeting! But—she thought nothing of me."

"She did. She thought enough to make me jealous. I'll tell you what, Pat, when I go to visit my people in the autumn, you must come too—you've promised that visit, you know. Between us we'll cut out this puppy. By God, he shall not have Adeline!"

Pat Crawshay smiled a conspirator's smile, but all he would say was, "What else is in the letter?"

"Nothing except a rave over the delicious food they had at the dinner. Christian has no heart."

Nine

The Dinner Party

To be free once more from engagements, from railway time-tables, from the tyranny of public life, was enough to fill Finch with contentment. Added to this was his happiness in Sylvia. She was, he felt, the perfect wife for him. What a contrast his life with her to his life with Sarah! Married to Sarah he had had little respite from her enfolding presence. She had been as a heavily scented flower—a pale lily whose leaves had shut out light and air from him. Sylvia demanded nothing. She was elusive. She seemed at times to be hiding from him. He would go through the house and into the garden calling her name and, when she answered, a sudden joy surged through him. He would take long strides to reach her, as though he feared she might escape him.

To Sylvia all they owned seemed precious, because it was theirs. She took pleasure in polishing the fine wood of tables and cabinets, especially the piano, through which it seemed to her the soul of Finch reached out to her. Now that the child was out of the house the disappointment of their relations, his antagonism to her were dimmed. She thought of him as needing her love, as being in a sense dependent on her. She would go into his bedroom and picture his return at the end of the summer, coming home, full of the doings of the camp, yet glad to be with his parents again.

Dennis returned sooner than expected. The day before the dinner party celebrating the engagement of Adeline and Philip, there came a telephone call from the owner of the boys' camp. His robust, genial voice came over the wire to Finch, who had been at the breakfast table.

"Hello," said the voice, "is that Mr. Whiteoak?"

"Yes," said Finch, scenting trouble.

"I'm afraid," went on the voice, "that we can't keep your son at the camp. I'm sorry to tell you this but I really think he'd be better at home."

"What has he done?" demanded Finch.

"Nothing in particular. He's a nice boy but he's badly adjusted. I'd say he is emotionally disturbed. He's a boy that's better at home."

"But he goes to boarding school," said Finch. "He's been at boarding school for years. I can't understand this."

But the man persisted, talking on, repeating his clichés. The receiver shook in Finch's hand. He was trembling with anger. "Send the boy to the telephone," he said.

Sylvia came to him. "What ever is the matter?" she asked.

"It's Dennis. He's giving trouble at camp. They're bringing him to the telephone."

"What sort of trouble?" she whispered.

"You ought to know what he's capable of." Finch did not realize how harshly he spoke. The severity in his voice caused Sylvia to flinch, to draw back from him. At that moment he bore an extraordinary resemblance to his grandmother, old Adeline Whiteoak.

Now he turned back to the telephone on hearing the treble voice of his son.

"Hello, Daddy."

"Dennis—I have been hearing very disagreeable things about your behavior at camp."

"Yes, I know. Am I to go home?"

"You are not. You are to stay where you are."

"But I want to go home."

"You'll be sorry if you don't stay there and behave yourself."

"I don't think Mr. Brown wants me."

"Dennis—listen." A cajoling note (much against his will) entered Finch's voice. "Listen," he said, "if you will settle down in camp and try to be like other boys, you will be rewarded when you come home."

There was a moment's silence, then the childish treble replied, "But I want to be with you."

Finch groaned in anger and frustration. Sylvia interrupted, "Let him come! On, do let him come."

"Be good enough not to interfere," Finch said with severity.

Now the man's voice came over the wire. "I'm afraid it's not possible for us to keep your son here, Mr. Whiteoak. It's not good for him and it's not good for the other boys. I'm sorry."

"Send him along," said Finch.

His bacon and eggs were cold when he returned to the

table. He pushed them aside. Sylvia poured him a fresh cup of tea. He gave her a sidelong glance, saw her pallor and laid his hand on hers.

"Don't look so tragic," she said. "After all, it's just the coming-home of a child, a little sooner than he was expected."

"He'll behave himself when he comes," Finch said fiercely, "or I'll give him a walloping he won't forget."

Dennis arrived just as Finch and Sylvia were dressing for the party. He looked tidy and cool, considering the heat of the day, and carried his small belongings to his room with composure.

"We passed Uncle Renny on horseback," he said, "just at his gate, and he said I was to hurry home and dress. He wants me at the party. May I have a bath?"

"Of course you may," said Sylvia, and she longed to take his slim little body into her arms.

Finch followed his son into his bedroom and shut the door after them. He said, "After your bath put on clean things and don't be long about it. Remember, you are in disgrace. You must toe the mark from now on or get into serious trouble. As it is, you should be hanging your head in shame, instead of staring at me as though nothing were wrong."

"Out of my green eyes," said Dennis.

"Are you trying to be funny?" Finch demanded.

"Oh, no. But people say they are." He blinked, as though their color dazzled him.

"Well," said Finch heavily, "remember what I've said."

"Yes, Daddy."

"Get a move on."

"Yes, Daddy."

Dennis began to pull off his clothes. In no more than a moment he was stark naked. On his way to the bathroom he wheeled and ran through the living-room. Sylvia, dressed for dinner, was putting the room to rights. She turned, startled, and Dennis faced her with embarrassment. "I've left some of my belongings in the porch," he explained, and smiled at her. Again the arms of her spirit opened to him.

He returned from the porch carrying a paper bag. "It's full of apples," he explained. "Sweet ones. I bought them for a present. Twenty-five cents." He carried them to the kitchen, where Finch followed him. The "daily" had left. Finch said, "Don't you know better than to run about naked, in front of Sylvia?"

"No," returned Dennis, almost curtly. His interest was

centred on the bag of apples, the bottom of which fell out as he was about to set it on the table, and the apples were scattered over the floor. Dennis broke into loud treble laughter. He picked up an apple and was about to bite into it when Finch, glancing at his watch, exclaimed:

"You little fool. Gather up those apples and be quick about it."

Still laughing, Dennis cried, "Catch, Daddy!" and threw the apple at Finch. It struck Finch's glasses, knocking them off.

The kitchen floor was tiled, The frame of the glasses snapped in half. The two lenses lay staring up from the tiles.

Sylvia had appeared in the doorway. Now she cried out that the glasses were broken—as though Finch did not know it!

Finch picked them up. "I have another pair," he said crossly, as though rebuking her for her emotionalism.

"It was my fault," Dennis said loudly. He snatched up an apple and struck himself on the forehead with it. Violently he wished to attract Finch's attention from Sylvia and the glasses to himself. Again he struck himself on the forehead. "Look, Daddy," he shouted. "This is what I get!"

The three were the last to arrive at the dinner party.

Already in the house were Piers and his family, the prospective bridegroom looking rather too scrubbed, like a schoolboy brought in from the playing fields and tidied for a Confirmation class. And indeed Philip wore a grave expression, as though determined to become his new position. Piers, with his nostrils widened in pride, regarded his son as though he would say, "I begot this young wonder." In Piers's mind the achievement of Archer in winning a Rhodes Scholarship was insignificant as compared to Philip's in winning Adeline.

With Pheasant it was very different. Her thoughts were with her loved first-born. If only Maurice might have married Adeline—Maurice, who had so constantly loved her . . .

Little Mary clung to Piers's hand. She wore a new white dress, with frills and a blue sash. She wished there were not so many voices, talking loudly above her head, which felt hot and rather confused. Her father's hand, to which she clung, was moist with perspiration. She said "perspiration" several times to herself. She knew it was rude to say "sweat." Her mother had told her so. Then why did Philip sometimes say he was sweating like a horse? Because Philip was rude, there was no doubt about that.

Dennis was not rude but he was looking at her with eyes that made her uncomfortable. Archer was asking him:

"Been in a fight?"

"No," said Dennis. "I came home from camp."

"How did you get that bump on your forehead?"

"I did it myself—with an apple."

"I hear," said Archer, "that you've been sent home from camp. I'm not going to ask you what you did, but I will say you have the perfect face for a juvenile delinquent."

"What kind is that?" Dennis asked, interested.

"It's pale and inscrutable, with somehow the look of a martyr. Your family will be blamed for whatever you do."

Adeline, overhearing this, said, "Stop it, Archie. He's conceited enough already."

Dennis said stiffly, "I came home because I am needed."

Meg had eyes for no one but her granddaughter, Victoria Bell, who lay on the leather couch in the library with the old knitted afghan that had seen so much service spread over her.

"Oh, the precious lamb!" cried Meg, hovering over her—if one of Meg's bulk could be said to hover. "I've never seen a finer child! Whom does she resemble, I wonder?"

"Not me, thank God," said Humphrey Bell.

"I know," Meg said, as though inspired. "She looks like Patience's father. Oh, how proud he would have been!"

The Rector too bent over the baby. "I see no resemblance," he said, "except in the receding hairline."

Renny joined them. He blew a whiff of cigarette smoke into the infant's face, which at once puckered and emitted a tiny sneeze.

"Always like to see them sneeze," he remarked. "Does them good."

It was now time to move into the dining-room. Little Mary had been given her evening meal before leaving home and she remained with the baby, for she was to be trusted. Therefore sixteen people sat down to table. Alayne, though opposed to this betrothal, had gone to great pains to make the dinner a success. She had decorated the table with old-fashioned, sweet-scented roses. The roast ducks were of the tenderest, the green peas were fresh from the garden, the asparagus succulent and, when it came to the dessert, the Rector declared that the strawberries were at their most perfect—the very hour before they became overripe, when their flavor was at its most seductive. As for the cream from the Jersey cows, it came out of the fat silver jugs in golden blobs. Mrs. Wragge had baked two angel cakes, not the sort out of a package but made with eight large eggs apiece. Renny had, as promised, provided champagne. After a health had been drunk to the young couple, who sat smiling at each other across the table, he proposed another—this to the earlier Philip and Adeline, who looked serenely down at this festive gathering from their massive gilt frames.

The sixteenth member of the family to sit at table was Roma Whiteoak, the niece who lived in New York. She had arrived only that day and had gone straight to the Rectory, for she had lived with Meg for some years. Though she was only two years younger than Adeline, she gave the impression, at first sight, of being almost a child as compared to her, for she was small and her face retained the contours of childhood. Her golden-brown hair waved softly about her cheeks. Yet a closer look into that artless-seeming face would reveal an expression of cool resolve, a bend to the lips that could easily harden into a sneer. At table she had been placed next Archer, who looked her over with a good deal of curiosity.

"Do you like living in New York?" he asked.

"Well, at least, there's something to do there," she said. "Not like this place."

"Have you made friends?"

"As many as I want," she returned with a shrug.

He inspected her more closely. "You have the face," he observed, "of the genuine heartbreaker. You don't even know you are doing it."

She liked that. Attacking her shrimp cocktail she asked, "How did you find out so much, at your age?"

"Don't you know you're talking to a classicist? I have qualified," he said, "for a Rhodes Scholarship. I have read the classics."

"Helen of Troy and all that?"

"Mostly all that."

"I haven't time for reading," she said, "except condensations."

"With all the best parts left out," he commented.

"You can cover more ground that way," she said.

"Is it a cause for conceit," he asked, "to cover more ground?"

Alayne leant forward a little to overhear this conversation.

How these young ones were striving to be grown-up, and how
much they had to learn! And possibly with pain. Her heart
yearned over her son. She wished, though she would not acknowledge it even to herself, that he had something of the
warm, responsive nature of Adeline. Yet when he smiled—
which he did so rarely—how sweet was that smile! Now, as
she caught his eye with her look of yearning, he returned it
with one of frosty condescension.

They sat long at the table, the cool night air blowing gently
in at the windows, the leaves of the Virginia creeper, that
overlapped in their exuberance of growth, making a scarcely
heard murmur. When the family returned to the library they
found little Mary fast asleep, her hair falling over her face,
while Victoria Bell's florid countenance was puckered in
protest at the delay in her feeding. Their two mothers swept
them upstairs, Patience undoing her blouse as she hastened to
uncover her flower-white breast. This was attacked by Victoria Bell with infant fury. Pheasant had captured a dish of
strawberries and cream for her child before putting her down
to sleep.

Alayne, who had come upstairs to tidy her face, glanced in
at them. She thought, Women and children always in evi-
dence . . . They are hopelessly rumpling that bedspread. She
said, smiling, "Having a little nourishment, eh?" And saw
how Pheasant was feeding Mary, like another baby. The little
girl's eyes were shut but she mechanically opened her pink
mouth to receive the luscious red strawberries. Cream trickled
down her chin. Alayne thought, One's own children are
enough. Why should one be asked to put up with other
people's?

She turned away to discover Dennis standing behind her.
His eyes were fixed on the baby.

"Is that the way I was fed?" he asked, as she reached the
door of her own bedroom. There was something in his
voice—an unchildlike note—a tone of fierce, contemptuous
curiosity.

"What do you mean?"

She turned into her room.

"I mean," he said, "the way Patience is doing. Was I fed
that way?"

"Why should it matter to you?" she asked. Her back was
to him. She examined her face in the mirror.

He was like a peddlar with his foot in the door who would
not budge.

"Because I want to know."

Alayne tried to think. "I can't remember," she said. Then—"No. You were fed from a bottle, I think. Now run along." She came and closed the door.

He ran down the stairs and out into the languid summer night, heavy with the scent of flowers. The picture of the red-faced infant tugging at its mother's voluptuous breast haunted him, filled him with disgust. Many a time he had seen animals suckling their young, but this was different. It filled him with angry repulsion. "I hate women," he said to himself. "They are cows. I hate them." He saw Adeline and Roma standing together beneath the dark leaves of a maple and turned aside to avoid them. Through the window of the dining-room he could see the men still sitting about the table. His eyes sought the figure of Finch and he said aloud, but softly:

"I only love my father. My father." And he kept repeating those words. "Women are cows."

Standing in the darkness Roma said to Adeline:

"I've something to tell you."

"What?" Adeline asked with mild curiosity.

"I'm engaged."

"To whom?"

"Guess."

"Do I know him?"

"You used to. You thought quite a lot of him—once."

Adeline looked down at Roma, trying to see her face.

"I can guess," she said. "Is it Maitland?"

"Yes," breathed Roma. "Do you mind?"

"Not in the least."

"I thought you'd perhaps be hurt. Or angry."

"Why?"

"Oh, I don't know. . . . I thought perhaps you'd feel you still had some claim on him."

"For heaven's sake," Adeline exclaimed, "be reasonable. I couldn't care less who marries him."

"I wanted him to come and make our announcement at the party but he wouldn't."

"I wonder why," said Adeline. The thought of such an announcement at that time was shocking, painful—or was it funny? She chose to think of it as funny and gave a short laugh. "That would have been a good joke," she added.

Roma was annoyed. "I don't see anything funny about it,"

she said. "If Mait and I choose to fall in love, I don't see anything funny in it."

"Of course not," said Adeline. "When are you to be married?"

"Next fall."

"Have you told Sylvia?"

"Not yet. There she is coming toward us. I'll tell her now."

Sylvia came across the close-cut dark lawn, on which a heavy dew was falling. She had a way of looking strangely alone. There was about her an air of solitariness even as she joined Adeline and Roma.

"What a lovely night," she said. "Too lovely for staying indoors."

Adeline put an arm about her. "Prepare yourself for great news," she said. "Roma has something to tell you."

"You tell her," said Roma, suddenly young and shy in manner.

"Is it about my brother and you?" asked Sylvia.

Roma nodded, her hair falling softly about her forehead.

"He has already told me," said Sylvia. "I had a letter from him two days ago." She bent to kiss Roma. "I hope you will be very happy," she said.

The three stood there in silence. The voices of the men came to them, as they emerged from the house. Roma said, "I think I shall go and break the news to Uncle Renny." She gave a childlike little skip as she crossed the lawn. She tossed her hair and ran and caught Renny by the arm. He smiled down at her.

She said: "I've a secret."

She was like a little girl, he thought, and let himself be led to the path that found its way, through grass and ferns and wild flowers, into the ravine. There the stream was singing in the darkness and there was the smell of moist earth.

"Uncle Renny," she said, now that she had him there—speaking in an almost matter-of-fact tone, as though the childishness had been but play-acting—"I'm going to be married to Maitland Fitzturgis."

If her news had not caused the sensation she had expected when she told it to Sylvia and Adeline, certainly there was no disappointment for her in Renny's reception of it. He had been about to light a cigarette and the flare from the match showed his astonished face.

"Marry Fitzturgis?" he repeated. "Why—I can't believe it! I thought—well, I thought you had no more than a passing fancy for him. Roma, are you sure you care enough about him to marry him?"

"It's pretty obvious that I do," she said coolly. She opened a little sequined evening bag and took from it a ring set with small diamonds. She slipped it onto her third finger. "I didn't want to wear this till I had broken the news," she said. She put her head on one side to admire the ring, which shone mildly in the moonlight that now drifted through the branches of trees growing so close together that their leaves allowed only narrow shafts of light to penetrate.

Renny Whiteoak reflected on how his daughter had for two years awaited the coming of Fitzturgis from Ireland, had loyally awaited her marriage to him—and now here was Roma, who had wrecked that engagement, primed herself to marry him. Yet always he had appeared to Renny as an unlovable man.

"It's a pretty ring," he said. "Fitzturgis seems to be doing well in New York. I hope he's in a position to keep you properly.

"We shall manage," said Roma in a tone that did not invite questioning.

She had told him her news and had little more to say. Voices and laughter came down to them from the lawn above and then the sound of a Chopin waltz played by Finch. Renny took Roma by the hand, kissed her and led her up the path to the house.

When the guests had gone, he drew Adeline into her own room behind the stairway, the room that had for so many years been occupied by his grandmother. Even to-day, with the belongings of a young girl scattered about, the atmosphere, the flavor of the room could not be subdued. Renny could not enter it without seeing again the bent figure of the old, old woman, her penetrating gaze beneath the lace frill of her cap, her beringed hands, her mordant grin. He could see again the green plumage of her parrot, perching on the painted bedstead.

"Tired?" he asked Adeline.

"No. It's been a lovely evening."

"What do you think of Roma's engagement?"

"Don't ask me."

"Why?" he persisted.

"Because I don't know. My brain is all confused where those two are concerned."

"Mine isn't," he said. "I think they'll lead each other the devil of a life."

"I don't see why. They are, both of them, pretty tolerant—not jealous and quick-tempered—like me." She took off her dress and, opening the window wider, leant out toward the night breeze.

Renny dropped a kiss on her shoulder. She was like a fresh flower, he thought, a new-blown rose, set in a rococo vase. "You're like me," he said, "and like Gran. How she would have admired you! You and Philip."

She said over her shoulder, "He's a nice boy." In that moment she was remembering Fitzturgis and the wild surge of her love for him.

"Philip has developed tremendously since his engagement to you," said Renny.

"Has he?" She turned and faced him, as though in mild surprise.

"And so have you."

Now she gave a little laugh. "That's funny," she said, "because I feel younger. Almost a child again."

"It's a good way for a woman to feel. Let the man do the planning—and worrying."

He said good-night to her; closed the front door, against which the three dogs were leaning. They longed to go to bed and followed him gladly up the stairs and into Archer's room.

The boy was sitting on the side of his book-littered bed, reading a French novel. "I'm trying to enjoy it," he said glumly, "because I hear that all Paris is enjoying it."

"I thought," said Renny, "that you disliked doing what it is 'the thing' to do."

"Very true," Archer agreed. "I do. But I shall be going to Paris. I must make some little preparation."

"Now, look here, Archie," said Renny, "no one in Oxford or Paris will care what you read or whether you're able to read."

Archer laid down the book. "I suppose they'll ask me questions about Canada—a country in which I'm not particularly interested. I don't, in fact, know one totem pole from another."

"You're a queer egg," said Renny, to whom his son was a constant source of amusement, while he filled Alayne with a confusion of mingled pride and humiliation.

"*Quid dem? Quid non dem?*" mused Archer. "*Renuis tu quod jubet alter.*"

"Hm," said Renny, "that's Greek to me."

"It was Latin," Archer said politely, "to the one who wrote it. It's not a very apt quotation, but the only one I can think of at the moment. These family parties leave me flattened."

"Better get to bed," said his father. "It's late. You should have plenty of sleep before you carouse in Oxford and Paris."

"Mercy!" said Archer.

The dogs were so eager for bed they yawned and whined in pleasure as Renny turned into his own room. The cairn terrier leapt straight onto the bed, while the bulldog and spaniel went under it. Renny remembered how the room which was now Archer's had been the bedroom of Uncle Ernest. That dear man—how interested he would have been in Archer, as indeed he had been in all his nephews.

Renny thought of his brothers—his half-brothers they were, but closer to him than many a full brother: Eden, dead this many a year; Piers; Finch; and Wakefield. It was a disappointment that Wakefield had not been able to come to the party because of an engagement in New York. Wake's love affairs, his delicate health had been a source of anxiety to Renny. He had given Wake a more fatherly affection than ever he had given to Archer. And now Wake was a man of thirty-eight and a successful actor.

As though to crystallize Renny's thoughts, a letter from New York caught his eye. It lay on the table beside his bed and was addressed in Wakefield's handwriting—a small scholarly hand, taught him by Uncle Ernest. How proud the family had been of the little boy's writing, so different from Finch's scrawl. . . .

When Renny had opened the letter and read it he went straight to Alayne's room.

Ten

The Letter

Alayne was already in bed, graceful in a lace bedjacket. She was reading a book of essays to calm her for the night. She raised her eyes from it to look inquiringly at Renny. He came at once to the foot of the bed.

"I've had a letter from Wakefield," he said. "He's ill."

All her married days she had been used to Renny's periods of anxiety over this youngest brother's health. He had had a weak heart. He had suffered (often willfully, it had seemed to Alayne) from his nerves. He had been a posthumous child, a precocious child, and the family had shown a solicitude toward him that had been denied Finch. It had been Alayne who had first realized Finch's talent and had urged music lessons for him. Wakefield was talented too. Eden, Finch, Wakefield—poet, pianist, actor—they were remarkable, these brothers, she had often thought, and what a contrast to Renny and Piers!

Now, looking concerned, she asked, "What is wrong? Nothing serious, I hope."

"Terribly serious, I'm afraid. His right lung is affected. He's been having treatments. The doctors say he must rest for several months, in bed. They say rest will complete the cure, but—can we believe them?" Renny's forehead was furrowed by apprehension. "Oh, Alayne, what if he should go, as Eden went?"

Resolutely she put that image away from her and said—in a reassuring tone—"Wakefield will recover. Care and rest will cure him, as the doctors say."

"He wants to come home," said Renny—eying her to watch the effect of his words—"home for the rest they prescribe."

She sat up straight in bed. Her eyes looked almost fiercely into his. "To come here," she said, "where there are two young people? He can't—he can't possibly do it."

"He does not suggest coming into this house. What he

wants is to come to Fiddler's Hut. You remember Fiddler's Hut?"

"Fiddler's Hut?" she repeated unbelievingly. "Surely not. Why, I haven't seen it in years! It must be a tumbledown ruin by now." She might have added that she hoped never again to see it.

"It is not a tumbledown ruin," he said defensively. "Although it stood here when my grandfather bought the property, it was built of stones from the fields. It's solid still. In the old days a fellow called Fiddling Jock lived there and my grandmother—"

"I've heard that story a hundred times." She spoke in sudden uncontrollable anger. "I know how he lived there and how he died and how I nursed Eden there through his first illness. Fancy your asking me if I remember it!"

"Well, you often say you forget things."

"Not that sort of thing."

"Alayne"—his eyes were dark with foreboding as he repeated—"what if Wake goes—the way Eden did?"

"He won't—not if he has the right care, and guards his health in the future, which Eden never did." Now she spoke calmly, reassuringly. "But I cannot think that tumbledown shack—" she reiterated.

"It's not a shack and it's not tumbledown."

"Call it what you will," she said wearily. "All I'm trying to say is—how can Wakefield get the proper care? Who is to look after him?"

Renny avoided her eyes. He said, in a low, almost conciliatory voice, "Molly is coming to nurse him."

His words appeared to electrify Alayne. "That girl!" she said violently. "It's impossible. They've been living together—without marriage—and you are the one who knows why. They are of the same blood."

"You forgave me that," he said, "and it was long before I met you."

She felt that she had borne more than any woman should be asked to bear. She put a hand to the back of her neck. "Do you want me to lie awake the rest of the night?" she said, her voice shaking with anger.

"All I said was," he repeated, "that Molly was born long before I ever met you and, if you could have known the circumstances—"

"My God," she cried, "do you imagine that I will endure

to hear the details of your randy youth? I want to settle down and sleep—if I can."

He flung out of the room. But, in his own room, one word she had used rankled in his mind. He returned to her.

The bedside lamp was still burning but the sheet was drawn up to her chin and her eyes shut tight. She opened them just a slit when he entered.

"You used a word about me just now," he said, "that I don't like."

"A word," she repeated, as though mystified.

"Yes—a word—and I want it explained."

She looked self-conscious now. "What word?"

"Randy. You spoke of my randy youth."

"Did I?"

"Well—I've heard the word before and, as I've said, I don't like it. I don't like the idea of your going about collecting odd words to throw in my teeth." And he marched out of the room. In the doorway he turned to say, "I've been called many things in my life but never—"

She sat up in bed. *"Sh!"* she commanded. "Archer will hear you."

He banged the door after him and she heard him go down the stairs with his light, quick step. He was clever, she thought, in his own instinctive way, to have put her in the wrong with something as flimsy as a word offensive to him; yet—and she smiled to remember it—he had been genuinely hurt.

The dogs, too, had heard him go downstairs but it was not till he opened the front door that the cairn terrier jumped off the bed and the spaniel and the bulldog came from under it. They were so afraid he would leave the house without them that they bundled themselves down the stairs and shouldered each other through the doorway in panic. They overtook him on the drive and created, with whines of pleasure and gambolings, a reunion as though after long separation. "Good boys," he said, patting each in turn—and added, "It's well that somebody loves me."

The least Alayne might do, he thought, was to show some concern over Wakefield's illness. He was deeply troubled by it. These half-brothers of his, he reflected, with the exception of Piers, had not much stamina. They had had a delicate mother—a pretty, graceful woman, but fragile.

He turned his steps past the stables, for the very thought of the sanguine beasts it housed was comforting. The path led to the back of Finch's property. A stile had lately been built where a fence divided it from Jalna and Renny now perceived, perched on it, the lanky figure of Finch. The dogs, too, had discovered him; and, after a few warning barks, ran joyfully to greet him. A tender summer haze enveloped all.

"Hullo," called out Finch. "That you, Renny?"

He clambered down from the stile.

"Why are you about so late?" Renny asked.

"Well, I couldn't sleep and the night is lovely."

"Yes." Renny absently looked up into the night's radiance, then said, "Come for a walk. I have something I want to tell you."

Finch peered into his face. "Not bad news, I hope."

"Not good. Come with me and I'll tell you."

Their two tall shadows merged together as they moved along the sandy road that led past the orchard to the woodland, the lesser, capricious shadows of the dogs darting about them. Almost overnight, it seemed, tiny green apples had formed on the trees.

Renny told his news in a low, almost laconic voice.

Few could be more impressed by bad news than Finch. He flew with open arms, as it were, to receive its impact. His lively imagination pictured the worst to come. Yet it was he who was most excited, moved to joy by good news.

"I'm afraid," Renny said, "that Wake is a very sick man, though he does not write despondently."

"But it will be terrible to him to give up his work. It's his life. And Molly too! You say she is coming to nurse him. That means they both give up. Why, their lives are dedicated to the stage!"

"What nonsense you talk," said Renny. "Neither is giving up. They are taking a much-needed holiday."

"But I keep remembering Eden. I saw so much of him, in Devon and later—when he was so ill. He wore a light blue dressing-gown. Sometimes I dream of him—in that dressing-gown. I see him so clearly. And the strange thing is that, as time goes on, I see him even more clearly and I understand him better. . . . Last night I dreamed of him. And Wake was there too—as a little fellow . . ."

Finch was becoming wrought up, and his excitement had the effect of calming Renny. As often before, he felt ashamed for Finch's emotionalism. He said, "Come along with me. We'll find the Hut. That's where Wakefield plans to rest. Did I tell you? I think it's a good idea."

Now, in unison, they strode toward the Hut, scarcely large enough to be called a cottage, that was half-buried in a neglected part of the estate. So buried was it in the luxuriant growth of summer that it was difficult to find. The path leading to it was obliterated. A mingling of weeds and wild shrubs grew waist-high. Among these hid small garter snakes and above circled bats, singing their nocturnal song, heard only by themselves. But above the other growth flourished an exuberant wild grapevine. It covered the windows of the Hut, wound itself about the latch of the door, fixing it as with a bolt. Its great leaves shone in the moonlight, as though lacquered. Its strong tendrils hung in wait for anything they could capture.

Renny was engaged in tearing the vine from the doorway, releasing the latch. Even as the vine, ripped from its stronghold, hung limp in his hand, its tendrils reached out for something to cling to.

Now he was able to open the creaking door.

Their nostrils were met by the smell of mould. They could just make out the shapes of a few pieces of furniture that had been left there. A melancholy place. Finch said:

"How long since it was occupied?"

"It must be twenty-five years."

"Good God! . . . It surely isn't the place for Wake."

"When I have cleared it up it will be."

"It feels so damp."

"Eden recovered his health here."

"But he died—later."

"Only because he went to Europe and knocked himself about. I shall come here tomorrow and set to work. You'll be surprised by what I shall do to-morrow."

"To-morrow!" exclaimed Finch. "To-day! Look."

Through the open doorway they could see the clouds above the treetops tinged by the coming dawn. The moon had sunk. The two brothers stood looking upward, conscious of the towering mystery of life. In that dim little dwelling they stood surrounded by shadows of the past.

The two became suddenly more visible to each other. A greenish light from the east had penetrated the lush growth and showed their hands and faces as though seen under water. The bats had retreated but a small bird burst into song and a mysterious movement was felt, rather than seen or heard, through the woodland.

"I shall get a few hours' sleep," Renny said, "then come here after breakfast to clear up. Want to help me?"

To do something with Renny was exhilarating to Finch. He agreed and they retraced their steps, hearing the first cock-crow as they neared the poultry house.

Going softly up the stairs to his room, Renny noticed that the light was still burning in Alayne's room. He opened the door quietly and put in his head.

"Still awake?" he asked.

She gave him a look.

"Did you expect me to sleep," she demanded, "after hearing you go out at such an hour?"

"Now, look here, Alayne," he said with the arch grin of his grandmother, "if you have been lying awake, worrying over that word you used about me, forget it. I have forgiven you."

Eleven

Preparing the Hut and
the Arrival

It was eleven o'clock in the morning when Renny and Finch, armed with scythe and axe, arrived at the Hut.

He looks as fresh as ever, thought Finch, if he can be said to look fresh with that weather-beaten complexion.

Looking Finch over, Renny remarked, "You certainly need the good rest you're getting."

"I find it hard to relax," said Finch. "I don't quite know why."

"Nothing will do you so much good as manual labor. Here—begin by pulling this wild grapevine up by the roots."

"It's very pretty," Finch said regretfully.

"It's smothering everything for its own satisfaction. Pretty but ruthless—like some women."

They set to work.

Now the vine lay in a great leafy mound, its tendrils reaching out as though for succor, for something to cling to, even in its death. Shrubs and saplings were cut down, trees were felled, undergrowth and bracken torn away. Sunshine and breeze came pouring in. Small creatures that had reveled in the sequestered greenness came hastening out. In the height of the work they were joined by Dennis, whom Renny set to collecting brushwood and placing it in a mound for burning later on. The boy threw himself into the work with zest, showing no embarrassment at having been sent home from camp, appearing rather to be pleased with himself, and above all to be happy to be working with Finch and Renny.

"He's a nice little fellow underneath all his queerness," remarked Renny, when Dennis was out of earshot. "Don't worry about him. He'll be all right."

"I wish I thought so. I can't tell you how he irritates me."

Renny laughed. "And I can't tell you," he said, "how Archer irritates me, but he amuses me too. That's the way with boys. Just when your patience has reached breaking point they make you laugh."

"Dennis doesn't make me laugh," Finch said grimly. Then he added, with sudden childlike yearning, "Used I to make you laugh?"

"By jingo," said Renny, "you used rather to make me want to cry."

The mound of brushwood grew. More light and air came into the Hut. Meg and Patience, Adeline and Philip visited and brought their advice. Within a week a path was made to its door. Its inner walls were tinted. Its windows polished. Furniture was brought from Jalna, but it was Alayne who made curtains and ordered a supply of groceries for the kitchen. Something of the spirit of pioneer days was reborn. When all was made ready Philip remarked to Adeline:

"D'you know, I shouldn't mind living in this little cottage."

"Do you mean you and me?" she asked.

"Yes." He spoke shyly. Never did he feel quite sure of himself when alone with Adeline.

"It's too small." She spoke with decision. "I like lots of room about me."

"Room for what?" he asked. "Here we'd have all outdoors and nobody in the house with us."

"The *house*," she mocked. "You call *this* a house?"

"We'd be alone here." Fearful that she would think him sentimental, he added, "I'd like to lie in bed and smell my bacon cooking in the morning."

"Who'd be cooking it?"

"You, of course."

"Don't deceive yourself. I'm used to being waited on."

"Do you mean to say"—and he looked more astonished than he felt—"that you'd refuse to cook my bacon?"

"If bacon was to be cooked," she said, "you'd do it."

"All right," he said sulkily. "I'd do it. And you'd lie in bed—a lazy wife—smelling it. My mother makes the breakfast. So does Patience. Do you think you're different?"

"Certainly I could do it, if I had to. But I'm used to coming down to breakfast and finding it ready. Also I like quite a lot of people about me."

"Waiting on you, eh?" Philip spoke with heavy youthful sarcasm.

Adeline looked him over without answering; then she asked a question. "Do you know what you make me think of, standing there?"

His nostrils dilated a little in expectation of a compliment.

"You are," she said, "a cross between a Hussar—"

He exhaled in pride. There was the resemblance to his grandfather, naturally.

"A Hussar," she finished, "*and* a Dresden china shepherd."

He gave a "Humph" of disgust. He searched his mind for a clever retort but found there nothing of the kind. But he felt it right that he should have some authority over her. She had turned away and was looking in at the neat white bedroom. He followed her and looked over her shoulder.

"You mustn't come here," he said, "after those two arrive; you know that, don't you?"

"If you mean I might get the disease—well, there's no danger of that. Uncle Wakefield is not much affected. But—I have promised Mummie."

She turned her head. Philip was close behind her. He looked compellingly into her eyes. "Your mother has a better reason," he said.

"A better reason?" she repeated, surprised.

"Yes. Those two—aren't married."

"Who told you?"

"My brother Christian."

"Why?"

She was startled now. He had a sense of power over her and spoke with gravity.

"I don't know," he said. "Perhaps she has a husband living. Anyhow, I think your mother is right."

"I don't need anyone, thank you, to keep me in order."

"But I just wanted to tell you," he said, "Molly and Wake aren't married."

With a tantalizing glance she exclaimed, "What fun!"

Philip would have liked to be sentimental in this little white nest, would have liked to feel nobly protective toward Adeline, but this last remark of hers made him almost wonder if he really wanted to marry her. As for her lovely looks, he was so accustomed to being with her that he scarcely noticed them. It was more important to him that he resembled his great-grandfather. A Hussar—a soldier—certainly not a Dresden china shepherd.

"It's a good thing," he said, "there were no other fellows about, to hear you make that remark."

"What did I say?" She tried to look artless. She wanted to hear what her words would sound like on his lips.

"You said," he now spoke with severity, "that it would be fun not to be married."

"Well," she laughed, "I still think so. Now take us. Do you

like the thought of being tied to me for the rest of your days?"

It was as though she had read his mind—that moment's wavering—that brief disloyalty. "Yes," he said instantly. "I do like it. I don't want anything different."

Without knowing how he had done it, he realized that he had pleased her and also asserted his masculine authority. His look of solid tranquillity returned.

They saw then that little Mary was standing in the doorway. She looked ready for flight, like a small bird that had alighted there. But Adeline welcomed her. "Do you know," she said to Philip, "when Mary was tiny, your brother Maurice and I promised each other that we'd never get married to anyone and that she would be our little girl."

"I can't imagine Maurice agreeing to that," said Philip, "for he always wanted to marry you. He'll be pretty sick when he hears of our engagement. Have you written to tell him?" Philip tried to keep the triumph out of his voice.

"No. I have not written. I don't think Maurice will mind. Have you written?"

"No. But Christian has. He thinks Maurice will be awfully sick."

"For goodness' sake, stop saying people are going to be sick."

"I only said Maurice is."

"You said it twice too often."

She left the Hut, her light walk expressing her irritation. She could not have said why Philip so easily irritated her, why she either chafed at his assumption of masculine authority or found his schoolboy vocabulary ridiculous.

Mary watched the two of them go down the path and out of sight. Adeline had not led her away as she usually did when they met by chance, but had gone without even a good-bye. But Mary did not mind. She was indeed pleased to find herself in possession of this tiny cottage that was like something in a fairy tale. Mary would not have been greatly surprised to see the Three Bears ambling in at the door or to discover Red Ridinghood's grandmother in bed. She tiptoed from one small room to another, happy in her sense of seclusion. A square of sunlight fell on the stone floor, shadows of leaves fluttering in it like birds. Yet she neither heard nor saw any living thing. Philip and Adeline had disappeared down the·path. If they never had returned Mary would scarcely have been surprised. People came and went, came out of the leafy strangeness of the outer world, disappeared into it. Mary did not question where or why. She had no curiosity about their doings, which sometimes gave her a sense of fear by their strangeness. She knew that her father had returned from the war (in her fancy she pictured it as men in armor fighting with lances) and that, sometime later, she had been found beneath a rosebush in the garden—a tiny baby, with no clothes. She knew that her father had "lost a leg" in the war, and it seemed to her strange indeed that he should lose something so large and substantial as a man's leg.

In her times of solitude Mary reflected on the strangeness of life. Her thoughts were not clear but confused and intermingled like shapes under water. Sometimes she remembered a visit she had made with her mother to her brother Maurice in Ireland. She would recall the towering black rocks of the shore, with the eddying dark waters beneath and the thousand waves rippling as far as she could see, with the little sea pinks blooming on the rocks. She did not see it clearly in her memory but as a confused picture, of which she was the centre. All the world seemed to revolve round her, yet often she longed to hide herself from it. Exciting things were always moving relentlessly toward her but, unlike most children, she did not long for excitement. She wanted things to remain always as they were.

This little hut pleased her by its leafy seclusion, its smallness. Through the open doorway a spider swung on an invisible thread. He swung joyously—lighter than air—free as the breeze—in at the door and out again, disappearing into the greenness beyond. Her hands clasped in front of her, Mary stood watching him in rapture.

But she was not long alone. Her cousin Dennis came running in through the back door. He ran three times round her and then stopped behind her and took a handful of her hair. "Who said you could come in here?" he demanded.

"I just came," she said, and she moved away from him a little fearfully as he released her hair.

"I'll bet," he said, "that you don't know who is coming to live here."

"Wakefield and Molly—because he's going to get well here." She was proud to know, but Dennis, because of the way his eyes held her, made her feel less certain.

"They're actors," said Dennis. "They'll be rehearsing terrible plays. They'll be shouting and screaming. You'd better keep away, if you don't want to hear them. It might frighten you to death. Did you ever know anyone who was frightened to death?"

"No." She was breathing quickly, her eyes wide.

"I did," he said. "And she was a grown-up woman. She was the stepmother of a friend of mine. She died a terrible death—from fright."

"Was your friend sorry?" Mary asked, fascinated.

Dennis thought a moment. "Yes. He was sorry because he hadn't meant to do it."

"What did he do? I mean that frightened her?" Mary's heart was beating fast.

Dennis looked puzzled, then—"I forget," he said.

He darted about examining everything. Two candlesticks, with tall white candles, caught his eye. He found matches and lighted the candles. "Now," he said, "we're ready for the ceremony."

"What ceremony?" Mary asked.

Dennis began to chant a meaningless jargon, in his high boy's treble. He genuflected and crossed himself. The thought of the sea came to Mary. A roaring of waves surged through her nerves. Its burning brightness dazzled her. Why this strange behavior of her cousin's should have brought the strangeness and wonder of the sea to her, she did not know. But she knew she was afraid of Dennis.

Yet soon he was only a schoolboy again. He went to a cupboard and brought out a tin of shrimps. "Have a shrimp, Mary?" He shook the tin in front of her. "Say the word and I'll open it for you." She backed away. "Have a Romary biscuit, Mary? No? All right. Don't have one." He put the tins back in the cupboard, and turning in a flash caught her round the waist. "Mary," he said, "do you want to grow up to be a cow—like other women?"

"What women?" she breathed fearfully.

"Patience—you've seen her nursing her baby? Isn't it disgusting? And my stepmother—she'll be having one before long. Shall I tell you how I know?"

Mary tore herself from him and ran out through the door. She heard voices approaching. To escape she ran through the undergrowth, past the heaps of brushwood, into a little clearing where a vegetable garden had been made. She stood in its midst, crying a little, then noticed the green pods of peas among the leaves. She picked a pod, squeezed it till it opened with a tiny plop and disclosed the perfect row of peas. These she ate greedily and suddenly felt happy again.

Dennis stood his ground in the cottage but he swiftly blew out the candles. When Wakefield and Molly entered he was standing erect as though to receive them.

"Why, here's Dennis," Wakefield exclaimed. "How he has grown! Look, Molly—here's Dennis."

"Have I grown?" asked Dennis. "Everybody says how small I am for my age." He walked up and down in front of them.

"Well, perhaps you are rather small," said Wakefield, "but you look a fine fellow to me."

Wakefield was consciously pleased to be at the Hut. He was eager to make Molly feel that all would go well there, to make her feel she was welcomed by the family. He was tired after the journey but not so tired as Molly, for she had had much to do in the preparations. Now her first thought was that he must be put to bed to begin his cure.

Finch, having met them at the station, now returned with their luggage in a station wagon. Dennis ran to meet him, putting all his small strength into the carrying of suitcases along the path and into the Hut.

"What a darling boy," Molly exclaimed to Wakefield. "I'd like to steal him. Did you notice the adoring look he gave his father?"

"Yes," said Wakefield, "and did you ever see a son so unlike his father?"

The luggage stowed away, Dennis was hanging on Finch's arm. Finch stood irresolute, not knowing whether to go or stay. Finch was embarrassed by Molly's presence. It was one thing to visit them in their apartment in New York, that mighty city which could make all within it seem unimportant. It was quite another thing to see them together at Jalna.

"Is there anything more I can do for you?" asked Finch.

"Not a thing," said Molly. "I'm going to tuck Wake into bed and then get some lunch ready. There's all sorts of food in the kitchen and a quantity of the richest milk I've ever seen."

"There's an up-to-date oilstove too. Renny has just had it put in."

At mention of that name Molly's color flamed, but it was without effect on Wakefield, except to bring expressions of gratitude from him. "Renny's been wonderful," he said. "I could not have believed Fiddler's Hut could have been made to look so inviting. What a wilderness this part of the woods was the last time I saw it! And I well remember when Eden was ill here."

"Eden?" said Molly. "That was your brother who died, wasn't it? Why did he come here? What was wrong with him?"

Finch and Wakefield exchanged looks.

"Did I never mention it before" said Wakefield. "Eden had tuberculosis."

"Well," said Finch, "we must be getting along. Come, Dennis."

Twelve

The Two in the Hut

Scarcely had Finch and Dennis disappeared when Renny and Rags came into sight. Renny came first, wearing a frown of anxiety lest he should upset what he carried, which was a skillet containing a broiled beefsteak. As for Rags, his face looking more wizened than usual in the bright light of day, he was laden with an immense tray with covered dishes of vegetables and a raspberry pie.

"All nourishing things," said the master of Jalna; "and see to it that you leave not a crumb."

He set down the skillet, put both arms about his brother and kissed him, giving him at the same time a sharp look, as though for signs of the ravages of disease. He then shook Molly's hand with an air of distant (though not unfriendly) dignity, and again urged them to enjoy the steak. Rags almost tearfully welcomed Wakefield, reminding him of their romps together when Wakefield was a small boy. He addressed Molly as "Madam," begging her to call on him for help in case of need. He then proceeded to lay the table. Renny opened a bottle of stout and brought a glassful to each of them. Then he and Rags departed, as suddenly as they had arrived.

Wakefield, attacking the beefsteak with zest, smiled across the table at Molly. "It's not so bad here, is it, dear?" he said. "I know you didn't want to come, but I think you'll soon feel that I was right."

"Why did he look at me like that?" she burst out. "As though everything were my fault!"

"I saw nothing of the sort in his look. Surely he could not have made us more welcome than he did."

"He made *you* welcome—not me."

Wakefield pushed his plate away from him. "Very well," he said petulantly, "we'll go. I can't bear to stay here, if you are going to be unhappy. . . ."

Molly's profile was turned to him, with its tip-tilted nose

with a few freckles, its well-cut chin. So often had he studied that profile, found it both courageous and charming, that this downward bend to the lips was unbearable to him. He repeated—"We'll go."

She sprang up, full of contrition. "No, no," she said, putting her arms round him, pressing his head to her slender breast, "we'll stay and be happy and you'll soon be well again. We have a right to be happy, haven't we? In the beginning we were innocent."

"I think I have no conscience," said Wakefield. "If I have, it certainly has given me no trouble. I feel as innocent as the day I was born."

"And so you are, my dearest," she cried. "If either is to blame, I am the one. The woman should always be the stronger. Come—eat this good food, and then I'll tuck you up in your bed. But first take a sip of the stout." She held the glass to his lips.

They talked with determined gayety and ate heartily, for they were hungry. Molly investigated every corner of the Hut, discovering each moment something new and exciting. If her gayety was a little forced Wakefield was not aware of it. Obediently he undressed and got into the inviting white bed. "Why, Molly," he exclaimed, "I remember this bedstead very well. It's one that Eden used to sleep in, but it has a new mattress. And that little chest of drawers was Uncle Ernest's. Oh, there's nothing here that I don't remember at home! I can't tell you how clearly I remember everything—every inch of Jalna. I wasn't strong enough to go to school, and so the Rector used to give me lessons at the Rectory and sometimes I'd play truant and wander through the fields and woods. But I was afraid of Fiddler's Hut and never came here. God—if I could have looked ahead and seen us two sitting at the table together!"

"Do try to settle down and rest for a bit," she urged.

"Bring me something to read, then. I saw some books on a shelf by the window. Did you notice how the window frame has been painted a pretty green?" She brought a book to him and he was delighted to discover that it was *The Little Duke*. "See, Molly, what's written in it: *For Wakefield, a reward for good behavior, from his sister Meg.*" Wakefield gave a shout of laughter. "Oh, Molly, this is delicious! 'A reward for good behavior'—she was always complaining of my naughtiness and thought nothing of taking her slipper to me. But how she spoilt me, too. I used to sit next her at table—on a volume of

British Poets to make me taller—and I remember how she would cut every scrap of fat from my meat to please me. I do wonder if Meg will come to see us—now that she's married to a clergyman . . ."

Thirteen

Goings and Comings

Dennis was proud to stride homeward with Finch, stretching his legs to keep pace with those longer legs. He hoped with all his might that he would be tall like Finch. As they strode along the dusty unpaved road, he looked up with admiration and love into Finch's face. He caught Finch's sleeve in his hand the better to stride with him. Dennis had looked forward with a certain dread to his home-coming from camp, but it had been easier than he had expected. The dinner party had drawn attention from him, and now there was the coming of Wakefield and Molly. He felt himself to be no longer in disgrace but an important member of the family, with Finch always as the lodestar of his existence.

When they reached home (during the walk Finch had been lost in thought and had not once spoken) they found Patience and Victoria Bell with Sylvia. Patience had also brought her poodle, which sat, statuesque and almost too intelligent, at her knee. The poodle considered that Patience and Victoria Bell were its special property. The three had contrived to take possession of the house, while Patience informed Sylvia of details of the infant's care. Patience had become all wife and mother, living but to serve husband and child. When she was not in a position to caress them with her hands she did so with her gentle gray eyes. She thought how wonderful it would be if Sylvia were to have a baby and they could spend happy hours discussing their babies and their wonderful husbands together. Then there were Adeline and Philip. They, in their turn, would produce a family, to be nurtured and discussed. Babies—and more babies—oh, the wonder of life!

As a treat for Dennis, and because she thought there was something touching about the little boy, she put the baby into his arms, as a treasure to be enjoyed.

"Now, isn't she a darling?" exclaimed Patience. "Your

113

latest cousin. Oh, I do wish I had my camera here so that I might take a snap of the two together! Look, Sylvia."

When Dennis felt the warm weight of the fat baby against his chest a voluptuous delight stirred him. He gazed into its face fascinated. Its red wrinkled features, its moist lips that kept moving, its glazed slate-colored eyes roused in him a feeling of protectiveness, approaching tenderness. He would have liked to squeeze it hard against his chest and run with it into the woods.

"Aren't they sweet together?" said Patience.

Dennis raised his eyes to hers and gave her a tranquil look. Indeed, this mood lasted after she and Victoria Bell had departed. He had a feeling of goodness, of purity. He wanted to be helpful about the house. The daily woman was ill and unable to come. Sylvia prepared the lunch and Dennis laid the table. He ran lightly from room to room doing little services for her. Sylvia was astonished and elated. Scarcely could she believe her eyes to see him like this. Finch had sat down at the piano and was playing some gay music. Bending over him she whispered, "Watch Dennis—see how he's helping me. He's quite different."

A little later she relaxed into one of the comfortable armchairs, for she was tired. Passing behind her Dennis dropped a kiss on her head. It was almost unbelievable to her that she should have had a caress from him. She was touched and even thrilled by this gesture of affection from the odd little boy.

"Finch, what do you suppose?" she whispered, when she had him alone. "Dennis kissed me! Oh, I'm sure we shall be friends from now on. All he needed was time to get used to me."

Finch was relieved, but he could not wipe from his mind, as Sylvia seemed to do, the memory of that night when the boy had so ruthlessly frightened her. The presence of Dennis in the house was like a small cloud that cast its shadow on the sunny field of his happiness. He had to keep a guard over himself when the boy was with him. It was so easy for him to lose his temper. Once, quite suddenly, he cuffed Dennis, who, instead of looking subdued, caught Finch's hand in both his and kissed it. What would Renny have done in a like case, Finch wondered. Given the boy another, harder cuff or kissed him in return? He was a great kisser, this master of Jalna, Finch thought. He'd seen him kiss every member of the family, from prickly-skinned old Gran down to Victoria Bell.

The fruit crop ripened and was plucked. The grain crop ripened and was garnered. The leaves turned from light and glossy green to dark lacklustre green. Blossoms became seed pods, it seemed overnight. Small birds gathered into groups and talked of their journey south. Humphrey Bell's cat, which had produced two kittens in the spring and been a doting mother, now turned against them—bit and scratched them when they tried to snuggle up to her; told them, in fact, that they were grown-up and to keep out of her sight.

Archer prepared to leave home for Oxford, but Alayne, unlike Humphrey Bell's cat, yearned tenderly over her son. He was so young to go so far away!

"Archer dear," she said, "it will seem strange without you. I shall miss you greatly."

Archer was packing and he stood looking at her with a collection of neckties in his hand. His high white forehead, which summer's sun never tanned, lent an air of chill distinction to what he said.

"This family," he remarked, "has been the structure of all our lives. We don't think about it. It's like the air we breathe. It's sacred to us. I wake in the morning, feeling myself a part of the family. I go to bed at night, knowing that I'm a part of it. It's time I went away into another country. But I daresay I shall come home again."

"Oh, Archer," breathed Alayne, almost in tears.

Seeing her drooping toward him, he moved a little away.

"I shall miss him," Adeline said to Renny. "I can let off steam on him when I'm out of sorts and he never loses his temper."

"He's a cold little brute on the surface," said Renny, "but underneath he's one of us."

He said as much to Archer when the moment of parting came. "You'll be back for the centenary of Jalna," he said. "I shall book your passage from this end, so there'll be no nonsense about it—"

"Like taking the money and shipping off to Greece," said Adeline.

Archer gave her one of his rare smiles. "My dear sister," he said, "nothing would induce me to miss the centenary. It will be something to boast of when I am ninety. I shall bore your great-grandchildren to extinction boasting of it."

"When I am a centenarian," said Adeline, "I shall lay a wreath of snowdrops on your grave, with the inscription: IN EGOTISM HE SURPASSED ALL OTHERS."

Archer went, and there was no doubt that he left a blank
at Jalna, for in the holidays he was always at home, having
few friends and no inclination for camping or canoe trips.
Yet he rode a horse well, and could swim strongly enough to
save himself in an upset, as he said.

Philip was to return to the Royal Military College for the
three approaching terms, and in early summer he and Adeline were to be married. Their relations were still cousinly
rather than loverlike. Indeed, Adeline was inclined to be lofty
with him—at worst supercilious, at best patronizing. He accepted all with good nature, yet occasionally gave her a
glance which showed that this might not always be so. He
was extremely well pleased by the position in which events
had placed him. He looked forward with tranquillity and
pride. In his mind he saw pictures of himself and Adeline living happily in an unchanging Jalna, to a great age. He accepted with pride the traditions of his family and, because of
his striking resemblance to his great-grandfather, saw himself
dedicated to their preservation. After the death of his great-
uncle Nicholas, he had been given Nicholas's old-fashioned
gold watch by Renny. This he never forgot to wind before he
went to bed. When he felt the stem of the watch between his
firm forefinger and thumb, heard the smooth response of the
mechanism, a look of pride would brighten his matter-of-fact
boy's face.

He was pleased that Adeline occupied the bedroom of their
great-grandmother and looked forward to the time when he
should sleep in the old painted leather bed with her. No
sensual image disturbed this anticipation. He was not yet loverlike toward her. In truth, they were scarcely to be called
friends. When he crossed the fields to say good-bye on the
morning of his return to college he considered what he ought
to say to her. What he really wanted was to get the good-bye
over and return to his fellow cadets. He had been told by
Renny not to make public his engagement, and he was glad
to keep it secret, for the present. He did not wish to be either
congratulated or chaffed about it. A few of his friends were
engaged or tentatively engaged, but none of these alliances
were so important as his.

Adeline was cross-legged on the grass, gently taking a burr
from the spaniel's ear.

"Oh, hullo," said Philip.

"Hullo." She just glanced up. The spaniel whined. "You're
not being hurt, my darling," she comforted, "so be good."

Philip observed her deft hands and the engagement ring that had been old Adeline's. "Well, I'm off," he said.

"Have a good time."

"I expect I'll have a lot of hard work ahead of me," he said, a little pompously.

"That'll be something new."

He was nettled. "You have no idea," he said, "how stiff our curriculum is."

She patted the spaniel. "Spaniels have such lovely ears," she said, "but they're terrible for burrs."

"Yes," he agreed, "they're pretty bad for burrs."

"And he had a canker in his ear once. That was misery, wasn't it, pet?" The spaniel, rocked by self-pity, lay down on his back.

"Scotties are the worst for cankers," said Philip.

Adeline sat on her heels and delivered a brief lecture on the treatment of cankers.

Again Philip said he must be off, and gave her a compelling look.

"Oh, good-bye," she said.

"I think we should kiss," he said soberly. "But, of course, if you don't want to . . ."

She jumped up and faced him, feet a little apart, toes a little turned in. She pushed out her lips in his direction. Certainly she was at her least alluring. Philip planted a kiss on the extended territory and left her. He hesitated a space in front of the house, giving it a possessive look. A row of pigeons stood on the edge of the roof, peering down at him in curiosity. Well might they stare! he thought. They were beholding the future master of Jalna.

Philip returned across the fields, with a vigorous stride and a look of gravity on his handsome face. He stopped at the Rectory to say good-bye and found Meg and the Rector enjoying a cup of morning coffee. In addition to this she had a plate of scones before her and some sugared cookies.

"Dear boy," she said, "I am always glad to see you." She spoke in a sentimental tone, as though they did not often meet—though in reality she saw him almost every day.

"Do have some coffee and a scone," she said.

"Thanks, Auntie Meg. But I must hurry along. I still have packing to do."

But Meg insisted. She poured coffee for him and put a scone into his hand as though he were ten years old instead of double that age. Looking about the room, he thought it was very full of furniture. Meg, when she made her second marriage, had brought to the Rectory the possessions she had not sold or given to Patience.

She now remarked to Philip, "I'm afraid you think this room is overfurnished, Philip. You young people have a taste for scanty furnishing, but I confess I like my house to look like a home and not a barracks. I could not resist bringing a few sticks of furniture with me, and fortunately Rupert loves to see it about me, don't you, dear?"

The Rector good-humoredly assented, though he was still bumping into pieces of furniture to which he had not yet become accustomed after several years.

"And speaking of one's belongings," went on Meg, "there is a dear old silver cruet at Jalna—real Georgian—which my grandmother always insisted I should have, but which, for some reason, Alayne does not want to part with. I do hope, Philip, that when you and Adeline are married, you will try to influence Alayne to let me have it. You will be in a position to be quite firm about it."

"Oh, Auntie," Philip said, deprecatingly.

"I know what you're thinking," said Meg. "You're thinking what a stubborn nature Alayne has but, as Adeline's husband, you should have influence with her."

Philip had never given a thought to Alayne's nature, neither had he ever considered influencing a grownup, but he was flattered and said, with gravity, "I'll see what I can do about it, Auntie."

"I do hope," said Meg, "that Alayne will not try to tyrannize over you young people. With her dominating nature it will be hard for her to refrain."

"She'd better not," said Philip.

"More coffee, please," said the Rector.

"The holidays are over," said Meg. "It's been an eventful summer."

"It's been a wonderful summer for me," said Philip.

He rose, and was about to go when Meg said:

"I've been thinking what a good idea it would be for you both to go into the church together and send up a little prayer of thanksgiving for the way Philip's path has been smoothed and for guidance in the future for him and Adeline." Meg took another bite of scone and looked benignly at the two males, who cringed perceptibly.

"Oh, no, Auntie," said Philip.

"The difficulty is," said Mr. Fennel, "that I have a churchwardens' meeting, and before that I have a sick call to make."

"Rupert, dear," said Meg, "I think nothing should stand in the way of this little act of devotion. Only yesterday, in your sermon, you said we should bring our religion into our daily life and you can see how this poor boy is longing to do it." She took a mouthful of coffee.

The Rector rose with a sigh.

"You'd better come, too, Auntie," said Philip.

"I'd love to," said Meg, "but I'm almost breathless already with the things I have on hand. And I somehow feel that it would be more effective if you two only were present. 'When two or three are gathered together,' you know."

"But you'd only make three, Auntie," said Philip. He strongly felt the need of support in this project, in which he found himself as helpless as a child, although it gave him a pleasant feeling of his own importance.

"Sorry, dear, but I can't do it." Meg took him in her arms and fondly bade him good-bye.

The Rector had left them for a moment but now reappeared with a rolled-up magazine under his arm. On their way to the church, which was just the other side of the cedar hedge, Mr. Fennel disclosed to Philip that he had a bottle of Scotch rolled up in the magazine. "It's for the sick call," he explained. "There's nothing I can do for poor old Brawn that will put so much heart into him." And the Rector gave a wink.

In the churchyard they passed the plot where Philip's great-grandparents, grandparents, great-uncles and uncle, Eden, were buried, as well as several infant Whiteoaks. Meg had put fresh flowers in the metal containers by the graves, and little Mary had that very morning laid a few daisies and a prettily colored dead butterfly on the smallest grave because she felt sorry for the baby down there.

"They look very nice, don't they?" remarked the Rector.

"Couldn't look nicer," said Philip, and he moved apprehensively toward the church door. "I really haven't much time to spare," he added. He stood very erect.

"We'll make it brief," said the Rector.

"Auntie should have come," said Philip.

"Ah, she's a busy woman," said the Rector loyally.

He opened the door into the vestry and, after he had disposed of the magazine and its treasure within, he said cheerfully:

"You go into the church and kneel at the chancel rail. I'll be with you in a moment."

Philip tiptoed into the church, which was cooler than the outdoors and where a shaft of rosy light from the window above the altar lay across its dimness. He knelt, looking upward into the window, which was a memorial to his great-grandparents. He felt himself being swept along helpless into a situation he would not have thought possible. He was not a religious boy, though at the time of his confirmation he had for a time felt an impulse toward things spiritual, said his prayers regularly, and taken care not to use "bad" language. That phase had passed, leaving him inclined to be devil-may-care and pleasure-loving; but always he was respectful toward tradition and, since his engagement to Adeline, he had moments of feeling nobly dedicated.

Now the Rector, seeing him kneeling at the chancel steps, likened him to a young knight making his devotions before setting forth on a crusade. He knelt down beside Philip and there was silence except for the twittering of a flock of small birds gathered in a tree beyond an open window. They were preparing for their migration to the south and their talk was of its difficulties and of the necessity of keeping together.

The Rector was a great lover of birds; therefore, raising his voice, but still low and reverent, he prayed:

"We pray Thee, most merciful Father, to send one of Thy special angels to guide and protect the small birds on their arduous and dangerous flight to the South. At this moment a number of them are collected near this Thy House. We pray Thee to have a mind to them on their journey."

There was another silence during which Philip's head drooped to his knuckles. Then Mr. Fennel continued:

"We pray Thee to guide Thy child, Philip Whiteoak, who kneels before Thee, on the road to noble manhood. Make him strong to resist spiritual sloth. Help him to value the things of the spirit. Spread the wing of Thy goodness over him and his affianced bride during all their life together. This we earnestly pray. *Amen.*"

Philip, whose voice had recently become a good baritone, joined in with an *Amen*, considerably louder than he had intended. Hastening along the road toward home he felt rather as he had felt when as a boy at boarding school he had been summoned to the headmaster's study and, instead of receiving punishment, had been told of an advance in the school team.

He found his parents, his brother Christian, and his little

sister already at lunch. Looking at him across the table, as he swept his plate clean, Mary thought: He is going away and that is good. There are too many men.

Pheasant said, "I hope you remember that your packing is not finished."

"I don't need to be reminded of that," he returned, with his mouth full.

"What you need reminding of is your manners," said Piers.

"Sorry." Philip flushed and looked at his plate.

Little Mary surveyed him critically.

To put him again at ease, Pheasant enquired whether he had got all his good-byes said.

"Yes. I did some of them yesterday. This morning it took longer than I expected."

"Hard to part with your girl, eh?" said Piers.

"It was Auntie Meg." He had a mind to tell of going into the church but thought better of it.

"Good Lord," exclaimed Christian.

"Hard to part with your girl, eh?" said Piers.

Philip's favorite pudding was brought on, as a treat, and as it was being eaten with gusto Pheasant said, "What do you suppose? You'll never guess, Philip. Well, I shall tell you. Your Uncle Renny wants to have portraits painted of you and Adeline to hang in the dining-room at Jalna beside the great-grandparents. Isn't it a lovely idea?"

Philip was both amazed and flattered. He mumbled, "Oh, I don't know."

"Capital," said Piers. "It's a fine idea. Is Renny prepared to pay for the portraits?"

Pheasant nodded vigorously. "I'm sure he is. He says he wants them done by a good artist."

"We have the artist right here," said Piers. "Christian shall do the portraits and keep the money in the family."

"Oh, Dad," the young artist exclaimed in despair, "I can't paint portraits!"

"Not after all that time in Paris? Of course you can."

"No—but really—I'm not a portrait painter."

"All you need to do," said Piers, "is to get good photographs of the pair and use them as models."

"It isn't often," Pheasant put in, "that an artist has such handsome subjects."

"I shouldn't like the style to be too modern," said Philip. "I mean the sort of thing that you can't tell what you're looking at."

"You would hate the portraits I'd paint," said Christian.

Philip was pleased by the prospect of having his portrait painted, for, with the exception of snapshots and school groups, he had never seen a picture of himself since the photograph Pheasant had had taken to send to Piers overseas. It had been taken by the best photographer in town and showed himself and Christian (then nicknamed Nooky) at the ages of eight and eleven. It was a charming portrait and, framed in silver, stood on a table in the living-room.

The meal over, Philip finished his packing and, with something oddly final in the atmosphere, as though he were going on a very long journey, he said good-bye and set out.

Mary stood in the doorway and watched the car disappear. Her heart felt light as she went, with a lively step, to the studio. As Christian had driven Philip to the railway station, she got it into her silly little head that he too had departed. Now the studio was her own—her own, that is, till he returned, which she hoped would not be for some time. She liked him well enough, but life was much pleasanter for her when all three brothers were away. Then it was that she felt more safe.

She investigated every corner of the studio, as though to make friends with it again, opening cupboards to peep into them and investigating drawers full of sketches. She did not like a single one of them. But a picture of young birch trees, standing on an easel, rather pleased her. She had just picked up a palette and brush, that she might pretend to be an artist, when Christian's shocked voice came to her from the doorway.

"Mary! What are you up to?"

She fled and, in the kitchen garden, among the pungent-smelling tomato plants and their scarlet fruit, shed a few tears.

Fourteen

Tea with the Wragges

Wright had dropped in to take tea with the Wragges and, as so often happened, Noah Binns joined them.

"Evenin' folks," he said, as he stumped down the several steps from the outer door.

"Evening, Noah," said the cook. "You're just in time for a nice cup of tea."

Rags placed a chair for the old man, who cast a greedy eye over the table. "You on a slimming diet?" he inquired.

"It's true we 'ave no cake," said Rags, "but we always eat a snack at bedtime. The wife is boiling a negg for me now and she'll put one on for you, if you say the word."

"I'll say the word twice." Noah leered at his own wit.

"Fine," said the cook and popped two more eggs into the boiling water. She turned then to Wright. "Will you have eggs with your tea, Mr. Wright?"

"No, thank *you*," returned Wright. "I'll be going home for supper shortly. I thought I'd just drop in and say hello and ask what's the news."

He drew up a chair and the cook poured him a cup of strong tea and pushed a plate of cookies closer to him.

"Things go along quiet in the house," said Mrs. Wragge. "The excitement all comes from the stables. I can tell you we were screwed up to concert pitch by East Wind's big win yesterday. The boss went to a party last night and if he didn't come home tight I miss my guess. His dogs was barkin' like all get out at three o'clock this morning."

"I never knew a man," said Noah, "who carried his liquor worse."

"Him?" cried the cook. "It's a libel. I've worked in this house for half a lifetime and I never seen a man carry his liquor better. If he gets tight he has good reason for it."

Rags said pontifically, "I 'ave fought with 'im in two wars and I'll s'y he can drink or let it alone as the case may be."

"Meaning," said Noah, "if there's drink to be had he'll drink it."

"The Whiteoak men," said Wright, "drink like gentlemen."

Noah scraped out the shell of his first egg and attacked the second. "I was brought up totalitarian," he said, "and totalitarian I'll die."

Rags winked at Wright. "Noah's a man of 'igh principles," he said. " 'E's severe, but 'e'll mellow with the years."

"I am against drink," declared Noah, "horse-racin', and lotteries."

"What are you for?" asked Rags.

"I'm fer a better world, but I ain't seen no signs of it. The climate gets worse and folks' behavior gets worse. It's a sorry sight to see so many young ones comin' on."

"Oh, Noah, don't say that!" cried the cook. "Think of the lovely young couple who are to live in this very house next year! Think of the lovely kiddies they'll have."

Noah had a trickle of egg yolk on his chin; still he contrived to look scornful. "I don't give no heed to sex," he said. "Hot or cold—rock or roll—it's all the same to me."

"I'd like to know where you'd be if it hadn't been for sex." She filled his cup, putting in extra sugar.

"I might still be an angel in heaven," he said with satisfaction, then sought to drown his straggling moustache in tea.

"One thing is certain," observed Rags, "the young pair won't 'ave much say in the management of the place—not while the present master and mistress are aboveground."

"I've been a gravedigger all my days," said Noah, "but I don't calculate to dig their graves, not unless they're carried off within the next ten years."

"By gum," said Wright, "you don't look as though you'd strength to dig a grave for a grasshopper."

Noah teehee-ed. "Don't you fool yourself," he snickered. "I'll outlast you by many a month. You're just the powerful kind of man that goes off quick. I'll be ready to dig a good six feet for you."

"Speaking of sickness," said the cook, addressing Wright, "how is Mr. Wakefield coming along, at Fiddler's Hut? My husband and I don't go to call there now, as the lady wasn't too friendly last time we did."

"She's shy," said Wright, "but she's very nice, and devoted to him. Regularly spoils him."

"He always was spoilt," said Rags.

"A perniscuous truant and snake-in-the-grass," said Noah.

"But what eyes!" exclaimed the cook. "And what curly hair! I couldn't refuse him anything."

Noah asked, "Is he doomed, do you think, like his brother was?"

"Not he," said Wright. "He's put on weight and talks of going back on the stage soon."

"In his ordinary life," said Noah, "he was a danged bad actor."

"Ah, he was a sweet boy." Mrs. Wragge sighed deeply. "I can't bear to think of him being ailing. I do like small boys. There's that little Dennis. He's a dear little boy. I hear he's to have a baby brother or sister in the New Year."

"It's chose a bad time to be born," groaned Noah. "All signs pint to a bad winter and a worse spring and summer to follow. It'll be a wonder if any of us is alive at this time next year. A terrible end is prepared for this world, and we're moving towards it fast."

"Have another cup of tea," urged the cook.

"I don't mind if I so. And this time don't be so stingy with the sugar. I need something to contradict the voluptuous behavior I see all around me."

The cook put three extra lumps of sugar in his tea.

Wright remarked, "I don't think that's a nice way to talk in front of a lady."

Noah stared. "Do you mean to say the carryings-on I witness ain't voluptuous and explosive? I seen 'em in ditches."

"There's no call to think about it," said Wright. "I like a little refinement."

Noah gave the table a thump with his fist. "It's the first time in my life," he said, "that I've been accused of loose talk before a female. I've reverenced the female sex. I've reverenced them too much to marry them."

"That's a loss to some woman," said Rags.

Noah was not mollified. He looked glumly at the table, then drained his cup and got to his feet. Walking waveringly to the door he stood with his hand on the latch and said:

"I like misery."

Then he disappeared.

There was silence for a short space, silence except for the noisy bubbling of the teakettle. Then the cook remarked:

"That old fella'd make a dog laugh."

Fifteen

Wakefield and Molly

Fortunately for Wakefield's progress the weather was almost continuously fair and he was able to spend his days outdoors. The richly colored tapestry of leaves fell from the trees and made a carpet below. The oak leaves were the last to fall, but already the glossy acorns strewed the ground and were collected and buried by squirrels that immediately forgot where they had hid them, and frisked up and down the massive tree trunks and made friends with Molly and Wakefield, as though there were no such season as winter. Birds lingered in this woodland retreat, seeming to forget the necessity of migrating. The flaming color of a cardinal would shine out like a lamp and a few bold notes from his spring song would enliven the air. He indeed had no intention of migrating but intended to spend the winter here. In early dawn the honk of wild geese came down from the misty sky.

Of the two beings isolated here, Wakefield was the least unhappy. At times he was almost content, for he felt the continued improvement in his condition and the doctor who came regularly to see him was satisfied. Renny kept him supplied with the necessary funds. He was in correspondence with managers who would, he hoped, offer him an engagement when it would be possible for him to accept it. *And* he was writing a play! He had already written an unsuccessful play, but this new one would be different. His heart was lifted by hope as he worked at it and, when he read scenes aloud to Molly and saw how her mobile face reflected their mood, he felt ready to fly with eagerness.

Molly knew that she could get a part in London or New York. Both managers and audiences liked her. She had been on the point, she felt sure, of attaining stardom when Wakefield's illness had cut short their careers, at least temporarily. Of the two, Wakefield had felt the shock of this most deeply. For a time he had varied between deep melancholy and a distraught uncertainty. But once he had decided he wanted to go to Jalna he became calmer. His spirit lightened as he looked forward in hope, instead of into a chasm of despair. To be at Jalna, to be near Meg and Renny, made him feel a child again. He accepted Molly's sacrifice, he accepted all that was done for him, as a child accepts the care that is given it. He did not lack company, for the family, with the exception of Adeline and Alayne, came to visit the Hut. Alayne could not bring herself to come, and Wakefield took a certain mischievous pleasure in her unease. She made him feel reckless and without compassion. He accepted Molly's devotion as something she longed to give and even told her that the rest in this lovely spot would do her good. The warmth, the almost continuous sunshine of the autumn days brought bright tints to her cheeks and hair, which she had cut short. She had not made a very good job of it but it became her. In an old cotton dress she would wander about the woodland, keeping from the paths, and fill her little basket with wild blackberries. Standing in the heat among the bushes, with trees obscuring all but a patch of the azure sky, she would remember the wild bare hills of Wales where she had spent her childhood, the wind that blew across them—her sisters, all scattered, her brother killed in the war.

While Wakefield was recovering his health and even enjoying the life thus thrust on him, Molly fretted ever more deeply for opportunities lost, for all that she felt slipping away from her. Sometimes a feeling of active rebellion shook her. She would wake in the terrible stillness of the woodland and long desperately for the muffled roar of traffic in a great city; would picture herself putting on her make-up in her dressing-room at the theatre or the return to their apartment after the play. Here, she felt less close to Wakefield—who, in a strange way, seemed absorbed by his family. He would talk by the hour of his boyhood at Jalna: of his grandmother and how she would feed him sops of sponge cake dipped in her glass of sherry; of his uncles, Nicholas and Ernest, and what gentlemen of the old school they were; of how he had gone to the Rectory for lessons, rather than school, because of his weak heart; of how, for the same reason, he had always slept with Renny. He would hug himself in laughter as he recalled, "Even when he brought Alayne to Jalna as his bride, she had to creep into a room by herself, because I was sleeping with the bridegroom!"

Renny continued, or so it seemed to Molly, sedulously to avoid her. He would come to see Wakefield when he knew she was out of the way. She, equally painstaking, would go into another room or hasten outdoors if she heard his step.

But on this morning of Indian summer he came suddenly upon her as she neared the Hut. Neither could escape, and they walked, with outward unity and inward unease, to the long chair where Wakefield sat in the sun. Renny bent over him and looked down into his face.

"Good boy," he said, "you look fine."

Wakefield raised his eyes to Renny's with the look of a son into an indulgent father's face. "When shall I be done with all this?" he said crossly. "I've finished the first draft of my play and I'm tired of being an invalid."

"I saw your doctor yesterday. He says that another three months' rest will cure you."

Wakefield gave a groan. He stretched his sunburnt arms as though in despair; but in truth he was, for the present, content with things as they were. The weather was glorious. He was indolent in its hazy blue bewitchment. He looked up at Molly. "What do you feel about another three months here, Molly?" he asked.

"It will be all right so long as you are getting well."

"And Molly has blackberries for you," Renny said heartily, but he did not look at her. When she had gone into the Hut he said to Wakefield, "I guess it's rather dull for you sometimes."

"I have my play to work at," said Wakefield. "We have visitors. Christian comes a lot. I like that boy. But I wish you came oftener, Renny."

"I'd come every blessed day, Wake, if it were not . . ." He hesitated, then went on: "Perhaps the time will come when you and Molly will go your separate ways. On my part I should be glad to know you had separated."

"We've no thought of such a thing. We're perfectly happy together."

"Perfectly happy, eh? That's remarkable."

"What do you mean, Renny?"

"I mean what two people are *perfectly* happy together? Is there such a thing?"

"We are not chained together by law. That's so much the better. It's a voluntary union and we're satisfied to have it so. Molly has been wonderful to me. If ever she feels restive she hides it. Anyhow, in three months, I shall have completely recovered and we'll be ready for work again."

"You will have Christmas at Jalna."

"Renny"—Wakefield's brilliant eyes sought his brother's —"would you invite Molly and me for Christmas dinner?"

"What a question! Of course, we should."

"Well, I'm glad to hear you say that, but we'd not embarrass Alayne by accepting. Possibly we shall be back in New York by then."

To change the subject Renny said, "We are to have visitors from Ireland. Maurice and his friend Patrick Crawshay. They're arriving soon and making a long visit. They're going to travel during the cold months and be back at Jalna for the centenary and the wedding."

"I'll be glad to see them," said Wakefield. "But what will Maurice feel about this wedding?"

"He will be quite reconciled to it, you may be sure. People do get over these infatuations and are none the worse for them. I've had them, myself—and recovered." He looked hard at Wakefield, who said, "But you're happily married, Renny."

"Yes—tied up this many a year."

He went on to talk of his horses and his plans for the fall shows. Molly slipped out through the back door and found a sequestered space among the trees where the ground was covered by pine needles. There she sank, first to her knees, then at full length, shaken by hoarse sobs. She could not have told why she wept, excepting that the gathering heartache of the past weeks had culminated in this. Yet she knew she should be happy, for she saw Wakefield in renewing health. But—the long isolation in this closed-in wood, where one knew there was a wind only because one saw the treetops swaying . . . her yearning for the active life of the theatre and for opportunities lost . . . above all, her feeling that Wakefield was being reabsorbed into the family. . . . As she lay there sobbing, the face of Renny Whiteoak rose before her. She saw his slanting eyes turned away from her. He hated the sight of her, she thought, and had within himself the power to take Wakefield away from her—and would take him away. He wanted to separate them; and he would separate them.

She lay for what seemed a long while on the harsh comfort of the pine needles, in their heady scent. She was thankful she had shed no tears but could return to Wakefield undisfigured by the tempest that had torn her.

He had got biscuits and milk for himself, and gave her a rather injured look.

"What makes you so unsociable this morning?" he asked.

"You seemed quite happy without me."

"I've been alone for the past hour."

"Poor boy. Is there anything more I can get you?"

"Scarcely—on top of this milk. I hope I took it from the right bottle."

Molly flew to the refrigerator to find out and flew back to him. "It's *not* the fresh milk!" she cried. "How could you be so stupid, Wake? You know that the morning's milk is always on the right-hand side!"

"How the dickens do you expect me to remember about milk bottles with all I have on my mind?"

"Oh, I've nothing on *my* mind, of course," she snapped. "Here—give me that milk. You can't drink it."

He began to drink. "It's all right. There's nothing the matter with it."

"It's stale!"

He took a determined gulp. She struggled to interfere. Between them the milk was spilt.

"Now see what you've done!" Wakefield, with his handkerchief, mopped at the milk on his sleeve. It was ridiculous, but it made them unhappy.

The next day Renny brought a car to where the path began and took Wakefield to the stables to weigh him. Wakefield returned jubilant, not so much over his gain in weight, though it was substantial, as over having been once again swept along in the current of life at Jalna.

"How real it is!" he cried. "What man in his senses would choose to live in a smoky filthy city when he might work in the fields or with those magnificent horses! Some two-year-olds were being schooled in the paddock and men and horses enjoyed it equally. I went with Renny where he was selling a colt—a lovely creature, and doesn't Renny know how to make a sale! Piers was taking a load of apples to the railway station. What gorgeous apples! Look—I've filled my pockets for you."

Molly accepted them gratefully, not reminding him that already they had more apples than they could eat.

"Patience was there," he went on, "and her baby—what a cute baby Victoria is—and Adeline, galloping like all possessed. D'you know, Molly, I felt as though I'd been dead for months—no, years—and just come to life again? Oh, Molly, you don't know what it is to love the country—to hunger for it, not as a refuge after illness but as a glorious place for living." He snapped off a bite of apple with his white teeth.

"Have you gained any more weight?" she asked.

"Seven pounds. Renny's delighted by the speed of my recovery. Three months more and I shall be stronger than ever."

"Three months . . ." she repeated. That very day she had had a letter offering her a part in a New York company—a small part, but just the sort she enjoyed playing. But she did not tell Wakefield.

"Why on earth do you look so gloomy?" he demanded. "Everything is turning out well. Think what we might be feeling if I were worse instead of better."

"I know. I know. And I won't be gloomy. It's the time of year. The leaves are beginning to turn—then they'll fall—then there'll be snow."

"You *are* gloomy—you *are*." He flung himself on his cot. "Oh, God, how tired I am."

Now she was all contrition for a fault of which she was unaware. "You have overtired yourself," she said, and she covered him where he lay and patted his back, as though he were a child.

"Why will you talk of snow and falling leaves?" he demanded, still bent on being hurt. "It's morbid. It makes me miserable."

"I won't do it again," she said—and she did not, but more and more she longed for freedom to express what was in her.

One day by chance Renny met the priest who had been Wakefield's confessor after his conversion to Catholicism. Renny, moved by a shrewd understanding of his brother, asked the priest to go to see Wakegeld. The appearance of the kindly old cleric at Fiddler's Hut almost caused a panic in the pair living there, but there was no need for panic. There was nothing formidable about the priest. He was accustomed to the frailties of human nature and said no word of censure. He talked to them of country life and of the Belgian hares which he bred, and of the cure for poison ivy, and of a famous recipe he had for blackberry cordial. This would be good for Wakefield, he said, and promised to bring him a bottle. This he did, and followed it with other visits. With each visit from him and Renny, Molly felt conscious of a web being woven about Wakefield, drawing him inexorably into a life she could not enter.

When the blazing colors of fall were at their wildest, with the blue tent of the sky hanging above the treetops and frost white on the grass when Molly prepared Wake's breakfast, the two visitors arrived from Ireland: Maurice Whiteoak and Patrick Crawshay. They were to stay at Jalna—because Piers's house was too small for so large a family—till after Christmas. Alayne was not disinclined to having the two young men in the house, but she would have liked to be consulted in the matter—which she was not till the visit had been arranged. That was always the way of it, she thought, with wry resignation. The Whiteoaks did what was most convenient to themselves, without considering the trouble it might be to others. Alayne realized that the presence of two visitors would mean a great deal of extra work for the Wragges, who were growing old; but they accepted the news gladly because it came from Renny, who never gave a thought to their powers of endurance.

As for Adeline, she was, in these bright-colored days of autumn, strangely exhilarated. She told herself, in her extravagant youth, that she was like a ship that had been buffeted by storm and had now found harbor. This harbor was all the calmer because the golden-haired harbormaster was away, finishing his education. Although she fancied herself as a buffeted ship, she felt childishly irresponsible. Everything had been arranged for her. Inside the circle drawn for her she was as free as air. Never had Renny been so pleased with her. He lavished so many endearments on her that an observer might have thought her father was in love with her had it not been obvious that just as many flatteries were spoken to his horses.

Adeline met Maurice with more warmth than she had given him in many a day—possibly more than she ever had given him. For one thing she was sorry for him. For another she wanted him to believe in her radiant happiness which could include even him. Maurice met her with a dignity for which she was not prepared. He was sober but not sombre, as he said, "Congratulations to young Philip."

Adeline imagined a slight stressing of the word "young," for Philip's youth was a tender point with her, but she achieved a smile and said, "Congratulations to us both. We're very happy."

The young men had come prepared for sport. Mountains of luggage, guns and fishing rods were carried upstairs. Their heavy boots littered the floor of the bathroom. Towels were thrown on the floor. Both were accustomed to being waited on by plentiful servants. But their manners were so delightful and they were so charming to Alayne that she forgave them. They were in such contrast to the violent immaturity of modern life! Often she reflected on what would have been her father's reaction to it. She pictured his look of cautious wonder. He never had been quick to condemn. Even while she never was able to feel near to her own children, she was thankful that they were moderately congenial to her. She envied Renny—and was sometimes almost bitter in her envy— the close bond between him and Adeline, the queer congeniality between him and the aloof Archer. Life for him, she thought, was so easy, so instinctive.

In the very hour of arrival from Ireland, Maurice went to see his mother. She was just where he expected to find her: in the garden, potting geraniums. He came up behind her and put both arms about her.

Pheasant, looking down on his hands, exclaimed:

"Mooey, darling—it's you!"

The pet name was sweet to him on her lips. He turned her round to look into her face.

"You look well," he said, and gave the impression, both to himself and to her, that he had been anxious about her health, though in reality he had been thinking only of his own doings and Adeline's engagement.

"I am well. Never worry about me. Mooey—how wonderful to see you!" She poured out questions about his journey, about his friend Crawshay. She noted with pleasure the clearness of his eyes and complexion, while, his arm still about her, he sniffed the familiar scent of her that had added the scent of sweet geranium leaves. At last he said:

"Aren't you wondering what I think of this engagement?"

"I am indeed."

"Well, if you really want to know, I think it's damnable."

"Scarcely that, Maurice. On my part I think it's dangerous."

"It's damnable, I tell you. Adeline will be miserable."

"They may get on together better than we think. The danger is that both are so strong-willed—and yet so immature. Of course, lots of very young people are getting married, but—these two are different."

Maurice demanded, "Who arranged this? Surely they didn't do it themselves. Lord, I should like to have overheard that proposal."

"I can tell you," said Pheasant, "the young man is very pleased with himself, and so are his father and his Uncle Renny pleased with him."

"I'll bet they are," said Maurice, and added bitterly: "They never wanted *me* for her."

"Tradition is all very well," said Pheasant oracularly. "I like tradition; but Jalna is a Canadian estate, not a dukedom. Your great-grandmother and great-uncles are dead, Maurice, but they left behind them a tradition that's living and strong. What does it matter who marries whom, so long as the couple are happy?" She brushed the earth from her hands and raised her lovely eyes to the shining October sky. "I don't see happiness in this arranged marriage."

In the studio, over a drink, Maurice allowed his brother Christian to see further into the depths of his hurt and resentment. "Nobody," he said, "except Mother, thought I was good enough for Adeline. She was influenced against me— I'm certain. Dad never has liked me. You're aware of that, aren't you?"

"He's not demonstrative," Christian said uncomfortably, "toward any of us but Mary. Uncle Renny's fond of you, I know. I've heard him say so. But he's possessed by the idea of another Philip and Adeline at Jalna."

"What of Archer?"

"Managing Jalna is the last thing he would choose to do. He's a queer boy but I like him. He's so clever he'll be quite able to provide for himself. I expect he will inherit Aunt Alayne's money—that is, if she has any left."

"*Hm,*" grunted Maurice, digesting this information—and added, "Uncle Renny tells me that you are to paint portraits of Adeline and Philip."

Christian made a gesture as though he would hurl the palette he held to the floor. "Did you ever hear such nonsense? As though I could!" He looked really distressed.

To distract him Maurice said, "I do like that picture on your easel—all those glorious autumn colors. I'd like to buy it to take back to Ireland, but—there's something in it—a feeling so intense—a loyalty to this place—it would hurt me to have it."

"I understand," said his brother. "I wish to God I could sell a few pictures. It would encourage Dad, after all he's spent on me."

Maurice could not keep his mind off Philip and Adeline. "They'd be good subjects," he said.

"They would," agreed Christian. "There's something about us Whiteoaks, we have old-time faces. We're so damned individual—the way people used to look, before everybody was in a hurry. I find that I can't guess what a man is by looking at him. It seems to me they all look alike—that they could change faces and never notice the difference. They all look like businessmen on their way to a conference. We're different. Is it a good thing? I don't know."

Patrick Crawshay admired the picture Christian was just finishing, and bought it on the spot, also a second one to take home to his mother. He soon became as one of the family at Jalna, and popular with the men about the stables. He had the look of happy youth that has never been crossed. Having met Adeline on her visit to Ireland—the visit which had brought about her former unfortunate engagement to Fitzturgis—he thought of himself as a suitor. His mother would have liked to see him settle down in marriage. Maurice, on his part, had a mischievous hankering that his friend might yet break up Adeline's engagement to Philip. Philip was away from the scene. Adeline could not possibly be in love with him. Maurice did everything he could to bring her and Patrick Crawshay together. Unsuspected by his elders, he wove a net of mutual regard about the pair. He contrived to isolate them. When the three rode together he would fall behind on some pretext. When they walked he would drift away to rediscover some haunt of his childhood. When they sat together before a blazing fire at night he would put on a record of passionate or romantic music. Jealousy of Philip was his strongest emotion.

Sixteen

This and That

The two young men from Ireland, accompanied by Renny and Finch, went on a fishing trip. Later they went duck shooting. On this outing Finch did not join the party. As he matured, the thought of taking the life of birds, of causing suffering to them, was abhorrent to him. In all excursions, in life at Jalna, Pat Crawshay took part with happy zest. He had enough to live on, to live well. No one had ever suggested to him that he should make himself a useful member of society. His spirit was so untrammeled that it expressed itself in a remarkable way through all his body. Adeline found that she enjoyed being with him more than with any other, with the exception of Renny. He fascinated Wakefield, who found himself imitating his speech and mannerisms—acting the part, as it were, of Sir Patrick Crawshay.

In the lovely weather of Indian summer, an excursion was planned to one of the not too distant northern lakes. A son of the Rector, a boyhood friend of Finch's, George Fennel, who had married a rich widow, offered to lend Finch a cottage on this lake. In the manner of the country it was called a "cottage," but, in reality, was a roomy stone and stucco house, with fine gardens, overlooking the lake.

Sylvia was pregnant and had become enervated by the heat of the summer. Finch felt that a change would benefit her. He himself was tired by the stress of composition, for he took everything the hard way, and would be glad of the northern air. Sylvia's condition was not yet noticeable. They decided to make a party of it—not a large party but only those who would be congenial to Sylvia.

Would Renny be congenial to her? Finch wondered—but there was no need for conjecture: Renny was committed to preparation for the horse show. Patrick Crawshay, Maurice, and Adeline eagerly agreed to be of the party. When Christian was invited, he said at once, "I'd love to go, Uncle Finch. I shall do a picture there."

"Good," said Finch. "It's settled then. There'll be six of us."

"What of Wakefield and Molly?"

"Is he well enough, do you think?"

"Quite. I saw him this morning. He tells me he's mad for a change. In fact, he's heard of the party and wants to join it. His doctor says it will do him good, if he is careful not to overtire himself."

"Good Lord," said Finch, pulling nervously at his underlip. "I hadn't though of that contingency."

"What contingency?"

"Molly."

Christian stared in puzzlement. "But surely she would enjoy the change. She's had a pretty monotonous summer."

"I know," said Finch, "but there's Adeline. She's never been to the Hut since they came."

"How strange. I hadn't heard. Is it by Adeline's own wish or her parents'?"

"Of one thing I'm certain," said Finch. "Alayne would be most unhappy if Adeline were to go where Wake and Molly are of the party."

"Why in the name of reason," exclaimed Christian, "don't that pair get married?"

"I've no notion."

"Possibly Wake is like me"—said Christian—"reluctant to part with his freedom. I marvel when I see how some fellows—my own brothers, for instance—are ready to stick out their necks for the yoke. Look at Humphrey Bell. Nobody can make me believe that he wasn't happier before Patience and her fat baby planted themselves on him. . . . I'll never do it. Never." And firmly he squeezed the paint from a tube.

"Marriage certainly brings an awesome responsibility," said Finch. "I've been twice married."

"Of course there are the dear little children," Christian continued, in a sweet conversational tone. "I'm sure Humphrey enjoys the squalling of his daughter Victoria. And you have your own dear little boy, and before long you'll have another dear little boy. Oh, Uncle Finch, it makes me so glad for you!"

Finch left him, with a grunt of mingled chagrin and amusement. There was no one from whom he could ask advice in this predicament. He made up his mind to go straight to Wakefield. He began to wish that George Fennel had not offered him the cottage or that he and Sylvia might have gone alone to it.

He strode along the path through the wood, which, because of the thinning foliage, seemed suddenly open to the sky Along its edge fragile Michaelmas daisies grew, and sturdy goldenrod. Finch had a reckless holiday feeling and, when he glimpsed Wakefield, sitting outside the door of Fiddler's Hut with a book, he shouted: "Hullo—Wake! What do you think of this for a morning?"

"It's fine," Wakefield called back, delighted to have a visitor. "Come and sit down."

"What are you reading?" asked Finch. He peered to see the title of the book.

"It's Hardy's *Woodlanders*."

"Appropriate to this place, but scarcely a book I should have expected you to choose."

"I didn't choose it. It is one of an armful Renny brought from the house. It was Alayne who chose them."

Finch sat down and, after a space, Wakefield said:

"I long for some activity but I don't quite know what it's to be."

Finch said—desperately—"George Fennel has lent me his summer cottage for a week. If this weather holds it will be lovely there. I'd like to invite you and Molly to join us, Wake, but . . ." He halted, then got out— "There's Adeline."

Wakefield stared, not at first understanding. Then he muttered, "I see. I quite understand. It's all right."

Finch was relieved. "I'm glad you understand, old man. I was afraid you might be hurt."

"We have Alayne and her prejudices to consider. I don't believe Adeline would mind—even though she hasn't been here to see us."

Finch's mind was lightened of its load. After some desultory talk he hastened away to make final arrangements for the holiday. There was a supply of food to be ordered and a new warm coat for Sylvia to be bought. She was clinging, in these days of her pregnancy. Whatever Finch bought for her she would like. He tried to remember what Sarah had been before the birth of Dennis, but he could not. He could remember only her almost savage possessiveness after the infant's arrival.

When Finch had left him Wakefield folded his arms and bent his dark brows to the point of looking tragic. He felt himself to be a martyr to his loyalty to one woman. He felt that, not for a long while, had he wanted to do anything so badly as he wanted to accompany Finch and the others on this stay of a week by the lake. He had not through his illness, after the first sombre shock, pitied himself, but now he was fairly overcome by self-pity. He remembered how in childhood he had seen one after another of the family depart on some pleasure jaunt, and he left at home. Now he was not even at home. He was marooned in an island of greenery, in a multicolored sea of autumn leaves. He was a cast-away.

He was sitting in this attitude of dejection when Molly, returning after a shopping expedition to the village grocery, discovered him. She laid her heavy bag on the kitchen table and hastened to him. She had ready an imitation of the shopgirl to amuse him, but seeing his frown, his bent head and folded arms, she hesitated and said:

"Everything all right?"

"I suppose so." He raised his eyes and added, "Finch was here."

What would Finch have said, she wondered, to hurt Wakefield? She asked, "Had he any news?"

"Yes—of a sort. George Fennel, an old friend, has lent him his summer place. In this weather it will be lovely. Right on a lake, two hours' drive from here. Finch is making up a small party."

"Oh." Molly tried to think what there was in this news to hurt Wakefield, for he was hurt—she was sure of that.

He said, "Of course, we're not invited."

"But, in any case, you couldn't go, could you?"

"Certainly I could go. I spoke of the possibility to my doctor when he called yesterday and he said it would be good for me if I took care not to overtire myself."

"Then why not go?" Her face which had been serious was now lit in bright expectancy. If there were any obstacle in the way, she would overcome it.

"Because," said Wakefield, "we are not respectable."

Now she saw clearly the reason for his pain, his disappointment. Like a child he was hurt because he was left out of a picnic.

"Don't let's mind," she said. "We'll do something else— something better." And she cast about in her mind to discover what that something could be.

"There's nothing for us to do."

"Wakefield—did Finch make it clear to you?"

"Absolutely clear. It's not his doing—or Sylvia's. It's Alayne who could not tolerate our presence."

"She is one of the party, then?"

"No, but her daughter is."

"Would Finch invite you—if I were not to go?"

Wakefield sat upright and looked her in the eyes. "Don't be silly," he said. "Nothing would induce me to go without you."

"But, Wake," she said, "if I tell you I don't want to go—that would be different, wouldn't it? There's all the difference in the world between leaving me to sulk or mourn here in the Hut, and leaving me to do the hundred things I want to do before the cold weather sets in. We've nearly three months more to put in here, you must remember." She dwelt almost ruthlessly on those months, as though she pressed herself deliberately inside a hair shirt.

"I will not leave you here alone," he said doggedly.

"But I shall be so busy! I shall be too busy to miss you."

"Busy doing what?" he asked with severity.

She sat down beside him and took his hand in hers.

"Listen," she said, "what is a week but seven days? They will pass like the wind. I shall be glad to get you out of the way for a bit while I put our clothes in order, house-clean the Hut, and make jelly out of a huge saucepan of blackberries I've gathered. You do like blackberry jelly with your toast for tea, don't you? And I have so much mending to do."

He weakened. He consented—though grumblingly.

When Finch came later in the day, with books for Wakefield and a box of chocolates for Molly, Wakefield said:

"I told Molly that you can't ask us to join your party because we're not respectable."

"Oh, no," Finch said miserably. "Surely you didn't say that to her."

"I did; and the odd thing is she doesn't want to come. She has a thousand things to do, she says, and would be glad to be rid of me. Naturally I don't want to leave her, but my doctor insists that a change would be good for me—at this stage."

"All right," said Finch, eager to have this galling affair settled. "Come along. We'll be glad to have you. Of course it would have been better still, if you both might have—"

He did not finish because Molly had joined them. He turned to her, his long sensitive face swept by embarrassment. But she showed no such feeling. She was so calm, so friendly, that he left the Hut comforted by the thought that she and Wakefield were a sensible and not too emotional pair. He wished that Sylvia and himself had as much sound sense.

There was not much time for preparation. It kept Molly busy to get Wakefield's clothes in order for the outing. The fair weather held, and in warm sunshine he left the path through the wood and joined Finch, who was waiting for him in a car where Wakefield's suitcase had already been placed. Molly had held him close and looked long in his face.

"Are you sure," he had said, "that you don't mind my going off like this?"

"It's what I want. It will give me leisure to do things. Have a good time, darling. Don't worry about me."

He was gone and she was alone in that golden woodland that now had become a prison to her, a prison whose walls were falling, leaf by leaf, a prison from which the birds were escaping, not one by one, but in flocks. She gathered up the bedclothes from the cot where Wake had slept, and neatly folded them. She was washing the breakfast dishes when suddenly, in the doorway, little Mary appeared. She advanced, shyly but steadily with a few sprays of chicory and Queen Anne's lace in her hand.

"I brought these for you," she said.

"How kind of you!" said Molly. "This blue flower is just the color of your eyes."

Mary looked on with satisfaction while Molly placed the flowers in water. Then Molly asked:

"Why have you come all this way alone? Are you allowed?"

"I heard Daddy say Uncle Wake had gone on a picnic. I thought you might be lonely—so I came."

"You came and you brought me flowers—that was sweet," said Molly. "Now will you sit down in this little chair while I finish my work?"

"Where there are men," said Mary, "there's always work to do."

"True," said Molly, "but it's sometimes nice to have them about."

Mary looked steadily at her. "I think it's better," she said, "when they go away."

Molly could not help laughing, so quaint the little girl looked, sitting there, with her fine hair falling about her face, and uttering such words. "But you'd not want your daddy to go away, would you?"

"One man is useful," said Mary. "He can hammer. He can sharpen the carving knife. Too many men make a noise going up and down the stairs. They're always wanting something to eat."

"I know, I know," Molly said sympathetically. "Men are like that."

"I'd rather," said Mary, "dry the dishes for you than sit here."

"Good." Molly put a tea towel into the deft little hands.

When Mary had dried the dishes she stood on a chair to put them into the cupboard. This done, she asked:

"Are you going to live here alone?"

"For a little while."

"It's better to live alone." Mary gave a smile, almost mischievous. "Then you can hear all the nice things and not the noise."

"What sort of things, Mary?"

"The secret things." And the little girl laughed, with the air of a conspirator.

Now they both were conscious of the sound of steps scuffing the dead leaves on the path. Startled, they turned, to see Piers's fox terrier looking in the door at them, then Piers himself. He was as sound, as well-colored as an apple that might take a prize at a country fall fair. He nodded, in his offhand way, to Molly and gave her his offhand smile.

"Deserted, eh?" he said.

"For a short while." She smiled nervously, wondering what he had in his mind.

Nothing, apparently, but the quest for his daughter. "You oughtn't, you know, run off by yourself like this," he said to her with a show of sternness.

"She's been drying dishes for me," said Molly.

"That's the way with young'uns," said Piers. "When her mother wants her to do something, she runs off."

Mary went to him and slipped her tiny hand into his large warm one that closed on it with tender paternal possessiveness.

"Shall you mind being alone?" he asked Molly.

"I have lots to do." She spoke defensively.

"But not what you'd like to be doing, I'll wager."

Still with that offhand smile he added, "What a little fool you are."

"What do you mean?" She spoke scarcely above a whisper.

"Wasting your life here. *And* your talent. I don't know

how good an actress you are but you're a very pretty woman, and I tell you there's no future for you as Wake's mistress." Suddenly he looked serious. "Don't be angry, or hurt," he said, "I mean to be kind. I like you, Molly, and now that you have Wakefield nursed back to health I think it's time for you to think of yourself. . . .

"Come, Mary." With his daughter, and his fox terrier, he disappeared along the path looking, it seemed to Molly, all the more resolute because he had an artificial leg.

She was left alone in the silence, where there was only the beating of her own heart. She wished Piers had not come, for her mind had already been made up. Through the open doorway she could see the falling leaves, some dun-colored, some still green, but mostly varied in scarlet and gold. They were, she thought, as the minutes in the hour, the hours in the day, the days in the year, the years in a lifetime.

Seventeen

Seven by a Lake

Wakefield was tired when Finch's car turned into the drive, behind the high cedar hedge of the house that was built of stucco and stone, with a green roof, and two massive stone chimneys. The lake was hidden by trees. Finch, Sylvia, Wakefield, and Adeline were in this car. Already the other car stood at the door, empty, and its occupants—Christian, Maurice, and Patrick Crawshay—were exploring the house.

"Tired?" Finch asked of Wakefield with solicitude, for he had a responsible feeling for him.

"Not in the least." Wakefield straightened his shoulders. "Just excited. It's such an adventure—after all those months of resting—and being bored."

"You must choose your room," said Sylvia, "and lie down for a bit. I'll bring you some milk."

"Milk be damned!" shouted Wakefield. "I hate it." And he ran into the house and out the other side.

"If he's going to behave like that," said Adeline, "we shall wish we hadn't brought him." She looked after his agile figure with severity.

"Don't worry," said Finch. "I'll attend to him. Fetch his milk, Adeline, and I'll see that he takes it."

Finch stared about him at the expensively furnished summer residence and remembered his boyhood pal, George Fennel, tousle-headed George who seldom had two coins to rub together in his pocket. He had married a rich widow and was growing bald, but still was just as tranquil.

Along a grass path, bordered by frost-nipped flowers, down steep wooden steps to the lake's sandy edge Finch followed Wakefield. The lake spread itself before them—a small lake, as compared to the great lake to which they were accustomed; on a clear day its opposite shore might easily be seen. It was not blue beneath the blue sky but rather of a changeful greenish color. It had islands on which tall trees rose stately from the rocks and cast their shadows on the lake. To

Wakefield, long confined to the woodland about Fiddler's Hut, it appeared gloriously free. His first thought was, "Oh, that Molly were here!" but he was too proud to give voice to it. Instead, he remarked in a matter-of-fact tone:

"If this weather holds, we shall have a week to remember. You can't imagine what it is to me. It's like a new lease of life."

"I can well imagine," said Finch, whose too active imagination found little impossible. "But you must come indoors and choose your room and rest awhile."

When they went in, the girls already had chosen a room for Wakefield, a single room that overlooked the lake. Stripped of his outer clothes and wrapped in a dressing-gown he tumbled into bed, drank a glass of milk, exclaimed at the luxurious comfort of the mattress, and slept like a log for two hours, in spite of the only half-muffled noises of the others settling in.

Of these other six, Finch and Sylvia took possession of the "master bedroom," as George Fennel called it, which he and his wife occupied when in residence. Adeline took for herself a pretty single room that, like Wakefield's, overlooked the lake. Maurice and Christian shared a room; while Patrick Crawshay was given one that opened on to a vine-embowered veranda. All were on the ground floor, which gave a carefree familiarity to the party. All seven were eager to make the most of this Indian summer outing—expense-free in another man's house.

Two discoveries brought added pleasure. One was that, moored a short distance from the shore, was a large sailboat. Finch had known there were canoes but this was a delightful surprise. The other discovery was a piano in the living-room. Finch recalled, with amusement and some tenderness the George Fennel of their youth, when George could make shift to play on any sort of instrument, when he and Finch had got together a small orchestra, in the hope of making a little money.

"How splendid," said Adeline. "Now we shall have music in the evenings."

But in the evenings they were mostly content to sit about the fire and talk. When the sun sank it was fall indeed: but during the sun-drenched days it was summer. They wore thin clothes, and taking their lunch with them, explored the lake in the sailboat. The lake that throughout the summer was the playground for small craft of all sorts but principally the

noisy outboard motors, was now deserted. It appeared as remote as when Champlain discovered it.

Wakefield, Finch, and Sylvia left the handling of the boat
to the others. Although a dreamy Indian summer haze hung
over the lake there was usually enough breeze to fill the sails.
Once they were for several hours becalmed, and twice the
wind strengthened till they fairly flew across the wavelets.
Maurice, who had felt in command of himself and that his
love for Adeline was something to be remembered with resignation and even detachment, found that when they two sat in
the bow together, the breeze blowing back the hair from her
face, her eager forward-looking profile turned toward him, he
wished with passionate longing that they might be the only
occupants of the lively craft. He no loonger sought to draw
her and Pat Crawshay into dangerous intimacy.

Yet effortlessly those two came together, first in the mere
physical pleasure of sailing the boat, then in long walks along
the deserted beach or on the quiet country road. It made
them happy to be together. They delighted in the same things,
needing no more than an exclamation or a look exchanged to
express their pleasure. A rhythm marched in unison through
their bodies, coming miraculously to rest in their faces or
even their hands, so that, for a brief while their hands seemed
to be the real home of the spirit. They felt themselves to be
part of the dreamy Indian summer landscape even as were
the trees. Adeline, in these days, gave no more than a passing
thought to her coming marriage. Since Philip's return to
college she had had no letter from him, nothing but a bright-
colored post card of a steamer on which he had spent a week
end on the St. Lawrence. He did not even say—"I wish you
were here." Neither had she written to him. She accepted
their engagement as something seemly, worth while, to which
they were willingly bound, but her friendship with Patrick
Crawshay came to her as an excursion into real and
mysterious regions.

In these days the others of the party found something
oddly magnetic in Adeline. They liked, for one reason or another, to touch her. And in its simplicity and vitality her
nature responded. When Finch would play the piano in the
evening she would sit with folded hands listening, in complete
uncritical absorption. She did not tan or sunburn, as the others, but retained a healthy flowerlike pallor, against which her
dark eyes were luminous. Though she greatly enjoyed Finch's
playing, she still more enjoyed the times when they sang in

chorus to his accompaniment. It was impossible for her unaided to keep on the tune, but singing in chorus she was safe, and let out her voice in pure enjoyment. Of all the seven, the best voice belonged to Pat Crawshay, and she would listen with delight when sometimes he sang old Irish songs.

Their constant cry was, "Oh, if only this weather will hold!"—and, day after day, the beauty of Indian summer was repeated, as though the earth had learned one song and was bent on its repetition. The air became even warmer. The sun was almost hidden in a lustrous mist. On the air there came a faint smell of distant wood smoke from forest fires in the north. All along the shore the colors became more startling. Vivid scarlet predominated and was reflected in the lake with the rich green of cedars.

Sometimes out of the misty radiance that enveloped the water, a sudden breeze would spring and send their boat scudding across the small bright waves. Then the crew of seven would shout and sing for joy. The lake seemed to be their playfellow; but, on the last morning but one it showed itself in a different mood. They had extended their stay by two days and this was the eighth day.

That morning the mist had cleared away and a steady wind blew from the northwest. It was a glorious day for a sail, they agreed. The girls made a larger lunch than usual and they prepared to make a day of it. The wind, growing stronger, swelled the sails. Patrick, who knew how to handle a boat, was at the tiller. There seemed no limit for the excursion but the farthest shore of the lake. They ate their lunch in the calm of a little bay, in the shelter of an island. It was on the way back that they encountered the squall.

Suddenly the wind took on a new note, screaming against the sails, blowing foam from the long curling waves that hurled themselves on the boat, that leaped over the gunwale, as she came about, and drenched those aboard. The lake turned to gray. The sun was gone and rain came down in a torrent. The distance they had covered, flying before the light wind, in two hours, was a struggle of four hours in the squall and its aftermath of uncertain gusts and choppy waves. Only Adeline, who had before stayed by this lake, was aware of its possibilities of fury. The straining and rattling of the rigging tranquillized rather than excited her. On her, it had the effect of riding a difficult horse at a show. But Sylvia felt alarmed and could not conceal it. She gripped Finch's hand and looked into his face for assurance. Because of her condition he was afraid for her; he found a small bucket and began to bail out the cockpit. Once when they came about and scrambled to the other side of the boat Sylvia fell. Wakefield shouted, "We're over!" and laughed in sheer wild excitement. He was soaked to the skin. Even in his excitement he wondered what Molly would think if she saw him now. What a lot he would have to tell her!

For a time the rain had ceased, but now the sky was blackening for another deluge. They were thankful when their own little bay came in sight. They had gone up the lake before the wind. Now coming back they had to tack and luff continually. Suddenly as they were bringing the boat about the boom swung over violently and, before she could crouch down, Sylvia was knocked off her feet and into the lake. She was not hurt but screamed in terror. Finch sprang in after her, and when they had been helped into the boat, she clung to him weeping. Maurice and Patrick were vigorously quarreling as to whose carelessness was the cause of the accident. Rain fell in torrents.

But at last all were safely indoors and the doors fastened against the storm. It raged and battered against the walls, sent streams of rain down the windowpanes and bent the trees as though it would uproot them. A huge fire was built in the stone fireplace, and steaming wet garments hung about it. The party shouted and laughed in hilarity, as though they had had a miraculous escape. They had changed into woolen pullovers and slacks, for they were shivering with cold. Sylvia had recovered her courage, and she and Adeline had the kettle boiling for coffee. Tins of soup were heated. Patrick Crawshay broiled what seemed a great number of lamb chops, but these all were devoured with gusto. In the happy abandon of warmth and safety they stood or squatted about the fire, on which they had thrown pine boughs and cones which crackled in resinous flames about the birch logs. When they had drunk their coffee, Maurice produced a bottle of cognac that he had saved, for this last evening. He, like the others, had been very temperate during those eight days, but now, flushed with drink, his eyes glowing in charmed devotion to Adeline, he sat beside her, a little apart from the others.

"Adeline," he said, his voice hesitating and thickened, "you never have looked as you look to-night."

"How do I look?" she asked.

"As though you could love me—a little."

"I love everybody to-night," she said.

He took her hand in his. "I wish I had drowned in that storm," he said.

"It would have spoilt everything."

"I don't care about myself," he exclaimed, "but you are all the world to me, and—to think that you are engaged to that young lout, Philip! Don't do it, dearest. He isn't worthy of you. Let's celebrate to-night by breaking off your engagement to him. If you won't have me—there is Pat. Look at him. What a man! He has no need to speak, because inner and outer are the one man. His body and soul cannot be divided."

Patrick Crawshay asked, "What are you saying about me?"

"Maurice is tight," said his brother. "He ought to go to bed."

Maurice rose and stood up very straight, resting his hands on the back of a tall chair. He said, with great gravity:

"I publish the banns of marriage between Sir Patrick Crawshay and Adeline Whiteoak, spinster, of this parish."

"For God's sake, go to bed," said his brother.

"I refuse to go to bed till I have performed this duty for two people very dear to me." He swayed a little, and the chair tilted. Adeline sprang up from the floor and seated herself on the chair, raising her face to his, as he stood behind it. He went and kissed her forehead. "Farewell," he said, "and, if for ever, still for ever, fare thee well."

"He's always like this when he's tight," said Christian.

"Somebody take him to bed," said Wakefield.

Pat Crawshay gently led Maurice away, who could be heard complaining of the lack of affection shown him by his family.

After this the company was a little subdued. For one thing, they were tired and there was so much to do before they left on the following day. Through all the house that had been elegantly tidy on their arrival, there was now supreme disorder. So early had been the morning start that not a bed was made. The kitchen and dining-room were a riot of dirty dishes. Wet clothing still hung about the fire in the living-room. The storm had passed, but the lake tumbled wildly against the beach, striving to uproot trees—eager, it seemed, to attack the very house.

Finch was anxious about both Sylvia and Wake. Though they had come triumphantly through the ordeal, he felt apprehensive about its effect on them. When he had them tucked safely in bed, he found Christian absorbed in preparing for travel the sketches he had made. He said, with a nod toward the kitchen—"We're not needed there."

Finch found Adeline and Pat Crawshay washing the dishes. It was two o'clock in the morning.

At dawn, a flock of wild geese flew overhead going southward. Their disturbing cries sounded above the roar of the waves.

Eighteen

Back to Fiddler's Hut

The wind blew bitterly cold from the north on this morning. It blew the leaves from the trees, almost to the last one, so that the trees stood naked; their lovely shapes, which had been veiled by the foliage, now spread themselves in intermingling limbs against the stormy sky. The seven who had so eagerly arrived were just as eager to turn homeward. To place Sylvia and Wakefield safe and sound at home again was Finch's concern. To return to his studio and finish the sketches he had made was Christian's. Maurice, in a mood of melancholy, wandered alone by the lake. Only Adeline and Pat Crawshay were concerned to leave the house in order. In her there was a fastidiousness that refused to leave confusion behind her. In him there was the desire to help her in whatever she did. He sought to make himself as much like the others as possible, yet so strong was his individuality that it could not be done. He could sail a boat, shout, sing, be half-drowned or half-drunk, but always was the product of a serene life.

Finch drove his car to the opening of the path that led to Fiddler's Hut. There Wakefield alighted.

"Your things will come in the other car," Finch said to him. "Are you all right? Shall I go with you?"

"I'm fine," said Wakefield. "I'll go alone and surprise Molly."

Sylvia was so tired that, wrapped in a rug, she was half-asleep in her corner of the car. Wakefield closed the door as quietly as he could, murmured a good-bye, and went off along the path. The golden leaves lay thick on it. Wakefield experienced a thrill as of childhood in scuffing through them. He moved leisurely along the path, scuffing the leaves, his face already alight for Molly's welcome.

The door of the Hut was closed and it pleased him to knock on it softly rather than to walk straight in. Molly must have been expecting him the day before. She would be anxious when he told her of all he had been through.

He knocked a second time but there was no answer.

"Are you there, Molly?" He called out and opened the door and went in.

How tidy the room was! Tidy and empty and silent as was all the Hut. He saw the letter lying on the table and snatched it up and tore it open. He read:

My very dear Wake,

Do not think badly of me because I am going to leave you now. I am sure it is the very best thing to do. We have had wonderfully happy times together, but I feel that now we must separate and go our own ways. I do not feel guilty in doing this. I have known for some time that it must happen—for both our sakes. Thinking it over in this lonely place, it all seems clear. I shall go back to the life that means most to me—more even than you mean to me. You will go to your family for a time—then back to your work.

I'm too excited to write more now. Good-bye, dear Wake—I shall always love you.

Molly

Wakefield stared wildly about the little room, so neat, so sunny. A pottery vase of pale blue Michaelmas daisies stood by the letter. Why had she put flowers there? Surely to mock him. . . . But she could not have gone like that—left him, as though theirs had been no more than a passing affair. It was too heartless. He went into the two tiny bedrooms, into the kitchen that looked so scrubbed, so tidy. Everywhere there was ghastly neatness, mocking emptiness. He could not believe in it. He could not face it. He felt dazed, giddy. He dropped into a chair by the table and buried his face in his hands. He gave a harsh sob which in that loneliness was exaggerated to a cry of anguish. I am alone—deserted—he thought. There is no one to care whether I live or die. He sat quiet there, feeling very tired. The ordeal of the day before had taken toll of his new-gained strength. He felt strangely excited yet unutterably tired.

After a time he raised his head and looked about him in the leaf-stirring, bird-twittering silence. He found that his eyes were wet. He felt as though he were acting a part in a strange play, and he tried, for a moment, to think of a play with a part in it such as this—a part in which a man who had given his loyal devotion to a woman was deserted by her just when he most needed her.

He went to the chest of drawers that stood by his bed and found the small thermometer, with which he took his temperature. He was shocked when he found what it now was. His temperature stood out to him as terribly important, as frightening. Now the Hut became unbearable to him in its isolation. He must find Renny, tell him of this frightening rise in his temperature, of Molly's desertion. His heart was thumping against his ribs. He felt dizzy as he ran along the path, where the thick carpet of fallen leaves now felt heavy to his feet. He tripped on the root of a tree and fell sprawling. He lay there sobbing among the wet cold leaves for some minutes before he gathered himself together and went on toward the house, moving slowly and irregularly.

The sun, coming out from behind a splendid white cloud, now shone full on the solid front of the house, which, stripped of most of its covering of vine leaves, showed the dim redness of brick and windows that looked out alert on the changing world—the world that was changing from fall to winter. A few leaves of Virginia creeper still clung to the house, and these ranged in color from a rosewood red to a pinkish shade, but the strong stalks of the creeper and its runners were evident.

As when Wakefield had been a child, he hastened to tell this eldest brother of his hurt. From the hall he could hear Renny's low whistle as he cleaned his gun in the sitting-room. Wakefield entered, leaning against the side of the door for support.

Renny, raising his intent gaze from the parts of his gun spread out on the table in front of him, exclaimed:

"Wake! What's the matter?"

"It's Molly," gasped Wakefield. "She's left me. She's not at the Hut. I'm ill." He looked ready to faint.

Renny put an arm about him and led him to the couch.

"Don't be upset, old fellow," he said. "I'll get some brandy for you. You'll be all right. There, there." He comforted Wakefield, patting him on the shoulder. He gave him brandy.

Incoherently Wakefield, between sips and spilling as much as he swallowed, poured out his story. He drew the crumpled letter from his pocket and thrust it into Renny's hand.

"She could write me a cool dismissal like that," he said, "when she knew what a shock it would be to me. I wrote loving letters to her from the lake. I wrote to her twice. And she could do this. Why, it might be the death of me. If you knew how ill I feel, Renny. . . ."

"All this has happened at a good time for you," said Renny, "because now you can come home. Cold weather is on the way. The Hut would be no place for you then. I can tell you I have worried a lot about you. Now, it's all settled. You'll go straight upstairs to a comfortable room where you shall be properly waited on. Before long you'll be yourself again. . . . Come now."

"You don't know what it is to lose your mate," sobbed Wakefield.

"Molly is a sensible girl," said Renny. "She knew that that situation could not go on."

"Did you say anything of the sort to her?" Wakefield demanded suspiciously.

"Not a word. What she did, she did of her own free will. You see, the stage is necessary to her—just as my horses and dogs are necessary to me. You'll find out, Wake, how sympathetic and comforting animals can be. . . . But now bed is the place for you, and I'll tell you where I am going to put you. In Uncle Nicholas's room. It is sunny, and has a particularly good bed. The dear old Uncle would like you to have his room."

So in that bedroom, so long occupied by Nicholas, Wakefield was installed. The doctor was sent for. Certainly Wakefield had had a setback, but it was not so serious as might have been expected. A few weeks in bed, with the right nursing, would correct the mischief. Soon all the family knew that he was safe at Jalna, and each according to temperament expressed approval.

Alayne was profoundly relieved to be rid of the presence of Molly, even though she had been hidden in Fiddler's Hut. She told herself that she breathed freer than she had in months. She saw to it that Wakefield was offered the most tempting and nourishing food. She sat with him, and he told her of the play he was writing. He gave her the manuscript to read, and, while praising it, she offered criticism which he found helpful.

Meg was not interested in his play, but she was passionately interested in him. She could not see him, lying there in bed, without poignant memories of Eden crowding in to tear at her heart. But she hid her anxiety, took Wakefield into her warm embrace, fussed comfortingly over him, brushed his hair, drank tea with him— "In the long run, al-

most everything that happens to us is for the best. When
have reached my age and look back over your life, you will
find this is so."

She remarked to the Rector, "Rupert, dear, it seems to me
that this would be a good time to tackle Wakefield on the
subject of religion. He is in a weak condition and might easily be drawn back into the fold. It's heartbreaking to think he
is a Roman Catholic, even though not a very strict one."

The Rector, however, stubbornly refused, saying that he
would not be party to any wobbling back and forth between
creeds.

Maurice and Patrick Crawshay now set out on a journey
to the Pacific Coast, planning to return to Jalna for
Christmas. A steady correspondence was carried on between
the young Irishman and Adeline. There was nothing in his
letters to be hidden, and, because of his comments, often
witty, on what he saw on his travels, Adeline read them
aloud to her parents. She read them with a jocular and almost possessive pride. She kept them in a drawer in her own
room—along with Philip's post cards—and replied to them in
kind.

Nineteen

Coming of Cold Weather

Early in December a letter arrived for Renny, telling of the approaching marriage of Roma to Maitland Fitzturgis, shortly to take place in New York. There was to be no church ceremony. They were to be married in a registry office, with only the near relatives of the bridegroom present. Any of the Whiteoaks who wished to give presents, wrote Roma, should remember the Customs duty and also that she would be going into a small apartment. She wished that all the family might be present and sent her best love to each and all. At a family conclave it was decided that they should club together and send the little bride-to-be a cheque, with which she might buy something really substantial that she could look on with pride for the rest of her days, point out to her wondering New York friends as a wedding present from her family in Canada. The amounts varied from quite small subscriptions from Meg and Piers—"Roma would scarcely expect much from a poor clergyman's wife or a poor farmer"—to quite large ones from Renny and Finch. All awaited with eagerness Roma's reply. She wrote five grateful little notes, with tiny bunches of forget-me-nots printed in colors on the corner of each, but the family waited in vain for details of what Roma had bought. The truth was that she could not have told them, if so she had willed, for she had frittered away the cheque on whatever had attracted her. Feeling suddenly rich, she had become suddenly extravagant—on herself. Nothing did she spend on Fitzturgis, and when he ventured to enquire as to whether the money had been deposited in the bank or spent, she withdrew into a cryptic and noncommital reserve.

Fiddler's Hut looked not less but more remote, with the coming of cold weather. Hidden among foliage, there was something mysterious and inviting about it, as though it were the home of fairy-tale dwarves. Standing among towering tree trunks, its doors and windows marred by withered leaves, it looked desolate indeed. Desolate, that is, to all but little Mary Whiteoak. To her it was always fascinating and she wished she might have had it as her own, for a playhouse where she could be quite alone with her fancies.

In a year or two Mary was to be sent to a girls' school, but at present she came, on five mornings a week, to Jalna, where Alayne gave her lessons in English, French, and history. Alayne did this not so much because she liked the child as because she had a natural bent for teaching and found the mind of this little one interesting. Piers gave her lessons in geography and arithmetic, Pheasant in sewing, and Christian in drawing. So that Mary was as busy as any eight-year-old need be. In truth she would have preferred to have fewer lessons, for she found life itself exciting and time never lagging.

One mild December morning Alayne was obliged to go to town, and Mary found herself unexpectedly free. She had been told to wait at Jalna till she was called for, but she decided that she would take a little walk in the direction of the Hut. There was in her an urge to visit the Hut which would not be denied. So she set out, walking sedately over the frozen ground till she drew near the path leading to the Hut. Then she began to run.

The door stuck against the ice along its sill, but she was able to open it and, without fear, stepped inside.

The Hut slumbered in a strange twilight, even though the sun was shining. It was so dim, so small, so tidy, that Mary's heart felt ready to burst with the sense of owning it, of belonging to it. Nothing she might find inside would have surprised her. But there was only twilight stillness, and a chill that penetrated her warm clothes. She remembered how Dennis had lighted candles there, and she saw that a fire was laid in the little stone fireplace. She found matches and touched the flame of one of them to the kindling. It was damp and was slow to ignite; but she blew into it and presently a crackling blaze was born. When Mary saw this blaze and its reflection on different objects in the room she gave a little cry of joy, and skipped about like a lamb at play.

Soon the room grew so warm that she threw off her coat and scarf. There was a sink and a tap in the kitchen. Mary filled the kettle and put it on the little oilstove. She intended to make some coffee, for she had found in the cupboard a bottle of Nescafé, and a tin of concentrated cream. Tea she drank every day, but coffee was a rare treat.

She was not quite sure how to make it, because the printing on the label had become blurred. But she was determined that it should not be weak. She put what she considered plenty into the coffeepot, then filled it up with boiling water. It was a large pot, and she wished she might have some guests to drink it up—not ordinary human beings but people out of a fairy tale, such as Humpty Dumpty or the Mad Hatter.

She chose the prettiest cup in the cupboard, poured coffee into it, then added cream. She drew up a chair and seated herself at table, waiting for the drink to cool. She had discovered a tin half full of Romary biscuits, and these she had arranged on a blue plate. Her heart was filled with happiness. She hummed a little nameless tune, and from the eave the dripping of melting snow made an agreeable accompaniment.

As she sat waiting, there came another sound—the sound of heavy boots on the path. They ceased and, for a moment, a shadow darkened the window. Then there came a resounding knock on the door. For a short space Mary was shocked into immobility by the sudden tumult of the knock, which must have been made by striking on the door with a stick. As she sat staring open-mouthed, the knock sounded again and almost immediately the latch was lifted and the door opened. There entered the bent, much bundled-up figure of Noah Binns.

"So it's you, is it, little lady?" he said, through his straggling, dribbling moustache.

"Yes, it's me, Noah," she answered, her voice trembling a little, but not really frightened.

"And you're sittin' here alone, drinkin' coffee by the smell of it."

"Yes, Noah," she answered proudly, and took a sip of coffee and a nibble of Romary biscuit.

He clumped close, after shutting the door, and peered greedily down at the coffeepot. Then he laid his heavy stick on the floor and picked up the pot, and hefted it.

"Nobody," he said, "ain't offered me a cup of coffee in a terrible long time. I've swallered gallons of tea this fall, but coffee—nary a drop."

"I'll pour you a cup of coffee, Mr. Binns," she said, suddenly becoming formal, with the air of a hostess.

The "Mister" pleased him. He dragged a chair to the table and heavily seated himself. Mary brought a second cup and filled it.

"Sugar?" she asked.

"Five lumps," he said, smacking his lips and helping himself to a biscuit.

Mary could not help giggling as she counted out the five lumps. She handed him the coffee without slopping any, and watched him anxiously as he gulped a mouthful. Noah had tasted strong coffee but never any so strong as this.

"Good?" she asked.

His mouth was burned, the coffee so strong that he could only nod, speechless.

"Drink it up," she said, in the firm tone her mother sometimes used to her.

Fairly hypnotized, he obeyed.

At once she asked, "More coffee?"

Noah Binns leered in pleasure as his cup was renewed. He said: "You plan to live here from now on, young lady?"

"I might," she said.

"How old are you?"

"Eight years old," she said.

Noah took a swig of the steaming coffee, and declaimed:

"When children take to the woods it's a sure sign of doom. All signs p'int to it. I've lived over fourscore years, and I ain't never seen doom so near."

"More coffee?" said Mary, and refilled his cup.

Noah demanded, "Why did you take to the woods?"

"I like this little house."

"Nobody will ever want to buy it off you. It's too lonesome. I had a little house, and I sold it in a subdivision. Do you know what a subdivision is?"

"It's multiplication the other way round."

Noah slapped his thigh and cackled with laughter.

"More coffee?" asked Mary, and filled up his cup. Noah drank and smacked his lips. "I live in one room now," he said, "and like it. Do you calculate to spend the winter here?"

Mary nodded and nibbled a biscuit.

"It's goin' to be a fearful winter," said Noah. "All signs p'int to the worst winter on record since William the Conqueror discovered this continent. Floods—blizzards—and pestiferousness . . . Don't you think you may be scared livin' alone here?"

"I may go home for Christmas."

"Christmas ain't what it was. Every Christmas fer three years I've been obliged to buy a card."

"Every year?" exclaimed Mary.

"Yeah," said Noah. "Every year. It's a terrible responsibility."

"More coffee?" she asked sympathetically.

"I don't mind if I do."

She filled up his cup, then inquired, "What did you get last Christmas?"

"One card. Two pairs socks. One shirt. One paper bag horehound candy. What I needed was overshoes."

"More coffee?" She did not wait for him to answer but filled up his cup. He added five lumps of sugar.

"I bought myself overshoes," he said, "and I have 'em here." He opened a parcel and displayed them. He said, "Two dollars and ninety-nine cents they cost. A fearful outlay." He set them on the table near the coffeepot.

"I have a new pair too," said Mary.

Noah craned his neck to view her small foot.

"It's a terrible thing," he said, "to think of all the pitfalls layin' in wait for them innocent little feet. Whatever way you turn there'll be pitfalls."

"My overshoes," said Mary, "cost three dollars. They are velvet."

"If I'd yearned for velvet," said Noah, "I'd have bought velvet."

"More coffee?" asked Mary.

Noah was beginning to feel more than a little sick. This was partly due to heat, for he was close to the blaze of the fire and he wore not only a heavy topcoat but a fur cap with earlaps which he donned at the first tentative snowfall. He was proud of this cap, and when not in use kept it in a paper bag with mothballs. Now the smell of camphor from the cap filled the room. Also Noah felt ready to burst from the amount of coffee he had drunk. He wondered if he would be able to get home. He rose unsteadily and, holding to the back of his chair, he loudly belched.

The impact of this escaping wind drove his upper denture from his mouth, through his moustache and out on to the floor. There it lay grinning up at them.

Mary was so frightened by this porcelain grin that she uttered a little cry, but then she gathered herself together and said:

"More coffee, Mr. Binns?"

Noah bent toward the floor to retrieve his denture. He became dizzy and fell, taking the chair with him, to the floor. At that moment the door was flung open and Mary's brother,

Christian, entered. Noah hastily restored the denture to his gums. His fur cap was over his eyes. He was helpless, unable to rise.

Christian grasped him under the arms and heaved him to his feet. Without a look behind, Noah shambled through the open door and down the path out of sight, scuffing through the dead leaves.

"What on earth," Christian demanded of Mary, "are you doing here?"

"Making coffee," said Mary. "Have some?"

Christian picked up the fallen chair and seated himself in it. Then he spied Noah's overshoes standing by the coffeepot.

"What are these?" he demanded.

"They belong to Mr. Binns," said Mary, and tears rose to her eyes.

"How disgusting," exclaimed Christian. He sprang up, took an overshoe in either hand and flung them through the door after Noah.

Mary looked after them in mingled sorrow and relief.

"Whew," said Christian, "what a stink!"

He fetched himself a clean cup.

"Coffee?" asked Mary. .

"Please. No sugar or cream."

She filled his cup. He sat down and lighted a cigarette.

"I have been sent to search for you," said Christian. "It's very naughty, you know, for a little girl to run off like this. Little girls should stay at home and behave themselves. My morning's work has been upset because of you." His hazel eyes gave her a clear look of disapproval. He sipped his coffee and remarked, "This is the worst coffee I've ever tasted."

Everything was now in his hands. He put out the fire, tucked the tin of Romary biscuits under his arm, and led Mary homeward. In experience she was poor, but in the world of imagination she was richer than he because she still moved freely in the realm of childhood—and that he had lost.

As she trotted docilely at his side, her hand in his, she saw Noah's overshoes lying among the dead leaves and shed a tear for them.

Twenty

Finch and Sylvia

This was a happy time for Finch and Sylvia. She awaited her confinement with more tranquillity than even a few months ago she would have thought possible. Rather than harming her by exposure and fatigue, the holiday by the lake had done her good. Despite the increasing bulkiness of her body, her spirit was light. She was given confidence by the knowledge that Finch was to remain at home till after the birth of her child. He would finish the composition on which he was working, before Christmas. After Christmas he was to go to New York to see a publisher. This sonata claimed him, as did his wife and the coming birth. Between the two his mind shuttled, never at rest, but without apprehension. The fates were smiling on him. All would go well.

The snowfall was light. They took long walks. In the evenings Sylvia would read aloud to him, or others of the family would come to spend an hour or two. Sylvia and Patience had confidential talks regarding the trials and triumphs of maternity. The marriage of Roma to Maitland Fitzturgis was a puzzling event to Sylvia. Brother and sister had passed through times of deep emotion together, intimate in spirit, alternately tender in their love, or angry when he had sought to control the vagaries of her past mental illness. Now that she was secure in Finch's love, Sylvia felt that she should be happy that her brother had married into the same family. Yet she could not be happy about this marriage. In their short acquaintance she had found little to attract her in Roma: she appeared not only cold, but shallow. What was there behind that charming face beyond a narrow self-seeking—an indolent distaste for exerting herself in the affairs of any but herself? And why had Maitland chosen to fall in love with two young girls—one after the other?

This question she put to Finch, as they sat together watching through the window the pheasants feeding on grain he had scattered for them.

162

"One after the other," said Finch, "is better than both at the same time."

"But it's not like him. He's not an impulsive, out-giving person. He's reserved. He needs understanding."

"Possibly he feels that a woman his own age would understand him too well."

"Oh, Finch, you must not be too critical of Mait. He's been so good to me."

"I know he has and I'm grateful."

"But you don't like him."

"I do—with reservations."

"What reservations?" She leaned forward eagerly.

"I don't need to tell you—you know him better than I do."

She sank back, closing her eyes for a moment. Then she said, "I understand what you mean. There's something in Mait that you can't get near. You wonder whether he is hiding his real self or whether he is just aimlessly drifting. It makes me angry with him."

"Not me," said Finch. "I seldom think about him."

"That's strange," she said. "I'm always thinking about him. I do wish I could see him."

"You will very soon," said Finch. "He and Roma are coming for Christmas." Then he added, "Oh, I shouldn't have told you that. Meg said it was to be a surprise."

"Meg—how could she know?"

"They are to stay at the Rectory."

"How lovely! And yet—"

"And yet," he repeated, "why not? I think it is a good arrangement. It would be too much for you to have them here and it would be impossible for them to stay at Jalna."

"I suppose so," she said thoughtfully. "Heavens—why should family relations be so complicated?"

"They're terrible," said Finch, "and wonderful. They're the very stuff of life."

A fortnight later Sylvia and her brother sat together in that same room.

"No need," he said, "to ask you how you are. I've never seen you look better. But it's strange to find you settled here in this lovely new house—an expectant mother."

"And you," she exclaimed, "settled in New York—both of us so far from Ireland! I can't say I've never seen *you* look better. You're paler, and, I think, thinner. But perhaps that's because you wear your hair shorter."

He passed a hand over his curly mouse-colored hair. "No Irish tweeds either," he said. "I'm trying hard to look American."

"You'll never succeed. But—the thing is: do you *like your job?*"

"As well as I like any sort of work."

Then she came out bluntly with the question—"*And* do you like being married?"

"Possibly not as well as you do, but better than some."

"One can never get a straight answer out of you, Mait."

"Give me a straight answer to this—how do you like being a stepmother?"

He saw at once that he had touched on a tender subject. Sylvia flushed and looked unhappy. She said—trying to keep her voice steady—"I've tried hard to get near Dennis but I cannot. Sometimes he's almost affectionate, but I feel no sincerity in him—except in his adoration of Finch. That's terribly sincere."

"And Finch? Does he dote on the boy?"

"Ah, that's one of my worries. Finch is so cold toward Dennis—it really hurts me. If his feelings toward Dennis were different—then Dennis might be more kind to me. I believe he blames me for Finch's attitude toward him. But Finch never has loved his son. He's told me so."

"Whatever our faults as a family," said Fitzturgis, "we have love for each other."

Sylvia gripped his hand, as though by that clasp she would sustain herself. "You've always been so good to me!" she said, and there were tears in her eyes.

"Why should you worry over this youngster?" he exclaimed. "Put him out of your mind. You have done your best—that's all you can do. How old is the boy?"

"He will be fourteen this month, and looks like twelve—rather a childish twelve."

"Fourteen! Boys of that age have usually got over hero-worshiping their father."

"Dennis is a very odd boy. In some ways he's precocious. In others he behaves like a boy of seven. I never know which side of him to expect."

At this moment Dennis entered.

Sylvia said, "This is my brother, Dennis. Do you remember him?"

"Yes, I do," said Dennis. "Only the other day my father

and I were speaking of you." He offered his hand to Fitzturgis.

"Something pleasant, I hope," said Fitzturgis.

"I forget, my father and I talk of so many people and things."

"Music, I suppose," said Fitzturgis. "Do you play an instrument?"

"I play the violin—as my mother did. Would you like to see my violin? It was hers, of course. She had been playing on it the very day she was killed. She would play—specially for me—the tunes I liked. I was only five. Would you like to see the violin?"

"Yes, indeed." As the boy moved away, Fitzturgis cast a look toward Sylvia that said, "What an uncomfortable youngster." His intent eyes then returned to the boy, who was taking the violin from its case.

"Someone has been meddling with this," said Dennis.

"You left it lying on the piano," Sylvia said sharply. "I simply laid it back in its case."

"I don't like it interfered with," said Dennis, and carried the violin to Fitzturgis. "It's a very valuable one," he explained. "An old Italian violin. Very valuable." He ran his small fine hand caressingly over the violin.

"Will you play for me?" asked Fitzturgis, from curiosity rather than desire to hear the boy perform.

"Some other time," said Dennis. "Just now I'm out of practice because of school exams."

He was listening. In a moment Finch came into the room.

He greeted Fitzturgis and sat down beside Sylvia. Those were the three males, she thought, most nearly bound to her—irrevocably bound—Finch, by love—Maitland, by blood—Dennis, by the iron forging of circumstance. She was deeply conscious of these bonds. At this moment they tugged almost painfully on the eagerness of her spirit to be strong and free for the ordeal which awaited her and which, in spite of her happiness, she mortally feared. She clung to Finch's protectiveness, yet shrank from his brooding hold on her. The presence of Fitzturgis brought all too painfully the remembrance of her unhappy illness, when he had heroically striven to save her from her despair. She could not look into that intent face without recalling scenes in Ireland that she would like to wipe from her memory for ever. As for the boy, Dennis, she felt toward him a kind of fear. In spite of his small frame, his pale and delicate features, she thought she sensed in him a stony cynicism, an almost insane hatred toward herself that frightened her. Yet, when Finch spoke sternly to him, her instinct, already maternal, spread itself like wings, to protect him from harshness.

After a little desultory talk between the two men, Fitzturgis said, "I hear that your son is talented too. He's promised to play the violin for me one day."

"May I not be here," said Finch, half-laughing.

Fitzturgis, seeing the boy look crestfallen, said, "I'm sure he plays very well. Anyhow, I'm not a severe critic. I'd like to hear him play."

Dennis, with a slanting look at Finch, said—with a catch in his breath—"I'll play for you, right now, if you like. If you can bear a few mistakes." Even as he spoke he picked up the violin, as though to make certain that nothing would hinder his intention.

"Good," said Fitzturgis, and settled back with a smile, to listen.

Dennis made a charming picture, the violin tucked beneath his chin, his right arm upraised with the bow.

Sylvia said, "Will you play the accompaniment, Finch?"

Without speaking, Finch moved to the piano seat. Dennis laid the sheet of music before him.

"Schubert," muttered Finch. "Can you really play this?"

"I'll try," said Dennis, and began.

Finch did not support the boy's unaccomplished playing as he might have done. The attempt ended in a breakdown, accepted by the boy with almost negligent calm—by Finch, with intense irritability. Fitzturgis, nevertheless, applauded. Shortly afterward he left. Outside, he stood gazing into the noble darkness of a group of pines that had escaped the fire which, a few years ago, had swept away the original house and many of its trees. These pines remained and would still be casting their mysterious shadow when the new house and its occupants were no more. He wondered about Sylvia. Was she happy? And why was she so affected by the presence of the boy Dennis? For she was strongly affected, Fitzturgis was aware of that. On his own part, he was oddly attracted by the boy. A vague wish flickered through his mind—a wish that Dennis might have been his son.

Inside the music-room Finch turned on the piano seat to face Dennis, who stood, still holding the violin.

"The next time," said Finch, "that you persist in playing,

don't ask me to accompany you. I want to be free to leave the room."

"I didn't ask you," said Dennis.

"I asked you," said Sylvia, and in agitation rose to her feet. "To me," she added, "it seemed that Dennis played very well."

"Then you weren't listening," said Finch. "It was atrocious. There is nothing so devilish as the squeaking of a fiddle can be. I refuse to listen to it."

Dennis stood transfixed. Beyond the window he could see the masculine darkness of the group of pines; set against them, inside, clear and heavy, the terribly female bulk of Sylvia. Rage surged within him, from bowels to brain. He raised his arm, and, pointing the bow of the violin at her, he said to Finch:

"You used to like to hear me play till she came on the scene."

The formidable weight of the words, the smallness of the speaker, might have made the scene almost ridiculous, but the effect on Sylvia was as of a blow. "No, no, no," she gasped and clung to the back of her chair for support.

Finch strode to her side. "Come," he said, "you must lie down." Keeping his eyes off Dennis, he supported her into their room and closed the door.

There she drew on all her strength. She stood upright. "What a fool I am," she said, "to let something said by a child upset me! He couldn't know how it hurt."

"He's a little devil," said Finch, "and I'll go out to him and break that damned violin over his back."

Between him and Sylvia he had a sudden vision of his dead wife, Sarah, playing on her violin—that same instrument which Dennis cherished to-day. Sarah was gazing at him with possessive intensity, gazing at him as though every inch of him were of extravagant importance to her.

"Let's not take this too seriously," Sylvia was saying. "Dennis was upset because—"

Finch interrupted, "I'll teach him a lesson. I won't have him insulting you."

She sank to the bed. "No, no," she sobbed. "I can't bear any sort of scene."

"You'll know nothing about it."

"I can't bear it," she repeated. "Please, please don't punish him."

"What do you want me to do?"

"Say nothing more. Dennis will be sorry."

"It's not in him to be sorry."

"Oh, Finch, he adores you, and it makes him madly jealous. We should not have let him come home and see me—like this."

"I'll send him away."

"You can't. Not just at Christmastime."

"I'll send him to Jalna."

She snatched at the relief of that. "Yes, yes," she said, "but don't tell them—everything. I should be ashamed for them to know. I'd look such a failure."

What she did look, to Finch, was infinitely touching. To give her peace he agreed and, making her comfortable on the bed, returned to the music-room. He did not close the door after him because he wanted to assure her that he would not so much as raise his voice when with Dennis.

When Finch went in to his son he found that the violin had been put away neatly in its case. Dennis, in his gray flannel suit, stood with bowed head, like a prisoner awaiting sentence. He held his clasped hands in front of him, as though they were manacled.

Finch said, in a controlled voice: "I should take you to Sylvia and make you apologize before punishing you. What I am going to do is to send you to Jalna, if Uncle Renny will have you, for the rest of the holidays. You are to understand that you are banished from here. Don't show your face about home. You're getting off very easily."

"But I don't want to go away," Dennis said earnestly. "I want to be with you."

"If you thought half as much of me as you pretend to think, you would realize that Sylvia's happiness is the greatest thing in life to me."

"I'll be different from now on," said Dennis. "Please let me go and tell—" He hesitated a moment, then brought out the word "Mother" in a still lower voice. "Let me go and tell Mother I'm sorry, I won't do anything like that again, I promise. But please let me stay at home."

Sylvia must have been straining her ears to hear. Now she called out, "Let him come!"

Finch stood undecided, dreading another scene.

Dennis looking up into his face said, "She wants me to go to her. May I go?"

"Very well," Finch said. "But be careful what you say. I'll be listening."

The small figure moved lightly past him and into Sylvia's room. She was on the bed, but leaning on her elbow. Dennis had the power of making her feel that a crisis of some sort was at hand. Now she was aware of this sensation as he came to her bedside. She noticed a bruise on his smooth child's forehead.

"You have hurt yourself," she said.

He gave a little laugh and put up his hand to feel the spot. "I don't even remember how I bumped it."

His eyes moved from her face and came to rest on the protuberance at her middle. Then he averted them and said, "I'm sorry. I don't know why I said what I did about you. I know it isn't true. Will you please forgive me and let me stay at home?"

"Of course, I shall—if your father agrees." She put out her hand to him. He caught it, bent over it, as though in curiosity to examine the delicate blue veins in its thinness. Then he wheeled and ran from the room to Finch and caught him by the arm.

"She wants me to stay at home," he said eagerly. "She says so herself. *Please* don't send me away, Daddy. I'll be different. I'll behave the way you'd like me to. I won't play the violin, or be cheeky—or anything. *Please.*"

"What I should like," said Finch, "is to see you behave more like other boys."

"I try," said Dennis, "but somehow I can't. At the camp they said I'd been spoilt at home. Do you think that's the trouble with me?" He looked ready, thought Finch, to discuss his disposition at length.

Sylvia was now calling from her bed, and Finch went to her.

"Have you told Dennis he's not to be sent away?" she asked.

"No. I think it would be better if he went."

"I can't bear it," she said. "A child sent away at Christmastime. No—no."

Finch returned to the boy. "We," he said, stressing the *we,* "have decided to let you stay here, if—"

Dennis interrupted—catching Finch's arm in his hands.

"How good you are, Daddy—how kind to me—both of you."

Twenty-One

The Snow Man

Ninety-nine Christmases had been celebrated at Jalna. In its
first Christmas Philip and Adeline Whiteoak had been young
people and their three children infants. Now all those five
were in their graves and the youngest to join in the
celebration were Victoria Bell, who arrived in her father's
arms, and the unborn Whiteoak, still curled up in his
mother's womb. Victoria Bell, strong of back and bright of
eye, sat upright, enthralled by all she saw. Boughs of spruce
and hemlock made every doorway seem the entrance to a
bower. Evergreens and holly were entwined on the banister.
Mistletoe was not forgotten. Victoria bore with patience the
dandling from one pair of arms to another, the compliments
on her complexion and on her dimpled knees. The smell of
roast turkey with sage-seasoned stuffing that rose from the
basement did not make her mouth water. The only smell that
interested her was the warm milky smell of her mother's
breast. But she enjoyed being the centre of interest on this,
her first Christmas. What were the thoughts of the unborn
Whiteoak in his slumberous retreat, it would be difficult for
the most fervent imagination to guess. Did those thoughts
ooze darkly through his brain, causing no stir, or did they
strike as a blinding blow, making him twitch and bound in
his effort to escape what they portended?

Nineteen members of the family were present in the house.
They were in drawing-room and hall, for the library (which
Renny persisted in calling the sitting-room) was where the
massive Christmas tree was enthroned. No one must enter
there till came the hour of present giving. In the meantime
they were a talkative, rather noisy gathering, and when Finch
sat down at the piano and played a carol the singing was
hearty, and especially that of the Rector, who had already
that day conducted three church services.

Alayne sadly missed the rather chill presence of her son,
which could, at time such as this, warm to a tolerable cheer.

Archer had sent no presents because, so he wrote, he could not afford them; he had lost count of the number of relatives; and he believed that the celebration of Christmas should be made in solitude. However, he had sent a card to each of his parents—to Alayne a picture of a pale, sad Madonna and child; to Renny, three emaciated Wise Men on camels. These cards Renny had placed in a position of honor on the mantelshelf. Unfortunately when Piers was adding logs to the fire he knocked them off and they fell into the blaze and were burned. At the time, no one but himself noticed the mishap. He stood, with dropped jaw, staring ruefully at the tiny conflagration. Then, taking from a table a card with a fat Santa Claus, and another showing rosy-cheeked choirboys, he placed them where Archer's cards had been.

Maurice and Patrick Crawshay were sadly missed, but they sent affectionate telegrams from California, of which balmy land they appeared to think they were the discoverers. As for presents, they had sent souvenirs of California to everyone. Little Mary, in particular, was pleased with these, and felt friendlier towards the young men than ever before.

Philip, in his becoming cadet uniform, showed—as the Rector declaimed, in his second glass of sherry—" 'Hyperion's curls, the front of Jove himself, an eye like Mars, to threaten and command; a station like the herald Mercury new-lighted on a heaven-kissing hill.' "

"Listen to the man," whispered Pheasant to her son Christian—"He'll make Philip more vain than ever."

"Impossible," said Christian. "Since this match has been made for him, he's like a young peacock."

Adeline that very morning had stood in the paddock watching while Philip schooled a nervous young show horse. Also there was Renny mounted on East Wind. East Wind was not a jumper but a racer. Still he could take these moderate jumps with ease. He showed an angular devil-may-careness. Nothing affected his nerves. He attacked every hurdle with a joyous stride. Not so the colt, who trembled with excitement, tossed his stark head in anger, champed his bit, and sought to throw young Philip, his rider. Adeline's eyes were bright with pleasure as she watched Renny on East Wind, critical of Philip on the dancing colt. Yet when, in a violent swerve, the colt threw Philip and he lay still, she gave a gasp of dismay, ran and bent over him.

Renny rode up.

"Are you hurt?" he asked.

"The ground felt a bit hard," said Philip. He got to his feet and ran limping to the colt who stood a little way off, making a grimace of disdain. Philip mounted him, and they again circled the paddock, this time taking the jumps with ease.

"Good man," called out Renny.

Philip bent to pat the colt's shoulder, then rode with casual grace to where Adeline stood. She saw a smear of blood on his forehead. "It's nothing," he laughed.

"I quite like you," she said. "I can't help myself."

As she watched the two horsemen she saw her life stretching before her bound up in these two men. They were comrades, in accord, prisoners of the traditions of Jalna, as no outsider could ever be.

It would have been strange if Philip had not been pleased with himself. Those of his elders whose opinion he valued most did not hide their enormous pleasure in the engagement. Those who were not pleased concealed their disapproval. Adeline chose on this occasion to make a felicitous picture with her fiancé. Wearing a new dress of shot mauve and gold taffeta, with a bouffant skirt, and leaning in Victorian fashion on Philip's arm, she looked happy indeed as they moved among their kin. Possibly the presence of Fitzturgis added something to her smile, made it a little fixed, for she could not forget the passion he once had inspired in her. He and Roma stood side by side in the corner by the china cabinet. Roma, with her cool appraising glance, looked the affianced pair over and remarked, "My, you look elegant. Almost too good to be true."

Philip tried, and failed, to think of something else to say. He could only caress the down on his upper lip and look haughty. Fitzturgis's intent eyes were on the cluster of auburn hair that lay on the whiteness of Adeline's neck. He said, "My congratulations. I hope you will be very happy."

"As happy as we are," added Roma.

The constraint of this meeting was overcome by the addition of Wakefield to the quartet. He was now fully recovered and in good spirits. In fact his spirits were more than good: they were in high hope. His play was to be produced by a repertory theatre in London and he intended to leave for England in the New Year. Twice had he written to Molly, but the first letter he had been ashamed to send, so full of self-pity was it. He had torn it up and later had written to her gently, saying that what she had done, though it had seemed cruel to him at the time, was possibly the right, the noble thing for her to do. Molly's reply had been so friendly, so free from the contrition he was sure she would and should be feeling, that he glared at her letter in anger, then laughed out loud, and hearing that hollow laughter, thought he had never heard laughter better done on the stage. He felt himself able to make the tremendous effort of putting Molly out of his life. Safe and loved in the bosom of his family, he was as a boy again—an experienced and worldly boy, but still a boy.

He was conscious of no embarrassment among the quartet he now joined. At the moment he forgot that Adeline and Fitzturgis ever had been engaged. He forgot all complications connected with the four. His own clear conscience, his bright prospects, were sufficient unto this Christmas Day. His mood was contagious. Chaffing and laughter turned to unrestrained high spirits. Wakefield put his arms about Finch and Christian and declaimed: "Make way for the artists of the family!"

The three, interlocked, executed a polka down the drawing-room. With scornful laughter for the artists, Renny, Piers, and Philip clasped one another, and, in spite of Piers's artificial leg, did a sort of gallop. "Make way for the horsemen of the family!" commanded Piers, who was panting.

Two faces remained unsmiling. One was the face of Patience, who was hurt because her dear Humphrey was not included among the "artists" of the family. The others might forget that Humphrey had had shorts stories in print, had had stories produced on television; never would she forget, and she was hurt for his sake. But Humphrey did not in the least mind. He was swept along by the high spirits of the White-oaks. He could not have told which trio he admired the more. To him they all were fine fellows.

The other unsmiling face was that of Dennis. He watched his prancing elders with an expression of cold aloofness. Yet, all during the day, whenever he found that either Finch or Sylvia was looking in his direction, he gave a little smile, as though dutifully. It chilled his small face throughout the present-giving, when Piers, for the sake of him and Mary and Victoria Bell, appeared in the Santa Claus costume brought down from the attic and smelling a little of mothballs. From the towering resinous-scented tree, Piers handed down presents for everyone, at the same time making jocular and highly personal remarks that, partly because of the champagne at dinner and the liqueur afterward, were considered witty.

Sylvia was tired when all was over, yet the exhilaration of the evening still upheld her. She decided that she would like to walk home. There had been a snowfall. A full moon was searching out the whiteness of the silent land.

"Are you sure the walk won't be too much for you?" asked Finch anxiously.

"Nothing is better for her," said Meg, "than walking—in moderation, of course. Sylvia must have no overexertion."

Sylvia's snow boots were put on, and her new fur coat. She felt excited, well. She, Finch, and Dennis set out. They left their Christmas presents behind, to be called for on Boxing Day. So crisp was the snow beneath their feet it made a cheerful crunching sound. Tiny moonlit particles floated on the dark blue air, there were icy patches on the road and Finch held Sylvia close by the arm lest she should fall, but Dennis ran ahead sliding on the ice. Suddenly he was laughing, full of life.

"Come and slide with me," he shouted.

"Go on—slide with him," urged Sylvia.

Finch objected to leaving her, but she insisted. In a moment father and son were running and sliding wildly together, while Sylvia in her bulk plodded after. Dennis was sparkling with delight. Never had he and Finch so enjoyed themselves together. They forgot everything but their pleasure in running and swooping in long slides over the glitter-ice.

"Don't let's go in," shouted Dennis. "I'd like to stay out all night."

But Sylvia was tired. Once, unseen by them, she had nearly fallen and, in righting herself, had strained her side. She began to long for bed and plodded ever more slowly. She spoils everything, thought Dennis, and a black wish that she would fall and kill herself sped like a hawk through the brightness of his mind.

Now they had left the road and were at their own gate. Carefully Finch supported Sylvia along the snowy path and into the house. It was deliciously warm inside. Finch turned on the lights and she sank, with something like a groan of relief, into a deep chair. Finch, kneeling, took off her snow boots and stockings and chafed her cold feet. Dennis, at a little distance, stood watching them.

"Would you like a hot drink?" Finch asked her.

"Yes, please. I'm ashamed to say it, but I'm rather hungry." How suddenly, thought Finch, Sylvia could look pale and wan. Over his shoulder he said to Dennis:

"If you want to make yourself useful, heat some milk for Sylvia. And bring biscuits."

"Do you know where to find things, Dennis?" called out Sylvia, as the boy went toward the kitchen.

"Oh, yes," he answered cheerfully, but his spirit was heavy with resentment.

He heated some milk, filled a glass and neatly arranged biscuits on a pretty plate. As he carried the tray to her, he was repeating to himself words he had heard on a record of *Under Milk Wood:*

Here's your arsenic, dear. Here's your ground glass.

He was so inwardly amused he scarcely could restrain his laughter. To Sylvia he appeared gently solicitous. When he had gone to his own room she remarked to Finch:

"Don't you think Dennis is developing greatly? He's outgrowing those little-boy clinging ways."

"I'm glad to hear it," said Finch. "I hadn't noticed any difference in him."

"He was sweet when he brought my tray."

"Was he?"

"I do so want to be friends with him."

Dennis, standing in the doorway of his room, strained his ears to hear Finch's reply but could not. He shrank from closing his door, shutting himself away in that room, leaving those two happy people together. His father's long lean figure, Sylvia's bulk, were silhouetted against his closed eyelids as he lay stretched out small and straight in bed.

Two days after the New Year, it was necessary for Finch to go to New York, in connection with the publishing of his sonata. It was to be a flying trip. He would be only two days away. He did not want to leave Sylvia, for even so short a while, but she urged him to go, promising that she would arrange to keep the daily woman overnight. The time of her confinement was not yet imminent. She was surrounded by the houses of relatives. Dennis was at hand. They two, she laughed, trying not to mind that Finch was going away, would look after each other.

"We're a pretty pair, aren't we," she said to Dennis—as they stood at the window, watching the car disappear along the drive—"we're a pretty pair, aren't we—afraid to keep house while your father is away?" She put her arm about him.

Dennis withdrew a little. He asked, "Why do you say we're afraid?"

"I was joking," she said hurriedly. "What I mean is—we're not used to responsibility."

If Finch had left Sylvia, as it were, in his charge, flattering his sense of power, he might have felt differently, but such a thing had not occurred to Finch and, if it had, he would have dismissed it as ridiculous. As it was, Dennis moved from room to room, savoring the thought that, with Finch away, he was master of the house; that there was no one here to control him. All that day he kept longing to come to grips with Sylvia, not only to show her that he could do as he liked but that he would force her to do his will.

Meg and the Rector spent the evening with them. They were a comfortable pair. In their presence Sylvia felt relaxed. She slept well. In the morning she discovered that there had been a heavy snowfall. She was astonished by the great white drifts which she had never seen equaled. Every branch and twig bore its breast-white burden.

"I'll tell you what I shall do," Dennis said at breakfast. "I'll build you a snow man. Ever had a snow man?"

"Never," she said, her eyes on his face, trying to read his thoughts.

He laughed. "Never had a snow man? That's funny. I make one every winter. You can watch through the window."

After breakfast he lounged in Finch's chair in the living-room, his legs stretched out, reading the paper in Finch's very attitude. Then he sat down at the piano and played a little piece, bending his head to listen to the music.

"That's pretty," said Sylvia, when he had finished. "What is it?"

"I don't know." He got up from the piano and went to the window.

"When are you going to build the snow man?" she asked, trying not to feel rebuffed by his curtness.

"When the right time comes."

She paid no further attention to him, and, after a little, he got a sweater from his room and went out. Sylvia peeped through the window and saw him rolling a large snowball across the white expanse of the lawn. He was conscious that he was being watched. He spied her, as the window curtain moved, and called out to her, his voice suddenly friendly and childish:

"Come on out. It's fun."

She was so eager to make the most of this mood of friendliness, to draw near to him, that she fairly flew to put on jacket and scraf. Outside, the air was marvelously light and crisp. A small bird, springing from a branch, sent down a dazzling shower of fine snowflakes.

"Why, it's lovely," cried Sylvia. "It's not at all cold."

"The snow is getting solider," said Dennis. "It's in good condition for a snow man. Want to help me?"

The ball he rolled was growing fast. Together they bent their backs and propelled it, as it accumulated more and more snow. Now the base was complete—now the body of the snow man. Now his head was firmly set on his shoulders. Sylvia and Dennis were positively overheated by the exertion. Her cheeks were scarlet and her eyes bright. She looked with pride on the snow man.

"His nose is good," said Dennis, "but now we need coals for his eyes and a pipe and a hat. You go into the house and get them."

She did not like the authoritative tone he used. He was plainly giving her an order. Yet so happy she was, in this newfound harmony with him, that she could not bear to strike the faintest note of protest. She hastened as well as she could to get what he wanted.

Dennis stood looking after her, his arms folded, his lips compressed. He had a delicious sense of power. He felt capable, as never before, of drastic action, utterly to subdue her, but he did not know what the action might be. He watched her with cool pleasure, as she came plodding back through the snow, with a pipe, an old hat of Finch's, and two coals in her hands. She was panting from the exertion.

"Now," she said, "let's put on the finishing touches, and he'll be quite a handsome fellow."

Dennis inserted the coals, stuck the pipe in the mouth of the snow man, put on the hat at a jaunty angle.

Sylvia clapped her hands.

"Splendid!" she cried, and felt that never before had she known what strength and joy could be born of outdoor exertion in the sunny cold of a northern winter morning. Then there was this new companionship with Dennis. She had dreaded Finch's going away. It had been almost frightening to be left alone in the house with this odd little boy. Yet how well it had turned out! Never before had those two been on such good terms.

She smiled into his face. "Aren't we clever?" she exclaimed.

He returned her look sombrely. "Clever?" he repeated. "I don't see anything very clever about making a snow man."

He pulled off his mittens and stuffed them into his pocket. He began to make snowballs with his bare white hands. He threw them with surprising force against the side of the house. Sylvia was suddenly tired. "I think I shall go in," she said.

"No, don't go," said Dennis. "Let's make another snow man. This man needs a son. Let's make him."

Full of energy he began rolling another snowball. Quickly it gathered more snow, grew in size.

"Come on and help," shouted Dennis, and, as though hypnotized, she bent her back over the increasing snowball and pushed and pushed.

"Come on—come on," he would shout, as though encouraging a team of horses.

But suddenly she could do no more. "I'm going in," she said, and with difficulty straightened her aching back.

"If you're going in," Dennis said casually, "you'll not need your scarf. You might leave it for the snow man." He began to draw it from her and, when she gladly relinquished it, he wound it about the snow man's neck and meticulously tied it.

Inside Sylvia lay down on her bed. The "daily" brought her lunch to her on a tray. She kept repeating to herself, "Tomorrow morning Finch will come home." In the afternoon she slept. Dennis had gone off by himself. The house was quiet, except for the cautious movements of the "daily." "You're looking poorly," said the woman. "Don't you think you should call in the doctor? You really do look bad."

"No, no. I'm feeling much better. I shall be all right."

She rose, and she and Dennis sat down to the evening meal that had been prepared for them. She could scarcely see him across the table, she was so weary.

"I'm sorry to be such a dull companion," she said, "but I'm a little tired."

"Why?" he asked, his cool greenish eyes on her face. With the same cool ruthless gaze he watched her heavy movements as she went to the kitchen to make the coffee. The "daily" had gone because of illness in her own family. Dennis sprang up to carry in the tray for her. She felt ready to drop, to sink to the floor in the misery that now almost overwhelmed her. But the coffee revived her. She chatted quite naturally with

Dennis, recalling happenings in Ireland that she thought might amuse him. She longed desperately to go to her bed—yet there was the boy, looking at her brightly, waiting to be amused.

His bright cruel eyes followed her with disgust and hate as she moved to the window.

"The snow man looks lovely in the light from the window," she said.

Dennis did not answer. She turned to look at him and was surprised by the pale contortion on his lips.

"What's the matter?" she asked.

"Nothing." He tried to smile.

She turned again to the window. To-morrow Finch will be here, she was telling herself. To-morrow—to-morrow.

"The snow man looks lovely," she repeated, and tried to forget that odd look in the boy's face.

Presently a terrible pain struck her like a blow.

She cried out in her shock and surprise. Then she said, speaking hurriedly—"Dennis—the doctor—telephone him to come," she said, repeating the doctor's number. She could not control her voice. The pain increased.

The telephone was in the hall. Dennis went out to it. He could not bring himself to dial the doctor's number. He wanted to be alone with Sylvia—to savor his power over her. He looked into the music-room and saw her moving heavily to her bedroom, her face ugly with pain. His hatred for her, his repulsion for her condition, surged through him, loosed in a morbid tide.

"Did you phone the doctor?" she asked.

"No." He looked steadily at her.

"Why? Why?" Her voice broke into a scream.

"I forgot the number."

She repeated it to him loudly. "Tell him to hurry—my baby is coming!" She laid herself on her bed, doubled up in her agony.

An extraordinary sense of power possessed Dennis. His small body was fairly shaken by this sense of power. He strode up and down the music-room, listening to her groans, but he would not telephone the doctor.

Presently she began to scream and continued to scream. He ran out of the house, leaving the front door open behind him. With his bare hands he made snowballs and hurled them with all his might at the snow man. Sometimes they stuck to the snow man, became a part of him. One of them flew past him and stuck the window of the music-room, leaving a blob of whiteness on the glass. Dennis aimed snowballs—and harder ones—at the window, hoping it would break, feeling great power within himself.

He longed for violence. After a little, he went to the open door and stood listening to the shuddering cries within. Then he ran, fairly flying, over the snow and among the tall black trees to the edge of the ravine. There was the stream, frozen but not frozen hard. He tore helter-skelter down the steep and on to the snow-covered slushy ice. He would like, so he thought, to run along the stream to the bridge and so to Jalna. But the ice was slushy and began to give way; so he scrambled back to land and climbed the steep. He was panting and his heart beating fast.

He returned to the house. All was silence.

Trembling with fear and that strange guilty power, he went to the door of Sylvia's room and looked in.

"Feeling better?" he asked.

Rolling her bloodshot bulging eyes toward him, she said thickly:

"A little. Is the doctor coming soon?"

"He says he can't come."

"But why—why?" She raised herself on her elbow and glared at him.

"He says he's tired."

"He must be mad." She rolled out of bed and onto her feet and somehow reached the telephone. But she had forgotten the doctor's telephone number.

"Tell me his number," she asked, in a strange harsh voice.

Dennis could only remember the number of the veterinarian. She dialed it and he heard her say, "It's Mrs. Finch Whiteoak speaking. Come quickly—for God's sake. . . ." She collapsed in pain over the telephone. Later she somewhat recovered herself and said:

"Dennis, are you sure you gave me the right number?"

"No," he said, "I'm not sure."

"The voice didn't sound right," she said, "but he promised to come."

She went back to her bed. Her movements were heavy, lunging. Dennis watched her with repulsion. Then he turned swiftly and strode outdoors. His very smallness and grace made his movements more striking. He walked up and down in front of the house.

Sylvia called out to him: "Shut the door! Oh, it's so

cold—I'm freezing—I'm freezing!" Her voice faltered against her chattering teeth.

In a sudden fury of antagonism Dennis shouted: "If you want the door shut—do it yourself!"

He strutted back and forth in front of the house, with each turn becoming more violent. He felt ready to burst with the wickedness let loose in him. He strutted, holding himself very straight, eying the house whence came those animal noises of suffering.

Now he ran to the open door and shouted: "Go ahead! Have your monster! That's what it is going to be, you know—a monster—a monster. My father doesn't want it—I don't want it—it's yours."

Out again he ran, in the black shadows of trees, into the glittering white of moonlight. Now he was out on the road—running and shouting. He ran past the church, with its peaceful graveyard. He did not know where he was going. He began to be very tired and turned again home. He must have been running a long while, he thought, for the moon was losing itself in the branches of the pines.

By the time he reached the cold, lighted house with the snow man on guard, he was moving slowly, timidly. All his fire was burnt out. He passed through the hall. There was icy silence like a frozen garment. Fearfully he looked into Sylvia's room.

What he saw made him turn and run out of the house. Outside he stood stock-still, trembling with fear. Where could he find help? Where—oh, where?

He became aware of the sound of an approaching car. He stood waiting while it raced along the drive and stopped with a jerk at the door. Out of it alighted the veterinarian, a burly kindly man. Against this man's bulk Dennis flung himself. He gripped the lusty figure in his small arms and burst into tears.

"Save me," he sobbed. "Save me!"

Twenty-Two

Winter

The light in the drawing-room was a grayish reflection of the snow-laden sky. Alayne had had a fire laid, but it still was no more than tentative little flames licking at the kindling. The faces of the three who were in the room, standing about the fire, were of a grayish tint also. Meg's iron-gray hair and Alayne's, of a silvery white, gave a touching feminine dignity to their pallor. The fading of Piers's ruddy color was to make him appear less robust, older, but not more dignified. In truth, his expression was one of rather boyish incredulity, as though he were saying to himself, What happened last night was impossible. He had been in bed when Renny had telephoned him, but had dressed and come at once to Jalna.

The three were almost silent, but cast anxious looks across the hall to the door of the library.

Presently it opened and Renny Whiteoak emerged.

As he joined them Piers said: "Well, how did he take the news?"

"Like a man. I can tell you I'm proud of him. I had expected a breakdown. You know what his nerves are. But he controlled himself marvelously well. I think he's dazed by the shock."

"Poor boy," said Meg. "My heart aches for him."

"It's a strange thing," observed Piers, "that Finch is the only one of us fellows to be widowed, and he has been twice widowed."

"It is not so strange, Piers," said Meg, looking full at him, "as your use of the English language. It is impossible for a man to be widowed."

"It is grammatically correct," said Piers.

"Neither is it accurate," Meg went on, "to speak of a man as a widower when his divorced wife dies, as Finch's first wife. I am sure Alayne did not look on herself as a widow when her divorced husband, our dear Eden, died, especially as she was already married again." Meg turned her full blue gaze somewhat accusingly on Alayne, who received the look in rigid silence.

Renny appeared not to hear this interchange. He said, "I think I had better bring him in here by the fire."

"Good idea," said Piers, and put on another log.

"And he should have a nice cup of tea, poor dear," said Meg. "He is probably hungry, and would enjoy a little buttered toast with his tea."

"Coffee would be more stimulating," said Alayne, "if he can take anything, which I doubt."

"When I met him at the airport," said Renny, "I took his suitcase from him and led him to my car. I said nothing, but there was something in the way I met him that made him suspicious. He gave me a fearful look and asked if everything was all right at home. I drove a little distance; then I stopped the car and told him. I told him straight. I thought it best."

"Lord, I'm glad I hadn't to do that," said Piers.

"What did he say?" asked Meg.

Alayne turned away and went to the window and looked out on the snow-muffled scene.

"At first," said Renny, "he seemed unable to take it in. He just stared and went very pale. Then I told him how the doctor arrived before the end but too late to help her. So she didn't die alone, poor girl."

Alayne moved from the window to the fireplace, and pressed her forehead to the mantelshelf.

"Did he speak then?" asked Piers.

"Yes. He said—over and over: 'Sylvia—my wife—dead . . . I should not have left her.' Then I told him he must come straight to Jalna—that everything was being attended to properly at his house. I had no trouble with him, as I said; he seemed dazed, and hasn't spoken since. I think it would do him good to come in by the fire."

"Will you order tea, Alayne?" asked Meg.

"I gave him a good stiff whiskey-and-soda as soon as I got him into the house," said Renny. He crossed the hall toward the library.

"He isn't able to take much in the way of spirits, you know," said Piers. He took a turn about the room, pausing to look into the cabinet of ivory curios from India, as though it were new to him. Indeed everything appeared strange and new to him on this grim morning. Now he said:

"What I can't understand is why Finch went off to New York leaving Sylvia alone, except for a young boy."

Alayne sprang to Finch's defence. "The daily woman had promised Finch to stay the night, but something went wrong at her home and she couldn't—or said she couldn't."

Piers persisted, "In that case why didn't Sylvia ask Pheasant or Meg or you to come?"

"That I do not know, but I think Sylvia felt quite secure for the one night. She was not expecting her baby for some weeks, you know."

"It was very foolish of her," said Piers. "Has anybody questioned Dennis as to just what happened?"

Meg spoke up, with tears in her voice. "The poor child is bewildered by it all. He looks really ill. Such an experience is very bad for him. Rupert says he should be allowed to forget it, if he can."

"But when he saw that Sylvia was ill, why didn't he telephone to someone in the family to come?"

"All this probing is in very bad taste, Piers," said Meg. "We are here to comfort Finch. This is a house of mourning." Alayne left the room for coffee as Renny returned with Finch.

Piers had drawn their grandmother's wing chair close to the fire that now brightly blazed. Finch went toward it, but before he reached it, Meg's maternal figure interposed. With outstretched arms she gathered him to her bosom and held him. Tears ran down her pale cheeks.

For a space, during which the only sound was the ticking of the clock on the mantelshelf, Finch submitted, then almost roughly disengaged himself. Piers came to him and held out his hand. In silence they gripped hands. Piers said, "It's hard for you. She was a lovely girl. I admired her greatly. Anything that Pheasant and I can do—you know."

"Thanks," muttered Finch. He sat down in the wing chair and held out his hands to the blaze. Against the pallor of his face his blue-gray eyes looked very large, tragic, but with no questioning in them—just silent acceptance of Sylvia's fate, of his family's ministering to him.

Alayne now came into the room, followed by Wragge, who carried a tray bearing a coffeepot and cups. He arranged the tray beside Finch, then said, in a discreetly low voice:

"May I beg to offer deepest sympathy from myself and my missus, sir."

"Thank you, Rags," said Finch—then added: "You did speak, didn't you?"

"Yes, indeed, sir. I was offering you most heartfelt sympathy."

"Ah, yes," Finch said vaguely. "It's very kind of you."

"Shouldn't you rather have had tea, Finch dear?" Meg asked, coming to him and stroking his hair.

"This will do nicely, thank you."

With a steady hand he raised the cup to his lips and swallowed a mouthful of the scalding liquid. It burnt him, and his eyes watered from the pain.

"It's not a matter," said Meg, "of making-do. It's the question of which drink will give you the greater comfort."

"Now that he has coffee," put in Piers, "let him drink it in peace."

"Really, Piers," said Meg, "the things you say are shocking. Surely if anyone can bring peace to Finch in this sorrow, it is his only sister." She continued to stroke his head. Gently he put up his hand, took hers away from his head and gently returned it to her.

She remained standing beside him and said, "One blessing you have in your loss, dear, is Sylvia's child that is left to you."

He stared up at Meg, not comprehending.

"Sylvia's child," she repeated. "Her baby."

"Don't!" Finch shouted hoarsely. He put out his hand as though to ward off a blow.

It was at this moment that Dennis came into the room. He moved slowly, shyly, his child's face bearing no imprint of what he had been through. He stood irresolute, looking from one to another of the grownups. He then moved beside Renny who put an arm about him. Finch did not appear to notice him.

Meg said, brokenly through her tears, "You have two sons now, Finch. Two dear children to live and plan for."

"Keep them out of my sight," said Finch.

Alayne came and took Dennis by the hand and led him from the room. He went with her, as though blindly, but, when they were in the library and he saw the television set, he went to it and turned it on, though softly. Alayne was surprised and rather shocked to see him do this, but thought: After all, he's only a child, and, if he can occupy his mind with this, so much the better.

"What was it my father said?" Dennis asked.

"He did not mean it," Alayne hastened to say.

Music was coming through the television set. The musicians were shown on the screen.

"That's the sort of thing," Dennis said, "that my father detests. We must keep it out of his sight."

So the child had heard, thought Alayne. And how deeply had he been wounded? There had been something odd in the way he had repeated, in his clear voice, Finch's very words.

"I think we had better turn it off," she said.

"You mean because there's somebody dead?" he asked.

She hastened to say, "No, no, but you might find music that would—" She hesitated, then finished calmly—"That would better suit our mood—our feelings."

"You mean funeral music?" he asked, almost brightly.

"I think your father would not like that."

"He can't hear it, if it is low," Dennis said argumentatively.

"Very well." Alayne turned toward the door.

"Auntie Alayne—" Before he spoke he had turned off the music.

"Yes, Dennis."

"Do you think my father will be fond of that baby? When he feels better, I mean."

"Of course, he will."

"Where is it?"

"It's at home. Pheasant is there looking after it."

"I hope they will keep it out of my sight." Dennis gave her a swift and penetrating glance, as though to observe the effect of these words on her.

As Alayne was considering what to say to the boy, Wakefield and Adeline came into the room, he looking overwrought, Adeline's eyes reddened and swollen from weeping.

Alayne's lips formed the words, "Be careful," and she glanced at Dennis. Wakefield, however, broke out:

"It's the cruelest thing that's ever happened to us."

"Has Uncle Finch come?" Adeline asked.

"Yes," said Alayne. "And for his sake, control yourselves. He's having coffee in the drawing-room."

Again Wakefield broke out, "He should never have left Sylvia—alone—at this time."

"She wasn't alone," Adeline said. "Dennis was there." She put an arm round the boy, in a comforting gesture.

He trembled and said, in an unsteady voice, "It was my fault."

"*Your* fault? What do you mean?" demanded Wakefield.

"I couldn't remember the doctor's number." He looked wanly unhappy.

"It's been a terrible experience for him," said Alayne. "We'll talk of it no more, please—not in front of him."

"I suppose," said Adeline, "I should go in to see Uncle Finch. But I dread meeting him."

"I'll go with you," said Dennis. "I want to see him."

"I think you had better stay here with me," Alayne objected, but only halfheartedly, for she felt something overriding in the boy that baffled her. Boys! Strange beings. And what an odd boy her own son Archer was. She had a sudden rush of gratitude for Adeline's frankness and warmth. She took the girl's hand in hers and pressed it.

"Don't go to Finch," she said, "not now. Wait will you get over the first shock."

"Better have it over with," said Wakefield. "We'll go together." He led Adeline and Dennis to the drawing-room.

"Everything is being attended to at your place," Renny was saying to Finch. "You had better stay here at Jalna."

"No, no," Finch said loudly, "I must go to her. To Sylvia." He got heavily to his feet.

Adeline, with a great effort, controlled her lips and spoke to him, but she could not control the tears that ran down her cheeks.

"Don't cry, dear," Finch said, comforting her.

Piers was saying in the low voice to Renny, "Do you think we should let him go?"

"Yes. Nothing else will satisfy him. But you must go with him. I couldn't possibly—not into that house." The eldest Whiteoak, after fighting in two wars, had an invincible abhorrence for the presence of death.

"Very well," said Piers. "I'll take him." Dennis was timidly touching Finch's sleeve. "May I come too?" he asked.

Finch, with his wide-open, dazed eyes, looked down at him. "I don't want you about," he said.

Meg hastened to add, "Dennis dear, what your daddy means is—not now. He'll very much want you later."

Finch turned to Meg. "Does Fitzturgis know?" he asked. "He was leaving to-day, wasn't he?"

"Yes. He and Roma were getting ready when the news came. It's terrible for him. He and his sister were so close."

"Were they?" said Finch, as though not comprehending.

"Better have another cup of coffee before we go out into the cold," said Piers.

"Tea would have done him more good," said Meg. "No drink is so comforting."

"I'll take the coffee, as it's here," said Finch.

He drank more coffee; then Renny helped him into his coat, as though he were an invalid.

The house was full of the resinous scent of pine and balsam which wreathed the banister and decorated doorways and pictures. The Christmas tree still towered in the library. Finch passed these evidences of the holiday season without appearing to see them, but outside he stopped to turn his tragic eyes on the pigeons that had come down from the chimney-warmed roof to peck at the grain Adeline had scattered on the drive.

A grimace of pain twisted Finch's lips, as he got out the words, "Sylvia loved birds."

"I know, old man," said Piers, and waited patiently while Finch stared, in lost bewilderment, at the pigeons whose coral-colored feet made attenuated imprints on the soft snow.

While the two brothers were on their way by car along the road, the small figure of Dennis might have been seen running through the ravine, climbing the steep path that led to Vaughanlands. Reaching the grounds, it stopped stock-still, as though in wonder to find the house still standing, to find all looking as it had yesterday.

Dennis was panting from the exertion of the climb, the running through deep snow, when he faced the snow man—stout, jolly, pipe in mouth, rakish hat, neatly tied scarf, coal-black eyes—and it was but a few moments before the car, driven by Piers, turned into the drive. Dennis darted behind the snow man and hid there. He must not let his father see him or he would be angry. "Keep them out of my sight," he had said—meaning his children. . . . "Keep them out of my sight."

The brothers got out of the car and entered the house by the front door. The curtains were drawn. Dennis had seen his father's profile turned, had made sure that Finch had not discovered the snow man. And never, never should he see the snow man, who had been the instrument of the evil that had befallen them. The snow man must be obliterated.

Denis walked about the snow man, moving with that pleasing sensation of power which made him feel capable of mastering all opposition. He walked lightly, almost jauntily, conscious of his power. He saw the gay plaid scarf that he had taken from Sylvia and tied round the snow man's neck.

Now, with an imperative gesture, he whipped off the scarf and then wound it tightly about the bulging neck. He pulled fiercely on the ends of the scarf.

"You're being throttled," he said to the snow man. "This is a garrotte. You're being garrotted. Do you understand? Well—I'll make you understand, you monster. That's what you are—a monster!" In an excess of fury he put all his strength into this act of retribution, for the snow man had become to him the symbol of his own obloquy.

"Why don't you turn purple in the face?" he growled. "Why don't your eyes start out of your silly head?"

Down fell the snow man's pipe, out fell his coal-black eyes. Next his hat was tumbled in the snow. "Monster—monster," growled Dennis. "Now you're getting what's coming to you."

The head fell off and Dennis kicked it up and down the snowy lawn till there was nothing recognizable left of it.

He would have attacked the body also, but it had hardened. He needed something more than his hand for its destruction. He remembered where the snow shovel stood, by the back door, and ran round the house to get it. He was startled to find a small black motor van outside the back door. A young man in dark clothes was in the driver's seat. Dennis went up to him and asked:

"Do you want to see somebody?"

"No," answered the young man, "I'm just waiting for the technicians who are in the house. We're from the Smith and Smythe Funeral Home."

Dennis stood dumfounded. This was his first experience of the trappings of death. He stared at the house, silent, though a tumult of thoughts thronged his mind. He made a movement toward the house. The man said, "You'd better not go in there, little boy, unless you're one of the family."

"I am one of the family," said Dennis. "How old do you think I am?"

The man looked him over, "About eleven, I guess."

"Well, you guess wrong," Dennis said. "I'm older—a good deal. I could go in if I wanted to, but what I want is this snow shovel."

"O.K.," said the man, as if shovel and house both belonged to him. He spoke with authority.

Dennis put the snow shovel over his shoulder, and, holding himself very straight, marched round to the front of the house. A sound of music was in his head, as though he marched to the distant playing of a band. Large, soft snow-flakes were beginning to fall.

He no longer felt rage, nor even resentment toward the snow man. Methodically he set to work to break him up, to beat the white blobs of his remains to softness, to spread the remains over the lawn. He threw the coal-black eyes into the shrubbery. He put the pipe into his pocket, and carefully folded the scarf. With it and the hat in his hands he returned to the back door. The undertaker's van was still standing there, but the young man had disappeared. The daily woman came out of the house, her eyes reddened by weeping. She looked very surprised to see Dennis.

"Why, you poor little soul," she exclaimed, "what are you doing here? Your uncle told me you was at Jalna."

Dennis handed her the hat. "This is an old hat of my father's," he said. She took it with a doubtful look, then spied the scarf. "I've seen the poor lady wear that," she said, and her reddened eyes filled with tears.

"Take it, too," said Dennis. He was glad to be rid of it. The sight of it made him tremble with a terrible sense of guilt. He put the pipe also into her hand.

"Are you hungry?" she asked, wanting to do something for the child. "Will you come into the kitchen and let me fix you something to eat?"

"No, thanks," said Dennis, drawing back. He wanted to ask what was going on inside that austerely curtained house that seemed no longer home, but only one question could his lips form. "Where is the baby?" he asked.

"Poor little mite," said the woman. "It's safe and sound with Mrs. Bell. She took it to her house this morning. Poor little mite."

The words resounded in the boy's ears. He said them over and over to himself on his way to the Fox Farm. Strangely, he was too tired to run. His legs were weak. He could not run and yet he must keep moving. Combined with extreme weariness was an inward something that drove him on. He would have liked to retreat to the safety of home, but he felt that he had no home. He pictured himself as homeless, alone in his guilt, wandering in a snowy world.

The mysterious snow-weighted trees reared their cloaked boughs about the small house. One might think nobody lived there, so silent it was, and no path made in the deep snow. Dennis went to the door and lifted the iron latch. He stepped inside where it was warm and there was the smell of soap and hot water—yes, and milk.

He stood there in the narrow passage, his sense of smell and hearing intent. From upstairs there came the faint sound of a typewriter; from the kitchen the sudden loud cry of an infant. He heard Patience moving about in bedroom slippers, speaking in a reassuring voice to her child. Then the crying ceased and he pictured Victoria Bell guzzling at her mother's breast. He went softly to the door of the kitchen and looked in.

Patience was gently rocking, in an old-fashioned rocking chair, the downy-haired blissful child in her arms. She was not startled by the sudden appearance of Dennis, but gave him a welcoming look and held out her hand, almost as though she had expected him.

He looked at her gravely and asked, "Where is the other baby?"

"On the couch in the living-room. Want to go and see it? It's just been fed. This bottle business is new to me and I was nervous, but I think it's all right."

Dennis bent over the crimson-faced mouthing infant, new-born, scarcely recovered from its terror of suffocation.

"He's all right," said Patience, "even though he does look miserable. It'll be nice for you to have a little brother."

"We must keep him out of my father's sight," said Dennis. "Both of us must keep out of his sight. He doesn't want to see his children about."

Twenty-Three

Aftermath

When Adeline went to Finch's house that same evening, she found Fitzturgis standing before the door trying to make up his mind to enter. Any embarrassment he had felt on their meeting at Christmas had now given place to a reaching out to the warmth, the almost painful compassion of her presence. She, too, remembered at this moment nothing of their past love, except that it was a common ground for their present sorrow. The hush of a heavy snowfall enfolded them. He said, in a low voice, without preliminary:

"You have been here before, I suppose."

"No. I had not the courage to come. Not till now."

"Neither had I." He looked at her questioningly and added, "This has happened, I suppose? I'm not dreaming?"

"It's happened," she said sombrely, and held out her hand to him. So, holding to each other's hands, they entered the cool, flower-scented house.

They could hear low voices from the back of the house but the music-room was silent and lighted only by candles. That was where Sylvia lay, surrounded by pale flowers.

In silence they stood looking down at her, then Adeline said, "How beautiful she is! I've never seen anyone so beautiful."

Fitzturgis did not speak but bent and kissed the marble-white forehead, on which the fair curls lay. He drew back from that cold touch and suddenly and utterly lost command of himself. He broke into wild sobs that shook him.

"No—no," Adeline said, in fear as much as in pity. "Mait—you must not."

"My sister—oh, my sister," sobbed Fitzturgis and, giving himself up to his grief, sank on his knees beside the coffin.

On an impulse that she could not and did not even try to restrain, Adeline flung herself to the floor beside him, put both arms about him and mingled her weeping with his harsh sobs.

Meg and Finch came in from the adjoining room.

Finch's tragic eyes accepted this abandon of grief as though nothing were too extreme to be fitting to the occasion—not even to the tearing of hair and the rending of garments. There was something almost noble in the kneeling figure of Fitzturgis—and his reiterated: "My sister . . . my sister."

Finch did not speak, but Meg laid a hand on the head of each of the kneeling figures. "Come—come," she said soothingly yet reprovingly, "we must try to resign ourselves to God's will."

Fitzturgis, with difficulty it seemed, got to his feet. He made as though to reply to Meg, but could only turn away his face and repeat, "My sister . . . my sister . . ." He came then to Sylvia and, laying his hands on the coffin, said, "She won't speak to me. I can't make her hear."

Finch touched Adeline on the shoulder. He said, "You must take Mait out of here. There are people coming. I hear a car. Please take him away."

Adeline rose and took Fitzturgis by the hand. He allowed himself to be led from the room out into the enfolding silence of the snow-bent trees. More snow was falling. For a moment they were in the bright light of a standing car; they heard low voices, then were alone under the trees. In silence they plodded along the quiet road. Now Adeline had the strange, new sensation of being the older of the two, and with this she experienced a new tenderness for Fitzturgis. She said gently:

"I'm not going to talk of my grief, Mait, because I know that yours must be far greater, but I never have had a sister and I loved Sylvia like a dear sister."

"She suffered so much in her life," he said brokenly, "and then this."

"You always were so good to her, Mait."

"No—I wasn't," he denied passionately. "Looking back, I think I was sometimes harsh with her. In Ireland, I mean, when her nerves were in such a bad way. You were there once, I remember." He wheeled, as he said the last words, and, pulling his hand from Adeline's, he began to retrace his steps.

"Where are you going?" she demanded, in sudden fear.

"Back to Sylvia," he said. "I must see her again."

But Adeline caught his arm and held him fast. "You can't—not now. You shall see her again to-morrow. Come—let us walk along this road and talk of her."

"Will you come with me to-morrow?"

"Yes, if you will be good and come with me to-night."

She spoke to him as to a deranged child. Standing there in the falling snow, she looked stately as a young queen. She had tied a black veil over her head and beneath it Fitzturgis could dimly see her pale face. He gained control of himself and said docilely:

"Very well—if it will not tire you."

"Nothing tires me," she said, and they plodded on through the snow that lay heavy on the road.

As they walked they talked of Sylvia. Adeline recalled her first meeting with her and of how their attraction for each other had flowered into love. "It was love on my side, anyway," she said, "and I do think Sylvia was fond of me. Did she speak of me as though she were?"

Fitzturgis tried to recall a time when he and Sylvia had talked of Adeline, but he could think only of his present grief for his sister.

"Sylvia had great affection for you," he said briefly, then went on to talk of youthful days in Ireland. As he talked, his nerves grew steadier. Adeline drew him by questions to recall the past. They walked on and on, their hands linked. At last he fell silent for a space. She too was silent, brooding on the monumental consequences of life, trying in her simplicity to understand.

Now he looked about him bewildered; the white fields, the gaunt trees that edged the road looked alien. The snow had ceased to fall and a wan moon moved in and out among the clouds.

"Where are we?" exclaimed Fitzturgis. "Do you know, Adeline?"

"These roads I know like the palm of my hand," she said. "We have walked a long way."

They turned back and again were silent, as though there were nothing left to say; but, as they reached the road that led to the church, he remarked, with sombre resignation:

"I have lost my sister and I have lost you."

"You still have a sister," she said, "and you have a wife."

"My older sister," he said, "means little to me, as compared with Sylvia. Any affection I am capable of giving Roma is slight compared to the love I gave you. Oh, we get along very nicely, but—somtimes I wonder how we came to marry. I suspect that Roma wanted a husband and I more or less filled the bill."

Adeline drew the width of the road, away from him. "You mustn't say that—it's wrong."

She gave him a look, almost of appeal, as though she doubted her own strength to deny what he, in this moment, might say.

Fitzturgis, however, went on: "And you can't make me believe that you are able to give that handsome boy, Philip, the love you once gave me. Oh, I know I'm nothing to you now, but I stick to it that we've lost something terribly valuable, and that we shall never find its like again. Do I flatter myself?" He tried to see her face but could not. He went on to say, "I'll wager you never give me a thought."

"I do think of you. I'm not one to forget. But—it's all over between us—I can't talk about it." She spoke with a sudden weary finality, as if she had borne all of stress and strain that she was able to bear.

"You are right," he said. "After all, we are no more than these snowflakes that are falling."

"It's stopped snowing," Adeline said, in a practical voice. They did not speak again till their brief, almost abrupt goodbye, when they reached Jalna and he left her to walk back to the Rectory.

"It must be very late," he said.

"I have no idea of the time." But, as she opened the door, they heard the clock strike two.

"It's two o'clock," she said over her shoulder. "Are you sure you know the way to Auntie Meg's?"

"Quite sure. Good night." He turned away and was gone.

As Adeline was about to close the door she saw a small figure standing close against the wall in the porch. It was Dennis.

"Hello," he said, coming into the light. "I guess I've frightened you."

"You ought to be in bed," she said, taking him by the arm and leading him indoors. "Why aren't you?"

"I don't know where to go."

"Not know where to go?" she repeated. "Where did you spend last night?"

"I don't remember," he replied, in his clear boy's treble. "I don't remember last night."

She heaved a sigh, as though his coming were indeed the last straw. "Very well," she said, "we'll go upstairs and find a bed for you. Come along. Keep your voice down."

But he clasped the newelpost and hung there. He raised his

eyes pleadingly to hers. "I'm afraid to be alone in there, Adeline. Please let me stay here with you."

"There's no bed for you."

"I'll sleep with you," he pleaded. "Please let me sleep with you." His lips quivered.

There was something in his face, in his voice, on the verge of tears, that made her agree to this added burden on this night of sadness. She gave a groan of sudden weariness as she went down the hall to her bedroom behind the stairs. She turned on the light and took warm pyjamas from a drawer.

"These will be miles too big," she said, "but, if you're as tired as I am, you'll not mind. You may go up to the bathroom first. You must be quiet. Then I'll take my turn."

Dennis agreed with almost passionate docility. Sleeves down to his knuckles, he crept into bed and lay, slim and straight, next to the wall. He put his arm across his eyes either to shield them from the light or to shut himself off from conversation.

"Did you wash?" inquired Adeline, reaching out toward commonplace matters for ease from the tension of the past hours.

"Yes," he said, almost in a whisper.

"You haven't said your prayers. Better get up and say them."

Dennis burst into tears. Beneath the bedclothes his legs kicked as though in agony.

"Don't ask me to pray," he sobbed. "I can't—I can't."

"All right," Adeline said hastily. "I'll say them for both of us."

She brushed the burnished chestnut of her hair and, going inside the clothes cupboard, took off her clothes and put on a nightdress. She turned out the light and knelt down beside the bed. She tried to say her prayers, but suddenly she was unutterably tired and could not remember a word. Kneeling there she fell asleep. She had opened the window and the frosty air blew in on her. Yet she slept, and was waked only when the boy's timid hand touched her.

"Hadn't you better get into bed, Adeline?" he said.

She grunted. Where was she? Had she been asleep? Was all that had passed a terrible dream?

"Hadn't you better come to bed?" Dennis repeated.

She opened her dark eyes on the darkness and crept into bed. She put an arm about Dennis and patted his back. She did not speak, but the consolation of her nearness drew him to turn over and press his face against her breast. Again he began to cry.

Now she was all awake.

"Stop it," she said sternly. "You can't go on like this. I tell you I've borne enough."

Now he was speaking, and she made out the words.

"I killed her. . . . I didn't mean to, but I killed her. . . ."

"Killed whom?"

"Sylvia. I made her help me with the snow man. I had her alone and I hated her but I didn't mean she should die. Oh, Adeline, I didn't phone for the doctor, but the vet!"

"That's all nonsense," said Adeline. "You had nothing to do with it. Sylvia would have died anyway. The doctor says so. A boy like you shouldn't be mixed up in such things, but I'll tell you this. Women aren't all alike. For some it's dangerous to give birth. Sylvia was one of those."

"I taunted her," he said. "I killed her."

He continued in his morbid self-accusations and questioning, which she quieted as best she could, till at last he fell asleep, holding fast to her, as though in her soundness he would hide himself.

She lay thinking. The scene with Fitzturgis, the strange, confused confession of the sleeping child, mingled in her mind like dark birds seeking rest. The death of Sylvia, the marriage of Roma and Fitzturgis, filled her with shrinking from the experience of marriage, of childbirth. The touch of a man's hand laid on her, even in tenderest love, was more, she thought, than she could endure. She put the thought of Philip away from her in fear.

Then, as though summoned by her thought of him, she heard Renny's light step in the hall. He opened her door a little and put in his head.

"Adeline, are you awake?"

"Yes, Daddy." Her heart began to beat quickly, in apprehension of she knew not what.

"Have you seen Dennis? I've been telephoning all the family and nobody seems to know."

"He's here. In bed with me. Fast asleep."

"Good Lord." Renny turned on the light and bent over the bed.

Adeline said, "Don't wake him, Daddy. He's been terribly upset—by everything."

"He can't stay here," said Renny. "If he must sleep with someone, it had better be me."

"Oh, Daddy, he'll begin all over again."

"He'll be all right with me. I'll carry him upstairs. He weighs nothing."

Renny drew the boy from beneath the blankets and laid him against his shoulder. Dennis lay inert, like someone rescued from drowning. Adeline, relieved of his presence in the bed, stretched herself and raised her eyes to Renny's face.

"Do you think we shall ever be happy again, Daddy?" she asked.

"Of course, we shall. This is a bad time. It's like a storm at sea. It rocks the ship but doesn't sink it. We'll recover and sail on. I'll carry this youngster up to my room, then come back and tuck you up."

She lay, awaiting his return, with an almost blissful melancholy. Her clothes and the boy's clothes lay on the floor. She shut herself off from the thought of Dennis—from the thought of Finch and of Fitzturgis—and waited only for Renny's return. She asked, when he reappeared:

"Did Dennis wake?"

"Yes, but fell right off again. He seemed dazed. What did he say to you?"

"He babbled in a strange way. I could make no head or tail of what he said—except that he blames himself for—everything. Daddy, what time is it?"

He looked at his watch. "Four o'clock."

"I'm hungry," she said. "If only I had a biscuit I could go to sleep."

"I'll get you something more substantial."

"No, no, just a biscuit."

He went across the hall to the dining-room. From the sideboard he took a biscuit jar, then filled two glasses with sherry and set them on a small silver tray. When he returned to Adeline she was sitting up in bed. She gave him a tremulous smile. He sat on the side of the bed and they ate biscuits and sipped sherry together. He began to talk of his horses, and on that healing subject, and in the power of his presence, Adeline found tranquillity. Scarcely had he tucked her up and left the room when she fell asleep.

Twenty-Four

The Tolling of the Bell

Sylvia's mother was prostrated by the shock of her daughter's death. That sweet-tempered yet rather vague Irish-woman had built high hopes on the coming of the grandchild who would, she was sure, complete the restoration to health which a happy marriage had begun. The older sister of Fitzturgis remained in New York to nurse their mother, but his American brother-in-law came up to Canada for the funeral.

The New Year was on the way and for it the weather had turned brilliantly but bitterly cold. A gusty wind, straight from the Arctic, blew the fine snow in bright clouds across the crusted surface of the deep snow in the graveyard. The snow lay so deep on the graves that they were almost hidden beneath it and showed only as gentle undulations in the sea of snow. The gravestones looked less than impressive, as any slant from the upright was made the more noticeable by the meticulous austerity of the surroundings. If the gravestones were of white marble they were inclined to look dingy against the immaculate whiteness. The graves of the family were, however, marked by a granite plinth which, unaffected by weather, stood up with sombre dignity to point out to the passerby where the Whiteoaks lay in their last rest.

Inside the church it was fairly warm, though with each opening of the door the outer cold rushed into the vestibule. The church was not warm with its accustomed Sunday warmth but with the sudden warmth of an unexpected week-day service. It was filled with people, in spite of the fact that it was the holiday season, the very season of the birth of Christ. But, here at the chancel steps, lay the body of a young mother who had died in giving birth to her child. Although Sylvia had lived in the neighborhood but a short while, she had been greatly admired and liked for her shy friendliness, her simple, unpretentious air of a woman of the world. Her sudden death had come as a shock. The hearts of

199

all went out in sympathy to Finch, sitting there among his brothers.

Throughout the service, Finch's eyes, when he was not kneeling, were fixed on the coffin, on the marble profile of Sylvia, as she lay, a lily among the lilies, a pale rose among the roses. Fitzturgis, on the contrary, continually shielded his eyes with his hand.

The Rector was so much moved when reading the service that more than once his voice faltered. Even when he was able to read steadily and with feeling, he found his mind wandering, recalling another burial service, when snow had covered the ground, when another young person from the same family had died—Eden Whiteoak. And there was Eden's little daughter, Roma, a grown woman, and married . . . How the years flew—the scene changed—yet the Church and its services remained the same. Surely something to cling to, in a changing world. He experienced, too, a certain feeling of gratitude toward the Whiteoaks for retaining, more or less, the quality of their forebears who had built and been loyal to this small church. His eyes, moving over the family as they sat in the pews below, rested a moment on the smooth head of Dennis, the youngest present, and he wondered what thoughts were in that little head, what the child would make of all this ritual, this intrusion of death into his young life.

The Rector spoke of Sylvia, of her gentle nature, and how she had endeared herself to all who knew her. He spoke but shortly, for he could not trust his voice to remain steady, not with the sight of Meg weeping in the pew below, of Finch's stricken eyes fixed on that lovely face in the coffin.

The moment came when the lid was closed, when the pallbearers raised their burden to their shoulders. The bearers—Renny, Piers, Wakefield, Christian, Philip, and Humphrey Bell—were followed down the aisle by Finch and Fitzturgis; close after them, Dennis and Sylvia's American brother-in-law; then the remainder of the family.

Fortunately only the surface of the earth had been frozen. The disfiguring yellow mound of this had been covered by an emerald-green run of artificial grass. The wind was bright with tiny snow particles. It sang its own heedless song to those grouped about the grave. It froze the tears on the cheeks of the women, and lay in waiting to freeze the flowers that were laid on the grave.

Now Mr. Fennel spoke the final words, the wind snatching

them from his mouth; but to those standing by the grave these few were clearly audible: ". . . cometh up, and is cut down, like a flower; . . . fleeth as it were a shadow, and never continueth in one stay. . . ."

At last all the dark figures moved away across the whiteness of the snow and the graveyard was deserted.

Twenty-Five

The Stolen Flowers

An unobserved spectator had watched the ceremony by the grave with keenest interest, yet little understanding or sympathy. It all was so new and strange to her. This was the small Mary Whiteoak who, dressed in a warm blue snow suit, was hidden behind a group of shrubs at the edge of the graveyard. White berries grew sparsely on these shrubs and birds came there to eat them. Just before Mary's arrival, a cardinal had tilted there, like an exotic blossom on this northern shrub, but her coming had frightened him away, and he was now hidden in the twilight of a massive spruce tree. From there, as the funeral cortège moved from the graveyard, he gave a joyous whistle, as though boldly to give voice to the life that was in him.

Now Mary emerged from her hiding place and cautiously drew near the new grave. Yet it was not the grave she wished to examine but the flowers laid by it. These delicate flowers, blooming in the wintry cold, were fascinating to her and she had a great longing to possess even a very few, to smell their perfume in that arctic air.

This longing was irresistible. Indeed, she did not try to resist but with nervous care chose and plucked two white roses, a golden lily, three freesias and a carnation. These she hastened with—taking care not to fall—away from the graveyard. She kept her eyes on them as she ran across the snowy field and the bare woodland, where there was a path, to the Hut.

It was not easy to open the door, which squeaked in protest, but she laid all her strength against it and it opened. Sheltered from the wind, it felt comparatively warm in the Hut, and so welcoming, and so truly her own, that her lips parted in a smile of pleasure to find herself there.

She well knew how to melt snow in a saucepan to make water for the flowers to stand in. This accomplished, she filled a vase and arranged the two roses, the lily, the three freesias and the carnation in it. She set it on the table in the middle of the room and gazed in rapture. She wished that Sylvia might be there to admire with her. But Sylvia, she knew, was in heaven, flying with beautiful wings, above green pastures and still waters, as in the Twenty-third Psalm. She was not to be pitied, yet Mary could not help pitying her a little for not being there to admire the flowers from her own funeral.

Mary had been given a real little wrist watch on Christmas, to make her more conscious of the passing of time. She viewed it with mingled pride and apprehension, for she was not at all sure that she was able to tell the time.

Now she examined its face slowly, trying to make sure whether it said twenty-five minutes to five or twenty-five minutes past seven. She turned her wrist this way and that, peering at the enigmatic face of the watch, but she could not discover. Then she heard the barking of dogs and a man's whistling. She peeped out of the window and saw her uncle Renny taking his dogs for a walk.

Suddenly the Hut seemed rather chill and lonely. A saffron cast from a saffron sky made the room strange. Mary thought she would like to join Renny and his dogs. Slipping through the door, she ran after them and put her small bare hand into his. He did not seem surprised to see her, but, gripping her hand, strode on. She noticed, then, that he was all in black, which seemed odd.

After they had walked a short distance, he remarked:

"You should learn not to drag your heels over the crusty surface of the snow. It will wear holes in your snow boots, and they cost money."

Twenty-Six

In Search of a Home

Two days later the women of the family were gathered at the tea hour, in the cozy warmth of the drawing-room at Jalna. But, though the room was cozy and warm, those concerned in this meeting were experiencing emotions which had neither of these qualities. They were, in fact, trying to settle on at least a temporary home for the infant left behind by Sylvia.

One thing Alayne felt she must make clear. It was that there was no place at Jalna for a crying baby. As she was explaining this, she was interrupted by her daughter. "But, Mummie," said Adeline, "I shouldn't in the least mind looking after him. No more than another puppy or a foal."

"You have no faintest idea of what such an undertaking entails," said Alayne. "But you do know that I have been suffering for some time with insomnia." She lowered her voice, showing how well she knew that such a disability was not worth discussing with the young. "There are nights when I have not closed my eyes before three o'clock."

"But this house is so large," said Meg. "The baby and his nurse could sleep in the attic."

"It's chilly up there." Alayne now spoke quite emphatically. "Also, quite soon I expect Maurice and Patrick Crawshay to return. I cannot heap too much work on Wragge and the cook. They are no longer young and often have too much to do." She now turned to Roma. "It seems to me," she said, "that, as Sylvia's sister has been married for some years and has no children, she and her husband are the natural ones to take the child into their home. Also her mother is there to help."

"They live in an apartment," said Roma. "They have no facilities."

"What about you and Maitland?" persisted Alayne.

"We live in an apartment," returned Roma. "We have no facilities."

"There is nothing I should enjoy more," broke forth Meg.

204

"than to welcome that poor darling little waif into the rectory, but I must think of Rupert. Never, never could he write his sermons with a crying infant in the house."

"I love having the little one with me," said Patience, "but I must think of Humphrey. Two babies in one small house are absolutely fatal to his work. Both of them were crying at three o'clock this morning, and, as though that weren't hard enough for him, I fell halfway downstairs with a saucepan of warm milk!" She held out a skinned elbow as proof.

"What unselfish wives!" exclaimed Alayne, with something approaching a sneer. "I confess I am thinking only of myself and my domestic help at Jalna. It's out of the question."

Pheasant had sat listening in silence to all that was being said. Now she spoke, rather breathlessly but with cheerful resignation. "I seem to be the only one," she said, "who is in a position to look after Sylvia's baby, and I'll gladly do it."

Oh, if only she had not brought Sylvia's name into the discussion! It stabbed the atmosphere like a sword and was followed by a wounded silence. This was broken by Meg. "Certainly Piers does no brain work that will be affected by a baby in the house. Nor have you domestic help to be imposed on, or insomnia to keep you awake, for I noticed that you nodded and almost fell asleep at the last meeting of the Women's Institute."

After these remarks by Meg, the feeling in the room became less strained. Wragge brought in the tea-things. Everyone looked kindly at Pheasant, who, with composure, began to eat a currant bun.

Patience went and sat close to her. She whispered:

"When may I take the baby to you?"

"Any time."

"It's terribly good of you. Do you think Piers will mind?"

"He'll think it's the right thing to do—and he likes babies."

Patience hastened to say: "Oh, so does Humphrey. He's sweet to them. It's just his work. I must guard that. Did I tell you that he's writing a play for television?"

Roma moved to sit near them. "Is it accepted?" she enquired skeptically.

"It's been practically accepted," said Patience proudly. "Of course, nothing is certain."

"There's more truth than fiction in that," said Roma.

"Humphrey," went on Patience, "puts everything he has into his work. He never considers what it is taking out of him."

"Everyone to his taste," said Roma.

Meg was rising to go. "I hope everyone understands," she said, addressing Alayne, "that I long to have the baby with me, and that nothing would prevent me if the Rector were not obliged to have a certain amount of seclusion. As Jalna is a considerably larger house, I should have thought . . ." She added, after a moment's reflection: "Especially as no important mental work is being carried on here—indeed no mental work of any sort—"

"It's impossible," said Alayne, "for me to have a newborn infant and trained nurse here at this time."

"If you haven't the facilities, you haven't," said Roma. "Everybody understands that. What I can't understand is why Uncle Finch cannot keep his two children at home. Why should he get out of his responsibilities?"

"For some reason," said Meg, "Finch appears to feel little affection for either child."

Alayne made a gesture of extreme weariness. "Finch," she said, "has been through an appalling time."

"Haven't we all?" said Roma.

"I must be going," Meg said. "You had better come with me, Roma. You have your packing to do."

"It's been done for days," said Roma, but rose, too, with her air of docility. She came to Adeline and held up her smooth cheek to be kissed. "When next we meet, it will be for your wedding." Her voice was as cool as the firm flesh of her cheek. Adeline had a momentary desire to bite it, but gave it a noncommittal peck. "That's a funny-smelling scent you use," she observed.

"French," said Roma. "Six dollars per quarter ounce."

Alayne went to bed early, hoping, yet scarcely daring to hope, for a good night's sleep at last. To make sure of this she had taken a sleeping pill. Were they losing their efficacy? she wondered. But, no—there was the gentle benign drowsiness stealing over her—beginning at her toes—creeping deliciously upward, along the stretched-out length of her taut body . . .

But there was nothing benign about the sudden opening of her door, the introduction of a stark, russet-colored head into the aperture. Even though Alayne could not see his face, she could picture that ingratiating grin of his, which, for some reason, she liked least of all the expressions that passed over his bony, mobile features—possibly because it appeared when he knew he was not wanted, or when he offered her an opinion best kept to himself. Or so she thought.

All Alayne's senses were acute, her sense of smell particularly so. This appeared to be the only trait which her daughter had inherited from her. Alayne and Adeline passed their days conscious of every odor, good or not so good, which came their way. They wrinkled their noses, curled their lips, over the unpleasant. They bumbled like intoxicated bees in the scent of flowers, of new-mown grass.

Now, as Renny came into the room that was full of scentless, snow-washed air, and leant over her, she drew back into her pillows with a distraught wrinkling of the nose. "Your soap," she moaned. "What is it? It has a horrid smell."

"It's something new in detergents," he said, bending closer that she might better sniff it—"guaranteed to kill all odors— even the smell of the stable."

"I've become used to the smell of Windsor soap," she said. "I quite like it—but this is something new."

"It is," he agreed cheerfully, as though it were eight o'clock in the morning and an hour when one could speak of something new. "Surely you have heard the singing commercials about it on the radio." And he began to sing, in an unmusical voice, the refrain which she had heard but once and instantly turned off.

His singing was the last straw to her load of misery. Beneath the bedclothes she kicked like a small child in a tantrum and said, with whining intonation, "Go away—please!"

"I'm going—in just a minute." He patted the bedclothes to quiet her. "But first, tell me—have you girls settled who's to take the baby?"

Alayne now gave herself up to a night of insomnia. "It's settled," she said.

"And he's to come to Jalna?"

She replied, in a clear, definite tone: "Pheasant is to take him in for the present."

"Pheasant! Good God!" he ejaculated. "Surely she's the last to undertake that job!"

"Why?"

"She does her own work—has three men and a little girl on her hands."

Alayne sat up in bed. "We are expecting Maurice and Pat Crawshay very soon. We have a wedding in prospect. Wragge suffers from lumbago, the cook from varicose veins. I will not speak of my own affliction."

"Affliction," he repeated bewildered. "What affliction?"

"Most people would call insomnia quite an affliction. I've been suffering from it for months."

"Now, Alayne," he said, "just let me mix you a good stiff drink before you go to bed and I'll guarantee you will sleep."

"It would have the very opposite effect. You ought to know that."

"Very—well," he soothed; then said, returning to the subject that stirred his emotions at the moment, "Adeline says she will look after the baby."

"Adeline is completely ignorant of such things. If the baby is forced on us it will have to bring a trained nurse with it."

"Well—well," he said again, and then added, "These matters always settle themselves in the end."

He had left the door open behind him and now a new odor assailed Alayne's sensitive nostrils. She scrambled out of bed, managing, in spite of haste and pink woolen bedsocks, to look graceful and even dignified.

"I smell something burning," she declared. "It come from the kitchen. I must go right down. Oh, dear, what ever can it be?"

For answer he picked her up and returned her to her bed. He left her there and ran down the two flights of stairs to the basement. Shortly after, he returned to find her waiting in the passage.

He gave her a cheerful grin. "It was only a saucepan that cook had left on the range. Giblets, by the look of it. Scorching. Stuck to the saucepan. I took it off and left a window wide open. It'll be nice and cold in the kitchen when she gets up. That'll larn her."

Renny's dogs, hearing his voice, had come to the door of his bedroom, to which they had retired some time ago, and scratched on it and whined—the bulldog on a deep, authoritative note, the spaniel ready to break into a bark, and the little cairn terrier in apparent anguish. Renny opened the door and the three came tumbling out.

"Oh, how rested they are," exclaimed Alayne. "Why can I never feel rested like that?"

"Because you don't go about it the right way, my darling," he said. "They lead an outdoor life—"

"When they're not sleeping beside the fire," she interrupted.

He continued, "They lick their dishes clean at every meal."

"And frequently bring up what they've eaten," she added sarcastically.

He paid no attention to this but went on: "When they go to bed they haven't a thought in their heads but what fun tomorrow is going to be. You would feel rested too, if you behaved as they do."

Now from the hall below, into which Adeline's room opened, came her voice, raised in excitement: "Daddy—Daddy—what ever is wrong? I smell something horrible."

"Giblets. In the kitchen," he said. "Go back to bed."

Alayne leant over the banister. "Isn't it horrible, darling?" she called down to Adeline. Mother and daughter sniffed together in congenial disgust.

Now the talking had disturbed Dennis, tucked up in Renny's bed. He woke from the nightmare that for the past nights had been haunting him.

"Save me—save me!" he screamed, and struggled wild-eyed to get from under the quilts.

The cairn terrier rushed at the bed, in a mood to bite the child, for he resented his being there. The spaniel sat down in the middle of the room and howled, while the bulldog bundled himself down the stairs and scratched at the front door to be let out.

Wakefield appeared from his bedroom, only half-awake. He had smelled nothing, but was thoroughly frightened by the confusion. He saw Alayne and Adeline in their nightdresses, Renny with the sobbing child in his arms.

"Wh—what's the matter?" stammered Wakefield.

"Stop staring," ordered Renny, "and go downstairs and let that dog out." He added, "By Judas—did ever another man have such a temperamental family?"

But there was no doubt about it that the eldest Whiteoak took a great deal of pleasure in his family and in his position as head of it.

Twenty-Seven

Winter Moves On

Roma and Fitzturgis were to leave for New York that night, but now, in the hard bright light of day, they had come to Jalna, in the Rector's old car, to make their good-byes. Roma's face, except for the seriousness of its expression, showed no trace of the emotions of recent days. Even though she had felt no deep emotion, she had seen those nearest her deeply affected, and she had experienced fatigue and loss of sleep. The face of Fitzturgis was, on the contrary, ravaged by grief. His brows were drawn together in a knot of melancholy concentration; dark shadows gathered beneath his eyes; deep lines marked the sombre bend of his lips; his skin was sallow; and even though he was fresh-shaven, he had the look of needing a shave. His dark gray suit would have been the better for pressing. But his strong, upright figure, of no more than middle height, showed no drooping of despondency, and his mouse-colored, curly hair stood upright.

"Well, it's good flying weather," said Renny, looking out of the window.

"I do hope you'll have a comfortable flight," said Alayne.

Roma gave a little yawn. "I expect to sleep all the way," she said.

"Have you been to Piers's to say good-bye?" asked Renny.

"I have," said Roma.

"Did you see the baby?"

"Yes. He's sweet. Auntie Meg thinks it would be nice to call him Ernest. Uncle Ernest was—I forget just what—but she thinks it would be nice."

"I agree," said Renny. "We couldn't choose a better name for him than Ernest or one with happier recollections. What does Finch say?"

"He hasn't said. I don't think he cares."

"Very well," said Renny. "We'll name him Ernest Nicholas or Nicholas Ernest."

Alayne said, in a low voice, "I think Sylvia might well have wished to name her child for her brother."

"No, no," Fitzturgis said hastily. "Not after me. Give him a Whiteoak name."

"Anyhow," observed Roma, "what's in a name?"

"I think," said Renny agreeably, "we shall stick to Ernest."

"Surely," Alayne said, with some tartness, "we are not in a position to name him. That must be done by his father."

"He couldn't care less," said Roma.

Adeline had stood silent during this conversation, wondering where and how she was to say good-bye to Fitzturgis. She stood by the window, looking out at the snowy silence of the scene, remembering their long walk at night, the agitation that had so stirred their hearts. There must be no emotion in their good-bye. She could not bear the pain of it—not because of her own suffering but because of his.

Roma was speaking in her low, matter-of-fact but pleasant-toned voice. "Mait and I," she was saying, "must say good-bye to Uncle Finch." She turned to Adeline. "Should you like to come with us?" she asked, on an almost pleading note.

Adeline thought, Roma wants to show off, in front of me. She wants to show how much Mait is hers now. . . . But Roma wanted Adeline's company for a quite different reason. She had, in truth, such an invincible shrinking from emotional scenes that she reached out toward Adeline for support in this meeting between Finch and Fitzturgis. She did not expect the two men to break into weeping. She did not know what she expected, and, like a child, she shrank from the unknown. The thought, scarcely formed in her mind, was, Why can't people be let to die, without all this fuss? She looked pleased when Adeline said, "All right. I'll go."

The three got into the motor car, Fitzturgis and Roma in the front seat, Adeline in the rear. She had on a shabby fur jacket which she kept in the little room at the end of the hall and in the pocket of which her straying hand discovered three chestnuts and half a chocolate bar. She sat silent fingering the nuts and gazing thoughtfully at the two in the seat in front. They did not speak either, except that Roma, driving, remarked on the bad state of the road.

Finch's house looked new, yet pleasantly secluded among its trees. Strangely the sound of the piano came from within, broken chords and arpeggios. Standing by the front door, as though on guard, was Dennis, looking even smaller and paler than usual. He had blue shadows beneath his eyes.

"I'm not sure that my father will want visitors," he said. "He's composing a piano concerto and he doesn't like interruptions. That's why I'm here."

"He'll want to see us," said Roma. "We've come to say good-bye." She said to Adeline, "You go in first."

"Coming?" Adeline asked of Dennis.

He shook his head. "Three will be enough in the room at a time," he said.

Adeline led the way. They entered the room, where a manuscript of music lay scattered on piano and floor; where Finch, in cold concentration, bent over the keyboard.

When he was conscious of their presence he took his hands from the keys and clasped them together. He rose and stood, gaunt and formal, to greet them.

"Oh, hullo, Uncle Finch," said Roma. "Mait and I are off to-night. We've come to say good-bye."

"Good-bye," said Finch, rather too promptly; then, as though realizing this, he added, "Won't you sit down?"

"Thanks, but we've no time. We've a thousand things to do." Roma was eager to have this leave-taking done with.

For something to say, Adeline remarked, "We saw Dennis outside."

"Really," said Finch and then spoke to Fitzturgis, as though just conscious of his presence. "It's good flying weather. You should have a pleasant flight to New York."

"A pleasant flight. . . ." Fitzturgis inaudibly repeated the words, as though savoring them without relish. He said aloud, "Yes, it should be all right."

"The roads are awful here," remarked Roma.

"I suppose they are," said Finch.

"Drifts," she said, "bumping along. But I don't mind. If you can't cure it, you can endure it." She gave a little shiver. "It's awfully cold too."

"I'm not cold," said Adeline, for the sake of contradicting Roma.

"You have on a fur coat."

"This old thing," said Adeline.

"You have another—a good one—at home," Roma said enviously. "I have none, and no prospect of one." She gave a sidelong glance at Fitzturgis, who received it imperturbably.

"We have no time to spare," he said. "We should be getting along."

"Then you can't sit down?" said Finch.

"I'm afraid not."

"Uncle Finch, what are you composing?" asked Adeline, her eyes on the scattered manuscript, as though from it she might discover an answer to the mysteries of life and death that troubled her.

"Just something I was working on before. . . ." he said curtly.

Roma hugged herself and shivered. "I'm so cold," she said. "I can't get warm. Even in here."

Finch looked at her contemplatively, then said, "Sylvia had a new fur coat. If you would like to have it, you may. I think it would fit you well enough."

Roma beamed. "That would be nice," she said. "Might I have it soon?"

"You may have it now. Come and try it on." He led the way to Sylvia's room, taking long quiet steps, his head forward.

The other two were left together in the chill disorder of the music-room. Fitzturgis said, "Let get out of here. I can't breathe in this house. . . . God—what callousness."

His expression was one of such poignant pain that Adeline hastened with him outdoors. He took her hand and they moved, as though for shelter, under a massive pine, a few of whose cones lay, sticky with resinous juice, on the snow.

Fitzturgis said, "I have lost Sylvia. You are lost to me, Adeline." He looked, with restrained passion, into her eyes that were on a level with his. " 'Love wakes men, once a lifetime each,' " he quoted, his burning eyes searching her face, his hand holding hers, as though desperately.

"Mait," she said, her hand still warm in his, but her mouth firm and almost severe, "I wonder if it is possible for you to be faithful to one woman, even for a little while. When I was engaged to you—There was Roma. Now that you're married to Roma—here am I."

He snatched his hand away. His forehead dark with a scowl, he said, "You've never understood me, Adeline, or even tried to understand me. While, for me, you've been the only—"

"Don't," she interrupted, shaken by a resurgence of her love for him. "I can't bear it."

His eyes were clouded with tears. "Spare me a moment of compassion," he said. "It's all I ask."

"I'm sorry," she said, in a shaking voice, "for both of us."

In the tenderness of her heart she went to him and put her arm about him. Her movement had dislodged the snow from a branch above them and it fell, enveloping them in a fine mist.

From among the trees Dennis appeared and came close to them. He looked up into Fitzturgis's face and said, "Adeline is very kindhearted. She took me into her bed when no one else wanted me. Now I sleep with Uncle Renny. When do you suppose my father will bring me and my little brother home again?"

Adeline and Fitzturgis regarded him doubtfully. They did not know what to say. Inside the large window they could see Finch and Roma, she wearing a handsome gray lamb coat. When she saw them she came out, walking elegantly, as though modeling the garment.

"What do you think of my lovely new coat?" she asked, her face rising warm and happily flushed from its embrace.

"Very becoming," Adeline said tersely. She had taken her arm from Fitzturgis's shoulder. Roma appeared to have noticed nothing.

"I hope," Adeline spoke as to a child, "you thanked Uncle Finch for it."

"I don't need to be reminded by you," said Roma. She darted back into the house.

Through the window they could see Roma throw her arms about Finch and hug him.

Fitzturgis pressed his forehead against the rough bark of the pine. "My sister—" he said—"and she scarcely in her grave . . . She was so proud of that new coat. . . . She put it on to show me. . . . Good God, it would scarcely meet about her. . . . And now . . ."

Finch and Roma came out of the house. "Come and say good-bye," she called.

The two men gave each other a perfunctory handshake. Again Roma hugged Finch. They left him standing alone in the open doorway. Dennis was nowhere in sight.

In the car Roma laid her beautifully shaped hands, with their red-lacquered nails, on the wheel. She made a visible movement of snuggling herself inside the gray lamb coat. After a moment she said, "It's an ill wind that blows nobody good."

Fitzturgis looked at his watch. "We'd better be moving," he said.

At Jalna, Adeline left them. She and Roma touched

cheeks. She and Fitzturgis touched hands. When they were gone, she dropped to the seat in the porch and closed her eyes, as though to shut out the white world that surrounded her. Any suffering of mind that she had so far experienced seemed almost trivial to her, as compared to the dead weight of desolation she now felt. She was very tired. Insofar as her healthy young body permitted, she felt weak. She asked nothing, she thought, but to be left alone. Snowflakes, drifting in on her, clung to her hair.

Now the pigeons discovered her and flew down, in a turbulence of gray wings, to seek her out for food or perhaps merely for the pleasure of being near her. Their jewel-like eyes stared at her; their coral-colored feet, cold from the snow, touched her hands, alighted on her shoulders and knees. As though they had discovered something new and quite wonderful, they reiterated their cooing notes.

They were scattered by a quick step crunching on the snow of the drive, and, with a great agitation of wings, they rose to the roof. When settled there they peeped down from the eave to see what it was that had disturbed them.

Philip, in his gray cadet's coat, came up onto the porch and seated himself beside Adeline.

"Cold, isn't it?" he remarked agreeably.

"Mm," she murmured.

"You shouldn't be sitting out here." There was solicitude in his voice.

"I don't mind the cold."

"But I mind it for you," he said, like a brave young protector.

Without warning, without preliminary, Adeline laid her head on his shoulder. It was the first time she had made a gesture of affection toward him, and he received it with dignity and concealed surprise. He put his arm about her, and gave her a pat.

"What we need now," he said, "is a little pleasure. Christmas seems a long way off."

"I forget what it's like to be happy."

"It would be good for us to go skiing. In Quebec. Lots of snow there," he said.

"Who would go with us? We can't go without a married person."

"My mother," said Philip, "would love to go with us."

"She can't! She's taking in the baby to-morrow."

Philip stared in consternation, then—"I forgot," he said,

and added: "Very well. There are hills nearby where there's a fair amount of snow. I'll put our skis in order. . . . Blast that baby. It would have been better if—" He broke off, feeling her start from him, glimpsing the shock in the pale face she raised to his. "I didn't mean that," he hastened to say. "I only meant that it seems hard my mother should almost be forced to take on a job like this when she has all her own work to do."

"I would have taken care of him," said Adeline, "if I'd been let."

"I know," said Philip. "I heard all about that meeting, when Auntie Meg had to protect the Rector, and Patience had to protect Humphrey, and Aunt Alayne had to protect her insomnia, and there was no one to protect my mother."

"You make us all sound horribly selfish," said Adeline, flushing a little and sitting up straight.

"Not you, Adeline," he hastened to say. "But you have no experience. You don't know the first thing about looking after a kid. Time enough for you . . ." He stopped and he too flushed. They fell silent, contemplating the towering possibilities of their future.

The object of self-protective discussions from those who did not want to undertake his care, of the shrinking of a father who could not endure the sight of him, of the morbid curiosity of a brother who had hastened his entry into a wintry world, took up his abode in Piers's house—well named The Moorings—the very next day.

He arrived in the arms of Patience, protected from the bitter cold by a white woolen shawl that had belonged to his cousin once removed, Victoria Bell. He was at this stage singularly unattractive, having a raw red complexion, a completely bald head and a mouthing, grimacing face. His eyes, with wrinkled lids, he kept shut except now and again to peer gloomily through a bleary slit. He was almost constantly wet but always yearning to take in more liquid. Piers had a look at him on the day of his arrival and drew back in dismay.

"Whew!" he exclaimed. "What an ugly little devil!"

Pheasant was insulted for the baby's sake. "He's not really ugly," she cried. "Just very new and rather premature. He's beautifully formed. See his darling little hands and well-shaped head."

"Let's hope he will improve," said Piers. "It's an awful

thought that Sylvia should have given her life for that. No wonder Finch can't bear the sight of him."

"Dennis sees him every day," said Pheasant proudly. "It's really touching to see his devotion."

Dennis did indeed come each day and hung, as though in fascination, over the crib where the infant lay.

"Do you suppose," he once asked Pheasant, "that the Christ Child looked like this?"

"Well, of course," Pheasant said thoughtfully, "He was a very special child. For one thing, He had a halo."

"That would be an improvement," said Dennis. He curved his white hands about the infant's head, to try the effect.

Another time he said to Pheasant, "Do you suppose they know when they're being born?"

"Goodness, no. They don't know anything about it."

"I don't see how they can help knowing."

"You ought," said Pheasant, "to keep you mind off such things. They're far beyond you."

"Far beyond me," he repeated, with his enigmatic smile.

"Yes. Just try to keep your mind off them."

"I can't," he said simply.

"When you feel those thoughts coming on," she advised, "say the Lord's Prayer to yourself. You can't think when you're saying that."

"Our Father," he said softly, "Which art in Heaven—"

"That's right," she said. "Keep saying it when you need help."

"The trouble is," said Dennis, "that I couldn't ever get past 'Our Father.' When I say 'Our Father,' I mean the father of us two—me and this little codger." And he gave three possessive pats to the little bundle in the crib.

"You are a funny boy," laughed Pheasant, but she did not really think he was funny. That night she remarked to Piers:

"I do wish that Finch showed a little affection for Dennis. He needs the understanding of a father. He's a lonely child." She could not help remembering how little Piers had understood Maurice, or tried to understand him.

"Finch," said Piers, "is completely self-centred. If he weren't, he'd never have had those nervous breakdowns when he was young. He's absorbed in himself and his music. Today I went to his house to take him a basket of apples—you know, he always like Talman Sweets. There he was, playing the piano, as though he hadn't a care in the world."

"We can't know what's going on inside him."

"And just as well we can't," said Piers.

On the day before he was to return to school Dennis looked in, through the large window of the music-room, at Finch absorbed in reading a book. Finch became conscious of him and raised his eyes.

"What do you want?" he called out. A pang pierced him as he remembered the summer night when the child's appearance outside that window had so terrified Sylvia. "What do you want?" he repeated.

Dennis entered by the front door and came into the music-room before he answered. He stood, small and neat, just inside the door. He said, "I'm going back to school to-morrow. I've come to collect my things."

"Oh," said Finch. "Very well. Go ahead."

Dennis disappeared into his bedroom. Finch could hear him rummaging, opening and shutting drawers. Finch felt uncomfortable and wondered if he should offer to help him. But, after a little, Dennis reappeared, carrying a suitcase.

"Got everything?" asked Finch.

"Yes, thanks."

"Like some pocket money?"

"Yes, please."

Finch took out some bank notes and held out a five-dollar bill.

Dennis took it with a murmured thank-you, then asked:

"Shall I be seeing you again?"

Finch thought: What a grammatical, precise, little fellow he is!—and recalled what he himself had been at that age. He noticed how pale were the boy's lips and the intensified greenish color of his eyes that were so like Sarah's; but hers shone beneath her jet-black hair while his hair was a pale gold.

Dennis was waiting for an answer. Finch asked instead:

"Is Wright driving you to the station?"

"Uncle Renny is taking me all the way to school."

Dennis spoke with a certain pride but no reproach. He was indeed thinking, If my father knew what I did, perhaps he would kill me right here where I stand. But he kept his eyes on Finch's face and the small steady smile on his lips.

"Good," said Finch, with forced heartiness. He held out his hand and Dennis put his hand into it.

"You do pretty well in certain subjects," said Finch and tried to recall what they were. He ended lamely, "I hope you'll work hard to improve."

Their hands separated. Both said, "Good-bye."

Dennis picked up the suitcase and, bending under its weight, disappeared. He reappeared for a moment, standing suitcase in hand where the snow man had stood.

Finch returned to his book.

It was an unusually long winter, possibly because of a series of snowfalls from heavy skies, each of which seemed the beginning of a new season of hidden earth, hungry birds, early nightfalls and late dawns.

But at last it was ended—the silence of winter—ended with a shout of springtime victory. There were noisy floods raging—noisy crows cawing—noisy animals in the streaming barnyard: a noisy stallion whinnying in his loosebox; noisy cockerels essaying their first crow. There were trees singing in the wind as they felt the sap stir in their trunks. It was miraculous.

The development of Finch's infant son during those winter months had been lovely to watch. So thought Pheasant and so agreed Piers. He had changed from a purple-faced, wrinkled gnome into a pink-and-white cherub. His bald head became covered by a curly down. He had dimples in his cheeks and smiled his good will toward all comers.

All the family (with the exception of his father, who still avoided him declared that there never was a nicer baby or a better-behaved one. Piers would take him in his two hands under the armpits and dandle him. Piers could pull funny faces to make Ernest laugh, but to Ernest all faces were funny and he always was ready to laugh. Pheasant loved him so dearly and found the care of him such a pleasure that she felt it scarcely honest to accept the generous allowance Finch gave her for her trouble. "I hate to take this, Finch," she would cry. "Baby is such a darling and as good as gold. Do come and see him in his bath. You'll love him. Of course, I know that you do love him already, but when you've seen him in his bath . . . Oh, Finch, do come."

But, on one pretext or another, Finch avoided this encounter with his younger son. "Finch," said Piers, "is going to be one of those fathers who don't like their sons. There are such, you know. I can't understand it."

Pheasant remembered Maurice, but she said nothing.

Of all those who admired Ernest, none was so fervent in homage as little Mary. He was her delight, from his first crowing in the early morning to the moment when he was

tucked up beneath the old woolly blanket that had served
Mary and her three brothers. He was better, she decided,
than any other of her treasures. Better than the cocoon out of
which the butterfly had seen the light of day. He was better
than a spider. Better than a rose. Better than the lilies and
carnations she had stolen from his mother's grave. He was
even better than the little silver thimble her Auntie Meg had
given her at Christmas. Mary did not much like sewing, but
when she took the thimble from its blue velvet case and
capped the middle finger of her right hand with it, that was
the signal for a delicious sensation of power. With the
thimble on her finger Mary felt ready to face the emergencies
of life.

But the baby Ernest was better than any of these. She
could scarcely bear to wait till spring when she might take
him out in the old perambulator that Piers had brought in
from the shed and given a fresh coat of enamel. Mice had
got into its cushions and Pheasant was making new ones. Ernest looked almost as interested as Mary in these preparations
for spring.

It seemed to Mary that this baby, this living toy, was especially hers. She was not prepared for the possessiveness of
Dennis when he returned to Jalna for the Easter holidays.
She was dumfounded, speechless, when he came into the
nursery where she was, as she felt, in complete charge, and
demanded, "Well, what do you think you are doing?"

She was, as a matter of fact, brushing the baby's curly fuzz
with a little old ivory hairbrush that had been used for all
Pheasant's babies. Surely Dennis could see what she was doing; but he repeated, in a hectoring tone, "What do you
think you are doing?" At the same time he looked at her out
of his greenish eyes in a way that made her uncomfortable.
His forehead was gathered into a frown.

She stammered, "I'm—brushing Baby's hair."

Dennis took the brush from her and threw it across the
room. "I'll let you know," he said, "when this baby's hair
needs brushing. He's mine."

"Yours?" she breathed. "How can he be?"

Dennis was smiling at her now, but his smile made her
even more uncomfortable than his frown.

"Because," he said, and seemed to be lost in thought. Then
he came and whispered right into her ear, "Because I saw
him born."

He drew back to see the effect of his words on her.

She looked no more than puzzled.

"You're not to tell," he said. "If you do, something terrible will happen to you."

"Something terrible?" she repeated.

"Forget," he said, and laughed out loud.

He looked hard at the baby. "How long," he asked, "has he been so pretty?"

"He's always been pretty," Mary said.

"No—he hasn't. He was ugly, ugly as sin. Do you know how ugly sin is?"

"He's pretty now," said Mary. "Can't I brush his hair any more?"

Dennis took the baby into his arms. He held him close, and rubbed his cheek on the curly fuzz.

Pheasant came into the room. "How do you like your baby brother?" she asked.

"Oh, well enough," said Dennis, noncommittally. "I'm like my father. I don't care much about babies."

Twenty-Eight

Conversation in the Kitchen

Mrs. Wragge had just taken a pan of buttermilk scones from the oven when Wright and Noah Binns descended into the warm basement kitchen from the chill outdoors. As yet there was very little spring growth, though the days were noticeably longer; even at this teatime the sun was slanting through the window to rest in rosy brightness on the copper urn that had been freshly polished.

"And what may that be?" asked Noah Binns, pointing a disparaging finger at it.

"That's a urn," answered Rags, "brought 'ere a 'undred years ago by the family. It came all the way from India, it did."

"What's its use?" demanded Noah.

"It can be used for tea but it's reely ornamental. It's kept in the library. It's a favorite of the mistress."

"I don't see nothing ornamental about it." Noah dropped heavily into a chair. "If it was mine I'd toss it into the dump heap."

Rags laughed good-humoredly. "I put a deal of elbow grease on it," he said, "to get that polish. Just see the glow where the sun strikes it."

Wright remarked, "It's the color of Miss Adeline's hair."

"In my young days," said Noah, "red hair was looked on as an affliction. In perticler fer young women. I look on it as an affliction to-day. I'll never ferget the first time I set eyes on the old grandmother. She was fairly young then and I was just a boy. I'd heard a lot of raving about her looks but what I said was, 'She'd be passable, if it wasn't fer her red hair.' That's what I said, and I'd make the same remark to-day about her great-grandaughter. She'd be passable, if it wasn't fer her red hair."

"She's a lovely young lady," said Wright, now seating himself at the cook's invitation.

Mrs. Wragge poured tea for everybody and heaped a plate

with the scones, which were of the sort to melt in the mouth. She handed about a square of honey in a comb. Noah leaned forward in his greed and was the first to take a scoop from the golden square. Liberally he helped himself to the rich dairy butter and dropped five lumps of sugar into his tea.

Continuing the discussion of Adeline's looks, the cook said:

"She has lovely eyes too."

"Ah," Wright agreed, "she gets them from her father."

Noah crackled with laughter. He laughed as he swallowed and had to be thumped on the back by Rags to relieve his choking. He said, when he was able to speak, "Well, I've heared funny things but *him* with lovely eyes beats all."

"They're inherited from the old lady," said the cook. "Mr. Wakefield has them too."

"They're welcome to 'em," said Noah. "I see all I need to see with the pair I've got. I've watched the world goin' downhill fer eighty years and longer. I look forward to more calamities before I pass on."

"You're a bit depressed after all that happened at Christmastime," said Mrs. Wragge. "Have some more tea and another scone."

Plate and cup replenished, Noah continued: "It was a hard season on everyone, and the hardest thing I had to do was to choose a Christmas card. It's a terrible responsibility to choose the right card. You've got to choose careful, and they get dearer every year."

"Do you send many cards?" asked Wright, with a wink at the cook.

"I send one only," said Noah. "Every Christmas it's the same problem. Sometimes I wish I'd never started it. Sometimes I'm driven to hope that, afore another Christmas, death will intervene and put an end to the worry of it."

"You might tell us who the lady is," said the cook, eaten up by curiosity.

"Wouldn't you like to know?" leered Noah. He was so overcome by the humor of the situation that again he choked.

When he had recovered and been given a third cup of tea and a third scone, there was silence for a space; then Wright remarked, "All our troubles seem small compared to the death of that sweet young lady."

"Don't start talking about her," said Mrs. Wragge, "or you'll have me crying, and when I start I can't stop."

"She's always been like that," said her husband, not without pride.

"That death," said Noah, "was a terrible disappointment to me."

The others at table stared at him uncomprehending.

"The weather," he explained, "was so danged miserable and my insides so upset after the Christmas feasting that I wasn't able to help dig the grave. I'd set my heart on that from the hour when I knowed the lady was doomed."

"Sakes alive," said the cook, "you give me the creeps."

"You couldn't know," said Wright. "It's impossible."

Noah struck the table with his fist. "I knowed," he said, "the last time I set eyes on her. That was three weeks before Christmas and she had on a new fur coat. 'It's a fine day,' she said, and she looked up at the sky. 'It's agoin' to be a fine winter,' she said, 'I look forward to it'—and, at that very minute, I saw the grave waitin' fer her and I said to myself, 'Noah, you'll dig her grave one of these times.' It was a terrible promonition."

"Gravedigging is a pleasure I can get on without," said Rags, his eyes on his wife, who was close to tears.

"I'm an expert at it," said Noah. "You need to love the work to be an expert. What I enjoy most is digging a grave for a young person. I know all the misery they're to be spared."

"That's a wrong way to look at life," said Wright. "There's just as much pleasure in it as misery."

"If you had your life to live over again, Mr. Wright," asked the cook, "what would you be, if you could choose?"

"Just what I am, where I am," said Wright sturdily. "It suits me."

"And you, Jack?" she asked her husband, with a coy look. "What would you choose to be?"

Rags threw back his head. "Me?" he said. "Oh, I'd be master of Jalna. I can't think of a better life."

"You can choose him, if you like," said Noah Binns, "but I wouldn't lead the life he's led, not fer a million dollars."

"He enjoys himself," said Rags, "as much as ever he did, and that's saying a good deal."

"Time takes away our pleasures," said Noah, "but there's one pleasure it's left me and that's champing my dentures." The others at the table sat spellbound while he, with obvious enjoyment, champed his false teeth together.

Twenty-Nine

Spider or Rose

Wakefield, restored in health, had sailed for England, in the hope of having his play produced—in the hope also of securing a part for himself in any play. He had, through his illness, lost so much time that he felt himself to be bankrupt in funds and in theatrical connections, though certainly not in talent and initiative. Renny was meanwhile supporting him generously, but with strict injunctions to return to Jalna in time for Adeline's wedding.

"But it will be impossible," Wakefield had exclaimed, "if I'm acting in a play in London!"

"You'll manage it somehow," Renny had said. "I find that when I very much want to do something, I usually contrive to do it."

Wakefield had given one of his trustful boyish looks at his elder. He could not have revealed how much more important to him were his own enterprises than the marriage of those two young people. Renny would not have understood, or would have chosen not to understand. A new and desperately urgent life was thrusting up out of the colonial past, but he ignored it, not so much in antagonism as in absorption by his own manner of life. He simply could not imagine a change in Jalna itself.

The vine-clad house, surrounded by its lawns, its meadows, its pastures and woods, were to him the enduring symbol of the life his grandparents had carved out of the wilds of a new country, and to which his uncles and parents had adhered. He saw no reason for changing it. The word "nationalism" had not occurred to him. He saw no stigma in the word "colonialism." He was proud of his country but disliked the idea of boasting about it. Some months ago he had been able to buy two hundred acres adjoining Jalna. A small house, badly in need of repair, stood in this, and a leaky barn. As was usual with him, he informed his wife of this transaction only after its completion. Yet he had, on occasion, consulted

225

her, but that was when he had wanted to borrow money from her. Alayne was not averse to his purchase of this property, because she knew that all about them prices for land were rising. He had bought this at a bargain. Now she counseled him to sell when a profitable moment came. He listened to her counsel gravely and nodded as though in agreement, but he had no intention of selling. He liked this neglected farm as it was. House and barn, put in order, would be very useful to him and to Piers. The two spent happy hours inspecting it. They looked with protective pride at its trees, of which some were fine. Never would these be cut down, they said, to make way for little boxlike bungalows.

The stream that passed through Jalna meandered also through this farm. Yet, early that spring, it had been in flood, done damage to the barn, swept away a poultry house with the poultry in it, and almost uprooted three immense willow trees. Though almost taken by the flood, the tenacious roots of the willows still held fast to the bank, and their drooping branches were graced by a cloud of golden-green leaves. Birds, attracted possibly by the singing of the stream, sang also there, one pair even going to the length of building a nest.

The two young men, Maurice and Sir Patrick, returned to Jalna in this springtime, after lengthy travels. So full were they of all they had seen that, for three successive nights, they talked till long past midnight. California, Arizona, Mexico—they were enthusiastic about all. The family, from four other houses, came to see and hear them. The reactions of the different members might have been interesting to the travelers had they found it possible to be interested in anything outside their own recitals in those first days. Alayne recalled her visit to Italy with her parents. Renny remembered incidents of horse shows in New York. But no one was interested. On the fourth night the Rector began to talk of missions in the North. Meg began to talk of the Women's Institute; Piers of breeding cattle; Patience of the television play Humphrey was writing; Pheasant of the baby, Ernest. At this point Finch, who had been present for the first time, excused himself and left.

"One would think," cried Pheasant, "that he'd be glad to hear how his little boy is thriving—even though his birth did bring tragedy. He's a perfectly lovely baby, and I know something about babies, having had four." Pheasant looked truculently at those present, as though daring them to deny it.

"Finch will come round," said the Rector comfortingly. "He'll come round."

"But little Ernest is so sweet, and Finch has never once kissed him or even given him one little pat."

"Has he ever shown affection for his other son?" said Piers and answered his own question. "No—and never will."

"It's high time for the baby to be christened," said Meg. "We must choose godparents and arrange a date before the wedding. There is also Dennis's Confirmation at his boarding school. How I love these ceremonials! As many as possible of us should go to see Dennis confirmed."

However, it turned out that Dennis was not to be confirmed that spring. The school chaplain wrote to Finch:

> I am rather anxious about your boy. After attending several of the preparatory classes, he came to me and told me he felt he ought not to be confirmed yet. When I questioned him, he refused to give a direct answer but gave me the impression that he is suffering from a sense of guilt. I am wondering if you may be able to throw some light on this difficult situation. I think that, if you could come to the school and have a talk with Dennis, it might be a great help to him, and also to me.

Finch read this letter and though, "Is it possible Dennis is remembering that fright he gave Sylvia when he appeared outside the window, smeared with blood? By God, he deserves to have a sense of guilt and no pity given him." Sylvia's terrifie face came between Finch and the letter. She had been brave, too, in her fear, and forgiven the wretched child, and now possibly he was justly suffering—if he had it in him to feel contrition. Through the wall of ice that divided Finch from his son, he saw his small white face distorted by emotion. He must go to the school, try to discover what lay behind all this. Finch was not driven to go by fatherly concern but by a chill curiosity. For the first time he had a desire to seek out Dennis.

The impulse moved him to lose no time. Within an hour he was on his way to the school. He sped through the blowy spring morning with a feeling of purposefulness he had not experienced since Sylvia's death. His heavy heart was lightened by it.

Less than fifteen miles on the way he was delayed by a train at a village crossing. Standing there also was a truck loaded with calves on their way to the slaughterhouse. Their anxious eyes looked out on the green world where they had been so lately free and now were captive.

The howl of the train whistle made their eyes start. They shuddered in fear and one of them raised its voice. The train passed. The truck jolted across the tracks, but the calves were so closely packed in the truck that they could not fall. They could not move.

Neither could Finch continue on his way. His reason was powerless to prod him to start the car. He wanted nothing but to turn back—if only it were possible to turn back on the road where Sylvia was lost to him . . .

The virtue was gone out of him. He could not move forward. Slowly he turned his car about and returned the way he had come. The spring wind blew in his face. The roots struggled in the chill bed of the loam to send up their shoots. Finch said to himself that he would write to the chaplain telling him not to urge Dennis to be confirmed; to let him come naturally to the point where he desired it. But that letter was not written. The chaplain's troubled letter remained unanswered.

When Finch reached the lately acquired farm which Piers had cleverly named New Farm, he stopped his car beside a gate that led into a stony field. He could hear hammering from where two farm hands were mending the roof of the barn. The hammering, softened by distance, was pleasant to the ear. There was an urgent rhythm to it. Finch left his car on the side of the road and went through the gate to where the three willows, dressed in wistful green, bent over a pool left by the flood of the stream. There was an oak nearby that had not yet put forth so much as a leaf, and there were the willows, exquisitely dressed. . . . A low-hung April cloud moved eastward and let the warmth of the sun full on the bank of the stream by the pool.

There must be small fish in the pool—suckers possibly, or sunfish—for a boy had left his fishing rod on the bank, gone off on some other boyish quest and forgotten it, or decided that there were no fish to be caught. The rod was no more than a willow wand, but it had a fishhook on a string and on the hook a writhing worm. It was long since Finch had fished. He thought he would like to catch even a very small fish. He dropped to the bank, in the sudden appealing warmth of the sun, and examined rod and bait.

His eyes became rivited on the writhings of the worm. Bloated and blindly twisting, it uttered a voiceless cry: Save me—save me!

Squatting on the bank Finch set about releasing it. He withdrew the hook, but the worm broke in half. Its writhing ceased. Ruefully he looked at it lying on his palm. The worm had waited long for this day and now had come to this—two half-worms, never to be joined together.

There was nothing for Finch to do but put it on the hook again, which he did, and, squatting there on the bank, dropped the bait into the pool. A feeling of something approaching tranquillity stole up through his body, beginning in his feet planted on the sun-warmed earth, and seeping, like sap through trunk and limbs of a winter-bound tree, up to his very scalp.

All about him green shoots were seeking the sun. Green leaves were in the very act of untying themselves from the rolled-up package of a backward spring. On a mossy stone a slippery green frog sat staring with calculating coldness at the budding world in front of him.

Suddenly Finch felt a lively tug on the line. It was more than a nibble. It was a bite—and he landed, with a grin of triumph, a small fish. Carefully he took the hook from its lip. It was scarcely damaged and, after an inspection of it, he returned it to the pool, where it vanished, as though it had never suffered such an experience.

Finch removed the body of the worm from the hook and proffered it to the frog, which refused it with a glassy stare—then, with incredible agility, leaped down into the pool.

Finch's housekeeper had made a package of lunch for him to eat on the motor trip. This he now opened and ate the sandwiches, sitting beside the stream. He dangled his legs over the edge of the bank in a freedom from tension unknown to him for months. The worm, the fish, the frog, glided through his empty mind as shapes in a crystal bowl. The meaningless murmur of the stream was music enough.

This New Farm was a place of the greatest interest to little Mary Whiteoak. Whenever she was given the chance she came to it. Especially was she fascinated by the farmhouse. It was being reshingled, painted inside and out. When it was in good order, Wright and his family were coming to live in it. But Mary, as much as was possible to the tenderness of her

nature, grudged Wright the farmhouse. She would have liked
to live there alone, with the baby Ernest. She knew so well
how to care for him—he was so happy with her—she would
wish for no interference from anyone.

Weeks passed. It was no longer spring but summer.

The time for Ernest's christening was near at hand. Next
came the centenary celebration of Jalna, and, following it,
the wedding of Adeline and Philip. To Mary, the christening
was by far the most important. She frequently talked about it
to Ernest, telling him how properly he must behave himself,
and that he was to wear the christening robe of his great-
uncle Ernest for the occasion, and that the robe was a mass
of the finest tucks and lace insertion, from neck to hem.

Already Pheasant had washed and exquisitely ironed the
robe, and it now lay between sheets of tissue-paper, in a
particular drawer that was scented by a bag of lavender.

There was no doubt about it—Pheasant and Piers were in-
fatuated by the baby. Piers quite simply doted on him. Now
on this morning in early June Piers had, at Mary's urgent re-
quest, brought her and little Ernest with him to New Farm.
She had sat beside Piers in the car, holding the baby on her
lap, as sensible as any little woman. As for Ernest, so intently
did he watch Piers's handling of the car that, as Piers remarked later to Pheasant, he might soon have it in his mind
to apply for a driving licence.

Piers had gone into the farmhouse to inspect the painting
and Mary was standing on the unkempt grass of the lawn,
with Ernest in her arms. Just to stand there and hold him
tightly was bliss. His first tooth was making itself felt. The
gum about it was sore and an excess of saliva gathered in his
mouth. He would thrust his round white fist into his mouth
and, when he brought it out wet, he would wipe it on Mary's
pink cheek or on her straight fair hair. But whatever Ernest
did was charming to Mary.

Now she was trying to draw his attention to a quite perfect
spider web on the grass where three captives waited to be devoured. The fact that two of them were honey bees, bound
round with glittering gyves, did not excite her pity. She was
completely on the side of the spider and, when she saw him
joyously descending on a gossamer thread from a briar rose
to his web on the grass, she laughed in pleasure. "Look, Ernest, look—look!" But Ernest only stared wide-eyed at her.

She kissed him on the mouth and cried, "You're better than a spider—prettier—prettier—prettier!"

Now she discovered that the briar had a pink rose on it. She tried to make Ernest see the rose but he saw only her. "Look—look—smell how nice!" But he just snuffled on her cheek.

She hugged him in delight. "You're better than a rose," she cried. Now, in a loud chant, quite unlike her usual voice, she repeated: "Prettier than a spider! Sweeter than a rose! Better than a spider *or* a rose!" She swayed with him in her arms, dipping him to see the spider's web, raising him to smell the rose. But he would neither look nor sniff.

Now she became conscious of another presence. Dennis was coming round the corner of the house.

"What's that you're saying?" he demanded.

She hung her head, speechless.

"I heard you," he said. "You were saying, 'Better than a spider. Sweeter than a rose.' What nonsense! . . . Give me the baby." He tried to take Ernest from her, but she would not let him go.

They struggled.

Just then Piers came out of the farmhouse.

"What's going on?" he asked.

"I'd like to hold my little brother for a bit," said Dennis, "but she won't give him up."

"Mary," said Piers, in an admonishing tone.

She let Ernest be taken from her.

"When did you come home, Dennis?" Piers asked.

"Last night. I'm ten days early because of chicken pox at school."

Piers looked at him thoughtfully. "Where did you spend last night?" he asked.

"At Jalna." Dennis spoke eagerly. "Wright met me at the station and took me straight home"—Now his voice took on an argumentative tone—"but my father wasn't ready for me. My room wasn't ready. Well—you couldn't expect him to want a boy in the house when he was composing a concerto, would you? And my room was not ready. He said for me to go to Jalna temporarily. It's different at Jalna. You can always go there because no one's ever doing anything important there." Dennis spoke fast, excitedly. He was proud of the word "temporarily," and repeated it under his breath. He kept his eyes on Piers's face.

"Your father," said Piers, "doesn't take much interest in his children."

"Oh, he's interested in us all right," Dennis said eagerly, "but he's an artist and you can't expect them to be like other people, can you?"

"You're coming on," said Piers, "but you haven't grown any taller this term."

Dennis hung his head and Mary stood up as tall and straight as she could. Ernest looked sweetly pensive, as he did when about to wet himself.

Piers put all three children into the car. He said: "I'm going to drive you to your father's, Dennis. When we get there I want you to go to him, with the baby in your arms. Let him see that you expect to be taken in—as you have a right to. Do you understand? I'll wait at the gate."

In front of the house Dennis stood, with Ernest in his arms, while Piers drew off with Mary. She was crying a little.

Dennis moved to where the snow man had stood, in front of the picture window. He could see Finch in the music-room. He held Ernest up, in front of him, as high as he could, and waited. His arms were aching by the time Finch discovered them.

Against the green outdoors Finch saw the two sons he had begot. One by Sarah. One by Sylvia.

Finch came through the front door.

"What are you doing?" he called out.

"Waiting for you," said Dennis.

"Go away," called out Finch, trembling from the emotions that shook him. "Go—and take that child with you." He went back into the house.

But Dennis did not go away. He stood, holding up Ernest, like a beggar soliciting help through his child.

Finch, looking through that hateful window, was shaken by anger at the boy's persistence. He rapped sharply on the pane and motioned to Dennis to go. Ernest chuckled and blew bubbles. Everything was a joke to him.

Piers was waiting by the gate, as had been arranged.

"Well," he asked, taking the little one from Dennis, "did you see your father?"

"Yes," said Dennis, with a smile. "He took us into the room where he was working. He was so glad to see us. He said what pretty hair Ernest has, and how big and bright his eyes are. He said how nice it is to have me home again."

Mary, in the back seat, was listening. "Better than a spider," she muttered; "sweeter than a rose."

Thirty

The Christening

As the car passed New Farm, Piers slowed it down that he
and the children might watch the entry of eight show horses,
through the gate into fresh pasture. They were being led by
stableboys, who were in such high spirits as they came down
the road that they whistled and sang. The horses were on
their way from Jalna to this new field, and seemed to feel a
certain distrust of the change. They moved warily and even
shied a little at sight of the standing motor car. The rich
locks of their well-groomed manes lay on their massive necks.
They lifted their feet delicately, as though it would take only
a little to make them sprout wings and fly. When they were
on the pasture they disdained to crop the grass but, once their
halters were removed, galloped whinnying to the other end of
the pasture, where they stood immobile as a group in bronze.

The head stableboy slammed the gate and called out to
Piers, "They'll soon settle down, sir."

"Yes," agreed Piers, "they'll settle down."

"The grass here is first-rate," said the boy and bent and
plucked a handful and examined it, as though he had a mind
to eat it himself.

Piers drove on. When he reached home he handed over the
baby to Pheasant, with a look of satisfaction on his tanned
face. "I've good news about Finch," he said. "Dennis took
Ernest to see him and apparently Finch was pleased and
made quite a fuss of him."

"Isn't that splendid?" she cried. "How could he help being
pleased by him? Such a darling baby. . . . But Ernest, my
pet, you're just as wet as possible." And she carried him off.

There were many preparations being made for the three
events shining on the horizon. New arrivals added to the excitement. Archer from Oxford . . . Wakefield from London
. . . Roma and Fitzturgis from New York.

Archer, in spite of his youth wearing an air of chill distinction, came early to The Moorings to see his relatives there. Not that he appeared glad to see them. The sight of them seemed to give him pain, rather than pleasure. He didn't even smile at Ernest, but remarked to Pheasant:

"I suppose that charity of this sort is its own reward."

"Ernest is a pet," cried Pheasant.

"Then I suppose," said Archer, "that you keep him, for the reason that we keep all our pets, because we can't help ourselves."

"Finch is very generous to me," said Pheasant.

"I should think," said Archer, "that it would seem cheap to him at any price to get an infant off his hands."

"You'll be a parent yourself one day," said Pheasant. "Then you'll understand."

"Parentage," he said, "is hidden behind the marriage ceremony. A dream come true. A nightmare you can't be woken out of."

Pheasant was ready to argue with him but Piers came into the room and, after greeting Archer, asked:

"Have you see New Farm?"

"I've see it all my life," said Archer.

"I mean since your dad bought it."

"Is it permitted to ask why he bought it?" asked Archer.

"Well," said Piers, "your dad thought, and I thought, it would help to round out the estate. There are so many insignificant little places going up all about."

"A Triton among the minnows, eh?" said Archer.

Piers said proudly, "It's been our tradition, Archer, to follow in the footsteps of our forebears. To be like them and even more so, if you know what I mean."

"Plus royalists que le roi," said Archer.

Christian came in to invite Archer to go into the studio.

When they were there, in the midst of the young artist's paintings, Christian inquired, "What do you feel about life in England?"

"I found nothing there that tempted me to remain permanently," said Archer.

"Then you're glad to come home?"

"I should scarcely say that," Archer replied distantly.

He looked with a dissatisfied air at a painting of the three willow trees by the stream.

"You don't like it," Christian exclaimed, a little hurt by the look on Archer's face.

"Don't mind me," said Archer. "I just go on in my own

natural way. I never have liked trees. They take up too much room both above and below. Particularly I don't like willows. They remind me of depressing things—like Gilbert and Sullivan—'Willow, tit willow,' you know."

"My brother Maurice," said Christian, "is buying this picture to take back to Ireland."

"I can't think of a better thing to take to Ireland," said Archer. "Weeping willows and wailing Irish. They can mourn together."

Christian began scraping a palette. He concealed the chagrin which he despised himself for feeling, and inquired, "Did you make many friends at Oxford?"

"I made friends of sorts," said Archer. "But when I discovered that they all hope to visit me in Canada I dropped them. Friends are too great a responsibility."

"Not even a girl friend?" probed Christian. "Not one on shipboard?"

"There was one I liked," said Archer, "but she became too demanding. I was forced to drop her. I had thought my youth would protect me. But no—she was out to marry me."

"You do well," said Christian, "to hang on to your freedom. It's the best thing in life—for a man. It's different for women. If they can grapple a willing slave, to work for them till he drops, they don't need freedom. For example, look at Patience and Humphrey Bell."

"I prefer to look the other way," said Archer.

He moved critically about the studio, examining sketches.

"Why, here," he almost exclaimed, "are two quite good attempts at portraiture—Adeline and Philip."

"They were a ghastly failure," said Christian. "Uncle Renny wants portraits of the pair to hang opposite the portraits of our great-grandparents, and commissioned me to do it. Of course I know I couldn't—not to satisfy him—but I took it on because I need money."

"Why?" asked Archer. "You have a perfectly good home here."

"A fellow likes some cash in his pocket."

Archer studied the portraits. "I think they are very good," he said.

"Uncle Renny called them caricatures," Christian said bitterly.

"I will buy them," said Archer, firmly, "as wedding presents for Adeline and Philip. As they are only sketches, I suppose you'll not ask a high price."

"I'll give them to you," said Christian, "free, gratis, for nothing."

"I couldn't agree to that," said Archer. "I'll pay you ten dollars apiece, if you're willing."

"O.K.," said Christian. "I'll be glad to get them out of my sight."

Archer looked lovingly at the sketches. "It will be amusing," he said, "to see my father's face when these portraits appear among the wedding presents."

The morning of the christening dawned pink and gold. The mercury, as though in celebration, flew up twenty degrees. It was summer. Ernest had not only got his tooth through, but another pearl-like point now was starting beside it. On the slightest provocation he laughed, exhibiting them in pride. His tucked and embroidered robe lay waiting on Pheasant's bed. He had had his bath and lay sleeping in his pram on the lawn, near a honeysuckle in bloom that drooped from the porch. Everything was in delightful order—that is, until Dennis appeared on the scene.

He trotted in from the road, round the corner of the house, and bent over the sleeping baby, with a feeling of enchantment, a rapturous feeling of possessiveness. Uncle Piers and Aunty Pheasant behaved as though the baby were theirs, but it was his. It was his very own. He had been there when it was being born. He would be beside it all its life.

He felt sudden anger because he had not been consulted in any way about the christening. This aunt and uncle did not realize that the baby was his. But he would show them. He would prove to them that it would be well for them to consult him before arranging ceremonies for Ernest.

Dennis lifted him out of the pram. He lifted him gently and cautiously, and carried him round the corner of the house, through the gate, into the road. Nobody saw him go.

When they had progressed some distance along the road, Ernest woke. He laughed out of the pure pleasure of finding himself awake. He showed his two teeth in pride.

"Little brother—little brother," said Dennis. "Who's running off with you, little brother? Who's going to take you away and never bring you back, little brother?"

A tiny convulsion of joy ran through Ernest's plump body. He kicked and laughed, and then looked pensive, as he wet himself.

"This is your christening day, little brother," Dennis said. "There'll be presents for you—if you're there to get them. I'll bet you that our father doesn't give you a present, because he doesn't love you. But I love you and I'm taking you away, so you'll be late for your own christening—the way I was late for my confirmation."

They had now reached the gate that led into New Farm. They were where the three willows grew by the stream. Where the willows drooped was a good hiding place. There Dennis carried Ernest and lay down beside him, as in a green grotto. They were completely hidden, and there was no sound but the whispering of the stream. It was very warm.

Dennis began by taking off Ernest's knitted bootees, watching with delight the curling and uncurling of the sensitive toes. Then, suddenly, with a masterful air, he took off the rest of his clothes, leaving him a completely naked baby on the mossy ground beneath the willows.

At first Ernest was surprised by this. He lay staring quietly up, as though watchful. He appeared to discover that he was still he, though outdoors without clothes on. Another small convulsive movement shook him. He was like a fish suddenly swept from pool, out on to the grass. But when Dennis laid a hand on his round white stomach, he laughed.

" 'Prettier than a spider. Sweeter than a rose,' " said Dennis. "That's silly girl's talk. But we know what's true, don't we, little brother? Our father doesn't want us. He hates us, little brother. . . . But he doesn't know what we know. . . . If he did, he'd kill me. . . . It would serve him right . . . serve him right . . . if I killed us both. . . ." Dennis said, with sudden savagery, "What he needs is a terrible fright."

He took Ernest into his arms and clutched him hungrily. Ernest hiccoughed and then cried a little.

"Don't cry, little brother," said Dennis. "No more crying for you or for me. . . . We'll be happy together. . . . No mother . . . no father . . . Do you know who I am? I'm Esau. My hand against every man's, and every man's hand against me."

Now Ernest chuckled and tried to push his fist into his mouth.

"How nice and cool you look," said Dennis. "We'll both be cool. Esau and Little Moses among the bulrushes. We'll be naked and happy, little brother."

Dennis took off his own clothes and lay down beside Ernest, one arm thrown possessively about him. The two lay lost in pleasurable sensations, breathing the June air through every pore.

After a while Dennis got up and, taking Ernest into his arms, went down into the pool where rushes, in their new greenness, grew and whispered.

Dennis raised his clear, treble voice and said, in a kind of chant:

"We're Baptists, little brother. . . . I'm going to totally immerse you, and baptize you. . . . I baptize you Moses . . . in the name of the father—Finch Whiteoak . . . the son—Dennis Whiteoak . . . and the holy ghost—Sylvia Whiteoak."

In the meantime a frantic search was taking place. Pheasant had dressed little Mary for the christening ceremony, then herself; she had left Ernest to the last because he was the central figure and his costume was the most important. Then she ran down the stairs and to the pram where he had been sleeping. When she found that he was missing she was not frightened but a little annoyed. Mary had taken him up, she was sure, and was really naughty of her to be so officious.

Pheasant called loudly, "Mary! Mary!"

Mary came running from the studio.

"Where is Baby?" demanded Pheasant.

"I don't know, Mummie."

"But you must know. You took him up, didn't you?"

"No, Mummie. He was asleep."

"For goodness' sake," said Pheasant, now really annoyed. "It must have been your father." And she went underneath the bathroom window and called up: "Piers! Piers!"

He put his head out of the window, one side of his face lathered, "I'll be ready in ten minutes," he called back.

"You should not have taken Ernest up," she called. "Where is he?"

"What? Where is who?"

"Ernest."

"I don't know. Ask Mary."

"Mary says she didn't take him up."

"Ask her again."

Pheasant did and Mary repeated her denial.

Christian and Philip now appeared from the house, immaculate for the christening. Neither one had seen Ernest. Piers came on the scene and Pheasant drew him aside.

"There's something odd about this," she said. "When I was dressing Mary I saw tears in her eyes and, when I asked her why, she said she wished the christening were over. I said it was a lovely thing, but she said it was cruel."

"I'll attend to her," said Piers.

With a purposeful air he sought out his daughter, hiding behind a huge snowball tree in heavy bloom.

"Now, Mary," he ordered, his voice deep but not threatening, "tell Daddy where you've hidden Ernest."

"I don't know," she said, looking vaguely into the snowball tree.

"Now, pay attention, Mary. It's time for the christening and we can't have it without Ernest. Where is he?"

"I don't know."

"Why did you say to Mummie that you wished the christening were over?"

"Because I did."

"Why?"

"I don't know."

Now came the sound of cantering hoofs. They stopped at the gate, and Renny, mounted on his handsome old mare, Cora, rode in. In his hand he carried a package tied with a blue ribbon. He rode across the lawn, calling out as he came:

"Good morning! All ready, I see. I've brought a christening present for young Ernest. It's the manuscript of Uncle Ernest's book on Shakespeare. He never was able to finish it, but what he wrote was first-rate. Even Alayne said so, and that pleased him greatly. It will be something for little Ernest to treasure all his life. . . . What's the matter?"

"He isn't here. We can't find him. He's gone," answered Pheasant.

"Mary knows," said Philip. "Dad's questioning her, over there."

"I'll bet she's hidden him in the cupboard in my studio."

Christian set off at once to search. Renny rode to where Piers and Mary stood.

"Hello," he said, from horseback. "Can either of you tell me where Ernest is?"

This was the right approach to Mary's good will—not to be singled out.

"I only wish I knew," said Piers.

"I only wish I knew," repeated Mary, but did not look as though she meant it.

Christian now came out of the studio. "He's not there," he said.

Piers said—coming close to Renny—"Mary knows, I'm pretty sure. Pheasant thinks so."

"If Mary knew," said Renny, "she'd tell. The baby has been kidnaped. We must call all the family and start a search. I'll telephone everybody." He sprang from his horse and strode into the house, Mary following.

"What is kidnaping?" she asked.

"Stealing a kid—a child. Don't worry, Mary. We'll soon find him." He picked up the receiver and dialed a wrong number, though he had not appeared to be flurried.

Before long he joined the others on the lawn, Mary by the hand. Piers had gone upstairs to finish dressing. The two young men were peering under bushes and searching sleuthwise for footprints. Pheasant was standing by the empty pram, almost distraught. She was very pale.

"I've phoned all four houses," Renny said. "At the Rectory, they were about to leave for the church. At the Fox Farm, Patience is setting out to search the ravine. At Jalna, Alayne was splendid. She's to get the young people organized, and the stablemen, for an intensive search."

"What about Finch?" asked Pheasant.

"He's on his way here. Will arrive any minute."

"Poor Finch. He's had so much trouble."

"This last may wake him up to his responsibilities."

Finch, when a few moments later he arrived, looked calmer than they. He asked, "Where is Dennis?"

Nobody knew.

"If we find him," said Finch, "I think we shall find the baby. He has a very possessive attitude toward it."

Pheasant repeated to herself the impersonal pronoun. To call one's baby son—and such a darling little son as Ernest—"it" . . . Her sympathy for Finch turned to something approaching anger. She stood silently looking into his face, while with her hand she joggled the empty pram.

Now began an intensive search. Piers was for notifying the police, but Renny and Finch were agreed first to explore every part of the estate. It was Adeline and Archer who discovered the children. On foot they were searching the fields of New Farm.

Archer exclaimed, "Those three willows! Let's sit in their shade. I'm hot, and tired of this."

"I'll not rest till we find Ernest," said Adeline, and ran toward the willows.

As she reached them, panting, she gave a piercing scream.

"Mercy," said Archer. "What's happened?"

She ran to the edge of the stream. "Dennis is drowning the baby!" she screamed. She had now run into the water.

"Oh, you young villain!" she screamed. "Give Ernest to me."

Dennis at once put the little one into her arms.

"We were having a private baptism," he said. "Please don't tell or I shall get into trouble." He came up dripping out of the stream.

"Archer, hold Ernest, while I attend to this young villain." She tossed the baby into his reluctant arms. She took up the willow wand that Finch had used as a fishing rod and had left on the bank. She caught Dennis by the hair and brought down the rod in fury on his shoulders. He bent forward, but did not struggle or again speak.

"What a temper you have, Adeline," said Archer. "Come—that's enough."

She desisted and threw down the rod.

"Shall you tell my father?" asked Dennis.

"I'll tell everybody," she answered. "Now get into your clothes, while I dress this poor little baby." She took the infant from Archer, who asked:

"Why did you do it, Dennis? . . . What you say may be used against you."

"I don't know," said Dennis. "But he liked it."

When the quartet appeared at The Moorings, Piers was about to call the police. Instead he set about to notify all the searchers that the little one was found.

In a surprisingly short time the family were gathered in the church for the christening. Indeed, they showed little trace of their ordeal. This was especially true of Ernest, who beamed his approval of both ceremonies. It appeared that he would have been cheerfully willing to be baptized into any sect. His lace-trimmed robe was so becoming to him, and he was so becoming to the Rector, as he lay in his surpliced arms, that Meg declared she would treasure the sight all the rest of her days.

At Jalna, where all were gathered for a substantial lunch, Archer came to Finch and said: "What are you going to do about Dennis, Uncle Finch? I know that Adeline has told you what he was up to. But I think I ought to let you know that she chastised him thoroughly, in case you contemplate doing it yourself. It would seem a pity to waste all that effort."

"I don't know what to do with him," Finch said heavily. "Look at him now—he's as bold as brass. I believe he feels a bit of a hero. Do you think, Archer, that he was actually trying to injure the child?"

"Naturally," said Archer. "Just what I should have done in his place. The murdering of younger brothers is a time-honored custom."

Finch, gripping his glass of sherry, turned away. He found himself face to face with Maurice. Finch said:

"That young Archer has a sadistic streak. He's obviously pleased by what Dennis did this morning."

"I don't agree," said Maurice. "I think Archer is kind really. He told me he was afraid you'd be pretty rough on Dennis."

"*Rough on him,*" repeated Finch—"I've a mind to skin him alive! But the truth is I don't know what to do."

"Now I have a suggestion," Maurice said eagerly. "Let me take him back with me to Ireland for a visit—not a punishment, not against his will—just a complete change that might be good for him and rather fun for me—to have a youngster about."

"Reward him, eh?" Finch said grimly. "Reward him with a nice visit to Ireland?"

"Think about it, Uncle Finch. But I hope you will decide to let me have Dennis for a while. I'm often lonely."

"I'd be glad," said Finch, "to get him off my hands."

Maurice thought, And my father was glad to get me off his hands, though I was not a troublesome boy. He said, "I hope Dennis will like the idea."

"I must tell you," said Finch, "that to-day I had a letter from the headmaster of his school, saying that he thinks Dennis should not return for the fall term. He says the boy is badly adjusted, whatever that may mean. I take no stock in this psychological lingo."

"It does not impress me," said Maurice.

After the christening luncheon Finch, taciturn and almost silent, took his son to Vaughanlands. He sat on the window seat in the music-room, with Dennis standing small and white-faced in front of him.

"I want you to tell me," said Finch, "whether you're as vicious as you appear to be."

"I don't know." Dennis looked him straight in the eyes. "I can't tell. Sometimes I feel good. . . . When I'm with you— just us two—I feel good."

"Why did you do what you did this morning?"

"I don't know."

"Did Adeline punish you?"

"She struck me with a willow switch. Would you like to see the marks?"

"No," shouted Finch. "You will go to your room and stay there for a week. Your meals will be brought to you."

Dennis looked thoughtful. "We'll be together," he said. "In the same house. I'll like that."

"*Hmph,*" Finch gave a sardonic grunt. "See that you keep out of my way."

Thirty-One

The Centenary at Hand

The house, in this year of its centenary, had been truly titivated for the occasion. The woodwork had been painted ivory. To paint the window frames it had been necessary to cut away some of the Virginia creeper which draped them, and it was only after profound consideration on the part of the master of Jalna that he agreed to this. But, once that it was done, and the windows and shutters looked brightly forth, no one was so delighted as he. He would stand entranced in the hot sun, on the gravel sweep, admiring the ivory paint on the window frames and pillars of the porch.

"Look, Alayne," he once exclaimed, "the house, which had got rather dingy, has come out a glamorous blonde!"

"It has 'that Ivory look,'" she said, with an ironic smile, and quoting from a radio soap advertisement.

Yet she took a sincere interest in the centenary, made a list of people to be invited; had rugs, walls and curtains cleaned, and concerned herself with zest.

Renny was grateful for her interest, because always he had regarded her as one somewhat aloof from such homely things as family celebrations. One arm about her waist, he pressed her to his side. He said, "How pleased with you the old uncles would have been for your interest in this celebration. They thought the world of you."

"And I of them," she said fervently. "Their sort isn't bred nowadays, and I guess it's a good thing—as they would not have enjoyed the world we live in."

Renny looked surprised. "I don't see why," he said. "It seems to me very enjoyable. And I think it's a remarkable coincidence that another Ernest should have been born just at the right time for the centenary."

"Little Ernest Nicholas . . ." she mused. "What, I wonder, will his future be? Such a tragic beginning he has had."

"I think Maurice's idea of taking Dennis to Ireland with him is a good one."

245

"Perhaps," she said doubtfully. "But—with Maurice what he is, and Finch what he is, and Dennis what he appears to be—I can't think what will come of it."

"Don't try," he said, kissing the little knot on her forehead. "It will turn out all right." He was in these days almost too exuberant.

He had, with some pressure from Piers, persuaded Christian to do other portraits of the prospective bride and groom. The young artist had executed these in a panic of speed. He feared that if he hesitated to consider what he had agreed to do, he would never finish them in time for the centenary. He was, at the same time, ashamed and amused by his own work, and ended by being rather proud of it. The portraits were done with an almost primitive simplicity. The quality of the materials of evening dress and uniform was even better than the best commercial art. There was no attempt to portray the souls of the subjects, who were candidly charmed by the portraits. It had been left to Christian to choose the frames.

On this morning of warm June rain, he and Adeline and Philip were in the studio for the very last touches to the portraits, when Patience, led rather than followed by her prancing poodle, burst in on them.

"What do you suppose?" she cried.

"Hang onto your dog," begged Christian.

"Darling," Adeline called out to the poodle and he at once pranced to her.

"What has happened?" demanded Philip.

"I've just come from the Rectory," said Patience.

"You're always just going there, or coming from there," said he. "It's nothing new."

"But this is different." She looked solemn. "Roma and Maitland Fitzturgis are there. They've just arrived from New York. They're on their way to Ireland."

The name of Fitzturgis so stirred Adeline to emotions that were complex and painful that Christian stared at her as though he had just discovered her. He looked from her to his portrait of her, as though he had half a mind to do another very different one.

"It appears that Maitland can't stand the strain of life in New York. Being on time at the office every morning, writing advertisements as though he believed in them—it was too much. And the crowds. He hated crowds. He was always late, and he was always cross, and he lost his appetite."

"How does Roma take this?" asked Adeline.

"She's wonderful. Says she doesn't mind. They're going to buy a small place and breed cattle, in Ireland."

"A sow, a pig, and three hens," said Philip.

"It's the best thing in life," said Patience, "to do what you are fitted for. Find out what it is and do it. Roma is developing. She says she likes public relations but, because Mait hates them, she's willing to give them up."

"Life in New York must be a great mental strain," said Philip. "I can't stand mental strain. It puts me to sleep."

Later that day Roma and Fitzturgis appeared in the studio. Ostensibly they came to see the finished portraits, but actually they wanted all the family to know that they had left New York of their free will, of their own desire to be free. Fitzturgis, indeed, looked as though he had already drunk the air of freedom. His step was lighter. He was more ready to smile. As for Roma, always was she agreeable to change, to adventure. The thought of a sea voyage ending in a picturesque place in Ireland was attractive to her. She wanted to see Maitland settled down and fairly content because, when he was unsettled and discontented, he was not easy to live with. Roma liked people who were comfortable to live with. That was the reason she was so fond of her Auntie Meg and the Rector.

The pair stood in front of the two portraits.

"I like them" said Roma. "I wish you'd paint portraits of Mait and me, but I don't know who would pay you for them. I suppose you are pretty expensive. Do you think Uncle Renny would pay for a portrait of me?"

"Never, if I can help it, am I going to paint another portrait," said Christian. "What you see is my second attempt at painting Philip and Adeline. Archer is giving me ten dollars each for the first attempts. Uncle Renny would have nothing to do with them. Said they were caricatures."

"Has Archer paid for them?" asked Roma.

"Not yet. They're to be a wedding present; but you're not to mention it."

"It's ridiculous," said Roma, "to have two portraits of oneself. Don't you think it's ridiculous, Mait?"

Christian now brought the earlier portraits from where they stood, face to wall, and displayed them.

"Myself, I rather like these," he said.

The eyes of Fitzturgis rested rapt on the pictured face of Adeline. "Both portraits are good," he said. "She is so various," he said, "if you painted a dozen portraits of her they might every one be the image of her."

Roma was a little annoyed. "Adeline looks silly in this one," she said, "and smug in this. Philip looks dandified in both."

The pair wandered off. They were in holiday mood, had money in their pockets, and appeared vague as to when they would go to Ireland. Renny felt tender toward Roma because she was the child of his dead brother, and she was small and appealing. He felt almost tender toward Fitzturgis, he was so thankful not to have him for a son-in-law. He remarked to Alayne, "I like Mait better all the time. He really is a charming man." He made this remark with his left eyebrow cocked, in a way that was highly irritating to Alayne. He appeared so affected.

Humphrey Bell, who had a friend in an important position in the broadcasting company, was able to arrange for three talks on Irish country life by Fitzturgis, who had a particularly pleasant voice. He and Roma were very pleased by this and worked keenly on the talks, sitting up late in Mr. Fennel's study at the Rectory. Though Roma knew nothing of the subject, she had a deal of sound sense and discrimination, and had listened to many radio and television talks in New York.

The first broadcast was a success. The second was even more so. For the first, the family gathered about the radio at Jalna, feeling distinctly nervous. It took place at eleven o'clock at night. As the talk proceeded they became increasingly proud of Fitzturgis. Piers expressed the opinion that the Irishman might do well to settle in Canada and take up broadcasting as a profession.

But the third talk was a disappointment. Fitzturgis was late for the broadcast and it had to be postponed. When it did take place he was suffering from a summer cold, spoke in a husky tone, was lackadaisical. So that was the end of the broadcasting. Alayne was greatly disappointed by this, for she had a sincere admiration for Fitzturgis. She would have liked to see him often and familiarly, for there were few about her with whom she could exchange her ideas, as with him. He was, she thought, two men. One of them congenial to her, friendly and very intelligent; the other aloof, hopelessly indolent; willing to bury himself in a life that would require no mental effort. This was the man who had married Roma.

Roma was not only willing but moderately eager to go to

Ireland. Several times she spoke of "fresh fields and pastures new," and seemed pleased by the prospect.

In the brief interval between the christening and the centenary celebration—which was to be a dinner, followed by a dance—two incidents which influenced several members of the family took place. One was that Wakefield went to New York to see if he could persuade Molly to return to him. She was acting in an English comedy that was drawing full houses. It was not easy to get seats for it, but by good luck he was able to secure one in the second row, though at the side. He had a clear view of Molly's entrance, early in the first act. She was acting the part of a very young girl. The immature lines of her figure, her eager face and voice, gave a charming reality to her performance.

To Wakefield it was almost unbelievable that she could be unaware of his nearness. His eyes never left her when she was on the stage. His thoughts pursued her into her dressing-room. So often had they acted together. He knew just what she would be doing. But he did not attempt to see her till after the play, for he knew it might be upsetting to her.

At last they stood face to face, as Molly was about to leave the theatre.

"Wake," she said, in a trembling voice. "What are you doing here?"

"I came for nothing but to see you," he said. "May I take you home?" He put the question almost ceremoniously, and kissed her lightly on the cheek. The familiar scent of her flesh made him unable for a moment to speak or even to think. Neither could she speak but nodded her acquiescence. He could see that she was trembling.

They found a taxi and moved through the bright streets, sitting with averted faces and urgently beating hearts. Molly was living in the apartment of a friend, an actress who was on tour. The small apartment was on the sixteenth floor of a tall building. The movements of the two who now entered it were so familiar to each other that it was as though the past long winter had not separated them. The room felt close, airless. Molly went to a window and opened it, letting in the night coolness. Their faces were bathed in the coolness.

"When will your play be finished?" he asked.

"This is its last week. Then the theatre closes for the summer."

"And you? Where shall you go?"

"To Wales—and rest."

"You don't look tired," he said, almost accusingly.

"It's the heat I mind—and the crowds. I long for the hills—the bareness." She turned to Wakefield, in sudden sweetness and solicitude. "Tell me all about yourself," she said. "Are you quite recovered? What of your play?"

"There's only one thing to talk about where we are concerned," said Wakefield. "That is our relations. We must not lose each other. You understand that, don't you?" She gave a little laugh at his dictatorial tone.

"Oh, Wake," she exclaimed, "you do not change at all."

"That is true," he said, with great seriousness. "I don't change. I'm still yours—and always shall be."

"Don't!" she said, in a shaking voice, as though his words brought emotions that were unbearable.

"What do you want me to do?" he demanded sternly. "Go?"

"Not yet. Not yet. Stay a little while—then you must go. . . . I'll make coffee and you must have some—nourishing food." The habit of nursing him was still strong in her. She put on the kettle, but could find only strawberries and rolls for food. "If I had known you were coming," she said, "I should have provided plenty of cream."

"I don't need cream," he said sulkily. "I hate everything milky." And he picked up a strawberry and ate it.

They drew a small table near the open window and sat there with the night air blowing in. It was so natural to them to be isolated together that this New York apartment became another Fiddler's Hut. Instead of towering trees surrounding them, tall buildings rose palely against the moonlit sky.

The ate fruit and rolls, drank coffee, and she asked questions about the family at Jalna. He had written to tell her of Sylvia's death. Now she said, "I wrote to Finch and had an answer from him—a very restrained answer. But he must be heartbroken. All his lovely plans for their future come to nothing."

Wakefield looked at her steadily. He was searching for words to move her. In a low voice he said, "And what of my plans for our future—yours and mine?"

"We have no future together. You know that."

"I will not believe it," he said violently. "You and I, Molly, were made for each other. We've known that from the first."

"What we did not know from the first," she said, "was what must always separate us. Nothing can change that."

"But *you* have changed!" he cried. "Before my illness you

were content—you seemed content—to live with me as my wife. What happened?"

"I saw our lives clearly. I saw the theatre as the greatest influence in my life."

"And in mine," he said eagerly. "Next to you. I will always put your influence first, Molly."

"I won't," she said. "Equally there is the influence of your family—your religion. You can't be yourself when you are cut off from them. You belong to them more than you belong to the theatre or to me. I have thought it all out."

He fretted up and down the small room, stared into the street below from the open window, then up into the moonlit expanse of the sky, and always, always talking.

"You talk so well," she broke out. "Always you have talked so well."

"Does that mean," he demanded, bending over her, where she sat on the side of the bed, "that all my talk is useless?"

"It means I see our two ways as separate. I'm too tired tonight to change things. They must stay as they are."

"Molly—my darling!" He sought to take her into his arms but she eluded him.

"No—" she cried. "You must not. . . . Talk as much as you will but—not that."

"Very well," he said gently. "I will talk, because I am sure I can make you see that we are necessary—each to each. There's no one else for me, Molly. Is there anyone else for you?"

"No—nor ever will be."

The other incident—and this at the beginning appeared a minor one indeed—was that Maurice and Finch told Dennis of his prospective visit to Ireland. This came at the end of the week during which Dennis had been ordered by Finch to remain solitary in his own room.

He had given no trouble. He had obeyed to the letter. An outsider might have come to the house, stayed there for days, without ever guessing that a boy lived under its roof. Noiselessly he went in and out of the bathroom. He took care not to turn the taps on full. He ate lightly of the trays which the daily woman carried to him. Her heart went out in sympathy to Dennis, but she could not persuade him to talk of his punishment, except to say that he and his father agreed that he should rest for a week.

What did he do in those long hours of solitude? How did

he pass the time? He was always listening. He knew exactly what were Finch's movements throughout the day. When Finch played on the piano, Dennis consciously drank in the meaning of every phrase, as he in his childish way interpreted it. He thought of himself as a skilled critic, as an unrecognized musical genius, as above all a devoted son. Yet that week seemed endless.

When it was over he appeared, neatly dressed, before Finch and Maurice, who were having a drink in the music-room. He appeared so quietly that the two men were startled. Maurice thought, How small, what a child he is. What he said was, "Dennis, I've been thinking of you."

Dennis gave a polite little inclination of the head toward Maurice, but his eyes were on Finch. They were asking, "Is it all right? May I come?" A slight smile hovered on his lips.

Finch returned his look soberly. "Sit down," he invited, as though to a visitor but not a visitor he desired.

Dennis gave his sudden spontaneous laugh. "I think I shall stand," he said. "I've been sitting all the week."

Maurice looked embarrassed. There was a moment's silence before he continued, "I've been thinking how much I should like to have you visit me in Ireland."

"Visit you?" Dennis repeated, as though he could not quite take this in. "Visit you . . . you mean visit you—alone?" Now he looked straight at Maurice.

"Yes. Just you and me. Do you think it might be fun?"

Dennis turned his eyes inquiringly to Finch. "I don't know," he said slowly. "You'd have to ask my father."

Maurice thought, "Why the devil doesn't he speak to Finch straight? Why this queer, slanting approach?" However painful had been the relations between himself and his own father, they had at least been direct—or so he thought.

"It's certainly very kind of Maurice to invite you," said Finch.

"What about school?" asked Dennis.

"I've had a letter from the headmaster," said Finch. "He doesn't want you to go back."

Dennis looked startled. "He doesn't want me back at school?" he repeated, almost in a whisper. "I wonder why."

"You'd better ask yourself that," said Finch.

Dennis appeared lost in thought. "I can't think why," he said, and Maurice had a sudden feeling of pity for him. Somehow, standing before them he looked a lonely little figure.

"I'll get a tutor for you," Maurice said, "if you come to visit me. A nice Irish tutor. It'll be better for you than school."

"How long should I stay?"

"That depends on how we get on together. I think we should get on well together, don't you?" Even as he said these words, a doubt assailed Maurice.

"I don't know," said Dennis.

"Well, in the first place," said Maurice. "Do you want to come?"

"No," answered the boy, abruptly. "I'd rather stay here with my father."

Finch rose impatiently, went to the window and looked out. Dennis kept his eyes expectantly on Finch's back. Maurice said:

"You must do as you choose. This may be an important thing for you."

"A reward, eh?" said Finch, his back still turned. "A reward for all he's done."

"No, no," said Maurice. "Pleasure for me and possibly some profit for him."

"When shall you be leaving, Maurice?" asked Dennis.

"Right after the wedding."

"That's a wedding you don't like, isn't it?" said Dennis.

Maurice was quite taken aback. "What gave you that idea?" he exclaimed.

"Oh, I see what's going on."

"You see?" stammered Maurice. "But—how?"

"Out of my green eyes," said Dennis.

Finch wheeled to face Maurice. "That's the sort of cheeky thing he says"—Finch spoke with bitterness—"after a week of being shut in his room for punishment."

"I try not to be cheeky," said the boy, with a humility that might be or might not be real. "The trouble is I don't know when I am." He stood with bent head and folded hands.

Maurice tried to speak lightly. "Can you be ready," he said, "in that time—if you decide to come?"

"If *he* decides," laughed Finch. "That's a funny way of putting it—if *he* decides."

"Well, I'm the one, aren't I," said Dennis, "who has to bear the punishments?"

"But this is different!" Maurice spoke eagerly, his brown gaze warm with sympathy. "It's to be an interesting experience for both of us—if it comes off."

Dennis took a step towards Finch. "What do you want me to do?" he asked, with an air of throwing himself on Finch's affection, rather than his mercy.

"I want you to go," said Finch.

There was silence for a space; then Dennis turned and ran out of the room. He ran with a child's grace and abandon. They saw him pass the window and disappear among the trees.

"You have been awfully kind, Maurice," said Finch. "I won't deny that you have solved a problem for me. I did not know what to do about Dennis. He's a problem that's beyond me."

"He's greatly attached to you," said Maurice.

"Oh, Lord, don't speak of that," said Finch.

Dennis did not appear at any of the family houses for lunch. There were plenty of ripe strawberries and of these he made a meal. Indeed, he was not very hungry.

Thirty-Two

A Hundred Years Old

A heat wave heralded the centenary celebration. The flowers of the garden drooped in the heat. Fruit ripened with unwonted speed. In the poultry runs young chicks scratched and pecked. Horses and cattle sought out the shade. The stream moderated its springtime flow and dallied with reeds and under the rustic bridge. In the five houses occupied by the family, every single member, not excepting the infant Ernest, had something new to wear. There was Jalna itself, in its new coat of fresh paint, its new mantle of Virginia creeper leaves that this season seemed larger and glossier than ever. There were all the family sporting new clothes for the occasion. There were the dogs, having shed their winter coats and grown summer ones and been groomed to the point where pride ends and annoyance begins.

In the afternoon, farmers and their wives, also acquaintances of the countryside, were invited to a garden party. In the evening there was a party for friends from a distance, and young people. A small orchestra was engaged. There was to be dancing. The day was to end in fireworks—with a bang.

At the Fox Farm, the Bells were dressing for the evening

"Thank goodness," said Patience, "it has got cooler. The temperature has dropped seven degrees."

"Why are you eternally consulting the thermometer?" said Humphrey, his features tied up tightly, as he tied his tie. "It seems to me a must fruitless occupation."

"It helps," said Patience.

"Helps whom?" he asked crossly. "How?"

"What ever is the matter with you, darling?" Patience gave him a maddeningly solicitous look. "Won't your tie tie?"

"I've been to one party to-day," he retorted. "Why should I dress for another?"

"After all," she said, "your new TV play is liked by the producer. That's something."

"Do you think that is all I ask for in life?" he demanded. The truth was that Patience had utterly spoilt him. Their little house was hot and breathless, yet try as he would Humphrey could not look hot, because of his extremely pale albino-like coloring, whereas Patience could glory in flushed cheeks and perspiring forehead.

To please him she said, "Victoria was greatly admired at the garden party this afternoon."

He tried to stop himself from making the remark, but he could not. He said, "She can't hold a candle to young Ernest for looks. He's a knockout."

During all their married life Humphrey had not before made such an unfeeling remark—and that was about their own little daughter! Patience stared at him, scarcely able to believe her ears. She feared he might be sickening for something. She was thankful that Victoria could not comprehend what had been said. She chose to ignore the remark. Still, it was right that he should be punished a little. "That cut on your chin looks rather bloody," she said. "I hadn't noticed it before."

Humphrey's beard, or lack of it, was a tender subject with him. He observed his reflection in the looking-glass. "Perhaps I'd better not go," he said dolefully.

"I'll put a bit of plaster on it," she comforted, "and it'll never be noticed. Otherwise you look quite passable."

A few minutes later they descended into the ravine, which was not yet sought out by evening coolness. They crossed the bridge and panted up the steep path to the small gate that opened on to the lawn of Jalna. Renny and Alayne came forward to meet them. They were the first arrivals. An enormous moon was rising, as though ordered for the occasion. There were lights among the rich leaves of the trees and a really strong one in the porch. The small orchestra was tuning up.

Renny Whiteoak peered at Humphrey Bell's chin. "I see you have cut your chin," he remarked genially.

Trying to keep his temper, Humphrey said, "I think I had better not stay—I'm in such a bloody mess."

Alayne, overhearing, was conscious of the word "bloody," and felt a moment's shock that the mild young man should use such a word, but Patience quickly put her right. "It's the heat," she said. "He bleeds easily in the heat."

Relieved, Alayne exclaimed, "Does he? I had thought he looks nicer than usual."

Adeline and Archer now came racing out of the house and were reprimanded by their parents for their dilatoriness.

"I had practically to dress Archer," said Adeline. "He couldn't find a blessed thing."

"How soon will the party be over?" asked Archer. "I love the end of a party. Just to see the guests depart. The race is run. *Consummatum est.*"

At the Rectory the car, with the Rector at the wheel and Meg at his side, was waiting for Roma and Fitzturgis.

"Two parties in one day," said the Rector, "are a burden in this heat. As we went to the garden party, we should not be expected to go to the evening party."

"Neither is a duty." Meg spoke as patiently as she could. "Both are pleasures. Long-expected pleasures—for we have been looking forward to this centenary for a hundred years."

"I shall be glad when it is over," he said, "and that I shan't be here for the two hundredth." He then said to the motor car, "Whoa, Nelly," remembering his old mare, which had been dear for many a year.

Meg was not amused. She said, "I do wish Roma and Maitland would hurry. She never kept us waiting till she married him."

"She married him promptly," remarked Mr. Fennel. "I hope she won't live to regret it."

"Maitland is a dear fellow," said Meg.

"I don't like this going back to Ireland," said the Rector. "It's never done by the Irish."

"My dear old grandmother," said Meg, "frequently remarked that she wished she were back, but of course she couldn't go—not with all us descendants. Dear me, why don't that pair hurry? Sound the horn, Rupert."

Inside the Rectory, Roma was giving a final brushing to her hair, which was folded like wings back from her temples. Fitzturgis was putting on his shoes and saying, "I hope I shan't be expected to dance."

"There's one thing about our parties," said Roma, "we always have plenty of men."

"Even if I were in the mood to dance," he said, "which I'm not, I couldn't dance in this heat."

"I could dance all night," softly sang Roma, then added, "Just listen to that motor horn! Does the silly old blighter think we'll be ready any the sooner for that?"

Fitzturgis stood waiting.

At The Moorings Piers and his family were on the point of leaving for the party when Pheasant summoned them to admire Ernest as he slept. They came on tiptoe, Piers gazing down with a doting smile at the infant; the young men, Christian and Philip, a little bored but still admiring.

"Have you ever seen anything so exquisite?" demanded Pheasant. "And when I think of the narrow escape he had on his christening day I tremble—almost drowned, poor darling! I shall never like that boy Dennis. He's not to be trusted."

The object of their admiration lay, with lightly folded hands, a tuft of fair curls on his crown, a smile on his lips, as though consciously posing.

Mary was calling to everyone to come and say good-night. They trooped into her room, bent over her cot and in turn kissed her. At that hour even the kisses of her brothers were welcome.

"Funny," said Philip when they had left, "how Mary seems to like you at bedtime. She'll give you a kiss and a hug then, as though she had some affection in her."

"That's because she is afraid," said Christian. "She knows that when the light is put out she'll be terrified. I well remember the feeling."

"If I thought," said Pheasant, "that Mary was afraid, I'd go straight back to her."

"Children love terror. I remember how I'd pull the bedclothes over my head, waiting for the strange shapes that came out of the darkness. I was terrified, yet I would not for the world have missed their mouthings and their eyeless faces. Yet I was frightened of the dark."

"That's the artistic temperament," said Piers. "I'll bet Philip had no such imaginings."

"My head scarcely touched the pillow when I was asleep," said Philip, with satisfaction.

The car from the Rectory passed them. Meg waved and, when Roma saw Meg wave, she too waved.

At Jalna a number of guest had arrived. As soon as it was possible for the young people of the family to leave the guests and collect in a body in front of the portraits of the young Adeline and Philip, which Renny had caused to be framed and hung in the dining-room, facing those of the great-grandparents, they did so.

"These new portraits," Christian said dolefully, "compare

very badly with the old ones. I wish I have never undertaken them."

"I like them," said Philip. "Adeline likes them. That ought to be enough." He put his arm about his fiancée's waist and looked possessive.

She was about to move away from him when she had a glimpse of the face of Fitzturgis, who had remained outside and now looked moodily through the window at the group in front of the portraits. With Roma and Fitzturgis regarding her through the window, Adeline could not resist languishing against Philip's shoulder and flickering her eyelashes at him. He flushed in pleasure and a dimple indented his cheek.

"Look at that young ass," Maurice whispered to Pat Crawshay, gripping his friend's fingers. "And Adeline doesn't really care a damn for him. She's just showing off. She couldn't care less."

"She's to marry him."

"My dear fellow, it was all arranged. They had little to say about it."

Pheasant appeared in the doorway. "Come, all of you," she cried, "and join the reception line on the lawn. Guests are pouring in."

They trooped after her.

Maurice and Pat Crawshay were the last to follow. Maurice already had had a drink. Its visible effect—for he carried his drink badly—was to lend an unneeded brightness to his eyes and a truculence to his bearing. Now he laid his hands on the portraits of young Philip and Adeline and pushed them askew.

"There," he said, with a humorous yet malicious glance at Crawshay, "that expresses what I feel about them. The whole affair is crooked."

The two left together and immediately Fitzturgis entered. He put the portraits straight, then stood before them in an attitude of reflection. The sound of the orchestra, the chatter of voices, came to him as from a long way off.

He remembered his first meeting with Adeline on board ship on the way to Ireland. He had been returning after a visit to his married sister in New York. She had been accompanied by Finch and Maurice, the three bound for Maurice's house. How excited she had been by the visit in prospect—how unreservedly happy. He had not wanted to fall in love with her but he could not stop himself. And she was so openly, so generously in love with him. Two years had passed

before he came out to Canada to make himself useful at
Jalna—if he could—and to marry her. He had done neither.
He turned from regarding her portrait and passed through
the hall and to the porch, to see her standing with her parents
welcoming their guests.

It was a gay scene: the orchestra playing a Viennese waltz,
the light dresses of women, the summer suits of the men, pale
against the majestic darkness of the trees. The trees
maintained their primeval darkness and grandeur, despite the
levity of the music, the laughter, and the Chinese lanterns
suspended from their luxuriant boughs. Every window in the
house was alight and it appeared to Renny Whiteoak to wear
an expression of reflective brightness, as though it remembered the lively spirit and strong heart of its first mistress,
that other Adeline Whiteoak who herself had lived to be a
hundred years old—a gallant and stubborn-willed
centenarian. Many of the guests still remembered her. Some
were descendants of families who were important in Province
in her day but whose names were now seldom heard. There
were quite a number of young people, and before long dancing began.

Renny remained in the porch, from which he could see,
through the French windows, the dancing in the drawing-
room and library. They looked crowded, especially as some
of the women wore the new bouffant dresses that took up so
much room.

Renny saw two figures approaching across the lawn, one
tall, one very small. He saw that they were Finch and Dennis
coming from the direction of Vaughanlands. He went to meet
them and said, in a welcoming voice:

"You're late. We've missed you."

"We were having a little argument," said Finch. "I did not
intend to bring this fellow along but he was determined. I
hope you don't mind."

"Mind? We'd have minded greatly if he hadn't come!
There's a nice girl in there Dennis, longing to dance with
you."

Dennis did not believe him. He stared about him in wonder. "How pretty everything looks," he said. "It's like a fairy
tale. I'd like to stay out here and listen to the music. I
couldn't dance well enough." He left them abruptly and ran
to look in at the dancers.

"How does he take take the proposed visit to Ireland?"

"He seemed quite calm about it—till to-night. Suddenly he said he couldn't go. He said it was too far away—that he wanted to here with me."

"He's very attached to you."

"I doubt it," Finch broke out. "He goes his own perverted way, without regard to my wishes. He looks so innocent—yet sometimes I think he's really vicious."

"No, no, I'll never believe that. How long will Maurice keep him?"

"The longer the better," said Finch.

Dennis came running back to them. "They look beautiful in there dancing," he cried. "But is it nice for girls to be nearly naked with they dance? Shouldn't they have upper parts to their dresses?" Without waiting for an answer he exclaimed, "I see lightning. There's going to be a storm." He seemed oddly, almost pleasurably excited, as though he would have welcomed a storm.

"I hope not," said Renny. "Rain would ruin the Chinese lanterns." He looked anxiously at the sky, where summer lightning lit up the scene with operatic splendor.

In spite of the heat the dancers continued in their rhythmic and graceful movements. Through the open French windows a cooling breeze now entered. Dennis ran back to the window that he might look in on them. "Women," he said in a whisper. "Cows. That's what they are. I hate them because they're cows."

Another figure emerged from the shrubbery and came to look in at the windows. It was Maitland Fitzturgis. Among the faces passing, glimpsed for a moment, then lost, he sought only the face of Adeline. Now he saw her dancing with Patrick Crawshay. She was wearing a yellow taffeta dress and topaz earrings and necklace. Both looked singularly happy. In contrast to them were Roma, her face calm and pale, expressing nothing, and Archer, who had chosen her because she made no demands on him. He steered her stiffly through the crowd.

"Why don't you dance?" came in the clear boy's voice beside Fitzturgis. Dennis's eyes, green in that light, were raised inquisitively to his face.

"I hadn't thought of it," said Fitzturgis. "But why aren't you dancing?"

"You know why," laughed the boy. "I'm too young. I shouldn't be here, but my father let me come because I'm so soon leaving for Ireland. Do you think I'll like living there? Do you like going back?"

"I think I do," said Fitzturgis. "It suits me better than New York."

"Did Jalna suit you?"

"Not very well."

"Wherever my father is suits me," said Dennis, and ran across the dark grass to where he could see Renny and Finch. He pressed in between them, absorbing with eager ears what they were saying. Renny was indeed trying to persuade Finch to go in with him and join the dancers. But Finch refused. His heart was heavy with the sorrow of Sylvia's death. If only she might have been beside him on this summer night!

"I'll just stroll about here," he said, with an effort at cheerfulness, "till they come out for supper." He went to the door of the marquee where the supper was being got ready, and exclaimed, "You certainly are doing well by your guests."

"There's plenty of champagne," said Renny. "This is an occasion. We shall never see its like again. It's seldom that the same family lives in the same house for a century. Of course that's not long in the Old Country, but it's a long while here."

Inside the house Adeline and Philip were dancing together. Everyone was aware of the nearness of their marriage and a number stopped dancing and smilingly watched them. Some clapped their hands. Already their portraits in the dining-room had been viewed with real or pretended admiration. The youthful pair were happily self-conscious.

To Maurice, looking on from a doorway, the sight of those two dancing together was one to make him feel dizzy with jealousy. Philip, he thought, was an abominable dancer, rigid and military, who translated the exquisite rhythm of the waltz into a soldierly two-step. He would himself dance with Adeline and show what they two could do together. He was placing a real importance on this dance. He took out his handkerchief and wiped his face and hands. He sought to wipe from his face any disagreeable expression and to replace it with a look of genial invitation. But, while he was so engaged, Fitzturgis had come in through the French window, gone straight to Adeline and asked her to dance. Other couples began to move about the floor.

Maurice was more than surprised; he was hotly resentful when he saw Fitzturgis place his arm about Adeline's waist.

It was in bad taste, Maurice told himself, watching the two as they began to dance. It was not only in bad taste, it was an affront to the family. Fitzturgis, who had been cast off by Adeline—daring to lead her out to dance!

But there was no doubt about it, the Irishman was graceful, an elegant dancer. No taller than Adeline, his movements were the epitome of rhythm. So well were they suited to her that she danced as she had never danced before. They were like one body moving in vitality and grace. Yet there was ordinarily nothing in the carriage of Fitzturgis to suggest this talent. They had never before danced together, or, if they had, she had forgotten it. Certainly it had not been like this. This was entrancing, and her delight was visible in her glowing eyes and smiling, parted lips.

As the other dancers had paused to watch Adeline and Philip, so now they ceased dancing to watch her and Fitzturgis; but with what a difference! Now they did not smile or clap their hands. The expression on the face of Fitzturgis was not one of pleasure but rather of sombre and relentless concentration. His dancing was altogether too good. To the minds of their rather conventional company it was embarrassing. They knew that the pair had been engaged to be married and that the engagement had been broken off. It was said that Fitzturgis had a shady past. He had been married to a London actress, been divorced; was again married, but a short while ago, to Adeline's cousin. What business had he to dance so superlatively well? Besides, they felt something antagonistic in him, something that repelled them.

Young Philip had not been a witness to this exhibition. After his dance with Adeline he had hastened out into the night air to cool off. But he would be back very soon to dance with her again, to take her in to supper. He thought that the evening had been something of a triumph for them both. He was proud of her, proud of himself, proud of Jalna, but he wished to goodness that he did not perspire so readily.

Three members of the family watched this dance with unmixed disapproval. They were Roma, Maurice, and Renny. She, standing in a doorway with Maurice, remarked to him: "They're making laughingstocks of themselves, that's what."

Maurice agreed, with a contemptuous curl of the lip. His feeling toward Fitzturgis at that moment was one of furious jealousy. Renny was in too genial a mood to be more than ruffled on the surface, but he did think Fitzturgis showed extremely bad taste in dancing with Adeline, and particularly in dancing with such professional aplomb. He had not looked even tolerably cheerful when dancing, but had worn an expression enigmatic, not to be described.

When Fitzturgis and Adeline had left the floor they went through one of the French windows on to the lawn. People were beginning to move toward the refreshment tent where waiters were ranged in readiness and Rags was being particularly officious. He was going out of his way to speak to friends of the family, to give orders to the waiters. To him Dennis attached himself, firstly because he wished to keep out of Finch's way, secondly because he was tired of being spoken to by some of the older guests as a little boy. He did not want to be patronized by them as a little, rather touching boy, because of the bereavement in his family. That seemed long ago to him—yet occasionally near, with a terrifying clarity.

Fitzturgis, from the darkness of the trees, saw Philip looking for Adeline. His tall boyish figure, with the blond head, was easily discernible, and Fitzturgis gave a sardonic grimace as he glimpsed the boy searching. Adeline saw nothing. Her hand still rested on the arm of her former fiancé. It would appear that she needed his support, for her dark eyes wore a dazed look. She had not indeed recovered from the rapture of that dance. She was at that moment like an instrument which, having been performed on by a master, still reverberated to that ecstasy.

"Shall I get some refreshment for you?" asked Fitzturgis, with old-fashioned formality.

"Not yet."

He turned his head to look into her face, pale in that light.

"Tired?" he asked.

"Oh, no." After a moment she added, "But we must not dance again."

He gave a little laugh, his face close to hers. As though they could not help themselves, her white arms were about his shoulders and their lips were pressed together. During all the period of their attachment they had never kissed like this. It was something new, and, to her, frightening—to Fitzturgis tantalizing, even maddening in the hopelessness of their situation. But he was willing to surrender to the seduction of the moment, with no more than one despairing glance into the future.

Their kiss was seen by no one, for they were in deep shadow; but Maurice saw their two figures—the faintest glimpse of Adeline told him who she was—the white shirt-front of Fitzturgis in conventional evening dress, for he did not possess one of the pale summer suits affected by the other men.

Adeline, seeing Maurice approach, almost fled in the direction of the marquee.

Maurice approached Fitzturgis, all his former dislike of him seething into hate. He said, scarcely knowing what he said, "Up to your old tricks, eh?"

Fitzturgis, in a sudden fury, said with contempt, "Get to hell out of here." He took a step toward Maurice. A flash of lightning illuminated this retreat. In it Fitzturgis looked formidable. Other people were approaching. Maurice turned away, but he thought, The time will come when I must knock that fellow down.

Thought lightning intermittently disclosed the animated scene with great vividness, the rain held off. Supper was served. Champagne was plentiful and the merriment became noticeably more enthusiastic. With the assistance of Philip, Renny began to set off fireworks. Rockets soared into the night sky and descended in a shower of stars. Renny had been extravagant in expenditure. Not only rockets, but designs in fireworks brought forth Ohs and Ahs of admiration from the guests. The last of these was a crown in stars and beneath it, clearly to be read, the legend 100 YEARS OLD. Obligingly this hovered right over the roof and the vine-clad chimneys of the house.

A few large drops of rain fell.

A little tired, but certainly not tired enough to go to bed, Renny Whiteoak was the last to stand before the house that night. A great stillness had fallen. A distant roll of thunder only accentuated this deep nocturnal stillness. Where he had kept his supply of fireworks he found one last rocket. This he set off; with a smile watched its swift, hissing ascent, its explosion into a bouquet of stars, and raising his hand said: "A salute to you, Gran."

All the long evening the dogs had been shut in their room at the end of the hall. Now he strode in to release them. They came tumbling out—the bulldog, the spaniel and the little cairn terrier. They rejoiced to be with him. He had a ham sandwich for each of them and one for himself. Together they ate them under a few pale stars that now appeared, and a brightness of dawn in the east.

Thirty-Three

Dennis

Finch was the first to leave the party. He had not waited for supper, nor did he feel that he could endure the spectacle of the champagne-exhilarated crowd hilariously watching the fireworks. He was on his way when he remembered Dennis and turned back. Where was the boy? he wondered. He had had no more than a glimpse of him since their arrival. Archer was standing alone with a cup of coffee in his hand. Finch went to him and inquired whether he had seen the boy. "He's at a table over there, with Aunty Meg and another elderly lady, eating chicken salad. How wretched he will feel tomorrow! Yet to-night it gives him confidence to sit with those two stout ladies, and it gives them confidence to sit in the company of one so young and greedy who can gobble all the food put in front of him without fear of getting fatter."

"I'm leaving," said Finch. "He'd better come."

"He'd miss the fireworks. He is just the right age to enjoy the fireworks. I well remember when I loved to set off a firecracker—on the twenty-fourth of May it was, I seem to remember, somebody's birthday. Boadicea's, was it?"

"I'm leaving," repeated Finch.

"Have you said good-bye to my mother and father?"

"Yes."

"And they let you go without a struggle?"

"They understood."

"She would understand," Archer said thoughtfully. "She's probably wishing that she herself might leave, but I can't picture him as understanding. To him the pleasure of a party consists in draining the cup to the dreary dregs. . . . But I'll tell you what I shall do—I'll run Dennis home in our car when he's ready to go."

"Perhaps he could spend the night here," said Finch hopefully.

"Scarcely," said Archer inhospitably. "We are pretty full

up. The spare rooms are taken by Maurice and Patrick. My mother's insomnia will be troubling her, and my father had already three dogs in his room—"

Archer would have continued but Finch abruptly said good-night and left.

But there was no need for Archer to take Dennis home. He set out independently when the display of fireworks was over, taking a short cut through the ravine. It was inky dark down there, for the moon had set and the few stars were powerless to penetrate between the luxuriant leaves of early summer. Now the voice of the stream could be heard in its dark communion with reeds and undergrowth. Dennis must go slowly, for the path was rather overgrown and sometimes not easy to find. Ever since the terrible night of Sylvia's death Dennis had felt a shrinking from the hours of darkness. He was actually afraid of the dark, as he never had been before that night. No longer had he the sense of power which had then malignantly whipped him. He knew what fear was. He had frightening things to remember. Yet he wanted to go home alone—to go into the house by himself and find Finch there.

He found him sitting in his favorite chair with a book in front of him, but he was not reading. Dennis stood looking in at him through the picture window, his heart swelling with possessive love. Yet he was fearful of Finch, and started and flinched as though rebuked when Finch, becoming conscious of his presence, looked out at him. Then he came quietly into the house.

"Who brought you?" asked Finch.

"Nobody. I came by myself—through the ravine."

"Did you tell them that you were leaving?"

"I forgot. I wanted to come alone."

"Why?" Finch fired the question at him, angered, he knew not for what reason.

Dennis hung his head. "I didn't want to be brought home like a little kid," he said, and added, "I didn't want to give trouble."

"It's the first time I've heard," Finch said coldly, "of your minding giving trouble."

The silence that followed this remark was broken by the ringing of the telephone. Dennis sprang to answer it, then halted, with an enquiring look at Finch, who said, "I'll answer it."

Alayne's voice came over the wire. "Have you seen Dennis? Archer was going to take him home but can't find him."

"He has just walked in, by himself," said Finch. "He wants to apologize." He held out the receiver to Dennis.

"I'm sorry," said Dennis in his treble voice. "I should have said good-bye. Thanks for a lovely party."

When he had hung up the receiver he inquired:

"Was that all right?"

"It will do. Now get to your bed."

Dennis stood up straight in front of Finch. He had the look of an almost too well disciplined child, but he had something he must say. "I want to know"—he spoke as though with difficulty—"how soon I am to go to Ireland."

"Right after the wedding." Finch strove to put cheerful reassurance into his voice. "Maurice has booked your passage. I wonder if you need some new clothes. Perhaps you will begin to grow very fast."

"Did you?" asked Dennis.

"I believe I did."

"Then I likely shall."

"In any case," said Finch, "there are good clothes to be had in Ireland."

There was a moment's constrained silence, then Finch said:

"Come now. Get ready for bed. I'm going too." He rose, put out the lights and went to his room.

A gentle rain was beginning to fall. Dennis was soon in his bed and, like the rain, gentle tears ran down his cheeks. He made no sound of weeping but lay flat on his face, his tears wetting the pillow. He felt unutterably lonely. He could not return to his school. He had been too wicked to be confirmed. If his father knew all, he would probably kill him. Half-awake, half-asleep, strange feverish dreams tortured him. Thoughts of violence at time made him tremble. He would surrender himself to trembling, with every inch of his prone body.

At last he slept, but was again awake at dawn. The air was vibrant with the song of the cardinal that, like an unseen flame, poured forth its comsuming joy. Dennis, at the first moment of awakening, was conscious of this joy; then he remembered his own unhappiness and burrowed into the pillow, trying not to hear the bird's song.

He did not know what to do next. There was no one who could help him out of his plight. His future had been settled for him. He was to be sent far away from home—from everything that was familiar to him—to a strange country—with Maurice, who himself had been sent to that same house in Ireland when he was a boy, and had never come home again except as a visitor.

At the thought of the inevitability of grown-up decisions a pang of panic shot through Dennis's nerves. He found himself standing in the middle of his room, possessed by one idea—the idea of flight from what threatened him, flight from what the grownups were going to do to him. If only Sylvia were here she would have protected him. Sylvia was kind—but he had killed her.

In silence he drew on the few light garments he needed; then, passing Finch's closed door, he stole out of the house. He knew where he was going, where he would hide and where no one would look for him. There was an unused stable in the grounds which had been untouched when fire had demolished the former house.

Dennis gently opened the door, shut it behind him; then climbed the ladder leading up to the loft that felt airless and heavy with the stuffy smell of hay long lying there. The sun had risen, and a ruddy beam slanted like a dagger across the loft. He squatted on the hay. He felt safe here. Nobody missed him till that night, when his bedtime came.

Finch came into the house expecting to find the boy in bed. When an hour had passed, sensing trouble—for he was suspicious of Dennis and longed for the time when he would be the responsibility of somebody else—he rang up the other family houses and, in a voice that he tried to keep calm, enquired for him. No one had seen or even thought of him that day. He had disappeared.

"He hasn't been here," said Pheasant, over the telephone. "Piers forbade him the house, after what he did to darling little Ernest. You will probably find him up to some mischief."

He was not to be found. Finch was composing a sonata. It was torture to him to break the current of this effort. His capacity for suffering was heightened. He found himself actually walking in a circle in his bewilderment.

"He is hiding somewhere," said Renny. "He'll turn up in the morning when he's hungry."

But he did not turn up through all that day. In its intense heat they searched for him. It was the height of the summer season, yet all the men were taken from their work to join in the search.

No one thought of looking in the unused stable. It was so close to the house, so easily accessible.

Night again came.

The moon, growing old, was still shining in a deep blue sky when Dennis stole down from the loft. He went to the field, where the strawberries grew sweet and thick in heat. Even in the moonlight they could be seen, shining like garnets among the clustering leaves. Dennis ate them greedily, for they assuaged his thirst, which had troubled him more than hunger. The coolness of the night air was delicious, comforting to his nostrils and throat, irritated by the dry dusty air of the loft.

But his freedom was cut short by the barking of Wright's Scotch collie. It bounded toward Dennis with furious barking, then, recognizing him, uttered loud cries of delight. Dennis ran in panic back to the stable, the collie leaping beside him, and climbed the ladder into the loft. For a short while the collie whined at the bottom of the ladder; then, satisfied that it had done its duty, trotted off.

The following midmorning little Mary Whiteoak happened to be picking flowers near the stable when a small door leading into the loft was opened and Dennis's voice called her name, but softly. She looked up.

"Is that where you are?" she asked without surprise, for nothing he did surprised her.

"Yes," he answered. "And I want you to come right up here. Don't let anybody see you." He directed her how to find and ascend the ladder. Soon she was sitting beside him on the hay, looking anxiously into his face. Certainly he looked odd, for his eyelids were swollen and pink, and his lips dark and feverish. His hair looked stiff and dry like straw.

"I'm hungry," he said, "and you are to bring me something to eat. You're to bring it right away."

"But I can't." Now she looked really frightened. "I don't know where to get it."

"To-day is our woman's day for going to shop for us," he said. "She'll be on her way now. You're to go into the kitchen and find something for me to eat. Anything will do. I'm so hungry I could take a bite out of you. I could take a bite of Ernest. Would you like to see me take a bite of Ernest?

Mary stared at him fascinated, the flowers she had gathered wilting in her hand.

"Make sure," he said, "that nobody sees you; but if my father should see you, tell him you're hungry. Whatever you can get hold of, bring to me here. If you don't—shall I tell you what will happen?"

She nodded, gripping the flowers.

"I'll kill Ernest," he said. "Nothing can stop me." That ruthless sense of power which sometimes gripped him now swept through all his nerves, to his very marrow. "When I make up my mind to kill somebody nothing can stop me. Now run and find me something to eat and be quick about it."

He sprang up and flourished his arm in menace above her.

The kitchen was, as he had foretold, empty. She stood looking about her, not knowing what to do. A pineapple lay on the table, and she wondered if she should take that. Then she heard steps and Finch, in shirt and trousers, appeared from the passage.

"Well, Mary dear," he said gently. "What do you want?"

"That," she said, pointing to the pineapple. The wilted flowers fell from her hand to the floor.

"But—why?" stammered Finch, astonished, because she was usually so shy.

"I'm hungry."

Finch put the pineapple into her hands. "Ask your mother to cut it up," he said. Then he added, "We still have no word of Dennis. I've called in the police to help."

Mary turned and ran out of the kitchen.

She ran along the path in the direction of home. Then she hid behind some currant bushes, whose glossy red berries hung in bright clusters. Remembering her flowers she shed a few tears. The sharp spines of the pineapple hurt her hands.

After a little while she came out from hiding and cautiously climbed up the ladder into the loft. Dennis was waiting for her, his hungry eyes on her timid face. Then he saw the pineapple. He stretched out both hands to snatch it. With her face expressing both patronage and disgust at his greed, Mary watched him take out his pocketknife, cut a thick slice from the pineapple and devour it. He seemed not to notice the juice that ran down his chin and over his front. But the fruit put fresh heart into him.

"Oh, how good," he said. "How good! You know, Mary, I

was starving, and my head aches. Have you ever had a headache, Mary?"

"No," she answered distantly.

He threw himself on his back on the straw. "Mary," he said, "lay your hand on my head and feel how hot it is."

She laid her hand gently on his forehead. "Oh, how nice," he murmured. "Keep it there—keep it there till I tell you to move it. . . ." After a little he said, "Do you know what, Mary? When we're grown up, I may marry you. Would you like to marry me?"

"No," she said, with decision.

He broke into laughter. "You're just an ignorant little girl," he said. "You don't know anything."

"I don't want to know," she said.

He turned his face away from her hand and rolled over in the hay, as though in anguish.

"I know everything," he moaned. "*I know everything there is to know*. It's a terrible burden on my soul, Mary."

She understood nothing of what he said. She looked at him with distrust.

Inspired by a new vitality he sprang to his feet and held an imaginary violin above his extended arm and under his chin. "I'm a great genius," he boasted. "I'm going to run away to Europe with my violin. Perhaps I shall run away this very night."

Mary sincerely hoped he would.

"My father is a great genius," he went on. "You can't have two geniuses in one house. That's why I'm running away. I have to make room for him."

"Then you'll not want me to bring you any more food," she said.

"Yes—you must bring me some to-morrow morning—in case I don't leave to-night." And he added, savagely, "Don't forget—because, if you do, I'll come steal Ernest. I'll take him to Europe with me and I'll play the violin and he'll be a little monkey for me."

"All right," she said.

"Cross your heart and hope to die."

She promised and escaped, leaving him again attacking the pineapple.

How frightening seemed the rest of that day to Mary, with to-morrow a threat like doom. She hung over Ernest in foreboding. She followed her mother like a thief. All she found to steal was a biscuit, a bun, and a banana. With these in a

paper bag she deliberately ran away from home and made
her way unseen to the stable, where Dennis was hiding. As
she climbed the ladder up to the hot dusty hayloft, she hoped
and prayed that he would by now have set out on his travels.
"Please God—don't let Dennis be here."

But he was there, lying in the hay, looking strange to her
and frightening in a new way.

He sat up straight, as soon as he saw her.

"I've changed my mind," he said, in a husky voice. "I
don't want anything to eat. "I'm going to kill myself. You are
to go to my father and tell him you've found me, and that he
will never see me alive again."

"All right," said Mary, eager to carry this message. She began to go down the ladder.

"Wait!" he shouted savagely. "Come here—see this rope!"
He pointed to a thick rope hanging over a beam, dangling,
with a loop at the end.

"I found that rope downstairs," he said, "and I am going
to hang myself by it."

"Oh," said Mary. "Can I go now?"

"Yes. Go into the house and find my father and say to
him, 'Dennis is in the loft over the stable. You will never see
him alive again. . . .' Have you got that straight?"

"Yes," she breathed.

"Then repeat it."

"I'm going to Uncle Finch and say you are in the loft and
he'll never see you alive again."

"Right. Now get a move on. I'm sick. I've been sick all
night. That pineapple made me sick. I vomited it up." This
was true. The air was heavy with a strange, sourish smell.

"Good-bye," said Mary.

"Good-bye." He flung himself back on the hay.

"Are you going to begin soon?" she asked.

"As soon as you go."

"I don't want to see you do it."

"You'd better not. It will be a horrible sight."

"Good-bye," she said again, then asked, "What shall I do
with the food I brought you?"

He sprang up and took the loop of the rope in his grimy
hands. "Will you go?" he shouted. "I'm going to hang myself
this minute!"

Mary went into the house and heard Finch moving rest-
lessly about the living-room. When he saw her he said:
"They've not found Dennis yet. Where do you suppose he's

gone, Mary?" His eyes searched her little face, as though for help in the troubles that had befallen him.

She did not answer him at once because she was not sure that Dennis would be ready to be found. She was looking at a little vase with a few flowers in it.

"Those are the flowers you dropped the last time you were here. I put them in water to save for you."

"Thank you, Uncle Finch."   Surely Dennis was ready now. . . . She raised her gentle blue eyes to Finch's haggard face. She said, "Dennis is in the loft over the stable. You will never see him alive again."

"Mary," shouted Finch. "What are you saying?"

"What he told me to. Come and see."

She led the way and he followed in a daze of bewilderment. Outside they met Archer, who had discovered footprints leading from the strawberry bed to the stable. He said, "I believe I've discovered him. I think he's hiding somewhere about here."

"He's in the hayloft," said Mary, and repeated with relish, "You will never see him alive again."

"Dennis is dead," Finch said hoarsely. "You must go up, Archer,—I can't." The blood had drained from his face, leaving it gray. He was shaking all over.

His expression imperturbable but his body brilliantly agile, Archer darted into the stable and up the ladder to the loft. They heard him exclaim, "Mercy!"

Dennis had been standing on a box with the loop of rope about his neck. When he heard Finch's voice he kicked the box from beneath him. The noose tightened. His face was congested when Archer caught and held him in his arms. The rope was not well tied. It was easy for Archer to free him. But he struggled.

"Let me go," he gasped. "I will hang myself! I will—I will."

He was bitterly disappointed. He had fully expected he would be discovered by Finch.

Now Finch, hearing his voice, climbed the ladder and appeared, followed by Mary.

Dennis held out his arms to Finch. "I'm dying," he cried melodramatically. "Forgive me—I'm dying."

He did indeed look terribly ill.

"I think I'll go home," said Mary. "Ernest will be wanting me."

A few hours later Finch walked through the ravine to Jalna. He found Alayne cutting blue delphiniums in the flower border. Even with his mind troubled as it was, he thought how becoming the graceful blue flowers were to her.

"Alayne," he said, and put out his hand to touch her.

She caught his hand in both hers and held it.

"You've heard?" he asked, in an unsteady voice.

"Yes, I've heard. Are you sure Dennis meant to—do what he did? Archer says not."

Finch made a grimace of pain. "I'm sure he meant to. My God, Alayne, the rope was there—round his neck. He looked terrible."

"What does the doctor say?"

"He's put him to bed with a sedative. He's to stay there for a couple of days. He fell asleep gripping my hand. I should have felt deeply touched, but—I simply shrank from his hand. The doctor says he's very sensitive—very young for his age."

"Yes, yes—very young for his age—that's what I think," said Alayne. "The way he clings to your sleeve—the way he boasts."

"And yet—" Finch turned away from her, as though he could not trust himself to speak of this—then turned again to her—"and yet there are times when he seems to me capable of anything. Alayne—often he made Sylvia unhappy. Consciously, I think, he made her unhappy. I never can forgive him for that."

"Surely you imagine that, Finch." Her pitying eyes looked into his. She was seeing him again as the unhappy boy she remembered. "You have a troublesome imagination, you know."

"I wish it were imagination," Finch said bitterly. "But—it was terribly real. And—another thing—I have a feeling that something happened—on the night Sylvia died—something Dennis feels responsible for. When we found him in the loft he kept repeating 'Forgive me—I'm dying!' But I have been haunted by a feeling—not explainable—when he and I are alone in the house together."

"You must put such thoughts out of your mind," Alayne said. "You must think of Dennis as an odd boy, but not as you are picturing him."

"He's so terribly like Sarah."

"He may seem so to you, but he is really just himself, and there is no doubt about his love for you." She gave a wry smile. "I should be glad if Archer showed a demonstrative love for either of his parents."

At this point Piers came on the scene, crossing the lawn toward them, from the direction of the stables. It would have embarrassed Piers to speak of the near-tragic happening of that morning. Instead, he remarked to Finch in a genial tone:

"If you were a race horse at stud, Finch, you would soon have no reputation as a sire, for you can't get an offspring that bears the slightest resemblance to you. Look at your two boys—Dennis, who is the very spit of Sarah, except for his yellow hair; and Ernest, who is going to be the image of Sylvia, and has her lovely nature too. There's the lad that's going to be the comfort of your old age, Finch. Come along over to my house now and meet him. I can tell you I wish he were mine. You come along too, Alayne."

"Shall we?" she asked eagerly of Finch.

But he turned away. "Thanks very much," he said. "But I've things I must do at home."

They watched his tall figure disappear down into the ravine.

Thirty-Four

The Wedding

The three sons of Piers and Pheasant were, on this July morning, passing an agreeable hour in Christian's studio. The young artist himself was intently scrutinizing a mixture of blues that he had on his palette. A midsummer landscape stood on the easel before him, but he was not satisfied that he had captured the exact blue of the sky.

"It must be fun to puddle about with paints all day," said Philip, rather patronizingly.

"Much more fun than getting married," Christian said serenely. "You must be growing rather nervous, old fellow."

"Me?" laughed Philip. "I leave nerves to the bride."

Maurice, from where he sat on a window sill, gave a groan.

"What's that groan for?" demanded Philip.

"For your youthful exuberance," said Maurice.

"When you come to think of it," said Philip, "it's odd that I, the youngest, should be the first to marry."

"In the fairy tales I used to read as a child," Christian returned happily, "the youngest son invariably married the princess—thank goodness."

"Tell the truth," said Philip, "neither of you would object to being in my shoes."

"We're green with envy," said Christian, squeezing green paint out of a tube.

"You remember those very modern portraits you did of Adeline and me that Archer bought?" asked Philip.

"I do indeed. I quite like them. Better than the second pair."

"Well, Archer is determined to display them with the rest of the wedding presents, but I tell him that Uncle Renny will never allow it."

"That remains to be seen."

"Like so much else," put in Maurice.

"Where is Pat Crawshay this morning?" asked Philip. "You're seldom without him, Maurice."

"He's off to buy you a wedding present."

"Gosh, I wish I knew what he has in mind," Philip said, from the bottom of his heart.

"Probably a clock," said Maurice, "or table silver. There's so little of that sort of thing at Jalna."

"That's our trouble." Philip looked rosily serious. "Adeline and I have everything we need for the house. But there are other things we should appreciate." Suddenly he asked, without embarrassment, "Look here, Maurice, do you mind telling me what you are giving us?"

"A cheque," Maurice said curtly.

Philip was delighted. "Nothing could be better." He spoke with warmth. "For if there is anything we're likely to be short of—it's cash."

"I'm so glad," said Maurice, but did not say of what.

"It's a pity"—Philip still addressed Maurice with great affability—"that you and Pat are leaving for Ireland so soon. You'll be gone when we come back from our honeymoon."

"Please God," said Maurice.

"What about young Dennis?" asked Christian. "Will he be able to travel so soon? He's been pretty ill, hasn't he?"

"I've quite given up that idea," said Maurice. "He doesn't want to leave home, and I don't want to take him—not after what happened."

"What actually did happen?" asked Christian.

"Archer says that Dennis tried to hang himself, but I never believe what Archer says. He talks just to hear himself."

"I'm afraid it is quite true," said Maurice. "It's been a shock to me and terribly disappointing."

Archer appeared in the doorway just in time to hear this. He advanced into the studio and spoke as a professor delivering a lecture from a platform.

"Disappointments," he said, "are generally pleasurable in the end. It's the rewards that are hard to take. Now I have in me the power of joyous abandon, yet I never find anything that moves me to more than a wistful smile. I have in me the faculty for great suffering, yet I am never moved to exclaim anything more heartfelt than 'Mercy!' That's what I said when I took the noose off Dennis's neck."

"How is he?" asked Maurice.

"I've just seen him," said Archer. "He was in bed doing a

crossword puzzle. He'll be up and dressed to-morrow and as troublesome as ever."

"He deserves a good hiding," said Philip.

"How did Uncle Finch take it?" asked Maurice.

"Very badly. At first I thought he was going to faint, but when Dennis clutched him and made noises of suffering he pulled himself together. When I went there this morning he was surrounded by manuscript. 'My work,' he said, 'of the past month.' 'Are you pleased with it?' I asked. 'Just this much,' he said, and tore it to bits."

"What a pity!" exclaimed Maurice.

"In a brief space," said Archer, "I have seen a child attempt to hang himself, a musician destroy the work he has sweated over—and in no time I expect to see a young man stick out his neck for the marriage yoke."

Philip laughed and blushed. "Whatever way you look at it," he said, "we're getting a lot of splendid wedding presents. I'm off to Jalna now to help Adeline arrange them. We're setting them out on tables in the library."

"I'll go with you," said Archer. "I want the two portraits I'm giving you shown to advantage."

At this moment Noah Binns appeared. He was carrying a large, flat, paper package. He gave a bleary wink at Philip and said, "I'll bet a dime to a doughnut that you can't guess what I've got here."

"A wedding present?" said Philip.

Noah's face fell. "You guessed right, but I bet you can't guess what the present is—not in a hundred years."

"A calendar?"

"No. Not a calendar. Look." Noah ripped off the paper wrapping and, appropriating an easel, set the present in view. He grinned delightedly when he saw the puzzled looks of the young men. "It's an enlargement," he boasted, "of a snapshot, took by a tourist, of your family plot in the graveyard. Gravestones and iron fence and all. I paid good money to git it enlarged. I bought the frame at Woolworth's. D'ye think the young lady'll like it?" Now he looked anxious.

"She'll love it," said Philip.

"It goes to show," said Noah, "what young brides and bridegrooms come to. Like the rest of us."

Philip grinned unbelieving, but Maurice exclaimed, "It's horrible. He can't give that to Adeline!"

Philip doubled up in laughter. "She'll love it," he said.

Noah rewrapped the picture. "I witnessed a terrible accident when I was in the city buyin' that picter frame," he said. "There was an old gray horse drawin' a milk wagon. I guess it thought it was the last horse in the city. Then along comes another old nag hitched to another milk wagon. The first old nag hadn't seen another horse since he could remember. He'd seen millions of cars. The driver told me he guessed the danged horse thought he was a car hisself. Anyways, when he saw this other horse it near scared the daylights outa him. He rared and kicked and busted the wagon to bits. It was a senseless sight."

Noah was exhilarated by his adventures. Now he rewrapped the enlarged snapshot with the remark, "I hope this here will be hung in a constituous position."

"It certainly will," said Philip genially.

Renny Whiteoak was surprisingly touched by this present from Noah and delighted him by placing it prominently. Yet he refused to allow the portraits first painted by Christian to be seen. "They're hideous modern caricatures," he said. "The place for them is the attic." Archer was resigned. "I shall take them with me to Oxford," he said, "to show how art progresses in Canada."

Adeline was not resigned. "After all," she said to Philip, "it's our wedding and we should be allowed to do what we choose with our presents."

How this remark endeared her to Philip! The "we"—the "our"—gave such body to the prospect which sometimes appeared to him dreamlike. The fact that he was going to live in the home of his bride, a house with which he was as familiar as with the house of his parents, made the union somehow unreal. He would be glad when the wedding was over and they were settled down. Yet he looked forward with confidence to their honeymoon. It would settle all emotions that perturbed him.

Two nights before the wedding day Archer opened the door of his father's bedroom and put his head inside. It was pitch-dark and midnight. Renny had just turned off the light.

Archer said, "I can hear Adeline crying in her room."

Renny sprang up and joined him in the passage. "You must have exceptional hearing," he said. "I can't hear a sound."

"Listen."

Now Renny could faintly hear his daughter's muffled sobbing. He went straight to Alayne's room and bent over her. She was, for a wonder, fast asleep.

"Alayne," he said, "you must go to Adeline, she's crying. You must go to her. I can't."

Alayne was startled into instant sensibility. She rose, put on a dressing gown and slippers. She looked concerned but not distraught. In Adeline's room a dim light was burning. Adeline lay stretched on the bed, face hidden in the pillow.

"What ever is the matter, darling?" Alayne put a comforting arm about the girl.

"I can't do it," sobbed Adeline. "I can't go on with it. I'd die first." Now that she was discovered she no longer restrained her weeping.

"Tell me—" Alayne spoke urgently. "You must tell me."

"I can't go on with this," Adeline sobbed, while Renny, Archer and the three dogs listened miserably in the hall. "I can't marry Philip . . . or anyone."

"If you are thinking of Maitland," Alayne said calmly, "remember he is not free."

"Why did you say that?" demanded Adeline. "I'm thinking of no one but Philip, and I can't have him in this room. I want to be my own—by myself."

Renny now came to the door. "We can put Philip in Uncle Nick's room," he said, "if you don't want him here." Alayne patted Adeline's back, as when she was a tiny child.

"You shall not marry," she said, "if you do not want to; but remember—you must return every one of your wedding presents, with a note explaining that the wedding is not to take place."

Adeline almost screamed: "Write fifty notes of that sort— on top of all my thank-you notes? I'd rather get married!"

Archer now came carrying a tray with instant coffee and digestive biscuits for all four. "I would feel the same if I were going to be married. I'd scream the house down."

Adeline laughed through her tears and hungrily ate more than her share of the digestive biscuits. From this time she moved forward to the ceremony without hesitation.

On the morning preceding the wedding Finch, accompanied by Dennis, came to view the presents. Renny went with them into the library. "A nice display, isn't it?" he said, with the very same expression he wore when showing the medals and ribbons won by his horses.

"Very nice indeed," Finch said admiringly. "Keep your

hands off them, Dennis," he added, as the boy handled one thing after another.

Dennis wore a white singlet and gray trousers. He looked fragile, yet alert and happy. With him out of earshot, Renny said to Finch, "What are you going to do about him, now that the visit to Ireland is off?"

"I have heard of a school in New England where they take in difficult boys and, as I have some concert engagements there, I'm going to take him along."

Dennis had caught the last words. Now he came, with a light, almost dancing step to Renny. "My father and I," he said proudly, "are to travel together. It's the first time we've done that since I was a little fellow and he brought me from California after my mother died."

"That will be fun," said Renny.

"Yes, won't it?" He caught Finch's sleeve in his hand and held it. He added, "I'm going to hear him play in two concerts. I've heard him practicing these pieces. I won't be like the rest of the audience. I'll know everything beforehand, and that's what I like."

The midsummer leaves made silken-green curtains for every window of the church. The day had come when Renny led his only daughter up the aisle to give her in marriage to the bridegroom of his choice. Young Philip, immaculately dressed, looked a young man to be proud of. He and his brother Christian stood at the chancel steps for what seemed a long time before the bridge appeared. The small church was packed with people. A sigh of admiration rose from them as Adeline, very pale and beautiful, progressed along the aisle. Renny led her proudly, protectively. Her only attendant was her little cousin, Mary.

Mary also was in white and carried a basket of rosebuds. It was a trial to her to be stared at by so many people. Entering the church, with the air vibrating with the clamor of the wedding bells, she saw Noah Binns frantically ringing them. "I'll ring them wedding bells," he had declared, "if it's the last thing I do." He put his creaking back into the ordeal and he survived, gasping and ghastly.

As Mary moved along the aisle, her downcast eyes were fixed on the sweet rosebuds in the basket she carried. She was not surprised to see among them a pretty little blond spider. Whether it was for the spider or for herself she did not know, but a tear shone bright on her pink cheek. Piers saw it as she passed close to him and could scarcely stop himself from wiping it away.

Both Philip and Adeline made their responses with admirable clarity. Firmly he placed the ring on her finger, and, led by the rector, said "With this ring I thee wed, with my body I thee worship, and with all my worldly goods I thee endow: In the Name of the Father, and of the Son, and of the Holy Ghost. Amen."

They knelt together, she who had held his hand and helped him to learn to walk. They who had pulled each other's hair in childish combat.

Finch was at the organ, and never in that church had the wedding march been played with such splendid dominion over the instrument.

The air was full of music and admiring congratulations. Adeline remained very pale, but Philip was rosy as a young god.

Renny Whiteoak had, for this occasion, bought a new car; and Wright, well turned out in dark blue, with chauffeur's cap, was to drive the newly wed pair to Jalna. Wright was proud of his part in these important doings. He drove the car slowly and with dignity. Behind him Philip and Adeline sat, a little embarrassed, as though surprised to find themselves alone together. He just touched the flowers of her bouquet. "Pretty," he said.

She drew away. "Don't," she said.

"O.K." he said, and took out his gold cigarette case, a wedding present, and lighted a cigarette.

"Don't," she repeated.

"Why not?" he asked, surprised.

"It isn't appropriate."

He sent a puff of smoke down his nostrils.

In a sudden fury she snatched the cigarette from his lips. They scuffled for it, but before he recovered it it had fallen on her veil and burned a small hole in it.

"Oh—I am sorry!" he exclaimed.

She tapped Wright on the shoulder. "Stop the car, Wright," she ordered, still in a fury.

Wright stopped the car. He looked inquiringly over his shoulder.

Adeline opened the door. "I'm getting out," she said.

"What's wrong?" asked Wright dumfounded.

"Everything," she raged. "Look at this." She pointed to the hole in her veil.

"I didn't mean to," said Philip—"I'm sorry."

"I'm getting out," she repeated.

"You can't," shouted Philip, and caught her by the wrist.

But she had the door wide open and was already, impeded though she was by train, veil and bouquet, descending into the dusty road.

This was the sight that met the eyes of Renny Whiteoak in the car following. In an instant he, too, was in the road coming to meet her. She poured out an incoherent story of the mishap, while Philip, very red in the face, followed her along the road. Other cars, filled with wedding guests, were collecting.

Renny took his daughter by the hand. "There's a good girl," he repeated soothingly. "A good girl. What's a little hole in your veil? Come, come."

"It's not only that," she said. "It's everything."

"There's a good girl," he soothed, as though she were a nervous filly. "There's a good girl."

"You've got to come in the car with us," she said. "I won't go in it without you."

To humor her, he got into the car with her; and so the bridge, the bridegroom, and the bride's father returned to Jalna together. They were silent, Philip gazing resolutely out of the window, Adeline holding tightly to Renny's thin muscular hand. When the car stopped at the door that stood in welcome wide open, Renny put off his air of tenderness and said authoritatively: "Now you will stand in the receiving line and behave yourself properly. No more tantrums or I'll take a stick to your back." But he smiled as he said it.

Something very like a smirk dimpled Philip's cheek. He offered his arm to Adeline and she laid her slender gloved hand on it. Little Mary had overheard this threat, for she was waiting in the porch. Now she stole to the corner of the dining-room and had a little cry.

But she was not left in peace. Rags soon sought her out. "They're asking for you, Miss," he said, "to stand in the line. And what a picture you look, to be sure!" He led her to the drawing-room.

How glad she would be when all was over and she was safe at home, in an old cool dress, and with Ernest to play with! It was a comforting thought to her that some of the men of the family would very soon be leaving. Philip was going on what he called a honeymoon. Maurice and Patrick were soon to go to Ireland. Uncle Finch was taking Dennis to the States; she hoped he would never come back.

Mary did not think of Ernest as a male. He was a baby—hers to play with and keep for her own, always. Now, in an old dress, she bent over him as he lay in his cot laughing up at her. The bright whites of his eyes showed round the bright blue of the iris. He had got two teeth.

Her face close to his, she sniffed the pleasing scent of his flesh.

"You're prettier than a spider," she said, "sweeter than a rose."

"What's that you say, Mary?" demanded Pheasant.

"Oh, nothing," said Mary.

Taylor Caldwell

☐	NEVER VICTORIOUS, NEVER DEFEATED	08435-9	1.95
☐	TENDER VICTORY	08298-4	2.25
☐	THIS SIDE OF INNOCENCE	08434-0	1.95
☐	YOUR SINS AND MINE	00331-6	1.25
☐	THE ARM AND THE DARKNESS	23616-1	2.25
☐	CAPTAINS AND THE KINGS	23069-4	2.25
☐	DIALOGUES WITH THE DEVIL	23714-1	1.75
☐	THE FINAL HOUR	23670-6	2.25
☐	GLORY AND THE LIGHTNING	23515-7	2.25
☐	GRANDMOTHER AND THE PRIESTS	C2664	1.95
☐	GREAT LION OF GOD	23790-7	2.25
☐	THE LATE CLARA BEAME	23157-7	1.50
☐	MAGGIE—HER MARRIAGE	23119-4	1.50
☐	NO ONE HEARS BUT HIM	23306-5	1.75
☐	ON GROWING UP TOUGH	23082-1	1.50
☐	A PILLAR OF IRON	23569-6	2.25
☐	THE ROMANCE OF ATLANTIS	23787-7	1.95
☐	TESTIMONY OF TWO MEN	23212-3	2.25
☐	WICKED ANGEL	23310-3	1.75
☐	TO LOOK AND PASS	14055-5	1.95

Buy them at your local bookstores or use this handy coupon for ordering:

FAWCETT BOOKS GROUP
P.O. Box C730, 524 Myrtle Ave., Pratt Station, Brooklyn, N.Y. 11205

Please send me the books I have checked above. Orders for less than 5
books must include 75¢ for the first book and 25¢ for each additional
book to cover mailing and handling. I enclose $_____ in check or
money order.

Name_____

Address_____

City_____State/Zip_____

Please allow 4 to 5 weeks for delivery.